Obscene Bliss

Obscene Bliss

Thomas E. Coughlin

"There are only the pursued, the pursuing, the busy, and the tired."
—F. Scott Fitzgerald

Fitzgerald & LaChapelle Publishing, LLC

Written, produced and printed in the United States of America

ISBN: 09666202-3-2

Cover Photography: Robert F. Hoffman, Nashua, New Hampshire

Cover Design: Lisa Atkins, Pelham, New Hampshire

Cover Model: Shelley Collins, Manchester, New Hampshire

Cover Location: Wells Beach, Maine

This book is a work of fiction. Names, characters and incidents are
products of the author's imagination or are used fictitiously. The
names of actual places were used largely with permission or as a
point of historical reference. Any resemblance to actual events, locales
or persons, living or dead, is entirely coincidental.

FIRST EDITION

Fitzgerald & LaChapelle Publishing
30 Amherst Street, Suite 7
Manchester, NH 03101
(603) 669-6112; fax (603) 641-4929
chestercpa@yahoo.com

Dedication

For Rachel Morin

In recognition for your love of God, family, and Wells Beach.
We miss you terribly, Ma.

Acknowledgements

Jim Cassin and the Tavern at the Bridge, Gary Leech and Congdon's Doughnuts, Dick Varano and Billy's Chowder House, Bob and Ruth Ann Cullinane for the use of their wonderful porch overlooking Wells Beach, Scott Labnon and the Town & Country Motor Inn, and Peter Mars, the true friend I can always turn to for help and encouragement.

1

A solitary gust of wind roared up the hill from the Atlantic, rattling the windows on the eastern side of the building. The man glanced toward the sound and then up to the clock on the far wall of the office, switching his attention away from the computer screen. His eyes widened in surprise, noting the better part of the afternoon was now behind him. He pushed himself back from the desk and peered outside toward the motel building, picking up on a remarkable bank of clouds traveling silently past. A Winslow Homer sky, he thought, billows of white, trimmed with darkened and pinkish edges. It was late afternoon in early spring. Crossing the floor and stepping out onto the porch, he descended a short flight of stairs and made for a grassy pathway between the adjacent buildings. Between the motel and a small cabin and perched at the summit of a long, sloping hill was the finest view of the Webhannet River, Rachel Carson Wildlife Sanctuary, and Wells Harbor from anywhere on Route 1, at least in his opinion.

Brian Kelly stood transfixed, content to let his senses take in everything this splendid vantage point offered. Only a few hours earlier, the plumber and his assistant had sent the town water surging back through the pipes of his twenty-eight cottages and a seven-unit motel building following the long, cold winter. Only the main building, housing the office and four additional tourist rooms, had been left open over the winter months. He took a few steps and rested his body against the porch of a small cabin. The sight of the already greenish lawn rolling downward to the border of the wildlife sanctuary filled him with pride. He loved this time of the year. It would be two weeks before the first overnight visitor arrived and until then he was not obliged to share the Atlantic Coast Lodge with anyone. However, there was no avoiding it, the summer season of 1995 was swiftly approaching and the tranquil workdays, made up largely of confirming reservation requests over the phone or on the internet, were soon to end.

Shooting a glance at his watch, he pushed himself away from the building. Brian Kelly was tall and trim, standing a tad over six foot, three inches in height. He was what some local women considered handsome, but with features more ruddy and coarse than many, particularly those who worked indoors and out of the elements. His thick, dark brown hair displayed more than a speckle of gray, normal for a man approaching his fortieth year on the planet. Letting out an audible sigh, he turned and crossed the driveway, making his way toward the Ford pickup parked in the shadows at the far side of the complex. The prospect of a ninety minute drive home was not a pleasant one.

Since his marriage three years earlier, he was forced to make the trek back and forth to Bedford, New Hampshire from his Wells, Maine business something on the order of three times a week. Ahead were two days away from the office. His long-time employee and assistant manager, Millie Pierce, would continue in his absence, taking reservations and plugging guests into available units over the spring, summer and autumn months. Following a final visit to the office, where he signed off the computer and secured the back door, he hopped behind the wheel of the Ford and pointed his vehicle westward toward New Hampshire.

The one and a half hour trip, door to door, found Brian operating the truck in the state of what he termed 'automatic pilot.' He no longer had to concentrate on the route, so routine by now was the task of motoring home. Home was an expansive colonial on nine acres in Bedford, an upscale bedroom community to the south and west of Manchester, New Hampshire. There, he anticipated being greeted by his sixteen month old daughter, Colleen, and her nanny. He did not expect to lay eyes on his wife, the former Margaret Keogh, until well into the evening. Margaret was one of the region's most successful businesswomen and certified public accountants. It was early April and she was still deeply entrenched in the battlefield that was tax season.

Brian found himself emerging from his highway trance as the truck turned onto Joppa Hill Road and began the two plus mile final leg of his drive to the house. Reaching the driveway, he steered the vehicle through the front gate. The exterior of the colonial was dimly visible from the ground lighting that bordered the long, horseshoe driveway. This impressive structure, his legal address since the 1992 marriage, never ceased to stir a sense of awe in him. This was not surprising. Raised in tenement flats, the young Brian Kelly had set his sights no higher than someday owning a three bedroom, family house in a quiet neighborhood somewhere. As a boy growing up in Lowell, Massachusetts, exclusive towns like Bedford were practically unknown to him. Now, following his marriage to the lifelong Bedford resident, the trappings of his wife's relentless drive and ambition were his. Pulling his vehicle a few feet beyond the front door, he decided this night to ignore his wife's wishes and immediately shut off the engine. This was in direct violation of one of Maggie May's ten commandments: Thou shalt not park thy crappy truck anywhere on the grounds except hidden, out of sight, in the garage. Arrival home proved to be a pleasant one. He had barely cleared the front door when his daughter emerged from the kitchen and raced toward him.

"Daddy," she cried out, arms outstretched.

"Jelly Bean," he called back, crouching to one knee. The sixteen month old crashed into his waiting arms, her nanny a few steps behind. The three would spend the next hour together dividing their time between the living room and kitchen.

It was nearly ten o'clock when the sound of his wife's BMW flooded the living room, temporarily drowning out the movie he was only half watching through glimpses up from the newspaper. His daughter, Colleen, had long since retired for the evening as had her nanny. Seconds later came the thud from a briefcase hitting the hallway floor. The door to the living room swung open and his wife stepped into the room. Margaret Kelly was an impressive woman. Above average in height and meticulously dressed, she presented to the world the image of a female with complete confidence. Blessed with a classically pretty face showcased behind piercing blue eyes, her facial beauty would, for most women, epitomize their strongest feature. However, for Margaret, this was not the case. This was due to a life devoted to physical exercise. Since her days in college, a period spanning nearly twenty years, the woman had committed much of her leisure time to jogging, tennis, weights and exercise equipment. The product of this devotion was a perfectly fit body, the crowning jewel being a pair of magnificently athletic legs. Learning early in her career of the inherent power of these physical attributes, she had used them over the years to distract, disparage, disorient, discourage, disarm and ultimately dismantle members of the opposite sex in both business and social settings.

"Your fucking truck belongs in the garage," she said. He shrugged his shoulders. "You can't begin to imagine the collection of assholes that streamed through my office today," barked out the woman.

"Many of which I'm sure you prodded and schmoozed to land on your client list. Don't feed me that crap Keogh. These are your people—rich, penny pinchers looking for you to make the rest of us middle class saps pay our taxes and half of theirs."

"Oh, thanks Brian, for the words of encouragement," she answered, leaning against the wall and slipping off her leather pumps.

"Oh—and while you're up my sweets—how about making us a nice hot chocolate?" She responded by scaling a shoe across the room in his direction. "If my memory serves me right, there's a can of whipped cream in the fridge—you know, to top it off." Her second shoe followed the first, this time landing close to his head on the back of the couch.

"Cut the clowning Kelly, I'm tired and I'm pissed. I hate this fucking time of the year!"

"We go through this every year, you know that. You're letting things get to you because you're so damned tired. It'll be over soon. You'll be fine."

She rolled her eyes and plodded across the room, finally allowing herself to collapse in a heap beside him. Brian pulled his wife sideways, allowing her head to rest on his shoulder. She closed her eyes, as if trying to blot out the world.

"In a few days you'll be able to jump in the car and join me up in Wells. Then it'll be walking the beach—and running—and bicycling—and taking the canoe or kayak out."

"I just don't remember it being this hard," she exclaimed. He pulled his arm around her head and applied a gentle head lock.

"Hello, McFly—is there anyone in there McFly?" he needled, mimicking a scene from the motion picture *Back to the Future*. His words were accompanied by the soft rapping of his knuckles against the side of her head. "I hear this same crap from you every tax season, McFly," he continued.

"Jesus, if you knew how much that McFly shit aggravated me you'd stop it for your own well being."

He reached around the woman and began the now familiar chore of kneading the tension from her shoulders. She responded by letting her body go limp. For the next few minutes there was no verbal communication. After grabbing the remote and turning off the already muted television, it was Margaret who broke the silence.

"I think I'm going to want some biting sex this weekend, maybe tomorrow night."

His fingers stopped momentarily, her declaration possibly catching him off guard. Biting sex, as she was prone to call it, was her occasional desire and need to intersperse the couple's lovemaking with an almost vampire like activity where she hungrily bit down on exposed flesh, leaving him bruised and sometimes even breaking the skin.

"How can you know that twenty-four hours ahead of time?"

"I can feel it coming on, and it's been a while since I did it. I'm overdue."

"God, there's not a spontaneous bone in your body. I'm not always in the mood for that stuff. I love it when I'm in the mood, Maggie May—but I've got to be in the mood for that."

"Christ, you're starting to sound like that fruit, Brad, all of a sudden! It's not like I'm asking for the sun and the moon here." The comment comparing him to her ex-husband was not lost on Brian.

"No, it's okay, mark it in the book—me and vampire girl."

"Don't be such a martyr, Kelly. Ninety percent of the men in Bedford would kill for a night with vampire girl."

"And the other ten percent?"

"Fruits."

Brian enveloped his wife of nearly three years with his arms and legs, the warmth of her body penetrating her clothing and reaching him. He kissed her perfectly styled hair, inhaling the faint fragrance from her shampoo.

"There's something else from the office that's got a knot sitting in the pit of my stomach," she added.

"Are receivables getting too high?"

"Yes, but that's not what's got me uptight. Gretchen took a call for me today. Thank God I was in a meeting. She took a call from Skip Emerson. Actually, it's the second call from him this week. He also called on Tuesday. I didn't return it. For some reason, after all these years, he's trying to get in touch with me."

Skip Emerson, the young man who impregnated the fifteen year old Margaret Keogh during her sophomore year at Southside High School, had gone practically unmentioned in the Keogh, then Olson, then Kelly households for the better part of twenty two years. The pregnancy and eventual birth of Margaret's daughter, Jenny, drove a wedge between the Emerson and Keogh families. So severe was the split between them that a formal, written document was drawn up and signed by the Emersons, forbidding them from any contact with the girl until her twenty-first birthday without the consent of the Keogh family, namely Margaret. To date and covering a period of over twenty-one years, Jenny Keogh had had no contact with the family of her biological father.

"Chances are he's done the math—knows he can legally see Jen—and he's calling to get her address and phone number," theorized Brian. There came no response from his wife, merely a distant, thoughtful expression. "So what are you going to do? You can't just keep avoiding him by not taking his calls."

"Wouldn't that be fucking ironic? Having her worthless father—whose family would have had me dispose of her—who offered to even pay for the abortion—to have those worthless fucks move in on her now and take her in as their own. They will—over my fucking dead body!"

The attempts by Skip Emerson to contact Margaret had not only opened one old wound but also a second. She and her grown daughter were estranged. There had been no communication between the two for over a year. The rift, which grew with the passage of time, started when a budding romance involving Jenny and another student on the campus of Brown University began to negatively impact the young woman's education, an education largely financed by her mother. On a visit to Bedford, a confrontation had broken out, a war of words between Margaret and the two lovers. In an account provided to Brian by Moira, their Irish nanny, the argument had gotten heated with Jenny's friend, Roger, accusing Margaret of being a small minded, ignorant, money grubbing, nouveau riche Republican who was sticking her nose in matters that did not involve her. Margaret's response had been swift and, at minimum, equally scathing. In a flurry of accusations, Roger's common sense, IQ, liberal principles and beliefs, physical appearance and masculinity had been dissected and found wanting by the well-spoken Mrs. Kelly. The entire ugly scene, as recounted by the young woman from the Republic of Ireland, came to a climax when mother reminded daughter of the long list of sacrifices she had made on her behalf over the years. With Jenny standing between these two people she loved, she was delivered an ultimatum: either sit down and attempt to intelligently talk through the growing problems arising from the current direction of her life or leave with her young man and never return. Jenny walked from the house that day, not even turning back for a last glimpse of her mother. From that day forward, Margaret chose to never speak of the incident or its consequences. In time, Brian learned, in the interest of peace within the household, not to bring up the matter of the absent Jenny or the causes behind the estrangement.

"You know, Keogh, for all we know it might be a case of Skip catching a glimpse of his long lost Maggie May at the mall or something—seeing those long, major league legs, and figuring he still had a chance of getting you back— you being married to a loser from Lowell and all."

"You might be right, Kelly, and here I was getting myself all worked up. It's probably what you say—the great legs—loser from Lowell explanation," she quipped, happy to lighten the conversation. "I'll call the asshole back tomorrow. He left me his work number. Leave it to him to call me during tax season, the inconsiderate bastard." Closing her eyes, she nestled her body back into Brian's arms.

"It'll be nice being back here for a couple of days—catching up on my time with Jelly Bean."

"I wish you'd stop calling the baby, Jelly Bean. It's infantile. You'll warp her mind calling her something like that," she snapped.

"What's wrong with jelly beans. It's a cute nickname. It's not like it appears on her birth certificate or something. Hell, Ronald Reagan kept a bowl of jelly beans on his desk when he was president," Brian reasoned. "What do you think Clinton keeps in a bowl on his office desk?"

"D-CON, if we've caught a break," came back Margaret. His wife's quick and cutting wit brought on a burst of laughter from her husband.

"Seriously though, maybe I'll surprise Moira and give her a few extra hours off this weekend."

"Don't give her any time off on Sunday morning. Save that for me," she added.

"So how's this tax season going, you know, compared to last year?"

"Billings up, collections up, profits up—slightly. But it's coming at a cost. God Brian, you can't believe how disliked I am in there. Oh, forget disliked, I swear they fucking hate me."

"Hey Keogh, lighten up on the bad language, will you? Next thing you'll be talking like that in front of the baby."

"Sorry, your holiness, I'll be more careful. Anyway, back to what I was saying. There isn't one person in the office I can kid or hang out with. And, of course, Claire is so busy with her precious James she doesn't have much time for lunch or anything. Damn it, I'm pretty much alone."

"Have lunch with some of those slimy lawyers you have referring work to you all the time."

"Sorry, I'm lonely, but not that lonely," she admitted through a chuckle.

"Well, Maggie May, I don't feel sorry for you. I can't remember how many times you've laughed about the people you profile and hire; boot licking 'yes' men—and women who can follow orders and know their stuff. Unfortunately, all your little sheep are too afraid to mingle with the big, bad Mrs. Margaret Kelly—leaving her with no one else but her precious Brian to talk to and have fun with," he teased.

"Keep it up, Kelly—keep up the needling—and the lack of compassion for your wife. You seem to have forgotten who you're talking to—and who'll be having biting sex with you tomorrow night!" Brian let out with a howl.

"Oh, no—beautiful lady. It is you who is totally in the right—and all others who are totally in the wrong," he clowned, injecting the sound of fear into the tone of his voice.

"It's too late with the phony respect. Twenty-four hours from now—I'm a sex crazed madwoman and you're a quivering piece of meat."

11

*F*ollowing less than a full night of sleep, Margaret gulped down her morning coffee behind the wheel of the car and made her way into the city. The roads, particularly Route 101, were essentially free of traffic. It was just before seven-thirty when the BMW crossed the town line into Manchester and made its way through the west side of the city toward the downtown area. The offices of Margaret Kelly & Associates, LLC were housed in a renovated, nineteenth century brick building on Stark Street. The building was the prize plum she had snatched up at auction during the region's real estate bust of the late eighties and early nineties. Unlike some, who almost reluctantly took advantage of those property owners who were forced to surrender their real estate investments when market values dropped precipitously, she had enjoyed the exercise. As she was happy to explain over cocktails to anyone who would listen, *the hapless victims of the recession were nothing more than greedy buffoons who overextended themselves, leaving themselves ripe for the plucking.* "To the law of the jungle," she had said on more than one occasion, her cocktail glass extended in the fashion of a toast. "Kill or be killed, eat or be eaten."

Pulling into her reserved parking space at the front of the building, she noticed Vern Butler's Toyota along with two other vehicles already in place. Entering the front desk area, she heard playful chatter from the staff room come to an end. Margaret walked toward the silenced voices, finally peering through the doorway.

"Just a little over a week gang, then some welcome *r and r*," she said. She spent a few minutes fielding questions from employees before withdrawing to her office where a stack of client folders sat on the corner of her desk awaiting her attention. An hour passed before she realized that her concentration level was being impaired by the Skip Emerson issue. She reached for the phone. She punched out the digits to his home phone and waited.

"Hello," sounded a voice carrying a sadly familiar tone.

"It's Margaret Keogh—returning your call," she answered, surprising even herself by reverting back to her maiden name.

"Oh, Maggie—thank you—thanks for getting back to me." He spoke haltingly, sounding nervous. "You must think I'm a lunatic, calling after all this time."

"No, I'm just curious."

"Well, as you've probably already guessed, I'm calling about Jenny."

"Go ahead, Skip—and please get to your point. This is a busy time of the year for me and this call is taking me away from a mountain of work."

"Yeah, okay—I'm just calling to ask for a little bit of help in getting a chance to talk to her."

"She's over twenty-one now—all grown up. You don't need my permission or blessing to speak with her," she snapped back.

"Maggie, it's just—"

"It's Margaret, not Maggie. My husband's the only one I allow to call me that."

"Margaret, it's not for me that I'm doing this. I need to speak to Jenny about possibly coming to visit my mother. My mom is not in the best of health right now. She's talking more and more about seeing her granddaughter before long—"

"You're talking to the wrong person. I'm probably the last person you should be asking to run interference for you here."

"Margaret, we don't have Jenny's phone number or whereabouts or anything. Believe me—I wouldn't have bothered you on this unless it was of absolute importance. We really need to reach her and talk to her quickly." Instantly the circumstances at hand in the Emerson household became evident. Skip was choosing his words carefully but his inflection and tone lent substantiation to Margaret's hunch. Mrs. Emerson was dying.

"I'll make a call tonight. I'm not promising you anything, Skip. I'm not even sure I'm in favor of this whole thing—but I'll run it by Jenny. You'll hear from me within twenty-four hours, one way or the other."

"Thank you. I won't say a word to mom until I hear from you."

For Margaret, the workday passed as quickly as a funeral procession marching into a stiff wind. It was just after five o'clock when she locked the front door to the office and left for home. Fortunately, she managed to isolate her conversation with Skip to the back of her mind, remaining focused on the logjam of tax returns on her desk. The ten mile ride to the suburbs sped by and she was warmly greeted in the hallway by Brian and Colleen, the child hoisted up in one arm by her proud father.

"There's mommy, Jelly Bean, Bedford's answer to June Cleaver," he joked.

"How is my baby?" The toddler smiled slightly but quickly snuggled closer to her dad.

"Come on now, Colleen, let your mommy give you a big hug. Daddy can't be hogging all the fun." Brian transferred the weight of the sixteen month old across his body and handed the baby to her mother. The woman, who only hours earlier was the source of her employee's stress, was now cooing in her daughter's ear, much to the toddler's delight.

"Good day at work?"

"It's not done. I got back to Skip this morning and now I'm stuck in the middle of something I'd rather not be. He's intent on getting in touch with Jenny and, stupid me, I've promised to call ahead and set things in motion.

"What! Now all of a sudden he wants to be Ward Cleaver, the All-American dad."

"Jesus, Kelly, what's with all this *Leave It To Beaver* crap?"

"No, really, what's the big deal all of a sudden?"

"Well, it sounds like his mother is ill, quite ill. She's probably figuring she's not going to live to see a grandchild from either Skip or his brother, his incredibly *gay* brother, and Jenny's the only game in town."

"So what are you going to do?" he asked, sounding less sarcastic and more concerned.

"I haven't spoken to my daughter, my other daughter, for over a year now. Speaking from a personally selfish point of view, this gives me the opportunity to break the ice without appearing to cave in to her and her worthless boyfriend."

"Ah, my sweet Maggie May, forever the opportunist."

"Take the baby. I'm going upstairs to make the call." She handed the little girl back to her husband and raced to the second floor and her home office.

Nearly half an hour after retreating to her office to contact her daughter in Rhode Island, Margaret descended the stairs. Brian glanced up from his newspaper and watched as his wife withdrew to the kitchen, only to return to his side a few moments later holding a glass of wine. In her absence, Moira had taken charge of the baby and brought her upstairs.

"Are you okay?" he asked.

"No, not really. I just got off the phone with Mrs. Burns, Jenny's landlady. I called her when I wasn't able to get through to Jen. It seems her phone's been disconnected. Mrs. Burns informed me that Jenny's been alone there for nearly four months. Roger, that piece of shit she's been living with, split just after Christmas and Jen's been trying to make ends meet alone. It sounds like she hasn't been keeping up with her phone bill for starters. Brian, I'm worried. The landlady also hinted that this month's rent isn't paid either."

"Why don't we drive down to Rhode Island tomorrow and talk to her—you know, make sure she's okay," he suggested.

"I would—any time but now. Jesus, why did this shit have to happen in April when I'm up to my neck with work?"

"Well, it sounds like we have to do something."

"Brian, would it be too much to ask you to go down there for me? I have to find out what's going on."

"I'd need an address and some directions. I was hoping to go to Lowell tomorrow to see my aunt and uncle but I guess that can wait."

"Why does all this bullshit have to come all at once—and during tax season," she lamented, her head now resting on her husband's shoulder.

"Don't get yourself all worked up, Keogh. Some good might come of this. If I do go down there alone, I'm going to need some instructions."

"Like what?"

"Well, for starters, what if it looks like she wouldn't mind coming home? According to her landlady, that idiot Roger has taken off. What's keeping her there? Would you welcome her back and not jerk her around?"

"Of course she'd be welcomed home. Tell her I promise not to reopen old wounds."

"Promise?"

"Yes, Kelly, I promise." He looked down at his wife, catching her staring blankly across the living room while bringing the glass of wine up to her lips.

"My blood pressure must be up over two hundred about now. God damn it, take a look at my hands—the way they're shaking."

"You do want her back home, don't you, Maggie May?" She nodded yes.

"Okay, it's settled. I leave for Newport tomorrow and make sure everyone and everything is okay." Her response came in a weak smile. "Now enough with this serious stuff—the problem will be resolved. However—there remains one more serious matter to take care of tonight."

"And what is that?"

"I've been psyching myself up all day, knowing that my vampire girl would be coming home tonight. I told you last night I had to get myself in the mood for biting sex—and, by God, I have. When we slip under the covers I want vampire girl—in all her sadistic glory—to swarm over me—just like she threatened she would last night."

"Kelly, you've got to be kidding! There's no way. I'm too uptight."

"Cut it out, Keogh, I'm practically moving heaven and earth for you. How many husbands would travel to Rhode Island—on their day off, mind you—to do their wife's dirty work?"

"I'll reward you when you return if you're successful. You're so stupid, for all I know you'll get lost on the way down and wind up in Connecticut—or maybe on the Cape. No Brian, no reward, no vampire girl, no nothing until you get things straightened out down in Rhode Island."

"I'm getting drunk," exploded Brian. Margaret hopped to her feet and bounded for the kitchen. She returned with a second glass and another bottle of wine.

"Join the club," she said, falling back on the couch next to her husband.

III

The clanging sound from Brian's dated alarm clock broke the quiet of the bedroom as he opened his eyes to the pitch black surroundings. His hand swished once, then a second time before making contact with the spring powered, Bulova time piece.

"Mother of God, Kelly, what time is it?" Margaret moaned from beside him.

"Five-thirty."

"Why the hell did you set the alarm so early?"

"I wanted to catch seven o'clock mass before hitting the road."

"Oh, I forgot I was married to the last practicing Catholic in the world. Screw it, I'll get up and join you," she added through a muffled yawn. She forced herself up off the mattress while he plodded his way across the wide bedroom floor and into the master bath. Fifteen minutes passed before he joined his wife downstairs in the kitchen. She was facing the stove, her back to the door, when he entered the room and made his way up to her side. He planted a kiss on the top of her head and followed up with a peck to the ear before taking a chair at the table. She continued preparing his breakfast in silence. Scurrying across the floor, he filled a mug with coffee and placed it down before him. He took a sip before making a playful grab at her rear end as she walked to the fridge.

"Don't tell me, let me guess—steak and eggs?"

"Oatmeal, the real stuff, not that instant crap," she responded.

"Do we have any brown sugar in the house?" From behind him came the clatter of her fumbling through the cupboard. Seconds later she placed down a small, glass bowl granting his wish.

Brian sipped on the piping hot coffee for a few seconds before having the bowl of oatmeal set on the table in front of him. He started on his cereal while his wife left the kitchen. A minute or so later she returned and took the chair to his immediate right. Reaching into her bathrobe, she produced a wad of bills which she dropped on the table between them.

"Here's Jenny's address. Also, here's a thousand dollars. I want you to make sure she's not doing without anything. Talk to the landlady—get her paid up to date. She doesn't have to know it's coming from me. Brian glanced down at the stack of money, then raised his eyes back to his wife's. There was an unmistakable sadness etched on her face. She realized as much, causing her to spring to her feet and position herself behind his chair.

"Kelly, I didn't sleep for shit last night thinking about Jenny—and worrying about her. All of a sudden it's really hit me—how much I miss her and all." The woman kneaded his shoulders as she spoke, careful to avoid eye contact with him. "Brian, I'm asking you to do everything in your power to bring my baby home. Do you understand? You're good at things like this. I want our problems resolved. I can't tell you the kind of thoughts and nightmares I had last night thinking about what could happen to her—alone in another state. At least before I always figured that useless Roger was there to protect her."

"I'll do my best."

"Kelly, don't fail me on this. Tell her I'm ready to finance her back into school, somewhere local so she can live here at home. Make sure she knows her bedroom is still there waiting on her. She'll listen to you. She likes you and trusts you."

"Keogh, I'll do everything I can—everything."

"No one has to apologize—not her anyway." There was genuine emotion in his wife's voice as she spoke in just over a whisper. Seconds later her fingernails dug into his shoulders while she wrestled to keep her sentiments under control. This was not the Margaret Kelly he and the rest of the world were accustomed to witness. He reached back and grasped one hand. She broke away, rushing from the kitchen. She stopped abruptly in her tracks only a few feet into the hall.

"I'll go to work today knowing that when I'm done——I'll return home to my Jenny. Brian, assure me you won't fail."

"If it's humanly possible I'll do it, Maggie May. Right now though—go upstairs and get a couple more hours of sleep."

"You'll do it, Brian. I'm not going to even worry about this anymore. This is the kind of thing you're really good at. People trust you."

"Go upstairs and get your rest, baby girl. I'll take care of things down at Jenny's. He listened as his wife's footsteps moved toward the stairway. Unexpectedly, they stopped.

"Brian, I love you very much."

"But I love you more, Maggie May."

Brian filled a thermos with his wife's coffee before speeding into Manchester and the nearest seven o'clock mass. A short time after eight, he pointed his pick-up south and began the long drive to Rhode Island. Stopping near the Massachusetts border to fill up, he invested in a road map. Sipping from his thermos from the side of Route 3, he eyeballed in the route he would follow down to Newport. The exercise presented him with a basic geography lesson. He learned, to his disappointment, that the city renowned for its ocean side mansions was located in the far southeast corner of the nation's smallest state.

Following what seemed like an eternity between the white lines along Interstate 495, and then southward through more Massachusetts and Rhode Island communities than he cared to recall, he crossed the town line and entered Newport. The commute had taken him in excess of three and a half hours. Having found the city, he decided against stopping at a gas station for directions. He saved that option as a last resort. Instead, Brian decided to trust his instincts. He knew Jenny lived on Bridge Street. According to Maggie, the house was centrally located and close to downtown. He reasoned if he followed the road signs to downtown, he might come across the street. That accomplished, he would park the car and search out the specific address on foot. Incredibly, the strategy worked. In the course of making his way through the narrow streets toward the waterfront, Brian looked up while halted at a stop sign to see he was sitting at a

Bridge Street intersection. Traffic was light on this Sunday morning. After turning left and traveling less than a block, a vacant parking space came into view. It had been too easy, he thought. After making sure windows and doors were locked, he exited the truck. Knowing Jenny's address and comparing it to the number on a nearby building, he deduced that her house could not be more than two or three blocks away. He had considered what he might say to the young woman, the exact words, during the trip down from New Hampshire. It was not until this moment that the importance of his mission came into absolute focus. His wife was counting on him to return home with her daughter. If that was not enough, a gravely ill woman was lying in a bed somewhere waiting to meet the granddaughter she had never known.

He had walked less than two blocks when he scampered across Bridge Street and approached a well maintained, gray, two storied house sitting a few feet back from the sidewalk. Stepping up to the front door, he observed twin doorbells, the bottom button identified by the surname of Burns. The top button had no identification. Brian climbed three steps to the porch landing and pressed the higher button. He pressed a second and third time, but elicited no sound or movement from within. Following a minute of hesitation, he rang the lower bell. It took only seconds before activity was heard from inside. Eventually footsteps approached the door and it swung in.

"You'd better not be here from the vacuum cleaner company, I'm warning you right now. I don't know how many times I have to tell you—I'm not interested!" The boldly worded statement caught Brian off guard. It was spoken by an attractive, petite woman who stood before him dressed in sweats and wearing a towel wrapped around her head, no doubt having just washed her hair.

"No, I don't have any vacuum cleaners to sell you—but I am here to let you know you may have already won—one million dollars!"

"Oh please—what do you take me for?" asked the woman, the words exploding from her mouth. Her response caused him to burst out in an abbreviated fit of laughter.

"I'm sorry, just kidding. Are you Mrs. Burns?"

"Yes, well actually it's Miss Burns—no, Ms. Burns. And you are?"

"I'm Brian Kelly. My wife spoke to you yesterday about Jenny—that's her daughter. I've come down to visit. You wouldn't know if she's home, would you?"

"Mr. Kelly, I'm so sorry. You must think I'm insane or something—with all that stuff about the vacuum cleaner and all. I must have sounded like a lunatic."

"No—just a frazzled consumer."

"Please come in," suggested the woman, stepping back and ushering Brian inside. "I'm afraid she's not. Jenny waits tables Sunday mornings. The poor thing's holding down three jobs right now—of course two are only part time."

"Well then, Miss Burns—"

"Bridget, it's Bridget."

"Well, Bridget—any idea what time she might be getting home?"

"She's usually home on Sunday by the middle of the afternoon—unless she's working somewhere else after. It's hard to keep track of that little thing. Listen to me—little thing. She stands head and shoulders over me."

"If you don't mind—and hopefully no one in the neighborhood will get spooked—I'll just be hanging around until Jen gets back. I really have to talk to her—family matters."

"Can I get you some coffee or tea, Mr. Kelly?"

"Tea, if it's not going to put you out," answered Brian, content to sit down and relax until Jenny's return home.

For nearly an hour Brian and his hostess shared light conversation over tea. The woman appeared happy to field a variety of questions from him, most concerning the history of Newport and the role the fabled mansions played in it. When Bridget explained she had a prior engagement and had to begin preparation for it, Brian was quick to excuse himself.

"Bridget, before I forget, Jenny's mother wanted to catch up on her rent," he said, pulling a wad of bills from his wallet.

"No, please, that's really not necessary," the woman answered, appearing embarrassed by her guest's offer.

"No, really, it'll take some of the pressure off of Jen and put her mom's mind at ease."

The woman relented. She sheepishly informed him that the monthly rent was nine hundred dollars. He counted out the full amount, sending the landlady in search of her receipt book. After filling in and tearing off the receipt, she invited Brian to make himself at home, offering him use of her apartment until Jenny's return.

Another hour passed while Brian poured over an assortment of books and magazines in the living room of Bridget Burns, a woman who had been a total stranger just hours earlier. The landlady had been gone for some time when he thought he heard the sound of a key being turned in the lock from the front door. The racket from the sound of the door being pushed in echoed throughout the two family house. Jumping to his feet, he made his way to the hallway where he caught sight of Jenny halfway up the flight of stairs.

"Don't run away, Jenny Keogh, you've got company," he called out. The young woman stopped in her tracks and stared down over the banister.

"Brian? I don't believe it! What are you doing here? Is everyone okay?"

"Everyone's fine. I'm just here for a surprise visit with my favorite step-daughter. I just hope I'm welcome."

She twirled around and quickly descended the stairs. Approaching her visitor without hesitation, she wrapped her arms around the man and hugged tightly.

"Mother's not with you, is she?" she asked.

"Your mother's up to her eyeballs in work back home, but sent me in her place." The embrace continued for the better part of thirty seconds. Finally, Brian pushed her back to arm's length and looked her up and down. Jenny blushed but held back her words. He thought the pretty, young woman seemed genuinely pleased by his presence.

"Am I going to be invited upstairs to see your place or are we going to stand down here and have you just describe everything in minute detail?"

She laughed and pulled on his arm, directing him up the flight of stairs and into the apartment. The front door led into the kitchen. To the right, Brian looked in on a sparsely furnished living room. Straight ahead at the far side of the kitchen and next to a dated, avocado colored refrigerator, was an open door to the bedroom.

"Don't mind the shortage of furniture, Roger took half of it when he moved out," she explained.

"I'm sorry to hear that—about Roger, I mean," he confessed, pretending to be ignorant of her circumstances.

"Don't be sorry, he certainly wasn't." Her tone did not try to mask a residue of bitterness. Jenny's expression recovered its brightness as she led her stepfather into the living room, directing him down onto a futon sofa. He looked up at the young woman, a beautiful girl who appeared slightly tired around the eyes. Again, as he had done so many times before, he marveled at her resemblance to her mother. His memory of a summer, not so long ago, spent with Jenny as a live-in employee came to mind. It was the summer of 1991, a summer of happiness, heartbreak and exhilaration. It had been the summer of Maggie May.

"This is such a wonderful surprise. Why are you here? You said there was nothing wrong at home."

"There's nothing to be too concerned about, but there's lots to talk about—but nothing to be too concerned about. Your mom, and grandparents, and baby sister are all okay and in good health. Us—well, we're a little worried about you. By the way, how long has Roger been gone?"

"He left just after Christmas. He took the car. I kept the apartment and a majority of the furniture—as hard as that may seem to believe," she joked, extending her arm and showcasing the half empty parlor.

"Anyway, I'm here for a number of reasons, not the least of which is the fact that your mother has been worried sick about you—particularly after she tried calling you yesterday and found out the phone was no longer in service."

"That's strictly temporary," interrupted the young woman.

"When your mom couldn't reach you she wound up being updated by your landlady. Now she's sent her personal secretary down here with instructions to bring her baby home."

"That's not going to happen!" she insisted.

"Listen, Jen, hear me out. Don't get all defensive on me. There's stuff going on at home you don't know about and people who love you who want you back—that being me and your mother—especially your mother."

"Then why isn't she here herself?"

"Come on, Jen, you know more than anyone—tax season. She's working just a little under a hundred hours a week right now—and worried sick at the moment about you." Jenny stared down at him for a moment before retreating across the room and by a window. "And by the way, how is Miss Burns downstairs getting nine hundred dollars a month out of you for this?"

"You have to pay a little extra for the ocean view. It wasn't a problem until Roger split. Right now, I'm a few days behind," she confessed.

"No, you're not. You're paid up through the end of the month. I took care of that already."

"Brian, you didn't have to do that. I'll have the money next Friday morning.

I'm paying you back every penny."

"It's your mom's money—and she can afford it. Wait a minute! Wait just a minute. What did you say just a few seconds ago—something about an ocean view?"

"That's right. From my bedroom there's a water view—and that demands a premium." He rose to his feet, extending a hand towards Jenny.

"Lead away, this I got to see—ocean view indeed," he said through a good-natured smirk.

She burst into laughter. Grabbing his hand, she pulled him through the kitchen, ushering him into her bedroom and up to a long, perpendicular window.

"Look out over the beige building across the way," she instructed.

"Okay, I see it, now what? Where's the ocean?"

"It's there. Look directly to the right of the chimney at the far end of the building." He moved his head closer to hers, squinting his eyes in an exaggerated manner.

"My God, no, it's got to be me. It's got to be me because I'm not seeing anything that even remotely looks like water where you're telling me to look. No—and now my eyes are beginning to hurt from the strain of looking for this water you're talking about." She chuckled before comically burying her face in the tuck of his shoulder.

"I didn't say it was the finest view of the ocean in the world—just that it was a water view," she confessed through more laughter. He draped his arm over her shoulder.

"Okay, okay, now I see it. How could I have missed it? My God, Jen, how could I have doubted you? And you're getting this view that Mrs. Burns could be getting ten times your rent for—like from a restaurant who could cash in on the ocean view—or maybe just from tourists who would line up around the block to get a peek at this. Now let me get this straight—you're getting this eye-popping view and the avocado refrigerator—"

"Sorry, Brian, the fridge is mine."

"I'm sorry, this view—this entire palace for a mere nine hundred dollars per month?" he jested.

"It's my first, real apartment."

"Cabin fourteen back in Wells with Trudy was your first, real apartment."

"That was a great summer—for me, anyway." He stepped in front of his step-daughter, applying a two-armed embrace.

"I probably should stop goofing around and get down to business. I'm really not here to play, little girl. Let's go back to the couch and sit down. You need catching up."

"Now you said everyone is fine, right?" Jenny asked.

"Good as gold."

Brian fell back onto the futon and Jenny followed suit, seating herself to his immediate right and resting her head on his shoulder.

"First, the reason you didn't hear from me after the blowup with your mom was because I thought the last thing I needed to do was to get in the middle of your family fight. Then again, I thought you were all safe and sound with your boyfriend. Okay, enough said on that. Anyway, this past week your mother was contacted by your father."

"My father?"

"Your biological father—Skip Emerson. I don't know what else to call him. Anyway, Skip talked to your mother and wanted to know how to contact you."

"What the hell does he want?"

"Jen, Jen—calm down and let me tell the story here. Save your questions until I'm done. He told your mother that your other grandmother, his mom, is quite ill and has made it known that she would like to meet her only grandchild before—well, before anything should happen to her. The Emersons know that you're over twenty-one now and free to see them without your mother's consent, but they didn't know where you were. So——your mother sees a chance to break the ice and save face—because she's missing you so badly. Anyway, she calls your number thinking that you'll talk and maybe the two of you will start patching everything up—and that's when she finds out your telephone's been disconnected. She got all flustered and called up Mrs. Burns—and things just started getting set in motion. I'm here to let you know about your other grandmother, because you have to know about that, but also, and this is just as important— maybe more so—I'm here to bring you home to Bedford."

"That's not going to happen, Brian, so get that out of your head right now. I may be in a little over my head, but I love it in Newport. And then there's the matter of my mother. I cannot face that woman—not right now. You know what she's like. I will not—under any conditions—crawl back to her."

"You won't be crawling back. Where do you get that idea? She wants you back. She's ready to help you get back in school, to get a degree."

"And have my face rubbed in this whole Roger fiasco. I know her. She'd bide her time and then—wham!"

"I won't let that happen. Jen, if she even starts to pull any shit with you, then you can come up to Wells. I'll hand my cottage down at Deptula over to you. You could live and work out of there—rent free—for as long as you want."

"I would never ask that of you."

"Jen, all I'm asking here is for you to come home with me for a visit. You don't have to make a decision on that thing with your other grandmother right now. Come home and see how things are with you and your mom. I'm telling you, she wants you back and I know there'll be no finger-pointing or placing the blame from her on anyone. You have to believe me here."

Jenny fidgeted next to him for a moment.

"I can't just pick up and go home for a visit. I've got too many commitments here."

"It'd be just a short visit. Jen, a move back home would go a long way toward your future. Let your mom and me help."

"No, Brian, I've got to be at the shop tomorrow morning."

"God, you're making this so hard. Okay, have it your own way, but now you're going to have a houseguest on your hands. There's no way I'm going back to Bedford and face your mother without you in tow. Fine, I'll take that empty room next to yours and sleep on the floor. What was that? Roger's studio or something?"

"As a matter of fact, it was," she answered.

"Oh, and I'll be wanting three meals a day. I'm useless at cooking, your mother and Millie will attest to that. I'll expect oatmeal every morning—not that instant crap, either—the real thing. And aside from playing the television too loud all night, and keeping the lights on all night—I'm afraid of the dark, you see—well, you'll hardly know I'm here, Jenny girl."

The young woman responded with a sweet laugh, a laugh reminiscent, he thought, to the ones he had heard from her mother almost twenty-five years before in the hallways and classrooms of Southside High School.

"Brian, as I said, there is no way I can return home with you, but your visit here is a wonderful first step toward putting this family squabble behind us."

IV

Margaret spent the majority of Sunday in her office buried behind a stack of tax folders. She and Vern Butler, her trusted senior employee, were the only two professionals to work on what was a beautiful spring afternoon. It was after six o'clock when she glanced up from her computer and saw Vern standing in her doorway.

"Ever sit back and ask yourself why we chose this God-awful profession?" he asked from behind a weary smile.

"Not a day goes by that I don't—especially at this time of the year. But hang in there, Vern. Just a little over a week to go before things return to normal."

"I hate these years when the fifteenth lands on a weekend, and the season gets stretched out just that much more." Vern, approaching his sixtieth year and an employee of Margaret's for the last ten years, extended her a comical, military salute before heading for the staircase.

Margaret hit the 'Save' button on her computer, then proceeded to shut down her system for the day. Her thoughts flashed back to her discussion with Brian that same morning. She wondered how his journey to Newport had gone. She had not heard from him all day. Walking to the car, she debated with herself on whether that was a favorable or unfavorable sign.

Margaret steered the BMW to the turnpike, avoiding the growing number of traffic lights dotting Manchester's west side. With minimum traffic on the roadways, the commute from door to door took just over fifteen minutes. Her eyes searched for any sign of her husband's pickup as she roared into the driveway and powered in the direction of the house. The large colonial was in near darkness, telling her that Moira and the baby were probably upstairs in one or the other's bedroom. Breaking the plane of the front door, she called out to Colleen. From the base of the stairway, she heard the sound of scurrying. Within seconds, the toddler was descending the stairs, assisted by her nanny.

"Mommy," the child cried out, quickening her steps as she neared her parent.

"She's been fed, ma'am, done her movement and taken a nice soapy bath," announced the nanny. Margaret swept her daughter up into her arms and showered the girl with a flurry of kisses.

"Any word from Mr. Kelly, Moira? Has he telephoned?"

"No, ma'am—quiet, it's been."

"Listen, I'll take care of this one now. She'll have to be going to bed in a short while, anyway. Feel free to take the rest of the evening off—unless you've got other chores to catch up on."

"Oh, that'd be grand, Mrs. Kelly. And sure I'm caught up with everything today. This little one's been an angel all day—she has." The Irish teenager gave the baby an affectionate squeeze to the leg and headed back upstairs to her room.

Mother and daughter retreated to the kitchen, where the baby was allowed to roam the room and climb between the table and chairs. Margaret prepared herself soup and a sandwich, all the while keeping up a stream of childish banter. However, in the back of her mind was the matter of Brian's success in Rhode Island. Finishing dinner, she placed the silverware, cups and plates into the dishwasher. It was nearly time to bring the baby upstairs for the night. She hoisted her daughter up by one arm at the base of the stairs and made a game of climbing to the second story. Colleen broke out in a fit of laughter as they neared the top of the staircase. She was a happy baby, happier and more gregarious than Jenny had been at this age. Margaret wondered if it was influenced by her father and his lighthearted disposition. By seven-thirty, the child was snugly secure under her bedcovers and already dropping off to sleep.

Following a short visit back to the kitchen, where she poured herself a glass of wine, she made her way to the living room. She retreated to the far end of the couch and, after removing her shoes, folded her legs beneath her and curled up for the wait. The thought of her daughter's possible return home had lifted her spirits throughout the day. Now, as time passed with no word from Brian, she became more realistic about the likelihood of his success. Her husband did not believe in cell phones, claiming the potential disturbances were too high a price to pay for the convenience. However, as she saw it, that did not excuse him from pulling over to a pay phone and updating her on the success of his mission. As time passed and she was able to mull over the circumstances at hand, she was convinced that a successful Brian would have called ahead, trumpeting his success and breaking the long silence between mother and daughter over the phone. It was eight o'clock when she raised herself from the couch. Returning to the kitchen, she refilled her wine glass. She held her breath when she heard a vehicle approaching the house. Picking up the sound of deceleration, her heart began to pound as the unmistakable sound of Brian's truck engine filled the air around the house. Margaret did not move for fear of missing a single clue, a voice or the slamming of more than one door. Finally, there came a roar from the engine, followed by complete silence. She hated this habit of his, one of his few, blue collar habits. Following a full minute of complete silence there came the slamming of a vehicle door. Or was it two doors in unison? She could not be sure. At last, the front door swung open and she picked up on the shuffle of footsteps. She stepped to the kitchen doorway and glanced down the hall. Momentarily it was empty, and then Brian emerged from behind the stairwell. He was alone. His body language appeared to speak volumes. His head was lowered slightly as he stared in the direction of his wife.

"Things aren't as bad as they seem, Maggie May. They really aren't."

"She wouldn't come?"

"My visit went a lot better than you might think. She said it was a good, first step," he explained from twenty feet away. Margaret walked toward him, the disappointment already showing on her face. Reaching her husband, she glanced up at his eyes. His expression was cheerless.

"She knows how you feel—how we both feel." The woman laid her head on his shoulder, allowing it to muffle the sound as she began to weep.

"I made the mistake of getting my hopes up. Does she know how much I want her back?"

"She does."

"What did you talk about all that time?"

"Mostly about how we both wanted her home and back in school. I told her I couldn't go home without her—not the way you felt."

"You did tell her how much I want her back, no questions—no finger pointing?"

"I told her over and over."

"Did she say when she might come home? How did she react to the news about Mrs. Emerson?"

"She wouldn't commit on the Emerson thing and going to visit her grandmother."

"She'd have to come home soon for that. It's not like the woman has all sorts of time," added Margaret, seeing a glimmer of hope attached to the dying woman's circumstances.

"She has no car at the moment. The only way she would have agreed to come back to Bedford was if I promised to drive her all the way back to Newport tomorrow."

"And you didn't offer?" she asked accusingly.

"I didn't say I didn't offer."

"So, did you or didn't you offer?"

"Jenny said our meeting was a good first step," repeated Brian.

"Why can't you just answer my question?"

"Jenny really felt our time together was a good first step, but I thought a second step would be even better."

"Kelly, stop jerking me around. Did you offer to drive Jenny home?" Brian turned his wife in the direction of the front door.

"Our meeting was a good first step, but now it's time for the second step. Go open the door, Keogh." Margaret's eyes refilled with tears as the meaning behind her husband's words became clear. She sprang toward the front door, pulling it open without a moment's hesitation.

"Hello, mother," said Jenny, standing directly below on the granite step. Margaret flung her arms around her daughter, crying out in joy.

"Honey, you're home. Thank God, you're home." The embrace was returned by the younger woman. From a few feet away, Brian looked on as the two remained wrapped in each other's arms for the better part of a minute.

"If you guys want to come inside and do some catching up in the living room, I'll put on some coffee." Mother and daughter did not respond or even flash eye contact. However, seconds later they turned and walked inside the house, eventually making their way to the living room couch.

Brian was able to pick up on the two female voices all the way in the kitchen as he prepared the coffee, even if the words were not intelligible. The voices carried a cheerful tone, with bursts of laughter penetrating the dialogue every few seconds.

V

*B*rian's eyes opened to a room almost totally void of light. He glanced to the illuminated face of his clock as it ticked away on the night stand close by his head. It was nearly five o'clock. Reaching across his body, he pushed down the alarm button. He let his head fall back onto the pillow and surveyed his mental state, searching his mind for a sense of how rested he felt. After nearly a minute of contemplation, he determined the results were inconclusive. He let his arm fall over his wife's warm body. She did not move or react to his touch. He curled up aside her, pushing his hand under the bed covers and eventually down inside her pajama top. Her body was warm and her breast soft.

"God, I love your breasts."

"Kelly, what time is it?"

"It's five o'clock. No, seriously, Maggie May, I do love your breasts."

"They're too fucking small and you know it. I can't believe you woke me this early in the morning to feed me this shit."

"I have to get up, get Jenny up, and start getting ready for the trip back to Rhode Island. I assume you want a chance to see your daughter before she leaves."

"We were up talking until two-thirty."

"Working out details?"

"She's coming home at the end of the month. We'll have her back in school next fall. It's all arranged." He craned his neck and softly bit down on his wife's ear.

"You do realize you owe me big time for this, right?"

"And why's that?" she asked.

"For starters, I'm losing a day of work today driving Jen back to Newport. Shall I continue?"

"No, spare me. As much as I hate to admit it, you did well—in your own clumsy way. When tax season is behind me, I'll return the favor. Be thinking about how you want to be rewarded." He reached over and kissed his wife, running his tongue across her lips as he pulled away.

"The complete absence of morning breath—Keogh, you're amazing." He rolled himself off the mattress and crossed the room to her side of the bed. "Alley oop, up we go, let's go wake your clone." He reached down and lifted Margaret from the bed. Seconds later, the two were calling to Jenny from the doorway of her bedroom. It was directly across the hall from theirs and had remained unchanged and unused in her absence. Following assurances from the twenty-one year old that she would promptly shower and dress, they headed downstairs together to prepare breakfast.

After gulping down his toast and cereal, Brian left mother and daughter alone at the table and retreated upstairs to shower before his long day's journey. Margaret and Jenny used the time to straighten out a few, final details and say final good-byes. By the time Brian emerged from the couple's private bath, his wife was already nestled under the covers, hoping to catch another hour of sleep. Making his way to the hallway, he paused by the bed and looked down on her. Seconds later, two objects dropped from his hands and onto her reclining form.

"What the hell is going on?" she asked, reaching out to grab one of the items now balanced on her torso.

"Just in case you thought you might reward me with a new tie or some piece-of-crap gift certificate, this will help point you in the right direction." She opened her eyes and pulled one of the objects to within view. It was one of a pair of knee pads she had bought him two years ago as a humorous Christmas gift.

"In your fucking dreams, Kelly," she spat out. Her declaration caused him to burst into laughter.

"Sorry, Maggie May, that's what I want—complete sexual servitude."

"I'm sorry, but—then again, I wouldn't even know how to use them—or even put them on—not the way you've been monopolizing them for the past couple of years."

"That's all the more reason for me to leave them handy, so you can familiarize yourself with them." She stared up at him from the pillow. He smiled.

"Okay, Kelly, leave them. But be careful what you wish for." Her eyes flashed behind one of her devilish smiles. Her words were followed by the sound of teeth snapping together in an exaggerated, biting motion.

It was late afternoon when Brian turned into the driveway of the Atlantic Coast Lodge. The trip down and back from Rhode Island had left him physically drained. Taking an alternate route on the way back to Maine, he had gotten turned around in Providence, causing him to do battle with midday traffic. In the end, what he had hoped would be a relaxing weekend in Bedford had evolved into a driving marathon. The pickup rolled to within ten feet of the office door before he eased it to a stop and jumped to the pavement. His body was stiff from hours behind the wheel. He was already looking forward to making his way down Mile Road to the cottage and a full night's sleep. The office had remained closed on this Monday. He had not bothered contacting Millie or Hal to work in his absence, reasoning the complex was still closed and he could always catch up on voice and e-mail later in the week. He pushed in the door and walked across the room to the front desk. A glance down at the phone system told him there were twenty-seven messages awaiting his attention. He let out a sigh and retreated to the next room. There he found comfort in an old, familiar chair. Throwing himself back, he paused while his mind journeyed back, as it often did, to a time now clouded in his memory. The room looked different then, the chair beneath him being the only constant to the past, the chair and himself. There was a hush trapped among the four walls, a pronounced quiet except for faint noises wafting in from nearby Route 1. He closed his eyes and conjured up thoughts of a time when this room literally shook from human voices. Peering out toward the office, he tried to imagine Lou Russo back standing behind the desk. Lou and

Bella Russo were gone and had been for fifteen years. Brian's mind flashed back to a day a few years before and a low key telephone call from Florida, a call from Bella. Lou had died, very suddenly, and Bella was beside herself. Brian flew to Jacksonville for the wake and funeral. He had not seen the couple in over ten years and had only occasionally communicated with his former employers, but Lou's death had shaken him nonetheless. He continued to stare out into the quiet of the next room, reliving, painfully reliving. Inevitably, he called upon the memory of the first day his eyes set on Angelique LaChapelle. She had stepped into the far room while he sat in this very chair. The banter, in French, between Lou and the LaChapelle family chimed in his head like a muffled echo. That was the day a teenage girl had emerged from the shadows and, for all time, left a mark upon his spirit. Brian thought back to the exact moment his eyes had met hers. It was the moment she took possession of his soul, his free will, and five senses. Alone in the quiet building and apart from any distraction, Brian thought he found himself connecting with his Angel's spirit. He felt he was climbing to another plateau of existence and drawing himself closer to whatever remained of her in this world. Come May, it would be thirteen years since that dreadful day and the phone call that had sent him racing to Quebec City. Next month would be the thirteenth consecutive year he would return to Canada and visit her final resting place. He stared out to the office. He longed for Angel to be standing there as she had so many summers before. He longed for the sound of Lou's voice, barking out orders to his upstart, sixteen-year-old assistant, Brian Kelly. Instead, only silence collected around him. Mercifully, it was broken by the sharp ring of the telephone from behind the main desk. He jumped to his feet, returned to the here and now, and lumbered into the office.

"Atlantic Coast Lodge," he recited into the phone.

"Hey, finally back. Weren't you due back yesterday?" It was Bobby Copeland, his longtime friend and occasional drinking buddy.

"I got detained in Bedford—or should I say Rhode Island."

"Rhode Island! What the fuck were you doing in Rhode Island?"

"It's a long story—a very long story—and you don't have the attention span to hear it all."

"Don't be a wiseass, Kelly. Listen, I'm calling about supper. Annie's asked me to fend for myself. No, that's not true. Actually she told me to get my own supper, just like that. She's getting uppity in her old age. But, it works out fine. I want to talk to you about teaming up with me. Supper's on me. I'll take you wherever you want, it's on me. But you have to hear me out. Maybe we can go over to Alisson's like in the old days?"

"Bobby, how many times do I have to tell you, I'm not interested," he exclaimed, showing annoyance at his friend's insistence on this particular matter.

"What, you're turning down a free dinner?"

"Bobby, you're wasting your time. I have too much time and money invested here to start something else."

"Humor me, buddy, humor me," insisted his friend of nearly twenty years.

"Okay, it's your money," he relented, agreeing to hear the sales pitch yet another time on the prospect of creating a partnership from Copeland's Lawn

Service and Property Management. "This time it'll cost you, though. I'm think-ing fisherman's platter and lot of Guinness—and I don't want any bitching from you over the tab."

"Tonight at seven—like in the old days," Bobby called out before the click of the phone.

Brian placed down the receiver and glanced up at the clock. He had ninety minutes of free time before dinner in Kennebunkport. Without hesitation, he flicked off the light and made for his pickup. He reasoned he could do with a short walk on the beach to unwind from his two day ordeal. He was happy to help with family matters and the thought of Jenny's return home lifted his spir-its, but the drive to and from Newport on two successive days had left him phys-ically and mentally drained. It was under a mile and a half down to his cottage on Deptula Lane, even less as the crow would fly. In less than three minutes he was turning the Ford onto the private road and slowly rolling in the direction of his personal retreat. His cottage, yellow and small, sat at the end of the roadway surrounded on three sides by the marshlands and wildlife sanctuary. The mod-est, knotty-pined structure was the object of sometimes good natured, sometimes not, ridicule from his wife. However, in spite of constant pressure from her to enlarge and upscale, he had kept the rustic lodge as he had bought it ten years before. The simplicity of this dwelling suited him. Perhaps, subconsciously, he found it akin to himself: humble and yet rock solid.

After tossing his overnight bag onto the porch, Brian headed due east toward the Atlantic Ocean. It was a short walk, less than three minutes, to the cement steps leading down to Crescent Beach. With his feet firmly planted in the hard-packed sand, he turned northward, his steps drawing him close to the foaming surf as it gushed, then receded, only a few yards away. He found the sound and smell of the sea therapeutic as he strode headlong into a fresh breeze from the north. It was at times like these that he loved his home by the sea and could not imagine setting roots anywhere but close by the ocean. As he often did, he made note of the nearby row of houses facing the Atlantic. For the past fifteen years or so, there had been a significant change in the character and appearance of the structures bordering the beach. Rapidly disappearing were the weathered beach homes of prior generations. He found nothing more pleasing to the eye than the sight of these dated houses, many sporting a distinctive wraparound porch. Often on these walks, he would stare up at these piazzas and imagine women standing about, adorned in large hats and the conformist, traditional garb of the 1920's. F. Scott and Zelda's people from the Jazz Age, he would think wistfully. Then, passing by a cluster of rocks half buried by the tide-sculptured sand, his thoughts drifted back to Bedford and Colleen. Moira was probably feeding his baby girl at this very moment, while Maggie May slaved at her desk in Manchester, oblivious to her daughter and husband. Her difficult season was practically over, he told himself. Soon she would join him in Maine, followed shortly after by his daughter and her nanny.

After walking past the dual cement staircases leading up to the public beach's main parking lot, he steered his footsteps away from the foaming surf, directing himself to one of Wells Beach's numerous right-of-ways and onto Atlantic Avenue. He had walked nearly a mile and his internal clock told him his time was growing short. He would have to return to the cottage, clean up, and make his way to Kennebunkport. On the walk back to the cottage he chastised himself for accepting his friend's invitation. The fresh, ocean air reminded him how tired he was but he had already given his word.

VI

The marshland surrounding his property was shrouded in fog as Brian sat at the small breakfast table in the corner of his porch. He was in good spirits on this Wednesday. He had not seen his family in two days but was already looking forward to arriving home in Bedford this evening. For as much as he savored his time at the cottage, these periods were largely spent away from his wife and daughter. Therefore, his schedule was a delicate, psychological balance between familial affection at home in Bedford and a sense of independence while managing the lodge in Wells. Sipping on a glass of orange juice, his eyes perused a local newspaper, making note of any happenings in town or county government that could impact his business. Such attention to detail was understandable for a man who was not only the general manager of the Atlantic Coast Lodge, but also one third owner of the corporation, not to mention the only active participant in daily operations among the three shareholders. The loss of a full day of work on Monday had prompted him to put in a fourteen hour day on Tuesday.

As he nursed his juice and picked at two slices of raisin toast, his attention was pulled from the newspaper when a small group of mallard ducks swam by through the narrow arm of the estuary, their presence revealed by a short series of squawks. A few seconds passed and the formation swam from sight, disappearing into a low hanging wall of mist. He had slept well on Tuesday night, certainly better than the night before after dining with Bobby Copeland. Dinner in Dock Square had been enjoyable, particularly with his friend picking up the tab. As expected, Bobby had tried to lure Brian into joining him as a full partner in the lawn care business, explaining he was being forced to turn away lucrative work for lack of another hands-on owner. After explaining his feelings about the lodge and his obligations there for no less than the fifth time, the conversation had moved on to more pleasant topics, as the pair reminisced about days past and on some of the young women who had left their marks, both literally and figuratively, on them. Now both on the cusp of middle age, the two men broke into gales of laughter on a number of occasions, causing more than a few heads to turn from their own conversations over the course of the evening.

Arriving at the office prior to eight o'clock, Brian began working on a 'to do' list for Millie. Among the tasks he wanted to delegate to his longtime assistant manager was the interviewing of applicants for chambermaid duties. He had knowledge of, at minimum, one position to be filled for the upcoming summer, possibly two. Next, he made a tour of the entire complex, testing the lighting, appliances, televisions, plumbing, heat and air conditioning in each unit, in addition to making notes for possible cosmetic improvements. He did not return to the office until late morning. Entering the room, he was greeted by the sound of the telephone.

"Good morning, Atlantic Coast Lodge."

"Brian Kelly, please," asked a male voice.

"This is he. May I help you?"

"Brian, this is Skip Emerson—you may remember me from back at Southside. Your wife gave me your number. We just finished talking a few seconds ago." The man's voice sounded strained. "She said you'd have a pretty good idea of what I was calling about. It's about my mother—and Jenny. My mother's very ill—and she's made it clear to the family that she'd really like to meet her granddaughter before anything happens to her. That's why I'm calling, Brian. I need your help with this. Margaret—well, your wife's not helping me with this at all. She's made it clear that she's dead set against me or my father bringing Jenny to see Mom. She's saying that she'd let Jenny come to visit Mom, but only under certain conditions. I guess Jenny has no car and is too young to rent one. Margaret won't agree to let her come here by bus and, so, it seems you're the only one I can turn to on this. Brian, if it's money you want—for lost work—for anything, just say the word and I'll make sure you get paid."

"Skip, it's not like Jenny's just around the corner. She's in Rhode Island. As it is, I just finished driving down and back a couple of times."

"I'll pay you whatever you want for this," the man added, making no attempt to veil his desperation.

"Skip, it's not the money. Please cut out the talk about money."

"Brian, trust me when I tell you that we don't have a lot of time with this. Mom is in very bad shape. Please talk to Jenny. We need her back here soon. My mother is holding on—I think, for that reason—and that reason only." Brian, his stomach now twisted from the stress of the call, felt himself groping for a way to escape the present circumstances.

"Give me your number, Skip. I'll call Jenny and find out how she feels about this. I already talked to her about it earlier in the week, but she never stated how she felt about visiting your mom."

"You'll tell her how much it'd mean to her grandmother—to everyone?"

"Yeah, I will."

After jotting down Emerson's cell phone and home phone numbers, the conversation was brought to a close. Within thirty seconds, he was back on the phone, dialing the offices of Margaret Kelly & Associates. Gretchen, the front desk secretary, took the call and forwarded it upstairs to her boss.

"Margaret Kelly," answered a voice in no-nonsense fashion.

"It's your husband. What the hell is this shit of giving Skip Emerson my number?" roared Brian.

"The asshole wouldn't get off my back, so I gave him your number. I don't have the fucking time to be listening to him whine about his mother."

"When did this suddenly become my problem? Just get him in touch with Jenny and let them work it out themselves."

"Absolutely not. I told you that before."

"Keogh, this whole god damn thing is suddenly in my lap. This is not my problem."

"You're right, Brian, it isn't. Just tell him to go fuck himself and be done with it."

"Maggie, his mother's dying! This is her last request. For God's sake, give a little here. Let him go get Jenny—if she agrees."

"No, not him—or his asshole father."

"If you feel that strongly about it, then you go down to Newport and get Jenny up here."

"In case you haven't noticed, it's tax season!"

"I just finished driving down and back twice—in case you don't remember."

"How can I forget? You won't let me forget."

"I can't miss any more work running down to Newport. You've got to know that."

"I do?"

"Just let Skip go—if Jenny will come back."

"No, I'll only allow two people to go—you and me. And we both know that I won't be going."

"Come on, Maggie May, give a little."

"Kelly, this conversation is starting to drag on and I'm very busy."

"And I'm not?"

"Brian, my time is worth more than your time. If you need evidence of that, then we'll just compare W-2's next January. That should put all doubts to rest." There was no immediate response from her husband. That came a few seconds later.

"I need Jenny's work number—or maybe her landlady's." Brian listened to the sound of desk drawers being opened and closed for the next few seconds before being given the telephone numbers he had requested.

"Don't be a total idiot, Brian. At least make them reimburse you for gas."

"Skip's already offered to pay me for my efforts."

"Yes, the Emersons are great at that. They also offered to pay for Jenny's abortion—if you recall."

"Well, Mrs. Kelly, I won't keep you any longer. We all know how much your time is worth, don't we?" He did not wait on a caustic response from his wife, quickly hanging up the phone.

Jenny was seated on the front steps of the house when Brian turned the corner onto Bridge Street. It was lunchtime and she was nibbling on a sandwich as she watched the Ford come to a stop in front of the house. Gulping down the last bite of chicken salad on rye, she jumped to her feet and scurried over to the vehicle. Brian leaned over and swung open the door from inside the cab.

"I can think of a hundred things I'd rather be doing than this," she said as she settled herself in the passenger seat.

"That's funny—I could only come up with ninety-one," he answered. "And to think that only a week ago, I was thinking how little I got to see of my step-daughter."

"What time did you leave Bedford this morning?"

"I didn't. I came in from Wells. Your mother and I had words yesterday—over this whole thing with Mrs. Emerson. I decided to spend an extra night up at the beach. We'll have plenty of time to go at each other tonight after we get home. I thought we'd go visit Mrs. Emerson as soon as we reach Manchester—get it over and done with."

"I don't know what I'm going to say to her. This is not something you deal with every day."

"Well, Jen, if it were me, I'd just tell her that you're glad she asked to see you—tell her you love her—call her grandmother. Don't even bring up anything from back when your mother had you. Just tell her everything you think might bring comfort to her. Put her mind at rest. Put her at peace." Jenny peered across the front seat at Brian, appearing to be running his suggestions over in her mind.

"Are you up for climbing behind the wheel and giving me a rest?" he asked.

"Absolutely," replied Jenny.

"We'll change seats when I stop to get us some coffee—which will be the first chance I get."

The drive back to New Hampshire was uneventful with Jenny not relinquishing the wheel at any time. Brian spent no less than half the trip with his eyes closed and his head resting back against the seat. However, he was totally alert when the truck crossed by the ENTERING MANCHESTER sign on the Everett Turnpike, causing Jenny to let out a long sigh.

"The sooner we start, the sooner we get it done and behind us," he said after the girl stared across the cab, nervousness showing on her face. He reached awkwardly into his back pocket and produced a folded piece of paper.

"The Emersons live in the north end of town. I'll guide you to the street and house. It'll be fine, Jen, relax. You're doing the right thing." Her response was a timid smile.

Following the set of directions provided by Skip a day earlier, Brian directed Jenny across the Amoskeag Bridge and into the north end, widely considered the city's most fashionable neighborhood. The street by street directions eventually brought them to the front of a meticulously maintained, brown Victorian, set back from the road behind a generous expanse of lawn. Jenny chose not to pull the pickup into the driveway. Instead, she parked the vehicle on the roadside and in front of a black iron fence that ran the length of the property's front boundary. The young woman turned off the engine and took a long, deep breath.

"An hour from now we'll be driving home to Bedford and this'll all be behind you," he said encouragingly, applying a gentle squeeze to her hand.

"I'm very uncomfortable," she admitted, stating the obvious. He rose from his seat and walked around to open her door.

"I'll do the introductions from our end," he said.

Stepfather and daughter walked deliberately up the driveway to the front door where they paused, admiring the stained glass windows before them. It was he who finally reached out and pressed the doorbell. A few seconds of silence

from behind the oversized wooden door was followed by the approach of footsteps from within. Moments later the door opened to reveal a tall gentleman with
white hair and dark circles beneath his eyes. He did not speak, choosing to just
survey the two individuals standing on the doorstep.

"We've come to visit with Mrs. Emerson. I'm Brian Kelly and this is Jenny
Keogh." The introduction caused the man to shift his eyes exclusively to Jenny.
Both waited to be ushered in, but the man continued to stare at Jenny while they
remained standing on the doorstep. Then, as if appearing from behind an invisible curtain, a younger man burst upon the scene.

"I'm guessing you must be Jenny and Brian. I'm Philip Emerson, Skip's brother. Skip's with our mother right now," said the man. He was thin, of medium
height and impeccably groomed. "Please come in," he urged them. "Dad—it's
Jenny Keogh—Skip's Jenny." The white haired man looked down at the young
woman yet again but remained expressionless. Finally, he turned from the group
and walked down the hall in the direction of a half circle of chairs.

"My dad's on a lot of medication right now. Please excuse his manners.
There's no harm or insult intended," explained Philip anxiously. Directing the
visitors inside, he took their coats and asked them to wait until he could produce
his brother.

Brian and Jenny sat down in leather chairs not far from the front door. They
sat in relative silence while Jenny's eyes darted from object to object adorning the
hallway.

"Think of it, in a few seconds I'll be meeting the man who is my father—bio-
logically, anyway." Brian nodded his head in acknowledgement but withheld
comment. Twenty five feet away, Mr. Emerson sat by himself with his back to
them, gazing perplexedly at the ceiling. The room's absolute quiet was broken by
the opening of a door. Walking toward them at that moment was Skip Emerson.
Brian rose to his feet, all the while focusing on every detail of the man's face. No
doubt it was Skip, he thought. Older, his face showing the effects of his mother's
illness, his formerly jet black hair was now evenly mixed with silver.

"Brian, I don't know how to thank you enough," he said, reaching out his
hand as his steps brought him to within arm's length.

"It's all right, Skip, not a problem." He paused. "And, of course, this is your
daughter, Jenny." The young woman rose to her feet and extended a hand.

"It's good to finally meet you, Mr. Emerson." Skip took a deep breath before
taking her hand.

"I'd have recognized you anywhere. You're the image of your mother. I'm sure
you know that."

"So I've been told," she answered.

"You're grandmother has been anxiously awaiting your arrival. Please, come
right along now. I'll introduce you to her." He put his arm around his daughter,
leading her in the direction of a room at the far end of the hall. Brian followed
close behind.

Skip opened the bedroom door, ushering his guests into a darkened room, the
only illumination coming from a table lamp positioned next to the bed. The

room's curtains had all been drawn, allowing only slivers of afternoon light to make their way inside the house. Across the room was Mrs. Emerson. For the moment, her eyes were closed. Skip escorted Jenny and Brian to the foot of the bed. Mrs. Emerson appeared to be about seventy years of age. Her face was lightly wrinkled, reflecting the aging process, but without the deep lines present in many others of her generation. Brian thought she must have been an attractive woman in her youth, making her current circumstances all the more heartrending.

"Mother, Jenny Keogh's arrived—she's here to see you," whispered Skip, lightly nudging his mother's arm resting on top of the bedcovers. Her eyes blinked open. She focused first on her son and then on the young woman standing beside him.

"Oh, my dear, you have come," exclaimed the woman, albeit weakly.

"And this is Mr. Kelly. He was kind enough to bring Jenny to the house." Brian smiled down from behind the introduction and gestured respectfully to her.

"I'm glad I could be of help," he murmured, keeping his voice soft and low. The feeble woman's eyes remained on Jenny. In a gesture that seemed to summon up the small amount of strength present in her weary body, she motioned for the young woman to sit herself in the chair at the immediate head of the bed.

"Skip, could I ask you and Mr. Kelly to leave us alone for a few minutes?" The men obliged, quietly leaving the room.

With the closing of the door behind the two men, Mrs. Emerson let her head turn sideways on the pillow, her tired eyes taking in every detail of her granddaughter's face.

"You bear a remarkable resemblance to your mother." Jenny smiled sweetly.

"Grandmother, you're not the first person to tell me that." The girl's words brought a contented smile in return, and the first hint of moisture to the woman's eyes.

"I can't imagine what you must have thought of us over the past twenty years. I do know that over those years not a day went by that you weren't in my thoughts." Jenny reached over, laying a hand down on the woman's. "It's clear your mother has done a superb job raising you. Your mother—she is an amazing woman. Will you tell her that for me?" Jenny nodded. "It was important to me that I should have the opportunity to speak to you directly, to speak—and to apologize. It was cowardly of me to allow everything to happen the way it did—to let your mother and her family bear the brunt of your upbringing."

"Grandmother, it's all right," interrupted her granddaughter.

"I should have stood up to your grandfather. We had no right to do what we did. But you have to know, you were always on our minds—and certainly in both your father's and my heart."

"I'm sure I was," Jenny added.

"More than you know, Jenny, more than you will ever know." The woman took a deep breath before breaking out in a smile. It was a smile prompted by a fond recollection.

"When Southside High put on *Our Town* in your junior year, your father and I took a chance by getting two balcony seats, knowing the Keoghs would surely be seated front and center. We arrived as the curtains went up and witnessed the finest performance of 'Emily' by any actress of this or any other generation." Her personal review, shamelessly superlative, caused the woman's tired eyes to sparkle, if only momentarily.

"You were there?"

"We were there—for all three performances. We were so proud of you."

Brian sat quietly in the Emerson's hallway, balancing a glass of sparkling water on his knee and waiting out Jenny's emotional visit to her dying grandmother's bedside. He had now been seated in the chair for over forty-five minutes. He found the experience reminiscent of visits he had made in his youth and in the company of his mother, to wakes back in Lowell. They were gloomy memories of stiflingly sober events, very Catholic and particularly final where words were in short supply and almost everyone had to explain to everyone else who they were and how they were related to the deceased. Finally, he caught sight of Jenny as the bedroom door opened. Pausing for an instant in the doorway, she turned toward him. Skip, who had been standing near his father at the other end of the long, carpeted room, quickly made his way in the direction of his daughter.

"Mr. Emerson, I'm very glad you made a point of contacting my family and asking me to come," she said, sounding equal parts sincere and sophisticated. Skip shook the young woman's hand, appearing at a loss for words. "If you'll excuse me, I'll just have a few words with your father." Jenny turned away from the man and walked to the far end of the room, joining the elder Mr. Emerson who still sat with his back to the family proceedings.

"I'll be driving her back to Newport tomorrow morning," explained Brian, more to break the silence than anything else.

"I wouldn't mind going in your place, if that works for you," suggested Skip.

"I'd take you up on your offer in a minute if I didn't know her mother would have my head." Emerson nodded knowingly, a sad expression taking possession of his features.

Jenny only spent a few moments with the elder Mr. Emerson. Their brief time together was concluded when she leaned down and gave the man a kiss on the cheek. Brian rejoined his stepdaughter at the front door where she extended her hand a final time to her biological father. Next, she surprised him with an innocent kiss on the cheek. With that, the formalities were concluded. The polished young woman gestured for Brian to escort her from the house. They were less than twenty feet from the front door when he leaned down and spoke softly to her.

"You are an incredible young woman, Jenny Keogh. You carried yourself perfectly back there—I mean perfectly."

"I am so glad I came," she admitted, before starting to sob. He wrapped his arm around her, directing her head onto his shoulder.

"How did it go in the bedroom with your grandmother?"

"She's a wonderful woman. It was painful sitting there next to her and seeing how fragile she was. We had a wonderful talk—very warm. There was no fool-ish small talk. She knows how sick she is—and so anything and everything she felt, she said. And in case you're wondering, she was the one who wanted me to go over and say something to her husband. That's how she put it. She asked me to do that one little thing for her." Jenny barely managed to force the words from her mouth before another wave of sobbing broke through her speech.

Coming to the road and climbing into the truck, the twenty-one year old reached over and grabbed Brian's arm before he could turn on the ignition.

"If it's not too much to ask, I'd rather that you didn't tell mother what I've told you here—you know, everything that went on at the Emersons. I'll tell her, maybe, in good time."

"Even if she beats me to within an inch of my life—your secret is safe with me."

"Brian, I've been around you two enough to know that that's not how moth-er gets things out of you. You've got to promise that you won't let her coerce any-thing out of you."

"If you're talking about that thing she does using baby talk and rubbing up against me—I'm way too smart for that now." Jenny flashed a knowing smile.

"Sure you are."

The pair arrived back in Bedford just as Moira was about to begin preparing something for herself and the baby. On the arrival of the duo, all plans for sup-per were scrapped when Brian offered to go out for pizza. A menu was pulled from a kitchen drawer and Moira and Jenny made their selections, while Brian carried his daughter from room to room perched on his shoulders.

On Brian's return with the pizza, the four spread themselves out in the living room and attacked their meal. He was particularly pleased to see Moira relax in the presence of the family. He tried to get the nanny to loosen up by asking her questions about Ireland. The nineteen year old responded with stories about her growing up in a small town called Doolin in County Clare. The teenager's face lit up as she described the village in grand detail, perched on the side of an extended, rolling hill and overlooking the sea with the stark Aran Islands only a few miles offshore. The Irish girl's tales of her native land were only interrupted long enough to allow her to get her young charge up to bed and snugly under the covers. Colleen's exodus from the room was only accomplished after her father and half sister had peppered the girl with an assortment of kisses and tick-les up and down her body.

At a few minutes past nine o'clock the headlights from the BMW shone through the front window. With Brian sprawled out on the couch and Jenny curled up in a well-cushioned chair, the front door flew open.

"I see my tomcat of a husband has finally decided to come home," roared Margaret, her voice raised to penetrate the closed door and living room walls. "I really don't appreciate not knowing where you are and when you plan on com-ing home. Oh, and how many fucking more times do I have to tell you to park your shit box somewhere other than at the front door? Brian, I'm pissed." The verbal assault came as the woman hung her coat and removed her shoes in the hall. She pushed in the heavy door and glared at her husband. Buried behind the back of her chair, Jenny was invisible to her mother.

"You know Maggie May—usually, the only time you talk this way is when you play 'bad girl' with me and want to be spanked on your bare, little bottom. Is that what this is all about?"

"What the hell are you talking about? You must be getting me mixed up with some little whore you have on the side up in Wells—unless you're getting spanking and kissing mixed up in your thick, Irish head!" He smiled, detecting the first sign of thawing in his wife's temperament.

"So do you think you can hold off until next week for that spanking?"

"I already told you, Kelly—once tax season is over I'm going up to Wells Beach and releasing my demons. You know what I can be like when I get like this. I told you, I'm sure I told you, I had Brad in tears once when I had to purge my demons after tax season. Of course, he was a fairy and I expect more from you." Her husband raised his eyebrows, stealing a glance at Jenny who sat absolutely still, her hand covering her mouth.

"And there you have it Jenny—Margaret Keogh-Olson-Kelly—unplugged." He returned his eyes to his wife and found her mouth open in astonishment. Stepping further into the room, she caught sight of her daughter snuggled deep within the chair.

"What—what are you doing here?" Margaret's tone had softened.

"We came up from Newport today and visited Mrs. Emerson. Brian's taking me back in the morning." Jenny jumped to her feet and embraced her mother.

"I can't believe I let you sucker me into that exchange," admitted the woman over her daughter's shoulder. "You are so going to pay for this little stunt."

"Yeah, yeah, yeah, so you say," he answered, mocking her with a shake of the head. "I'll leave you two alone for the time being. I'm off to bed." He gave Jenny a soft peck on the cheek then leaned forward, pressing his lips to Margaret's. She did not respond.

"Jen, this act here is for your benefit. Behind closed doors your mother will be on her knees begging for affection." His wife responded, making a quick grab for his crotch. He deflected her hand at the last instant.

"Your day is coming, smart ass," she warned, albeit through a faint smile.

Brian looked up from his *Boston Herald* as hushed, female voices filled the hallway outside his bedroom door. Seconds later Margaret entered the room, walking to her bureau in silence. It was almost eleven o'clock.

"Someone was in no hurry to rush up to her husband's side."

"I'm still pissed at you for not calling last night." She made her way to the side of the bed, applying moisturizer while she spoke. Following a moment's hesitation, she sat on the edge of the mattress.

"I was ticked off having that whole thing with Skip and his mother dropped in my lap."

"All you had to do was say no. It was as simple as that."

"Okay, no more arguing. It's all history now. Jen and I did what we had to do, the right thing to do. It's water under the bridge."

"I expect a full account from you in the morning on what went on at the Emersons. Right now I'm exhausted and I need some sleep." She replaced the lid on the bottle of moisturizer and slid beneath the covers.

"How many more days, Maggie May? When are you coming to Maine?"

"Five days more—I can't come until next Tuesday. The fifteenth falls on the weekend and then there's the state holiday in Massachusetts on Monday. I'll be up next Tuesday." He drew his body against hers, positioning her head on his chest and running his fingers lovingly through her hair.

"I know I've said this before—but this tax season is literally doing me in. I had one asshole after another parading through my office today. I'm like a spring wound up to the point of exploding."

"Just keep thinking of next Tuesday and coming to Wells—and you and me going out for a nice dinner—followed by one of my soothing massages."

"No, Brian, think again. I've told you a hundred times. I'll be purging demons. Think of it this way: you know how on the nature programs when they show the lioness running down a wildebeast and how she tears the poor creature to pieces—ripping his throat out in seconds."

"I never thought of myself as a lion," he came back coyly.

"That's because you're going to be the wildebeast, stupid! I keep telling you— I have demons in me, Kelly—from this tax season—and they need releasing— rough, biting sex—primal. Before we were married you used to love it. I'll be expecting it Tuesday. Don't be like that pussy Brad—*Margaret, the people at work will see the marks and bruises. Please Margaret, I think you're breaking the skin— ow, ow.* God, he was a pussy." Over the past three years she had learned that using her ex as a bad example was an effective way to move her husband toward accepting most any behavior from her. He ended her scalp massage with a light kiss to the top of her head.

"Just don't let me suffer, Keogh, okay."

"It'll be over in ninety minutes—two hours tops," she laughed, already on the verge of dosing off.

VII

There was a prevailing sense of anticipation in the air at the Atlantic Coast Lodge as Brian worked with Millie discussing the upcoming season. It was Tuesday, the eighteenth of April. The first guests of the year were scheduled to arrive the coming weekend and the two old friends were happy to be working side by side again. In the midst of explaining enhancements to the company's reservation software and the two vacation packages in place for June, Brian stopped, poured two cups of coffee, and invited his assistant manager to join him in the TV room. Settled in corner chairs, he went on to explain the chain of events that caused him to miss so many workdays recently. The woman reserved comment, opting instead to roll her eyes or shake her head in disbelief as he divulged the details surrounding Jenny Keogh's circumstances. Millie Pierce and Margaret Kelly's relationship could best be described as lukewarm, if not strained. However, each was conscious of the other's importance in the life of Brian Kelly.

"Well, mister world traveler, I think you'll be pleased with the new girl I've interviewed for chambermaid. Did you happen to see her application and my comments on your desk?" she asked.

"Mary something, right?"

"Mary Porterfield—and a sweeter little thing you couldn't find. I mean, she had me grinning ear to ear when she started talking about coming from Washington County and how poor she was growing up."

"You hired her, right?"

"No, I was waiting on final word from you."

"If you think she's that good then give her definitive word. Call her when we're done and tell her she's hired. She's probably filling out job applications all over the place. Don't let someone else steal her away. Chambermaids—good ones anyway—are hard to come by."

"She's a cute little thing—blonde. I thought she was still in high school when I first set eyes on her but it turned out she was twenty-three—with a seven year old son."

"Wow! That's awfully young to have a seven year old," exclaimed Brian.

"She's a little doll. She comes from some island up by Jonesport."

"Tell her she can start next week. I'd like to see all the windows washed and brass polished while we still have the time."

In the next few minutes Brian and Millie went over a few trouble spots he had found on the complex during an earlier inspection. She was instructed to avoid renting two specific cottages over the next two weeks until the problems could be addressed. They were finalizing details of the informal meeting when the telephone rang in the next room, sending him scurrying to the front desk.

"Atlantic Coast Lodge," he answered enthusiastically.

"Kelly, I'm sitting at my desk shutting down my computer."

"I'm sorry—and you would be who?"

"Who do you think? Oh, that's right, wildebeasts can't think. I packed the car this morning. I'm leaving the office in a few minutes. I just need time to put the fear of God into my staff—warn them about screwing off—and then it's off to Wells Beach. I have a surprise for you."

"Damn, that doesn't sound good. Tell me, Maggie May, will this surprise make me want to laugh or make me want to cry?"

"Both—first, nervous laughter—followed by begging for mercy—then lots and lots of crying."

"Will we have time for supper before my little Maggie May does me in?"

"Good point. We'll send you out for something when I get there. I believe wildebeasts are vegetarians so you might get yourself a salad. Oh, and you might want to make sure you have some disinfectant in the cottage. I have some major league demons to purge."

"Keogh, you're not backing off one bit on this running gag of yours—are you?"

"If telling yourself I'm just screwing with your head about tonight helps you cope, well, good luck."

"Shall I expect you in a couple of hours?"

"Yes—and Brian, I do apologize."

"For what?"

"For what I'm going to do to you tonight." She followed her words with a mischievous giggle.

"I don't know—I'm beginning to think this whole buildup of yours is going to be one of those patented *all talk* and *no action* affairs."

"You're dead, Kelly." Her words were punctuated by a click and the dial tone.

Brian was lying outside on the deck of their cottage when the BMW turned into the parking space directly in front of the building. The late afternoon was pleasant with a fresh, land breeze coming in over the marshland and estuary. Margaret exited the car and strode over the lawn toward him. She wore a smile, best described as devious. Reaching the railing of the deck, she rested her arms and addressed her husband.

"I must say you look very calm for a man facing what you're about to face." Still dressed in office attire, she wore a conservative, white blouse, gray, pleated skirt and matching heels. He stared at her in silence, considering his good fortune.

"I haven't done a thing as far as supper is concerned," he confessed.

"Kelly, you have to be the last man on the planet that still refers to dinner as supper. Now why don't you run out to Billy's or Jake's and get us something simple, haddock or something. In the meantime, I'll get things set up inside for the evening."

"So let me get this straight, Keogh—not only do I have to go out and get my last supper—I've got to *pay* for it, too?"

"Law of the jungle—when the lioness and the wildebeast dine together, the wildebeast pays. And trust me—tonight the wildebeast will pay."

Hopping to his feet, Brian sauntered in the direction of the pickup. His path brought him in close proximity to her. Margaret's eyes followed his progress. Reaching the Ford, he paused for a moment then walked back to his wife. Instantly, they were locked in a passionate kiss. Her hands reached for and snared a crop of hair at the back of his head, pulling it downward and level with her own. It was she who brought the flurry of passion to a halt by pushing his head away.

The couple shared a fisherman's platter on the deck while the sun descended, then disappeared, behind the line of trees at the far edge of the marshlands. Dinner conversation was light with sentences replaced by short phrases and simple observations, mostly regarding the weather and the air temperature which seemed to be dropping by the minute. In the distance, a bank of dark clouds made an appearance just above the horizon. By now Margaret had slipped off her shoes and had both feet balanced on her husband's lap. After dropping his fork and declaring an end to his meal, Brian tried opening the lines of meaningful communication.

"You already look like you're beginning to unwind. Is there anything I can do to further the process?"

"Back when you were courting me I didn't have to even ask for a massage. All that's changed now," she said accusingly. Without hesitation he began stroking the arches and balls of her feet. "And as far as unwinding, well, I guess I'd have to say I am. I haven't been up here to your shit box since December, I think."

"*Our* shit box," he said, correcting her.

"My mistake—our shit box." She wiped the corner of her mouth and coiled her legs back to her side of the table. "All right, the meal is ended," she declared, rising to her feet and pulling Brian from the table.

"I've got to pick up, he said while being pulled toward the front door.

"It's time, Brian," she stated emphatically.

"The seagulls, they'll get the food on the table and make a mess." Margaret guided him back to the table, her hand locked behind his neck, and allowed him to pick up the paper plates. However, only seconds later he was being marshaled through the front door and onto the porch. His progress toward the bedroom under her direction was swift and direct. After depositing the dinner scraps and paper plates into the waste basket, he reached out and swung open the bedroom door. She pushed her body against his, moving him backward and up against the edge of the bed. In this position it only took the slightest nudge to send him onto his back.

Brian looked up from the flat of his back while Margaret removed her skirt, pantyhose and blouse in what seemed like a fraction of a second. After disrobing, she rummaged inside her pocketbook for a moment before removing something. His eyes barely had time to focus on her long, magnificent form when she bounded forward, quickly straddling his torso and ultimately pinning his biceps under her knees. He looked up at her in a state of near helplessness, his chest and shoulders smothered under the woman's smooth, tan skin and weight.

"There's no defense for a man against a woman with your looks and devious mind. You have too many weapons, Keogh." She gazed down on him in a curious manner, clearly running something over in her mind.

"Kelly, you may be about to catch a break. I want you to know I had every intention of ripping you to pieces tonight—primal, aggressive sex. I do have demons, you know that. Anyway, last night before bed, I was flipping through a recent issue of *Cosmo* and I came upon this intriguing article on foreplay. It's a little out there but if you're willing to give it a whirl, I might cut you some slack and take it easy on you tonight." He looked up at her suspiciously.

"What are you talking about when you say *out there?*" Margaret reached behind her and produced a pair of leather cords.

"We've done some pretty far out stuff but never gone into the whole restraint thing. The article went into how one partner can really play with the senses of the other—really push some buttons."

"And, of course, I'd be expected to be the one being restrained, right?"

"Well—I am the one who read the article. If it proves to be a real kick then we can change roles—naturally."

"Perhaps after we've both had a chance to read the article," said Brian.

"It's a fucking article in *Cosmopolitan,* not some kinky piece of shit I picked up in a porn shop. Jesus, Brian—grow a pair! God damn it, you sound more like Brad every day." He rolled his eyes and let out with a sigh.

"All right—but not too tight." She leaned down, kissed him on the cheek, and proceeded to bind his left wrist.

"This won't be too tight. Watch, I'll tie you just tight enough so you could get yourself free in a minute or so. How does that sound?"

"Thank you my warrior princess." The left wrist secured to the bedpost, she went to work on the right.

"Whoa, whoa—way too tight, Keogh. You're cutting off the flow of blood." Unresponsive, she circled his wrist and the post over and over. Shifting her weight across his body and back to the left wrist, she proceeded to circle his hand and wrist again and again until all movement was eliminated. Peering up at his wife's maneuver, he was reminded of the plight of an insect caught in a silken web, defenseless while the spider wraps strand after strand around the struggling body. It was not until all movement subsided from beneath her that she spoke.

"Brian, when the hell did you ever see me reading a women's magazine? I can't believe you let me talk you into this. Consider what you've let me do. You have one thing, and one thing only, going for you when it comes to me—you are physically stronger than me. And now I've managed to rob you of that."

Her husband completely immobilized, Margaret lifted her body up from atop his. Brian's shirt was damp from the perspiration caused by her resting on him. She casually walked to the kitchen and opened the refrigerator door.

"You know I like bottled water—and I don't see any."

"There's plenty of fruit drink and soda. Bottled water is for chumps who can be marketed into paying for anything."

"I don't think calling me a chump is a wise course of action at this point in time, do you?" She pulled a bottle of kiwi strawberry from the fridge, removed the cap and swallowed a mouthful. The utensil drawer was just behind her and soon came the sound of silverware being examined. His eyes widened when she reentered the room carrying her drink and a steak knife.

"And what is this all about?"

She did not respond. After placing the beverage and knife on the bureau a few feet from her husband's bound, left wrist, she walked to the foot of the bed and removed boots and stockings. His pants were next, the belt undone and the trousers pulled off in one quick motion from his body. His briefs suffered the same fate, ripped from his torso in a no-nonsense fashion. Brian's white briefs joined his other articles of clothing in a pile in the far corner of the bedroom. Pausing over her helpless victim, she smiled down on his manliness and reached for the knife.

"Okay, Maggie May, stop screwing around," he ordered. Appearing oblivious to his directive, she remounted her husband and grabbed hold of his shirt.

"Don't you dare, Keogh—I love this shirt. It's my favorite."

"I wouldn't move much if I were you. This is no butter knife." He heeded her words and continued to lie perfectly still beneath her. Bringing the knife up shoulder high, she went on to cut the fabric, starting at the neck and continuing until the entire front of the garment was sheared open.

"That *was* my favorite shirt. Thanks a lot."

"*Was* is right." She was not done with her handiwork. Next, she cut along both sleeves until Brian's tee shirt was little more than tattered remnants. Finally, Margaret pulled the fabric from his body and tossed the rags onto the pile of clothing in the corner.

"Now it's simply one body sitting atop another—one in complete control, the other powerless."

"You do know you will pay for this?" he stated. She smiled down on him, widening her eyes as if on the verge of madness. She followed this by tossing the knife back onto the surface of the bureau.

"Now a person of normal intelligence in your position would probably be asking themselves about now what could possibly set a woman off like this. Brian, has this question crossed your mind?"

"No, not really—due to the fact that I already know you're mentally unbalanced and this is just par for the course."

"Oooh, do I detect bitterness from my captive? I should have expected as much. Anyway, I'm actually going to take the time to explain to you why I am the way I am this tax season—so you can more appreciate your role in allowing me to purge my demons."

"I can hardly wait," he said, his words sounding like an afterthought. She knitted her brow and edged higher on his chest, his shoulders disappearing beneath her knees.

"Sarcasm will only worsen your plight," she answered.

Margaret paused, repositioning her body for comfort. She followed this by reaching around and finding Brian's manhood behind her.

"Is it me or is someone starting to get off on this brand new experience?" she asked, commenting on the early stage of her husband's erection.

"It helped when you tossed the knife back on the bureau."

"I'll bet it did. Anyway Brian, let me share with you one story from the world of shit I call a life so you can see why I am in need of a sacrificial lamb—and why that sacrificial lamb has to be male. Now this is just one asshole—but my life is full of them. I've had this husband and wife client for a couple of years—both self-employed. For the past couple of years the wife's been trying to convince him to take the step and buy their own home. He's all antsy over the idea—having had experience with banks and all the shit they put self-employed people through to get a loan. He's been turned down in the past and has an aversion to the whole process. Anyway, the wife asks if I can lend a hand in helping her talk him into trying to buy their own home—which I do. And the crazy thing is—I don't even charge them for my time. They're in their twenties and I can identify with them and how I felt at their age."

"Oh God, my princess is growing a heart," called out Brian from beneath her.

"Quiet, slave," she demanded, grabbing a shock of his hair and pulling his head forward.

"I thought I was a wildebeast?"

"In ten minutes when I'm gnawing on you, then you'll be a wildebeast. Right now, you're a slave. Anyway, as I was saying before I was rudely interrupted by the inferior life form pinned against the mattress beneath me, I helped them through the whole process—even went to bat for them with the bank. The wife called me the day they moved into the house and told me how much my help had meant. That was last October."

"And you mean to say the Vatican hasn't put you up for sainthood yet?" joked Brian. Her response was to grab at his hair and pull.

"I'm going to finish my story and then you'll pay for all these wiseass comments. I hadn't talked to these folks since last year and in early April, when I was reviewing our client list, I noticed I hadn't heard from them yet. I made a follow-up call one evening and managed to catch the husband at home. When I asked him about his tax work for this year, he told me he'd engaged the services of another CPA and that the work had already been completed. Naturally, I followed up by asking if an error had occurred from the prior year or if our services had been lacking in any way. Then—he tells me no—this male slug tells me no, that it's nothing like that, that it was a matter of taking quotes from other firms on the tax work—and another firm had come in seventy five dollars under my fee! Seventy-five dollars a year, that's what my giving a shit and helping this fucking prick was worth—seventy five dollars a year!" She stared down at her husband. She was pleased to see he was looking up at her sympathetically. "Now after hearing a story like that—and that was just the tip of the iceberg, you can see why I need a sacrificial lamb—a male, sacrificial lamb."

"Did you even consider calling Brad?" he joked in a timid voice, causing her to burst into laughter.

There arose a patter of rain from the roof along with a series of wind gusts, telling the Kellys that the dark clouds seen earlier on the horizon had reached the coast. Inside, Margaret stared at her husband, then slid her body down his, stopping when their lips were aligned. Her expression had softened, the edginess visible only moments before replaced with a more sympathetic look. Following the briefest of deliberations, she forced her tongue by his lips and excitedly explored his willing mouth, her body beginning a series of rhythmic plunges. The friction created by her movement instantly set off his nude body. He felt himself becoming more rigid by the second, the weight of his wife's torso igniting his passion. Brian opened his eyes when his wife unexpectedly withdrew her mouth from his. Transfixed, he watched as her head deliberately made its way downward toward the pillow. Then, unannounced, her teeth came in contact with his neck, delivering a wave of pain. There was real discomfort, eased somewhat by the passion taking possession of his body. He held back a response, trusting his mate would keep her aggressive urges within check. Brian's thoughts became an erotic blur, the naked primitiveness of Maggie May's assault pushing the temperature of his blood upward. Her right hand grabbed at, then secured, a tangle of his hair while her athletic thighs squeezed against his ribs. She was alternating now between pressing his flesh between her teeth and drawing moisture from his skin. When her erotic onslaught caused an inadvertent sound from him, a groan prompted by his journey between pleasure and pain, she responded by sinking her teeth deeper into his flesh. With her husband's neck already a crimson red, she moved to his shoulder.

Margaret bit down again on her helpless mate, devouring his flesh and tasting the salty beads of moisture from the surface of his skin. She was moving toward her intended destination: a state of mind beyond reason, dictated to by sexual urge and need. Her mouth moved back to his lips, then to a region of his neck not yet wounded. Again and again she bit into his flesh. He attempted to resist but with no success, prevented by his tightly bound wrists. When he managed to pull his neck slightly back from her hungry mouth, she responded by again grabbing a handful of thick hair and pulling him back into position. With her teeth sunk into his skin and no resistance being felt from below, she was approaching her zenith, the release of ecstasy from deep within and the purging of demons. Beneath her own, Brian's body was wet with perspiration. Pushing herself up from the bed, she hastily tore the bra and panties from her body. Her eyes met Brian's, their heavy breathing for the moment in unison. His eyes remained trained on her while she inspected his neck from above. It was pink with patches of scarlet red already cropping up. He waited on her next move, a slave to the heat of his own blood as it pumped through his veins. She did not need to examine herself. She was conscious of her own wetness, a condition incited by anticipation. The pleasant scent of her sexual excitement hung in the air around the bed. Inspecting him, she saw he was aroused and firm. Climbing over him, she positioned their bodies and directed him inside her. Both acknowledged the other through a cry of pleasure. Outside the rain was falling in earnest and could be heard whipping against the bedroom window. Abruptly, Margaret's head flew back as a shockwave of pleasure shot through her body. Brian was deep inside her. She moved, first forward, then faintly to the side, allowing him to make contact with the front wall of her vagina. Drawing in long breaths of air, she repeated the movement, causing his erect penis to slide along this erogenous region. He was where she wanted him. Tightening her muscles around his fully erect penis, he let out with a moan that told her he was nearing climax. The marvelous ritual played on, orchestrated by a woman feeling herself move toward the moment of sexual fulfillment. She opened her eyes. Beneath her, Brian was writhing in pleasure.

"Don't leave me here, Kelly. Just a few seconds more," she cried out. His head flew back against the pillow. She leaned forward, her hands coming down on the back edge of the mattress. Finally, she let out a single cry while her manicured nails dug into his shoulders.

Brian opened his eyes to see his wife, her back arched, drawing in one long breath after another. Her hair, wet and tossed frantically over her face, gave her the persona of a wild beast. He went to reach for her but was prevented by the cords encircling his wrists. He moved his hips, reminding her he had yet to be satisfied. She remained in place, her face continuing to mirror the pleasure passing through her body while Brian pushed deep within her. Seconds passed before a cry of rapture came from him as he spent himself within her. Again, he tried to reach up for her in the waning moments of his climax, only to have her slide away through his fingers as she brought herself up to an upright, sitting position. Pulling the perspiration laden strands of hair from her face, Margaret drew in another series of deep breaths. Outside, droplets of rain pelted against the bedroom window behind a particularly violent gust of wind. The sound drew a sideways glance from the woman. An instant later, she slid herself from atop her husband and walked to the window, raising the Venetian blind to inspect the weather outside. Brian's eyes followed his wife's naked body. He still marveled, even after nearly three years of marriage, at her form, most notably the swooping line from her lower back to her perfectly rounded buttocks.

"If it wouldn't be too much bother, you could untie me now," he politely suggested. Her response was to smile and shake her head in the negative. She walked back to the kitchen. "I mean it, Keogh," he called out. She did not so much as give his command the recognition of a backward glance. The refrigerator door swung open with a thud, followed by the sound of ice being extracted from the freezer. Thirty seconds later, she reentered the room with a glass half filled with ice cubes. Walking to the bureau, she poured the remainder of the kiwi strawberry drink into the glass.

Brian watched as his wife stepped to the far end of the bed, easing herself onto the mattress beside him. She spent a moment silently staring into his eyes before slowly directing her glance in the direction of his exposed penis.

"How cold do you think this glass will feel on you?"

"Knock it off, Keogh." Paying her husband no mind she reached forward, allowing the glass to make contact with his warm skin. His body lurched but he remained silent.

"You're in no position to tell me what to do or not do. My God, this is turning into more fun than I could have even hoped for. For starters, I wasn't sure I was going to be able to talk you into this whole rope thing."

"Speaking of the ropes, they're starting to dig into my wrists." His words caused her to break out in one of her mischievous giggles.

"Poor baby. Face it, Kelly, you'd be bored married to some little, adoring dim-wit. You love me because I'm such a challenge—an unpredictable ball buster." She leaned back against the headboard and took a drink from the glass. The room became quiet for a few seconds, the two seeming to consider their relative positions. It was she who spoke next.

"You know, it's hard to believe that this is the same man who threw a pair of knee pads at me a week ago and ordered me to pay him homage. Hey, Kelly, how's that whole macho bullshit routine working out for you?"

"Not too well at the moment."

Margaret gulped down her remaining juice, placed an affectionate kiss on the top of her husband's head, and vaulted from the bed. Naked, she walked leisurely to the closet and removed a bathrobe.

"It's way too early to call it quits for the night. I'm going to see what's on TV."

"Come on, Maggie May, the rope—untie me." His words brought her back to the side of the bed. She tossed the bathrobe to the floor and let out with a mischievous laugh. Jumping back onto the mattress, she shimmied up his body and again pinned his shoulders beneath her.

"Oh, McFly—hello, is anyone in there McFly?" she called out while rapping her knuckles against his skull. "McFly—you're not getting untied anytime tonight, McFly. Get that through your head, McFly." She recited the words, mimicking her husband's taunts from so many other occasions. "No, Brian, I'm enjoying this period of absolute power too much to let you go this quickly. Christ, it's intoxicating! No—I think I'll let you just lie here for a while and think about how lucky a man you are—married to your sweet, innocent, obedient high school sweetheart. Think back to all those nights you lay in bed so many years ago, thinking how wonderful it would be if only you could win the heart of Maggie May Keogh—all the peace, joy and tranquility such a love would bring to you. Ah yes, Brian Kelly of Southside High by way of Lowell, Mass—be careful what you wish for—you might get it." Margaret ran her hand along Brian's naked body approvingly before dismounting her husband and putting on the bathrobe. Finally, after staring lovingly at the man for a moment, she blew her captive a kiss and closed the door behind her, leaving him in total darkness.

Brian emerged from a light and restless sleep to the sound of the bedroom door opening a few feet away.

"What time is it?"

"The news just came on, it must be eleven," she answered, responding as if this night was no different than any other.

"Are you going to untie me?"

"Not if you ask like that," she snapped back.

"Keogh, so help me God"—Brian stopped in mid sentence, deciding that a threat of any kind might only worsen his predicament. She slipped out of her bathrobe and slid under the covers beside him.

"You haven't let me brush my teeth."

"You can go a night without brushing."

"What if I have to go to the bathroom in the middle of the night?"

"Be strong."

"Keogh, I have to go now."

"That's horseshit."

"Maggie, I'm not even under the covers." She let out a sigh and rose to her feet. Pulling the bedspread and sheet to the bottom of the bed, she allowed him to maneuver his body beneath the linen. This was followed by another more exaggerated sigh. She climbed back under the covers and brought her warm, naked body next to his.

"Now, Brian, roll over and go to sleep. Oh, that's right, you can't roll over," she needled before resting her head on his chest. "I love you, Kelly—I really do."

Brian's eyes fluttered open to a darkened room, the only light seeping in from around the drawn window blinds. Outside, the cawing of sea gulls was audible above the distant roar of the ocean, the Atlantic not much more than a hundred yards to the east. Rolling his head to the side, he became conscious of the tender condition of his neck. She had literally broken the skin, he thought. Only that could account for the sharp pain caused by his movement.

"And how is my sacrificial lamb feeling this morning?" she asked, somehow aware of his consciousness.

"My neck really hurts. That shit you pulled last night was way over the line."

"Stop being a baby and help me with a dilemma."

"What kind of dilemma?"

"I need to figure out how to get my sacrificial lamb—my helpless prey—to prepare me breakfast in bed while still tied to the bedposts. Do you have any ideas?"

"Keogh, I really have to go to the bathroom. It's been all night."

"Now, I'm guessing that you—you with your little pea brain and all—I'm guessing that you would think that that would be absolutely impossible. Am I right?"

"It would seem so," he replied impatiently.

"Yes, and again Kelly, you would be wrong." That said, she catapulted up from the mattress and raced in the direction of the living room. She was only out of sight for a few seconds, returning to the bedroom with his phone receiver. Bounding up onto the bed, she remounted him.

"Stated simply, the problem is how does the beautiful, charming, cultured and incredibly intelligent Margaret Kelly get her intellectually overmatched husband to provide her with breakfast in bed while still keeping him tied to the same bed?" She raised her hand to her chin, as if trying to come up with the answer from out of thin air. "And the answer is—by phoning his sinfully overpaid assistant manager, Millie Pierce, and having him order her to come down to the cottage and serve this same Margaret Kelly breakfast—under threat of termination. I figure—that woman hates me so much as it is—how much lower in her eyes can I really fall? How do you think the holy roller would react to learn that her big, strong boss was tied to his own bedpost?" She lifted the phone to within sight and glared down at her husband. "I do believe you don't look concerned enough, meaning you don't think I'd go through with it." Expressionless, he stared up at her. She took to rapidly punching in the numbers.

"Okay, Keogh, what do you want?"

"I want breakfast in bed, catered and served by my husband."

"I agree," he relented. "Now cut me loose. I *have* to go to the bathroom." Leaning forward, Margaret began slipping loose the individual knots starting with his left arm. It took well over a minute for her to free her husband. The cords removed, he jumped from the bed and made his way to the bathroom.

It was a minute later and Margaret was standing in front of the fridge when Brian rushed at her from the living room. Still naked, he lifted her from the floor and carried her through the doorway, spreading her out under him on the bed.

"Get off of me, Kelly, I'm warning you." Paying no heed, he brought his full weight down upon her body. "Get off me!" she raged, her right hand grabbing a shock of his hair. Proceeding without a word, he brought his mouth down to her neck, his lips and teeth drawing in a sizeable portion of soft skin. "So help me God, if you leave a mark on me I'll have you arrested." His response was to suck on and lightly bite her flesh. "You fucker," she cried out, her arms now beating on his bare back. Meanwhile, his mouth continued to draw on her soft flesh as if tasting her perfumed skin for the first time. For fifteen, then twenty, then all of twenty-five seconds, he continued in his hold on her neck. Gradually, almost in the manner of a helpless victim to a snake's venom and bite, her struggle to free herself ceased. She gave herself to the moment and the act. With her surrender, he shifted his lips to hers. They lay together for the next few minutes, each content to share the warmth from the other.

VIII

*B*rian awoke to an empty bed and a quiet house. It was Monday morning. Over the preceding days the tiny, yellow cottage had reverberated with his daughter's laughter and his wife's feminine, albeit forceful, voice. However, mother and daughter had packed their luggage and after some fanfare headed back to Bedford late on Sunday afternoon. The weekend had been a joy as the busy parents doted on their toddler, providing their nanny with a much needed three day weekend away from the demanding Colleen. Stumbling through the kitchen, he made his way into the combination living room and dining room. Eyes still half closed, he grabbed the phone and punched in the digits to his wife's office.

"Margaret Kelly & Associates," sang out a female voice from the next state.

"Gretchen, transfer me up to the battle ax, please." The woman gave him a polite laugh and complied.

"Margaret Kelly," answered the stern voice.

"I'm guessing you're wearing a turtleneck this morning."

"Yes—and I'd be wearing a Nehru jacket if I could find one," she snapped back. "I don't appreciate looking like an oversexed teenager for Christ's sake."

"But it's okay for me to look like something that fell into a lion's cage?"

"You clean toilets and clean the hair out of shower drains for a living. Who's going to give a shit."

"You haven't the slightest idea about what I do over here and how much planning goes into this job."

"Oh, of course, major decisions—decisions like: Should I clean the pedestal or the inside of the bowl first?" He decided not to engage her in a war of words.

"Maggie, I was just calling to tell you how much I enjoyed having my two girls over here last week."

"When will we be seeing you again?" she asked.

"I'll be back late Saturday night. I'll close on Saturday and come home. I'm taking Sunday and Monday off."

"Oh, and bring Colleen home some cotton candy. She saw some at the store when we got gas and now she's haunting me about it."

"Where did she see it?"

"She saw it when we were getting gas at the place at the top of Mile Road."

"Okay, Maggie May—I'll be missing you and I'll call Wednesday and Friday nights."

"Not too late."

"And I love you, Maggie May."

"I'm glad," she responded curtly.

58

"I hate it when you do that!" exploded Brian. She broke out in her familiar laugh, the laugh that both beguiled and infuriated him, before hanging up the phone.

Brian took his time preparing for work on this day. Millie was covering the lodge and he was experiencing some lingering tiredness from the week of entertaining Margaret and Colleen. It was after ten o'clock when the Ford turned onto Mile Road and motored due west toward Route 1. Mile Road, so called because of the approximate distance it covered between the Atlantic on its eastern tip and Route 1 on its western, was bounded on both sides mainly by the marshlands that made up the Rachel Carson Wildlife Sanctuary. His complex, The Atlantic Coast Lodge, sat on Route 1 on the crest of a hill only a short distance from the traffic light at the top of the road.

He entered the office, interrupting Millie as she worked on the days deposit slip. There was a steady flow of deposit checks this time of year, allowing the corporation to rebuild its working cash balance. He brushed by the silver haired woman and made his way into his undersized, private office in the far corner of the building.

"Did you have a good time with the family?" Millie called out to him.

"It was really good. I love having Colleen up and carting her around. It was nice having Maggie May all to myself for the first couple of days too," he hollered back. She went on endorsing checks and entering data into the computer. Already tired of calling from two rooms away, he stuck his head around the corner.

"Do you get a feel yet about who the baby looks more like?" Millie turned from her paperwork and pondered the question behind a stare.

"She already has your dark hair—and a pretty, little face—not your wife's horse face. She's definitely taking after you, Brian. She'll be a beauty." He erupted into a fit of laughter, finding humor in his friend's over-the-top criticism of his pretty wife. "Oh, while you have a little time on your hands, why don't you take this check down to Mary. You two haven't met yet. She started full time today. I have her doing windows and a thorough cleaning, floor to ceiling, of the cottages. She'll be down around cottage sixteen or seventeen. Why don't you bring her her check and introduce yourself. Brian, I know you're going to absolutely love her." Not even waiting on a response, she thrust the envelope at him. He took the envelope, mumbled under his breath, and made his way out of the building and across the complex toward the cottages.

The walk down the grassy slope led him to cottage sixteen from where the sound of country music wafted out through the raised windows. Brian climbed up onto the deck and through the cottage door. At the far side of the unit, a petite woman crouched at the base of the sink. She was visible to him through an open bathroom door. She was working feverishly, all the while accompanying the female singer in a sad sounding ballad on the radio. Stepping completely inside the knotty pine cottage, he took a seat on the couch near the door and watched as the young woman toiled on the floor. Mary Porterfield had a full head of bright, blond hair of medium length. She wore a checkered, red flannel shirt tucked into a pair of denim jeans. The bottom of her sneakers reflected much wear with holes visible in the soles of each. Brian looked on for a few seconds, wondering for a moment if the beautiful shade of yellow of this woman's tresses was natural. Eventually, he decided to make his presence known and get his first look at her face. He cleared his throat loud enough to carry over the music and the young woman's voice. Her head shot up abruptly and she swung around toward him. His eyes met with hers, seeing immediately that she was little more than a girl. Mary Porterfield had a very appealing face, blessed with a quality that proved luminous when she smiled. Blue eyes and angelic features were set on a slightly less than perfect complexion. However, the scattering of small blemishes immediately noticeable to the eye did nothing to detract from this young woman's first impression.

"Hi, you must be Mary. Millie sent me down to introduce myself and give you your check for last week. I'm Larry. I'll be working with you this summer."

"Doing what?"

"Doing the same as you—cleaning up, changing sheets, laundry and stuff."

"You're a chambermaid?" she asked, seeming to be startled by the revelation.

"Actually, I prefer to be called a chamber–*man,*" corrected Brian, satisfied the young lady had taken the bait.

"You actually do this kind of work for a living—really?" He dropped his eyes to the floor, feigning to be offended. "No, I didn't mean it in an insulting way—it's just different."

"A lot of folks react just like you. I don't see a thing wrong with it. It's an honest living, that's how I see it."

"No, Larry—oh, I'm so sorry," she hastened, scurrying to his side. "You're a chamber *man.* You know, it could be a lot worse—you could be a chamber *pot.*" With that, the pretty blonde broke out in a fit of giddy laughter.

"Oh great, now you're out and out making fun of me," mumbled Brian, leaning forward and dramatically burying his face in his hands. Mary sat down on the couch beside him, placing a hand on his shoulder.

"Larry, you can't be so sensitive about everything. If you're happy doing this, then, that's all that counts." The blonde woman spoke in a motherly fashion and with a measure of concern. She also spoke through a heavy, rural Maine accent. Brian found himself touched by her sincerity as a mild sensation of guilt crept over him. He wanted to end the charade but was hard pressed to come up with an exit strategy. Half reluctantly, he continued on with the pretense. He lifted his head.

"I mean—this was okay when I was a kid, but I'm nearly forty years old and here I am stuck in this same rut. My God, people must be laughing at me behind my back. Look at me."

"That's just not so. No one's laughing at you—and if they are then they're laughing at me, too. You look at the bright side—and all the fun we'll have this summer working here together. Millie seems like a good soul and she says Mr. Kelly is a fine man, too. These are good jobs we got—so what if they don't pay a lot. Millie says Mr. Kelly gives bonuses at the end of the season to the people who stay on into the fall." Brian rose to his feet and smiled down on the girl.

"I suppose you're right. Oh—and here's your check." He handed Mary her paycheck and turned for the door.

"Have you met Mr. Kelly yet?" she asked. He nodded yes.

"And you?"

"No, not yet—maybe later today. Millie says I'll really like him." Brian whirled around and stepped out onto the deck.

"He's going to like you," he called back without turning to face the girl.

At noon, Millie contacted Mary by phone, inviting her to join them up in the office for lunch. After declining the invitation, she was given an order to report to the main office and join everyone for homemade chicken noodle soup and warm bread. Arriving in the lobby at the main house, the twenty-three year old found a table set up in the middle of the sitting room with a bowl of soup simmering atop it along with a basket of homemade bread. The makeshift dining room table was set for three.

"Pull yourself up a chair and join us child. Brian's upstairs, he'll be down in a second." Mary glanced around the room, her eyes popped wide open.

"Did Larry already go home?" she inquired.

"Larry who?"

"Larry—Larry, the chambermaid, I mean chamber *man.*"

"Chamber pot," called out Brian from the stairs. He turned into the room and approached the table while Millie ladled out the soup and Mary stared in astonishment at him. Speechless, the young woman covered her face in embarrassment, probably trying to remember exactly what she had said to her new employer an hour earlier.

"You have found us a little peach here, Millie—a little peach," he stated while removing slices of warm bread from the basket. "Wait—let me get you ladies something to drink. Mary, I'll get you a glass of milk—you being a growing girl and all. Millie, you and me, coffee?" He hopped up and walked off to collect the beverages.

"Child, if you brought a lunch with you then feel free to run down and get it. There'll still be plenty of soup left when you get back." Mary responded with a blush.

"Truth is, I had to give the baby sitter everything I had this morning, to mind my son when he gets out of school. I was going to just skip lunch today."

"I'll hear none of that. Don't you let yourself go without eating while either of us is here. I know how expensive child care can be—being short is nothing to be ashamed of," snapped the woman in a voice only loud enough to reach across the table.

"Please don't say anything to Mr. Kelly about this. He must think I'm a little soft in the head as it is. Did he tell you he was having fun with me down at the cottage a while ago?" Millie shook her head no.

"You're going to have to stay on your toes around here with him. He's a real practical joker."

The two women were sitting patiently over their soup awaiting his return when Brian emerged from the kitchen with two cups of coffee and a glass of milk balanced on a tray. In perfect waiter style, he placed the drinks down at each set-ting and returned to his chair. Mary, feeling very much the outsider, waited for her hosts to begin their meals before reaching for her own utensils. This proved judicious when Millie bowed her head and broke into prayer.

"Dearest Lord, thank you for the food on the table—for our good health—and for bringing Mary to us as we embark upon another season. Amen."

"Amen," added Brian, followed by the sign of the cross.

Brian and Millie had just begun their meal and were chatting about the treat-ment of the lawn for insect control when they became aware of muffled sobbing from their new employee. Reaching across the table, Millie grasped her hand.

"What's the matter, child?"

"It's nothing—really nothing," the young woman forced out between a short series of deep breaths. "It's just that I love this place—and I love working at this place—and I already love you two so much." Millie stared across at the girl behind a motherly smile.

"This one's got a good heart she does," she said, nodding approvingly at the girl. Brian's response was non vocal, content to gaze approvingly at his new chambermaid.

IX

*I*t was May. The full fledged tourist season would not arrive until the end of the month but the Atlantic Coast Lodge still had enough visitors during the week and drive ups on weekends to keep up with expenses. Millie had just enjoyed a long, four day weekend when Brian decided to visit his aunt and uncle in Lowell. He had not seen Uncle Jimmy or Aunt Martha since the St. Patrick's Day weekend and he reasoned this was as good a time as any to see family and visit the city of his birth. Trips back to Lowell usually included a visit to St. Patrick's Cemetery where his mother was buried. Walking in the midst of the National Park, a stroll by his old high school and a side trip along the well-preserved canals, many dug by his Irish ancestors, were the things that enhanced his visits home. The cobble stoned back streets leading off of Merrimack held wonderful memories for Brian from his youth. Time spent clutching his mother's hand and being guided along the sidewalks of Central and Merrimack Streets was practically the only memory he had of his pre-school life on the planet. For this reason, he would visit and revisit these places where the distant, shadowed memories of his early existence found familiar surroundings in which to evaporate.

Brian, as was his custom, telephoned the Clarke's the day before his visit. He had just worked out the details of an afternoon with the couple when his uncle casually made a statement that caused him to stop in his tracks.

"Oh Brian, did I tell you that I dropped into the Tavern at the Bridge last week and ran into your old friend, Perez. He asked me how you were doing and how often I saw you. I told him I expected to be hearing from you anytime now."

"Perez is back in Lowell! What's he doing back? Did he say anything about what was up with him?"

"No, he just asked about you and how you were doing."

"I can't believe he's back in the states. "How did he look?"

"He looked pretty good, considering I don't think I've seen him in ten years or so. It's been that long, right?"

"Yeah, just about," answered Brian, his mind already racing wildly.

"So when can we expect you on Saturday?"

"Sometime right around noon—and don't forget, I'm buying!" His uncle laughed and wished his nephew a good day while Brian's head swam from news of his old friend's return to Lowell. He hung up the phone and stared out the window to the horizon. He thought back, attempting to put together the jigsaw puzzle of years that was his life. Perez had gone home to Puerto Rico in the mid to late eighties, 1986 or 1987, he figured. He vividly remembered driving him to

Boston and Logan Airport. Perez, the man who had acted as mentor and friend to him in his youth, had functioned, in some ways, as a father to him. Perez's last few days before going home were spent as his guest at the cottage. Now he was back in Lowell. As hard as he tried, Brian could not conjure up a set of circumstances capable of bringing back his close friend.

It was shortly after eight o'clock when Brian tossed a duffle bag of dirty clothes into the front seat of the pickup and set off for Lowell. First, he would drive to the cemetery and visit his mom, then spend some time downtown. At noontime, he would join the Clarkes, perhaps taking them to a particular, favorite restaurant in Dracut. Knowing he was not due back in Bedford until the early evening, he would also use some free time in the afternoon to attempt to track down his old friend. He headed the pickup out onto Webhannet Drive from Deptula, turning south along the coast. The ocean was mildly irritated on this morning, sending water spurting over the sea wall. The road was wet and covered with strands of seaweed as he motored in the direction of Moody Beach. He had not been back to Bedford since Jenny moved home from Rhode Island at the beginning of the month. He shook his head while considering how the house was filling up. Following their marriage, he and Maggie May had enjoyed the peacefulness that an empty household offered. That was until Colleen and the need for Moira, the fulltime nanny. Now, Jenny had returned for at least the next two years.

The day passed extraordinarily well. In the morning he placed a single, white rose by his mother's grave, spending more time than usual speaking in a low voice to the woman who presided over the first seventeen years of his life. Following his visit to St. Patrick's Cemetery, it was on to downtown where he traced the paths of a number of canals and walked the passageways between the city's mill buildings, the massive relics of his hometown's glory years during the industrial revolution. This was always time spent in deep thought. It was in these familiar places where he often, for better or for worse, took stock of his life. On this day he had left his car near the small park dedicated to Jack Kerouac, one of Lowell's favorite sons. On the far side of the nearby canal sat housing units in the same brick buildings where his mother had labored in sweat shops only twenty five years before. Nostalgic sights like these had long played heavily on his consciousness, providing deeply moving emotions, which he was never able to articulate and or share with anyone else. He only knew they made him feel alive, sensitively, sometimes painfully, alive.

His visit home proved a warm one with his aunt and uncle showering him with attention. Sometime during lunch, in the midst of one of his uncle's stories about his grandchildren, Brian noticed the effects time had carved on the faces of his two relatives. They were no longer the middle aged couple who took him in after his mother's untimely death. How could they be? He would soon be middle aged himself. *Don't trust anyone over thirty!* Wasn't that once the mantra of his own generation? Now, here he was, within hailing distance of his fortieth birthday. These and other arbitrary thoughts swam through his mind, first at the restaurant, then later seated in the Clarke's living room. He took a measured sip from a nearly empty cup of coffee and glanced down at his watch. It was after three.

"Oh, my God, where has the time gone?" he called out, jumping up from the sofa.

"My dear, it always goes so fast when you come," added his aunt. He crossed the room and applied a hug to them both. The Clarke's two children, Barbara and Jimmy, Junior had married, started families, and moved out of New England. Brian could not even remember the last time he had seen either of his younger cousins. His aging aunt and uncle were his only link to his youth and upbringing in Lowell and he very much cherished their continued role in his life. Good-byes, this day, lingered on at the front door until he placed a final kiss on his aunt's cheek and turned away.

Pulling his pickup out onto the road, he aimed the vehicle in the direction of Bridge Street. He knew it was a long shot but it was a few hours before he was expected home in Bedford. His intended destination was the Tavern at the Bridge, the pub where his uncle had spotted Perez a week earlier. Brian's progress was slowed when he became gridlocked in afternoon traffic. After spending time at a traffic light in the shadow of St. Michael's Rectory and a rush of reminiscences from his youth in the parish, the Ford rolled slowly down the street toward the tavern. Twenty five years ago, this particular pub was called the Wonder Bar and Perez had frequented it often. Sometime over the years, the establishment had changed its name and appearance. However, the location, close by the river and straddling the corner of Lakeview Avenue and Bridge Street, remained constant. After parking the Ford in the lot behind the bar, he walked toward the one story, brick building trimmed broadly in deep, green wooden panels.

Brian swung open the door and stepped inside. Immediately taken with the change in light between the sunshine illuminated sidewalk and the inside of the pub with its subdued lighting and dark, wooden paneling, he paused for a moment, his eyes adjusting to the room. The tavern was roomier than he remembered, the floor space dominated by a horseshoe-shaped bar in the center of the room. He glanced about as he moved forward, hoping to notice his friend among the two dozen or so patrons. Barely settled in his stool, he was approached by an attractive, female bartender.

"What can I get for you?"

"Any kind of light beer will be fine—no real preference." The woman whirled around and walked toward the far end of the counter. He had seated himself apart from the line of what appeared to be regulars seated four or five stools away. Again his eyes scanned the room, hoping to spot his friend. In the short time it took for the bartender to return with his bottle and glass, he managed to take in the face and back of the head of every customer present. It seemed his exercise was not going to be successful, at least not on this day. Perez was nowhere to be seen. He decided to quietly listen to the banter around him, leisurely drink his beer, and then quiz the bartender about Perez when she returned to see if he wanted a refill. That plan, as it turned out, would prove unnecessary for it was only a few moments later when the door to the men's room opened and his friend emerged carrying a newspaper under his arm. He walked a few feet before depositing himself at a small table in the far corner of the room. He stared at his old friend, seated no more than thirty feet away, as if seeing an apparition. Perez, totally unaware of his friend's presence, unfolded the newspaper and took a sip from the glass of beer in front of him.

It was only a few seconds before Brian rose from his stool, beer in hand, and walked around the bar and toward the man who had befriended him in his youth. Perez, his eyes focused on something in the newspaper, did not glance up until Brian was standing directly over him.

"I'd say it's been a while," Brian muttered, taking in every detail of the man's face.

"Bri—where did you come from?" answered his friend.

"Uncle Jimmy told me he'd seen you here—and I was in Lowell today—visiting." Perez fidgeted momentarily before gesturing his friend to take a seat. Brian sat, extending a warm smile. "How long have you been back—and are you staying?"

"I came back in March, so it's been a couple a months."

"Why didn't you call?"

"I don't know—been a little busy." Brian was already picking up on the brevity of his former mentor's responses.

"I'd of been down in a flash if I'd known." Perez shrugged and shifted his eyes across the room.

"Are you staying?"

"Who knows?" Brian shifted uncomfortably in his chair, all the while focusing on his friend's facial expression and body language. When Perez showed no sign of entering into a dialogue, Brian decided to ratchet up the intensity of the conversation.

"Okay, come on buddy, something's up. It's me sitting here—what the fuck's going on?"

"Hey man, until a minute ago I was sitting here, minding my own business—that was until you came over and started with the twenty questions."

"It's been close to ten years since I've seen you—and all I get is this bum fuck treatment! Something brought you back to Lowell."

"Personal matters, that's it—personal."

"And how many times did I come to you with personal matters? Buddy, if something is wrong—maybe I can help—even if it means just listening." Perez swallowed, exaggerated as if trying to contain some emotion he wanted kept from his younger friend, then noticeably withdrew inside himself, looking away. "But it was okay when I came running to you? That was okay. Buddy, I know you as well as I know myself. Is there something I can do?" Peering across the table, he saw that his friend's eyes were unfocused and distant. It was becoming clear the man had no intention of sharing anything with him.

"Fine—then fuck you! Don't let someone who gives a shit be of any help. God forbid if I was ever in a position to give back to you one tenth of what you did for me. Fuck off pal!" Brian gulped the last mouthful of beer from his glass and slammed it down, the thud on the table causing two or three heads from the bar to turn in his direction. He pushed himself away from the small table and walked straight for the door.

Brian's eyes squinted as he cleared the front door of the tavern, the sunlight reflecting off the window of a car parked nearby. Frustrated, he drew in a deep breath and walked around the building in the direction of his pickup.

"Bri!" called out a voice. He turned to see his friend jogging up from behind. "Calm down, will ya." Then, the man reached forward and embraced him, patting him over and over on the back. He returned the hug. "How much time do ya have?"

"I should be back in New Hampshire by six-thirty, seven at the latest."

"You're back in New Hampshire! What happened to your place in Maine?"

"Oh, I'm still there, too—but I'm married now. Believe it or not, it's a girl I met way back when I went to school up in Manchester. I may even have told you about her. In fact, I know I did."

"Then maybe ya have time to go for one of our walks along the boulevard?"

"Absolutely, but of course there's no Cathay Garden anymore—some water treatment plant or something is in its place."

"Damn it, fuck progress—good Chinese food is more important than clean water." Brian grinned down at his friend as the two men turned and walked in the direction of the Lowell-Lawrence Boulevard. Over the next two hours they retraced their route from twenty-five years before, following the Merrimack River eastward before climbing up the backside of Christian Hill, filling each other in on the twists and turns of their respective lives. It was only after Brian had recounted the turbulent events leading to his marriage to the former Margaret Keogh that Perez opened up and detailed his eight years away. He learned that for the first two years home, Perez's plan for a comfortable retirement at age forty-two was playing out quite nicely. That was until he met and fell hopelessly in love with a nineteen year old beauty with brown eyes and long, brown hair that flowed down her back to her waist. Drawn to an older man with money to spend on her, she eventually moved in with him and found her every request, and there were to be many, fulfilled by Perez. The romance lasted for over five years, side-tracked only briefly on two occasions when she moved out. However, both times the relationship had been mended, thanks to a spending binge bankrolled by the middle aged man. In the end, Natalia Rodriguez crossed paths with a young doctor of comfortable means, turned his head as she had turned that of Perez, and the five year romantic escapade was over.

"I managed to piss away in five years almost everything I'd worked my ass off for twenty years to get," he confided as they walked along side the reservoir atop Christian Hill.

"So you weren't going to tell me any of this—like I'd think you were some kind of jerkoff? Buddy, it's not like you're the first guy to get screwed over by a woman."

"But I took up with a teenager—me, already in my forties."

"Were they five good years?"

"I was in love. In a small way I guess I still am."

"Then screw her—she's the loser in the end. Someday she'll realize what she's missing—and it'll be too late. I'm still surprised you're back in Lowell." Perez looked down at the ground, his face taking on a strained, cheerless expression.

"My mama died in January—and I was never real close to my brothers and sisters." Brian draped his arm over his friend's shoulder.

"I know what that's like—and you know that's not bullshit. I know what going through that is like—I don't care how old you are, it hurts. She's the one who brought you into the world and you could always turn to. Mothers always give a shit, that's what's so great about them." The man nodded back in agreement, appearing to appreciate his younger friend's concern.

"Now I'm back here and everything has changed. All of my contacts have dried up and people don't need the neighborhood bookie anymore. I'm just spinning my wheels—watching what cash I have left get lower and lower."

Following a quiet moment when neither man found anything to say, the men paused at the crest of Christian Hill and looked out over the city. From this spot, they could clearly see the line of mill buildings bordering the river. Behind the row of dark buildings was the Sun Building and downtown Lowell.

"Did you ever think about how the Indians must have stood up here before there was ever a Third Street and a city and the mill buildings and looked out over what was then Lowell? All they would have seen was the river and a lot of trees."

"And maybe a war party coming their way," suggested Perez.

"And maybe some really cute Indian girls—nineteen year old Indian girls," teased Brian whimsically.

"You're not going to start busting my balls over that story about Natalia, are you?" Brian burst out in laughter.

"Relax, Buddy, I have too many of those kind of skeletons in my own closet to do that."

They descended the hill and walked toward the front of the tavern. It was nearly five o'clock. The conversation had begun to lag in the last few minutes, the two men becoming mutually aware that their time together was drawing to a close. Brian stopped by the front door of the pub as a patron emerged. The stranger gave the two a hesitant acknowledgement and stepped off toward the bridge.

"I'll buy you a drink—if you'll join me inside and listen to a proposition I have for you," said Brian. Perez hesitated for an instant before gesturing to his friend to enter. Once inside, they crossed the room and reclaimed the table in the corner. They were barely settled in their chairs when the blonde from behind the bar came over and took their order. Brian got right to the point.

"I'd like you to come up and pay me a visit in Maine. You can stay at the cottage like you did before or even up at the lodge. There are always open units this time of year."

"And what am I supposed to do while I'm up there?"

"Leave that to me. I have an idea. Just trust me on this. Besides, it's pretty up there. It'll give you time to clear your head and just think." Perez looked squarely at his friend, searching for a clue to what might be being planned behind his piercing, hazel eyes.

"I pay my own way," he stated emphatically.

"Room is free—you can pay for your own food if you like." He shrugged his shoulders and relented as two glasses of beer arrived at the table.

"I'll be going back on Monday morning. I'll pick you up at around eight-thirty. Pack enough clothes for five or six days. Where are you living right now?"

"Lakeview Avenue—it's only a room. It sucks." He pulled out a piece of paper from his back pocket and jotted down his address. "I'll be out front on Monday. I'd feel better if you didn't see the room. My old apartment on Bridge Street wasn't available—naturally, so I took this. It's a dump."

*I*t was shortly before seven o'clock when Brian turned into the driveway and crept toward the house. He had not been in Bedford for nearly a week and he looked forward to seeing the two ladies in his life. He had barely turned the key on the ignition off when a voice called out from the front doorway.

"Put that junk in the garage, Kelly, or I'll have it towed." He let out a sigh, restarted the engine, and moved the vehicle into the furthermost bay. If the first words directed at him on this evening were borderline hostile, the second were anything but.

"Daddy," cried out Colleen, running down the hallway toward her father as he closed the front door behind him. In her eagerness to greet the man, the toddler tripped on the carpet but was snatched up by Brian just before making contact with the floor.

"Has my little Boo Boo missed her daddy this week?" He scooped up the child, cradling her in his arms as he made his way into the living room.

"Can we play together now?" asked the child eagerly.

"Listen to this kid talk," he commented to his wife who was spread out in a regal position on the couch.

"I've been working with her—reading her bedtime stories and pointing out words to her in her books. It's clear she has inherited my brains," stated Margaret proudly.

"Your mother's brains and my good looks—you've hit the jackpot, Colleen Kelly, you really have," he added, holding his daughter in front of him at arms length, his eyes beaming with pride.

"She *better* not have her father's looks. Christ, she'll wind up a fifty year old spinster still living with her parents," cracked Margaret. The commotion brought Moira scurrying in from the kitchen. At the sight of her nanny, the little girl cried to her father for help.

"Boo Boo, it's getting to be your bedtime. We have all day tomorrow together, I promise." He followed his words with a flurry of noisy kisses to his daughter's neck and arms. His actions caught her off guard, sending her into a fit of laughter. Then, sixty seconds later, after dutifully kissing her mother and father, Colleen was carried upstairs and off to bed.

"Where's Jen?" Brian asked while collapsing onto the couch beside his wife.

"Out with friends," she answered. "It's been a while Kelly," she added, commenting on the five days he had been away.

"And it'll only get worse when we reach June."

"How was Lowell?"

"Good, as usual. Jimmy and Martha hardly ever see their own kids these days so they seem to really enjoy the company. Plus, there was a bonus. I got a chance to visit with my buddy, Perez. I haven't seen him in eight years and now he's back in Lowell." Brian went on to fill his wife in on everything that had transpired over the afternoon. The two had a late dinner of franks and beans, preparing their food while Moira flitted around them in the kitchen. Jenny was out for the evening, having caught up with a high school acquaintance in her short time back in Bedford. The evening passed quietly, a rented movie from the video store providing the entertainment.

The couple flicked out the light in the living room early on this Saturday. Following a series of awkward hints from Brian, Margaret announced she was not in the mood for sex this night but dangled a measure of bait in front of him. In exchange for an hour long massage, she would guarantee a night of lovemaking the following night. In addition, she promised to share an incredible, true story over the course of her massage, a story so fascinating it would surely make the hour fly by for him. He agreed after only a brief period of consideration. The words scarcely out of his mouth, she fell backwards onto their king-sized bed and closed her eyes.

"Undress me and we shall begin," she said. He moved to the bottom of the bed where he removed her sandals and slipped her cutoff jeans off in one, fluid motion. Seconds later her tee shirt was off and he began taking position.

"Everything comes off," she added. She rolled onto her back and allowed him to unclip her bra. Lastly, the panties were slipped off and he was ready to commence.

"You'll find the lotion in the top drawer of my bureau."

"How long has this been planned?"

"I bought the lotion Thursday on the drive home from work."

"Ah, my spontaneous Maggie May." He squeezed out a line of the thick liquid from the plastic tube, applying it from the middle of her back down and onto her buttocks. Seconds later he was rubbing the cream along the surface of her skin. "God, I never get used to this body! If I ever start losing my faith in a Supreme Being, I only have to look at you, Keogh—and all doubt is removed. Nothing like this form lying in front of me just happens by accident. Evolution, on its own, could never come up with something as magnificent as you."

"I'm glad to do my part to reaffirm your faith, Brian."

For the initial two or three minutes of her massage Margaret lay still, without movement or speech. It was while Brian applied more lotion to her back and shoulders that she finally spoke out.

"I had lunch in town today with a new client—a female client from Nashua. She recently purchased a commercial building in Manchester not too far from mine. Our office picked her up as a client when her old firm split up and the CPA she was comfortable with wound up moving to Pennsylvania. As you know, I've been on the lookout for a new friend—Claire being so caught up with her precious James. Anyway, I played tennis this week with Mindy and—oh, before you ask, yes—I did kick her ass at tennis. Anyway, Mindy and I had lunch

together on Friday and she told me this incredible story. I guess she's been looking for some new friends too—and she confided this story in me."

"Is this going to be some investment story I couldn't give a rat's ass about?"

"No, Kelly, it's not. I don't think you've ever heard a story quite like this.
Now, if you want, I'll just stop here—but if I do, trust me, you'll never hear it—
ever. Okay? No more interruptions."

"Fine, go ahead."

"Mindy happened upon this building downtown in Manchester that she
became quite interested in. She knew the landlord was having some cash flow
problems and the property was leveraged to the max. She approached the landlord on the side and opened negotiations to buy it. You see, she already had a
ready-made tenant to occupy the first floor. The second and third floors were
occupied by small businesses—a yoga studio, an architect's office and some small
time professionals. Now, the owner had become interested in selling because this
property was running a negative cash flow. A few weeks into negotiations, Mindy
sits down and starts going over some of the minute, financial details. That's when
she makes her incredible discovery. One of the offices is occupied by this con-
sultant type, an engineer or something, and his rent is like eight months in
arrears. What's more, it seems like he's been living on the premises for over a year,
which is against the city's zoning laws—except he can't afford to pay for the
office, let alone an apartment. Remember, he's eight months behind on his rent.
The only reason he's still there is because the landlord is an old friend and a soft
touch."

"So she buys the building and tosses his ass out, right? A guy behind in his
rent is not an incredible discovery, Keogh."

"I haven't got to the incredible discovery, you brain dead Irishman—stop
interrupting. As I was saying, Mindy looks down at this guy's name and can't
believe her eyes. His name is quite distinctive and just happens to be someone
from her past. As a matter of fact, she shacked up with this guy for an entire
weekend twenty-five years earlier—and this son of a bitch used her and broke
her heart. It was a case of him being one of those really special people you can
never quite get over—at least for her. Kind of what I was—and am for you—you
know, how one person just owns another---lock, stock and barrel."

"I get the picture, Maggie May—you can go on with the story."

"Well, here it is twenty-five years later and she still thinking of this guy.
Anyway, she pumps the landlord for all the information she can get and finds out
he filed for bankruptcy just two years earlier. Now, you have to understand, this
guy comes from old money—or at least his family used to have old money. He
still walks around in expensive suits and drives a nice car—but he hasn't got a pot
to piss in! Now, Mindy comes up with a plan. She's going to buy the building
anyway, you see, but now she sees the opportunity for something else. She goes
ahead with her plan to buy the building but also arranges to buy the debt, the
eight months of back rent, from the landlord. Now, legally, the back rent is owed
to her. Are you following all this, Kelly?" Brian responded by running his hands
along the inside of her thighs, a motion that always got a heated rise out of her.
This time proved not to be an exception.

"I'll take that for a yes," she said, responding to his gesture. "So while the paperwork and financing for the purchase of the building is being put into place, she writes this guy a letter, reminding him of who she was and inviting him to join her up at York Beach at the Union Bluff Hotel where they had their first and only encounter way back in the early seventies. She tells him that she spotted him on the street in Manchester a few days earlier and this gave her the idea. She expected him to be flattered and maybe accept the invitation. The guy selling the place has clued her in on the fact that the guy is between girlfriends, twice divorced, and pretty much down for the count—romantically and financially. Mindy hints in the letter that she's very comfortable—financially, which she is sure will appeal to this idiot."

"She's putting a lot of time and effort into this thing," commented Brian.

"You bet your ass. Anyway, she gets an e-mail a day or two later from the guy and they arrange to meet at the hotel in York on a Friday night for dinner—and perhaps more! Moving ahead, Mindy and Carlton, we'll call him Carlton but that's not his name, they hook up downstairs in the restaurant. She tells me how he's trying to convince her that he remembers her and their weekend up there twenty-five years before, but she knows it's all horseshit. When the evening and the dinner progress nicely she invites him upstairs. On a hunch, he's brought an overnight bag, which he gets from the car, and the two settle in for the weekend. It's a romantic place near Short Sands, their windows overlook the ocean. She told me how they spent the next two days on the move during the day, driving up to Portland to shop in the Old Port then on to Freeport. She spent money on him and he must have been thinking his bad luck streak was finally coming to an end. Then, on Sunday night as the two sat on the terrace overlooking the sea, Carlton brought up the subject of an ongoing relationship and how glad he was she had contacted him after all these years. The weekend had reached its epiphany as she saw it. Mindy told me how her mood changed at this point. She went on to relate to him the events from twenty-five years earlier—how she remembered them. How after surrendering herself to this man and doting on his every whim, she was dismissed like a fumbling store clerk—her telephone calls totally ignored and a gut wrenching letter sent to him apparently not even considered worthy of a single sentence response. It was here that she began catching the guy up on her leveraged position in his life—how she now owned the building he lived in and the eight month's back rent he'd accrued. She explained to this piece of shit that she wasn't fooled by his wardrobe or late model car—she had studied his credit report, knew of his recent bankruptcy, knew his consulting practice was a joke, and knew his family was in no position to help him anymore. In brief, Carlton's financial back was to the wall and Mindy owned the wall. All he had left was his pride and his family name—and she was in a position to humiliate him but good back in Manchester. His old friend, the ex-landlord, had kept the secret of his financial woes quiet for some time now, but she would not be so Christian. She reminded him that she was highly visible in more than one civic and business group. An eviction or anything else she came up with would not be carried out quietly." Margaret paused and took a deep breath while Brian's hands found their way back along the inside of her thighs, his palms sliding up from just above her knees and stopping only inches from her vagina.

"So she just emptied both barrels in him?" he asked, his hands now fumbling for more lotion to lubricate his massage strokes. She closed her eyes, drawing in a deep, extended breath. "God, Maggie May, no woman your age should still have a pair of gams like these. Why—it's a good thing you have a husband like me—a lesser man would already have been destroyed by a woman with weapons like these."

"That's funny, Kelly—I'm hard pressed to even imagine a lesser man. Wait a minute, I seem to be getting close—a figure is materializing out of the haze. No, I'm sorry Brian—try as I may—I can't even picture a lesser man," she blurted out, following her words with one of her patented giggles. He shook his head and resumed the massage, his fingers venturing far up her outstretched legs.

"Brian, why are you trying to make this so sexual?"

"You're lying here—completely naked—not even a hint of modesty or shame in you. Why wouldn't I make it sexual?"

"You're saying I should be ashamed of my naked body?"

"Don't start Maggie May. You're getting a massage here—damn it. Finish your story." She closed her eyes, letting out with another deep sigh as her husband's hands slid up her legs and crossed into her pubic region.

"Carlton had become flustered and embarrassed by Mindy's threat. He asked if there was anything he could do to change her mind or make amends. That's when she gave him an option, the option she had in the back of her mind all the while she planned the rendezvous. She restated his first option—eviction, humiliation, and everything that goes along with it. But then she gave him a second option—an option where he might save face—sort of." She opened her eyes and shot Brian her devilish grin.

"Oh, God, this can't be good," he joked.

"She told him about her house in Hollis, a sprawling farmhouse badly in need of attention. She explained how he could be spared the humiliation of an eviction and all of the petty gossip associated with his financial problems. He could quietly and unceremoniously disappear from sight. He would move onto the premises with her in Hollis where he could function as a combination handyman, sharecropper, house boy and indentured servant. He would receive room and board from her and a nominal wage. From the wage he would pay taxes and repay Mindy for the debt arising from his back rent. By her calculations, he could have the debt paid off in just a little over two years. Naturally, he would have to turn in his leased vehicle and any penalty from that she would pay—and add to the total debt owed to her."

"Jesus, God, he didn't go along with that, did he?"

"She said he hit the roof—stomped around the room calling her a fat bitch that he still couldn't remember from twenty five years ago. She told me how he ranted for about ten minutes. Then, he grew serious, confiding in her how he'd been dogged by bad luck from the time he finished college. 'The world had it in for him,' that's what he thought. He said he didn't care what the assholes in Manchester said or thought about him. Finally, she said he became very quiet, staring out at the ocean, then back at her. By this time he was near tears, his circumstances and his lot in life crumbling down on him."

"What did he decide to do?"

"That was last September. He moved into the house in Hollis less than a month after this whole incident—and is still there. Mindy says it's almost like he's come to accept his lot there. She's happy. She's getting the placed fixed up while she has the guy she pined for as a teenager living and working under her."

"Man—that story is so bizarre."

"I see it as evidence of how great capitalism is—how Mindy was able to gain satisfaction from this piece of shit without anyone getting shot or beaten to death."

"I hope you'll wait a few years before you tell this to Jelly Bean as a bedtime story."

"I'll wait till she's in school anyway, if it makes you happy." Brian substituted a light nip to her thigh in place of a verbal response. She rolled her body to the side.

"If that's an attempt to initiate anything—don't bother—I told you, I'm not in the mood." He let out a sigh.

"Well then, this might be as good time as any to remind you that I'll be driving up to Quebec City and visiting the LaChapelles soon. I'll only be gone one night—two days and one night."

"Oh, for Christ's sake, not again! Do I have to suffer through another year of drama? It's been fifteen fucking years, Brian. Put it to rest." The source of Margaret's irritation was her husband's ritual of visiting the gravesite and family of Angelique LaChapelle, a young woman he fell in love with nearly twenty years ago and lost to a car accident. She harbored a deep resentment toward this young woman she had never known. As she saw it, Angelique LaChapelle, in a strange way, was a rival for her husband's love, a rival she could never defeat. Frozen in time at twenty years of age, this girl, beautiful by all accounts, was the female rival she could never outshine or overwhelm. His relationship with the mysterious Miss LaChapelle was one of the few episodes from his past life he kept under wraps, unwilling to share even the slightest details of their time together with her.

"Actually, it's been thirteen years—but who's counting." He rose from the bed and walked across the room, stopping directly in front of his bureau.

"I just think you do it to aggravate me," she snapped.

"No—it's true I do do certain things to aggravate you, Keogh—and I'm working on new things all the time. This, though, is not one of them." His voice dropped off, signaling her he did not want to pursue this topic of conversation.

"Fine—sulk—I'm going downstairs and work out. I'd like to work out on the weights tonight. Would it be too much to ask to have you come down and spot for me?" He turned and shrugged his shoulders. She took this for a yes. Brian trained his eyes on her for a lingering moment. She stared back at her husband of three years, reading his thoughts the way only spouses have the ability to do. In that instant he considered how his life might have turned out if a motorist had not plowed up onto a Quebec City sidewalk and snuffed out the life of Angelique LaChapelle.

XI

*I*t was midweek and Millie was alone manning the office when the phone rang and summoned her from the kitchen, her hands still wet from activity at the sink. Brian was away visiting Quebec City.

"Atlantic Coast Lodge," she announced, careful to hide her frustration from being called away from the next room.

"Hi Millie, this is Linda Turcotte, you know, Brian's old friend—Brendan's mom." The statement was followed by an extended pause.

"Oh, of course, Linda—I'm sorry, it's part of getting old—the mind doesn't work as fast."

"Millie, I thought before I tried reaching Brian down at the cottage or back in New Hampshire, I'd try here. Is he handy?"

"I'm afraid not, Hon. He left yesterday morning for Canada. He's only going to be gone a couple of days and should be getting back sometime this evening."

"Is there any way I might be able to reach him—before this evening?"

"I'm afraid not. He doesn't have a cell phone—doesn't believe in them. Is there anything I can help you with?" Millie thought she picked up on some frustration from her caller.

"You wouldn't have heard from or seen Brendan by any chance?"

"No—but I'm not sure I'd even recognize him if I did. He was just a little guy the last time I saw him. How old's he now?"

"Eighteen."

"Listen, Linda, it sounds by the tone of your voice that there's a problem of some kind. Maybe I can be of some help until Brian gets back. He doesn't always call in so you may not hear from him until tonight."

"I have reason to believe that he's on his way over to see Brian—over to Wells or maybe even down to New Hampshire. There was quite a skirmish here early on and he flew out of the house."

"I don't understand, what does Brian have to do with all this?"

"Well, it's clear that he's kept his word and not shared our secret, at least with you. Why doesn't that surprise me? Millie—seeing that the cat's out of the bag anyway, I might as well share this with you. It was only about seven years ago that even Brian found out."

"Found out what?"

"That Brendan was his son. I'd kept it from him for over ten years. Then, even after I told him, I made him promise not to tell a soul until I thought the time was right. Well, Millie, that time came this morning after Brendan started questioning some blood test results he got and comparing them with his brothers and sister. There was no getting around the truth. I told him that Brian Kelly and not Bubba Birch was his biological father. He became incensed and demanded Brian's phone number and address. I was afraid not to give it to him—he was in such a rage. He was always such a wonderful kid until recently, then—poof— he started changing, being more like his brothers who are anything but wonderful. They've been a bad influence on him for some time now, but it's gotten worse in the last couple of years. My hands are tied Millie. Jack, that's my husband, he hasn't been in the best of health for the last couple of years and I've had my hands full caring for him."

"What do you suggest I do if your son turns up at our door here?" asked Millie.

"Humor him—tell him Brian's on his way back. Oh, God, I'm so sorry to drop this in his lap—but the truth is—I think Brian can handle it."

"Maybe we'll get lucky and he'll call in on his way home," added Millie before assuring the woman that things would turn out all right and promising to get back to her once there were developments to report on.

Jenny poured herself a cup of coffee at the kitchen table and unfolded the newspaper. She had been up late the night before, gathering information off the internet for an article she was writing on undiscovered vacation destinations in New England. She and her mother were already busy at work trying to get her enrolled in a local college for the upcoming fall term. In the meantime, the twenty-one year old was pursuing an ambition she had all but abandoned her senior year in high school, freelance writing. With her mother's blessing, Jenny was dividing her time between creative writing and applying to nearby institutions of higher learning. From upstairs, the only sound came from the back of the house where her half sister Colleen was simultaneously being given instruction and entertained by her nanny. Jenny's eyes had scarcely moved from the front page headlines to the celebrity news on the back page when the pounding of a fist on the front door echoed through the downstairs. Momentarily startled, she rose from her chair and walked gingerly in the direction of the interruption. She approached the front door barefoot and still in her pajamas. A second series of heavy handed knocks followed before she slowly eased open the door.

"Yes, can I help you with something?" she asked, looking down at a male on the granite steps. He was young, still likely in his teens, wearing jeans and a sweat shirt. There was an intense scowl etched on his face as he stared up at her through hazel eyes.

"Is Brian Kelly home? This is his house ain't it?"

"It's Brian and my mother's house—but he's not home right now—and I don't think he'll be home until later this week. He works in Maine," she answered. The words had hardly passed her lips when she regretted having shared them with him. The information prompted the boy to turn his head from side to side as if looking for a plan of action. "Maybe there's something I can help you with?"

"I don't think so. I've come a long way—from Albany—and I've walked all the way up here from the highway." The teenager took a few steps back from the door and seated himself in the grass by the walkway. Jenny's eyes opened wide in astonishment.

"You can't sit here. This is private property," she insisted. From behind came the sound of footsteps descending the stairs. She turned to see Moira carrying Colleen in her direction. By now the boy was lying on his back, his eyes closed and the sun shining on his face. "Get off our property, I said," she ordered.

"Not till I talk to Brian. Until I see him, I ain't goin anywhere."

Jenny swung the door closed and threw the deadbolt. Ignoring Moira's questions about the identity of the stranger, she hurried to the telephone and rang her mother at the office.

"Margaret Kelly," barked the voice at the far end of the line.

"Mother, we have a little problem here at home. There's a kid lying on our front lawn who will not leave no matter what I tell him. He says he's here to see Brian and says he won't leave until he does."

"What do you mean—a kid—a ten year old?"

"No, a teenage kid—seventeen or eighteen."

"Where did he come from?"

"I think he said something about Albany."

"Jenny, this is insane. Has he threatened you?"

"No, not really—but he's kind of creepy—just lying out front on our lawn."

"What the hell could Brian have to do with a teenager from Albany? No matter, Jenny, I want you to go outside and tell him you'll call the police and have him arrested for trespassing if he doesn't leave immediately. That should get him to move his ass—and if he refuses, call the cops."

The conversation ended with her mother, Jenny walked back to the front door, phone in hand, and swung it open. She addressed the young man, the telephone in plain sight.

"Either you get off of our property immediately or I'll call the police and have you dragged off." The young man lay motionless for a few seconds. After a half minute of inaction, he pushed himself to his feet in a single motion. The three females watched in the doorway as the tall, dark-haired teen sauntered down the driveway, finally leaving the property. Leaving the yard, he turned back to the expansive colonial and proceeded to the opposite side of Joppa Hill Road. Reaching the far side of the street, he collapsed down onto the grass.

"Go away," called out Jenny in a loud voice before closing the front door with a thud.

The second report from Jenny on the mysterious boy from Albany prompted Margaret to action. She rang the Atlantic Coast Lodge in hope of contacting Brian. She was disappointed when instead, she reached Millie.

"Millie, this is Margaret Kelly. We have a situation back here in New Hampshire. There's a teenage boy out at the house who is spooking the household—hanging around outside—who says he's not going anywhere until he speaks to Brian. Do you have any idea what the hell is going on—and if not—when do you expect Brian back. He's due back from Canada tonight, isn't he?"

"Mrs. Kelly, I do expect him here early this evening."

"And the boy, do you know anything about what his problem is?"

"I have a suspicion—but I think it's best if Brian lets you in on that."

"Is this a disgruntled employee or something?"

"He's not an employee," the woman answered, being miserly with her words.

"He has Jenny pretty rattled. At least let me know if he's in any way dangerous."

"I don't think so, but then again I don't know him too well. His name is Brendan."

"Does he have a last name?"

"Birch."

By now Margaret gathered she was not going to pry any more information out of the woman. "Tell my husband to call me the minute he gets in—and Millie—be sure to let him know that I'm really pissed."

The circumstances at the house in Bedford unsettled Margaret. It was shortly after two o'clock when she tossed her appointment book and some professional literature in her briefcase and left for home. She sped across the city, the radio in her car off, attempting to come up with a logical scenario to explain the puzzling visitor camped out by her house. She had just passed the village center on Route 101 when the vision of a bloody massacre at the house popped into her head. She reached across the front seat for her cell phone before realizing it was back at the office. She drove the ghastly image of the three girl's bloody bodies from her mind, telling herself it was an insane overreaction. Nonetheless, she pressed down on the accelerator, turned onto Joppa Hill Road, and roared in the direction of her home. Two minutes later she slowed on her approach to the driveway, her eye catching its first sight of the intruder. He was lying in a patch of shade six or seven feet from the road's surface. His head bobbed up at the sound of the BMW's engine. Pulling the vehicle in to just beyond the driveway gate she stopped, pulled on the emergency brake, and stepped out of the car. Her two inch heels provided a distinctive clacking noise as she strove down the driveway and across the road. Knowing enough to display no fear, she walked to within six inches of his head as he lay resting on the grass.

"I want to know who the fuck you are and why the fuck you're here." She peered out over the adjacent field, not even allowing her eyes to drop down on the young man.

"As I told your baby sister up at the house—not until I get to talk to Brian Kelly. And—what is he to you?"

"He's my husband—and you?"

"You'll know soon enough," he answered coolly.

Margaret took a step backwards and gazed down on the teenager. He returned the glance and their eyes made contact. She had to hold back a gasp. The young man's intense, hazel eyes, the slant of his brows, and the color of his hair said more than any words he could have uttered. Without question, this young male resting on the ground in front of her was connected to Brian by blood. She spun around and walked in the direction of the car.

"Follow me to the house."

Climbing behind the wheel of the vehicle, she turned on the engine and slowly drove up to the colonial. A peek into the rear view mirror told her that their visitor had accepted her invitation. She remained in the car until the boy reached the house. With him standing at attention at the base of the steps, she exited the vehicle, brushed by the young man and through the front door.

"We've got company," she called out as she walked down the hallway in the direction of the kitchen. Behind her, the teenage boy tentatively made his way into the house, his eyes taking in the appearance of prosperity.

"Can I have my baby sister get you anything?"

"A glass of water—if you don't mind."

"That's it?" He shrugged his shoulders and nodded yes. She retreated back to the living room and saw Jenny standing by the couch, apparently eavesdropping.

"Sister, dear, would you get Brendan here a glass of water?" Jenny was slightly confused by her mother's words but set off for the kitchen.

"How do you know my name?"

"Brendan—I know much, much more about you than you think."

"Then he's told you about me?" She smiled and shook her head as if in disbelief.

"And Brendan, why exactly are you here?"

"Well lady, whatever your name is? Oh, I'm sorry—it's Mrs. Kelly, isn't it? Well, I'm here to thank Mr. Brian Kelly for never telling me a damn thing—and not to think for a fucking second he's my father. Cause he may have fucked my mother and knocked her up—and got to walk away from it and dump it on someone else, but it's Bubba Birch who's my real dad—and whose name I have."

Margaret turned to see Jenny in the doorway, a glass of water clutched in one hand with a look of absolute astonishment covering her face.

"Well, it's preferable to my other theory—my husband's been hanging around Wells High picking up girls and now one of their boyfriend's out for blood—preferable, but not by a whole lot," admitted Margaret to Jenny in a half whisper.

"He could be lying," she whispered back, the two just out of earshot.

"No, I've been on the phone with Millie. Plus, you only have to look at his eyes—and his hair. He's Brian's."

The two women seated themselves by the young man. Jenny passed him his water and for a few seconds nothing was said as mother and daughter sized up their unexpected guest. Brendan, his eyes focused largely on Jenny, gulped down his water in seconds and then seemed perplexed on where to place down the glass.

"I've left word at his office to have Brian call me immediately on his arrival," said Margaret. "However, they're not expecting him back until six at the earliest. That would mean he'll be getting back to Bedford, at best, at seven-thirty."

"I'll wait."

"Oh, I'm sure you will. However, I'm just wondering where you plan on staying for the night. The nearest motel is probably four miles from here. Do you have any money?"

"Don't put yourself out worrying about me lady, I can take care of myself," he snapped back.

The room grew uncomfortably quiet through a pregnant pause in the conversation. That was when the three turned at the sound of rustling in the doorway leading out into the hall. Standing there, Colleen stood, her arms wrapped around her nanny's leg. The eyes of both females were riveted on the male stranger in their midst.

"Ladies, let me introduce you to our visitor," said Margaret. "Moira, Colleen, this is Brendan Birch, who's come all the way from Albany, New York to be with us. He's here to see Brian." Her voice had taken on a formal quality. "Brendan, Moira is our nanny, here all the way from County Clare."

"Where's that?"

"Ireland. You've got to work on your geography. And the little one with the slightly dirty face is Colleen Kelly, Brian's daughter, my second, and if what you claim is true, your little sister—half sister." The teenager's eyes widened. The toddler made her way into the room and up to her mother, her eyes never leaving the unfamiliar male.

"And you two are sisters?" he asked, gesturing between Margaret and Jenny. His question brought forth a welcome spurt of laughter.

"No, that was just a small joke on my part," confessed Margaret. "Jenny is my older daughter—just a tad older than my seventeen month old."

Brendan settled back into his chair, attempting to digest the revelations unfolding before him. The living room soon began to echo with the sound of female voices. When Margaret sensed her guest's uneasiness, she came to his rescue.

"Brendan, perhaps I can interest you in something besides the woman's perspective? Brian's not going to be home for a few hours. Follow me." Gratefully, the young man jumped to his feet and followed his hostess out of the room and up the hall. Reaching the back of the house, she ushered him into the family's gym, a large room strewn with exercise equipment, small dumbbells and floor mats. "The real heavy stuff is in the cellar. When you get bored or tired of being alone, come back and join us."

It was just before of six o'clock when the telephone rang at the Kelly residence. Margaret and Jenny were throwing together a salad in the kitchen. Margaret snatched the receiver prior to the second ring.

"Kelly residence."

"Hey, Keogh, I'm back."

"And don't think for a moment your driving is over for the day. I want you in the truck and back here now."

"Yeah, I've heard from Millie kinda on what's going on. You're probably pretty pissed, huh?"

"Pissed is not the word for it. Wait a minute—I'm going upstairs where I can talk in privacy." The woman handed the phone to her daughter and made for the stairs and her home office on the second floor. It took less than thirty seconds for her to climb the stairs, enter her office, close the door, and resume the conversation. "How the fuck was it you never told me about any of this?" Her question was met with silence. "Hello—hello, earth to my asshole husband."

"I wrestled with it. I'd given my word to Linda not to mention it to a soul. Keogh, believe me. I wasn't even sure it would ever reach the light of day. I knew it would bother you—and how it might never reach the light of day. I didn't think it would serve any purpose telling you about it if it was to remain a secret forever."

"Now, let me get this straight—you were only thinking of me—is that it Brian? Cut the shit."

"I'll be on the road in five minutes. I've already spoken to Linda—"

"Whoa, there's that name again! You've already been on the phone with the mother of your first child. God—I'm getting this warm, fuzzy feeling all over," she said sarcastically. "It doesn't sound like you had to look very hard for that number."

"Keogh, relax. I just wanted to find out what was going on. When I get home we'll have to have a talk."

"What the fuck does that mean?" roared the woman.

"Relax, will you. I just means we have to decide what to do with the kid— under the circumstances. He and his family have problems."

"He's really pissed at you, Brian. I hope you know that."

"It sounds like he'll just have to stand in line," he answered, forcing a uncomfortable laugh from his wife.

Brendan was sitting alone in front of the television when the Ford came up the driveway. He hit the remote, turning the rerun of *Cheers* to a blank screen. He rose to his feet. From outside came the sound of a vehicle door slamming. Margaret, dressed in sweats and perspiring from an exercise session up the hall, appeared in the doorway to the room. The front door opened, followed by footsteps down the hall. She signaled her husband through a gesture and retreated back to the kitchen. Without hesitation, Brian entered the living room, setting his eyes on his son for the first time in over four years.

"You've grown a few inches," he remarked. The teenager glared at him, making no attempt to hide his utter contempt.

"Is that all you have to say to someone whose life you've turned into a joke?"

"Your life's not a joke."

"No, then what is it? All I know is a week ago I was one person and now I'm someone else. It sounds like a fucking joke to me."

"Okay, for starters, I don't want any of this language in the house. We'll talk this all out. Let's go outside—for a walk. You can vent and tell me where to go— but let's do it outside." He gestured to the young man. Brendan responded, walking past him and toward the front door. Brian hesitated for a moment, exchanged glances with his wife who was now stationed in the kitchen doorway, and walked to the front of the house.

"Back in a while," he announced, his voice lacking its usual cheerfulness.

Brian was surprised when his son chose to remain silent while they walked down the driveway. Passing through the front gate, they turned and started down the country road.

"I spoke to your mom before I drove back home. She's worried to death about you, Brendan. All we talked about was you and what would be best for you right now.'

"Spare me this 'dear old dad' horseshit, will you? It's a little late for that shit right now. Where the fuck were you when I needed you?"

"I was doing what your mother asked me to do—knowing there was a good reason for it. Damn it, for the first eleven years of your life I didn't know you even existed."

"Oh, so now it's her fault?"

"I didn't say that. She was in a tough situation. I don't think old Bubba would have taken kindly to the news that you weren't his."

"Watch your fucking mouth. Bubba Birch is my father—Bubba and Jack—more father than the likes of you will ever be."

"Fine—fine—whatever you say—but as I was saying before, your mother and I had a talk about things—about how bad things are at home with Jack being so sick and her having to care for him."

"What's it to you?"

"She asked me if I could help you both out," said Brian in a quiet voice.

"If you think for one minute I came here for your help—forget it! I came here to tell you that you're an asshole—that your little secret ain't a secret no more—and for you to permanently stay out of my life."

"She wants me to watch out for you for a short while," stated Brian calmly.

"Man, you don't get it, do you? I've been watching out for myself for a good, long time now. I know mom's got her hands full with Jack."

"Your mom's a good woman—a damn good woman. You have a chance to take a little of the pressure off of her. She's worried about you—but she wouldn't be half as worried if you were over here with us or with me back at Wells. Besides, it's not like it's that bad a place to hang out for a few weeks or months. Bedford's a nice town—and that's more than a nice house back there. If you decide to join me over at Wells Beach, well, there's nothing too shabby about that either—and it'll be doing a lot to ease your mother's mind. Plus—you've got a little sister that you probably had no idea you had just a few hours ago. For God's sake, Brendan, get to know her a little bit." Brian brought his argument to a conclusion, knowing he had just given his proposal its best shot. Glancing down at his teenage son, he could see his words were being considered.

Brian ushered the young man into the house, directing him back to the living room where they found Moira curled up at the end of the couch. The television was on, turned to a British comedy that, by all appearances, was amusing the girl.

"I wouldn't mess with the channel. Moira can get downright ornery," quipped Brian. "I'll be down in a couple of minutes. I've got to run things by the fishwife. Feel free to invade the fridge if you want."

Leaving his son in the living room, he scaled the stairs, making his way in the direction of Margaret's home office. Not surprisingly, he found her pounding away at the computer keyboard.

"So what's up? What does he want?"

"He doesn't want anything to hear him talk. It's more a matter of what he needs. I had a chance to talk to his mom—"

"Oh, don't tell me—that would be the wonderful Linda," exclaimed Margaret with no lack of sarcasm.

"As I was saying, I spoke with her and she told me she's really worried about him. She's got her hands full with Jack—he's fighting it out with cancer and Brendan's been on a rampage. He's quit school and is running around with a bad crowd back in New York—including his brother, Trevor. She said she was at the point of giving up hope—then Brendan stumbled on this information about me because of something he saw in some blood work—and him knowing his mom's and Bubba's type."

"Sounds like a fairly bright kid."

"Well, Maggie May, look at his biological father."

"I'll pass on that straight line."

"Anyway, cutting to the chase, Linda asked me if I couldn't put him up for a while, maybe a couple of months, and see if I couldn't get him straightened out a bit. He wouldn't have to stay here. He could stay with me at the cottage as soon as Perez moves out."

"Perez is staying at *our* cottage?"

"Just for a few days. He's got a business opportunity he's trying out."

"Wow, aren't you just full of surprises today—a son out of thin air and now Perez using our cottage. I guess I really don't rate being kept in the know. Is there anything else I should know while everything is coming out. Perhaps a mistress? Oh, I'm sorry, Brian, you already have Linda over in Albany."

"Cut the sarcasm Keogh, she's nothing like that."

"Now tell me, she's got to be older than you. What's the age difference?"

"Ten years—maybe a little more."

"And if my calculations are correct, you had to be all of nineteen on the night Brendan was conceived."

"Yeah, I think I was."

"And I'm guessing that you're erring on the side of caution with that ten year thing. That puts this woman in her thirties at the time of your magical night of bliss. Oh, how dare I call this wonderful, upstanding woman your mistress? Does Mother Teresa know there's competition in the race for sainthood?"

"Can we get back to the problem at hand?" She tossed him an icy stare, folded her arms, and leaned back in her chair. "I don't expect you to put yourself out for him. Maybe just a couple of days here and then it's over to Wells with him." His suggestion hung in the air for a protracted moment, his wife's blue eyes locked onto his.

"I've been thinking about this whole situation for the last few hours. I was pretty sure you'd come up with a plan that involved having your little love child stay with you—or us."

"Watch the sarcasm, Maggie May—considering your glass house," warned Brian, no doubt a reference to her own teenage pregnancy.

"I'll be totally honest—I feel a lot safer on the nights that you're staying over than the ones you're not. Today, when Jenny called and said there was a strange male knocking at the door and hanging around our yard—it shook me up. I'd feel better if there was always a male in the house. Now, if he'd be willing to take on some chores—the pool for instance—and the yard, he'd save us some money and put himself to good use. He could get a part-time job, too—maybe. If he wanted to stay around a little longer, I might be able to get him back into school—to, at least, let him finish high school. I mean—he's a blood relative to you and Colleen—and he doesn't strike me as being dangerous. Besides, he seems to show *us* more warmth than he does *you*."

"You'd be willing to do all that?" asked an astonished Brian.

"God damn it, Kelly, I'm not some complete, unfeeling bitch!" He reached forward, putting his hand to her forehead as if to check her temperature.

"And I'm not running a temperature and delusional!" She grabbed at his fingers, hoping to twist them in some painful direction.

"Admit it, Keogh, you're doing this because of me. Confess—you're so hopelessly and madly in love with me that no sacrifice is too much."

"Oh, God, I'm going to puke," she announced in response to his exaggeration.

"We can put Brendan in the guest bedroom."

"You know—it wasn't all that long ago, say the summer of 1991, that I had this whole house to myself. Brad was off living with his little whore and Jenny was up in Wells for the summer in that birdhouse you called a cabin. That left me with the house to myself and the peace and quiet that went with it."

"That was unhealthy if you ask me."

"It's turning into a commune here for God's sake."

"People—people who need people," crooned Brian, bursting into song.

"Oh, God, I'm going to be ill," responded Margaret.

"Are the luckiest people in the—

"I hate it when Streisand sings it—and I hate it even more when you do," she cried out, placing her hand over his mouth. He took the opportunity to slip one, then two of her fingers into his mouth for a moment.

"Thanks, Maggie May. It means a lot."

"You can start paying me back with an hour of massage tonight."

"You're not going to bite me, are you?"

"You wish. No, I've got to be in the mood."

XII

The clock on the office wall of the Atlantic Coast Lodge was sweeping its way toward noontime when Brian took a break from putting a fresh coat of paint on the Adirondack chairs spread out on the back lawn. He entered the main house and went directly to the phone. He punched out seven digits and waited.

"Hey, Buddy, I hope you're ready to join me for lunch?" A mile away at his cottage, a gravelly voice responded.

"Hey, Man, any excuse to get me away from the tube. You can just watch the boob tube and walk the beach so many times before it starts to get to you," answered Perez, Brian's guest since he returned from Lowell with him five days earlier.

"I'm leaving in two minutes,—be waiting for me outside."

"What do you take me for—some old broad that's going to spend a half an hour in front of the mirror?"

After assuring Millie he would take no more than an hour and a half for lunch, he bounded off the porch and quick-stepped toward the pickup.

"You're leaving us girls," sang out a voice from inside one of the motel units. He turned to see Mary standing in the doorway.

"Yes—but not for long. It's sort of a business lunch."

"Why do men get to have all the fun?" pressed the pretty, young woman.

"You know, you're right. Next week my sweet, it's Millie for lunch on Thursday and the magnificent Mary on Friday," he called out.

"You're kidding, right?"

"Absolutely not—it gives me something to look forward to in my otherwise drab life." His wisecrack brought a chuckle from her.

"You do know you're the best boss in the world, right?"

"I've heard that rumor floating around from time to time," answered Brian modestly.

"Don't go and disappoint me," she warned.

"Are you kidding? It's a date—lunch with the Washington County heart-breaker one week from this moment," he added, glancing down at his watch as if to commit the appointment to memory. "But I've got to run right now. Be sure to join Millie for lunch, she's got some homemade pea soup in there that smells great." Brian shot the young woman a broad grin and jogged toward the Ford.

Less than two minutes later, the pickup was barreling down Mile Road toward the Atlantic Ocean and his cottage. Midway en route was Billy's Chowder House, the only structure interrupting the tidal marsh and Rachel Carson

Wildlife Sanctuary. This one building sat alone, defiantly in the midst of the environmental land preserve. With no other buildings within a quarter mile in any direction, the commercial landmark appeared as if it could have been deposited there during a singularly, high tide. Passing the restaurant, he glanced out the right hand side of the vehicle and thought he saw Perez standing by the cottage in the distance. A minute later the Ford cruised down the private road to the house.

"If nothing else, Bri, you're prompt," announced Perez while climbing into the passenger seat. Brian nodded his head in agreement. "It'll be nice having some company for lunch for a change."

The two old friends drove back to Billy's engaged in light conversation. Upon arrival, they were escorted to the west room and placed at a window table looking out over the estuary. The tide was advancing, pushing salt water under an adjacent bridge and flooding the marsh.

"Table for three, please—and could you bring us another chair?" requested Brian.

"Three? You're expecting someone?" asked his friend.

"Yeah, I want you to meet someone."

"Female?"

"I'm afraid not, Buddy."

The spacious room was steadily filling up with customers. Both men lifted their heads each time parties were shown into the room over the next few minutes and assigned a table. Brian used this time to update his friend on some of the specifics surrounding his son's arrival in Bedford. They put off ordering anything beyond a beverage for ten minutes before Bobby Copeland appeared at the far end of the dining room, spotted Brian, and made his way to the table. He extended him a hand, shot Perez a halfhearted acknowledgement, and collapsed into his chair.

"I believe introductions are in order. Perez, this is Bobby Copeland, my absolute best friend up here in Maine—and Bobby, this is Perez, who I've known and been best friends with since I was in grade school back in Lowell." The men exchanged hand shakes and compulsory nods of the head. That accomplished, both sets of eyes turned back to their mutual friend for direction. What followed was a strained period of silence while Brian stared at one man, then the other.

"And?" Bobby asked.

"You both have a problem," exclaimed Brian. The men's reaction was the same to their friend's declaration, casting curious looks at the other.

"So I drove all the way over here from Cape Porpoise just to hear you tell me I had a fucking problem?" Bobby asked. "Let me clue you in my friend, I have more problems than Carter has liver pills—so you could have saved me the drive and called that news flash in." The remark brought a crackle of laughter from Brian and even caused the usually stoic Perez to grin.

"No, let me be a little more specific. You guys have a problem—and in Bobby's case, a universe full of problems—but I believe you also have a solution to one of each other's problems." Brian stared at one, then the other, seeing he had piqued both men's interest. "Bobby, for over a year now you've been bugging me about joining you in your business as a full partner—and I've told you over and over that I wouldn't—that I'm happy with what I'm doing. Buddy, trust me when I say this, I am never going to join you in that property maintenance business."

"Brian, it's more than a property—"

"Never—ever—Bobby."

The waitress, a pretty, petite girl named Betsy Chase, arrived at the table seconds later and asked if they had made up their minds on what to order.

"Haddock sandwich and coffee," answered Bobby instantly. "Oh, and sweetheart, where have you been all my life?" he asked, adding a dash of drama to his question.

"Well, for the first half of it, I don't think I was born yet," shot back Betsy to the other men's amusement.

"Oh, guys, lunch is on me," announced Brian.

"Add a large seafood chowder to my order—and replace the coffee with a light beer—any kind you got—I'm not fussy," added Bobby, showing no ill effects from the young woman's put down.

"A small chowder, clam roll and coffee for me," said Perez, shooting Brian a look after Bobby's abrupt upgrade to his order. Brian closed his menu and handed it to the waitress.

"Haddock sandwich—large chowder and a glass of lemonade—and could I have some ice water along with the meal, too?" The young woman collected the menus and made off toward the kitchen. "As I was saying, Bobby's got his problems with needing a partner. Perez, you on the other hand have to be moving out of your former profession and into something else—and I think this might work. Now ordinarily two guys who don't know each other from Jack Shit should never go into business together. But seeing that I know both of you—know you're not afraid of a day's work—and know that I'd never speak to either of you if you screwed the other—seeing that I love both you guys—well, there's our built-in control."

Brian's proposal was initially met with silence, both men taking turns staring at each other and their mutual friend. In the end, it was Bobby who spoke up first.

"I'm into outdoor work, lawn maintenance, tree removal, anything to do with yard and property work. In the winter I throw plows on my vehicles and move snow. You think you'd want to do something like that? Have you ever worked outside and with your hands?"

"Back in Puerto Rico when I was a teenager I did. I came to the states to get away from that shit—but part of the problem with that was that I was doing it for somebody else. I'd need some coaching at first if I did decide to do something like this," explained Perez. Brian was gratified to see that his longtime friend was remaining open-minded and not immediately dismissing his idea."

"I've been trying to get this guy to come work with me for over a year now. I think he thinks he's above it," commented Bobby. "I'm turning away fucking work left and right. Brian knows I'm not just looking for some stiff to work into the ground. I'm looking for a partner. Someone who'll take on his share of work and some responsibility—and who'll spell me once in a while so I can take a lit-tle time off to be with the wife and kids. Man, I've invested the last nine years of my life in this company."

"Hey, Man, if I decided to come on board, I wouldn't expect ya to just bring me in like some fucking brother-in-law. I've got a little money left from my fucked-up early retirement. I'd buy my half of the business—and I'd work."

"If I may make a suggestion, guys—maybe let Perez work for a couple of weeks—minimum wage because he's learning the ropes and seeing how much he likes it—and you're both finding out if you can stand each other. We meet back here at Billy's in two weeks and decide what you're going to do. You could both hate each other by then and blow this whole idea up—or, who knows, we could have the birth of the Fortune 501," teased Brian just as the chowders and bever-ages arrived at the table.

"I'll keep paying my rent down in Lowell in case this shit falls through—but I'll get a room up here, too—for the next two weeks," added Perez.

"Come on, Buddy, you don't have to do that. You're welcome at the cottage as long as you want."

"No Bri, the little woman's probably getting fucking sick of me hanging around. From what you've told me, she wouldn't be too shy to tell me to go pound sand and get the fuck out. I think I'll kinda move on before I start driv-ing a wedge between you two."

"Don't take any offense here Bri, but Maggie May can be a real ball buster," added Bobby through a mouthful of chowder.

"No offense taken."

"Have you met his wife?" Bobby asked Perez.

"I've never had the pleasure."

"Hell of a looker—I mean—a real looker. You're a lucky man Bri—until she gets her fur up—and then—watch out. Last year at the cookout in Bedford—man, she got on my case—cause—cause"

"Cause you started with the cannonballs at the pool and a few of her clients didn't like getting wet."

"Shit—she started in on me and, I swear, I wanted to crawl in a hole and hide."

"Yeah, Bobby, and after everyone left it was my turn. Hot tongue and cold shoulder—that's what was on the menu for me that night—hot tongue and cold shoulder." Bobby shook his head and glanced over at Perez.

"Maggie May is one damn hell of a looker. Oh, and speaking of lookers—I stopped by the lodge a few days ago when you were gone. Millie told me you were up north in Canada. But while I was there I caught sight of this little blonde—I mean a hot little thing. This kid had the face of an angel. Does she work for you?"

"You must be talking about Mary. Yeah, she's on the payroll."

"What is she—like fifteen?"

"Try twenty-three. She's got a seven year old kid."

"You've got to be shittin' me! Married?"

"No—living with some low life, though—and what do you care? Last time I checked you were the father of four."

"Oh, sorry, my apologies for living," came back Bobby while his eyes followed Betsy serving the adjoining table.

"So, when do we get the great experiment going?" Perez asked.

"How about Monday at seven o'clock?" suggested Bobby.

"That works for me," answered Perez. Extending a hand to their new, potential partners, the two men, total strangers a mere fifteen minutes before, began their business journey into the great unknown with a single pump of a handshake.

A few hours after his luncheon with Perez and Bobby, Brian received a phone call from Jenny. She informed him that she had attended Mrs. Emerson's funeral earlier that day. In a calm, measured manner, she briefed him on the experience. He learned that, at the family's request, she joined them at the front of the funeral procession. She asked him not to share this information with her mother.

XIII

Millie fidgeted in her chair while staring across the table at her boss. Fifteen years had passed since she was hired as assistant manager of the complex. This was the first of two lunches Brian had scheduled for the week. The following day he would escort Mary to Billy's Chowder House, her restaurant of choice. Millie had chosen Congdon's for her noontime meal, a short walk across Route 1 from the Atlantic Coast Lodge.

"I was never keen on going out to restaurants. I don't like having people wait on me like I was all high and mighty," she explained once the waitress was out of earshot.

"If everyone felt like you, Gary wouldn't have a livelihood and the cook and waitresses might be unemployed," reasoned Brian. "Is that what you want Millie, people out of work and no bread on the table?"

"Now you know exactly what I mean. Of course I don't. Never mind this foolishness. And now that we have some time to talk, I was hoping you'd catch me up on how things are going back in New Hampshire—with Brendan and all. How's he fitting in with the family and his new life?"

"So far, so good—as far as I can tell. Maggie says he's been pretty quiet and has kept to himself for the most part. She says he's gone out of his way to play with Colleen, but that's to be expected—everyone else though, strictly at arm's length."

"Blood's thicker than water," she added.

"That's true, except when it comes to me. So far there's been no warming up to me. It'll come in time though, I'm sure."

"Give it time," she assured.

"Unfortunately, we're coming to the time of the year when I can least afford to go over there and spend some time with him." Millie nodded knowingly while sipping on her coffee. "By the way, is it me or do the grounds and the cottages look especially good this year? I know I've kept ahead of the spot painting and the other maintenance."

"It's not your imagination. Everything looks well cared for."

"The other day I was walking behind one of the cottages and I swear I thought there was no glass in the windows. They were that spotless."

"No doubt after Mary had been through the place. I've never seen a harder worker in all my time here. Brian, that girl does the work of two—and I'm not exaggerating."

"She was a find—and I have my assistant manager to thank for it." He lifted his coffee cup in salute.

"And speaking of our little prize, I just want to go on record and warn you to be very careful around that one."

"What do you mean?"

"What I mean is—she's developed quite a fondness for you."

"Oh, come on, Millie."

"I spend a lot more time with her than you do. I can see it in her face when your name comes up. You don't know what her life is like at home. That boyfriend of hers doesn't sound like much of a man to me. On a few occasions when she's talked about things at home I get the impression she's afraid of him—like maybe he can be abusive. I've been around the block a few times and I've seen examples of this at the church when we've had to help women out of bad situations. There are warning signs—and I'm keeping my eyes open. Anyway, this little girl comes to work everyday from what might not be the best of circumstances and there's this man who treats her with respect and kindness—"

"I'm not going out of my way to—"

"I know you're not. It's just your nature. I think she's seeing in you what she wants in a man. That—and she sees you're successful—"

"Successful? She should talk to my wife."

"I'm not going to say a word on the matter of your wife. You already know how I feel about that woman—and anything else I said would not suit me as a Christian." Brian hesitated a moment before speaking.

"It won't be long before we'll be sending in our tax return. We're always on extension. I dread that day because she always makes a point out of comparing our earnings. And, I mean, I don't even get the feeling she's kidding around when she rubs my face in it. Now, I happen to know I make more than most people here in Wells—but she starts in on me and suddenly I'm feeling as small as a penny waiting for change."

"Someday, when you retire me and put me out to pasture—that's when the gloves come off and I'll give your beautiful, spoiled wife a piece of my mind she'll take to her deathbed."

"Beautiful? I thought you said she had a horse face?" His question brought laughter from the woman.

"Pretty, she is—for a horse." she added, causing both to laugh aloud and turn heads in their direction.

Following an enjoyable lunch, Brian and Millie traversed a busy Route 1 on foot and reported back to the office. There, a somewhat unnerved Mary informed him his wife had called twenty minutes earlier, leaving instructions to return her call immediately upon his return.

"What now?" he responded, picking up the phone and punching out her number at the office. Gretchen put the call through without comment. "I got word you needed to speak to me," he said at the sound of his wife's voice.

"That I do. About a half hour ago I received a call from Ethel Jeffords, Randy's mom. It seems Randy came home last night very upset and with swelling under his eye. His parents couldn't get a word out of him until this morning, and that was after he refused to go to school. His mother was finally able to learn that he had been worked over the day before outside of the mall by Brendan.

According to Randy, Brendan approached him and a couple of girls from school outside the mall and began mouthing off, probably trying to impress the girls. When Randy asked him to stop Brendan turned on him, taunting him and challenging him to fight. When he refused, according to Randy, Brendan hit him anyway. Brian, I never raised a boy. I don't know how to deal with this. You know Randy Jeffords, he's always doing things with the scouts, collecting for paper drives and things like that. He's not the type to instigate something like this. I want you home tonight to deal with this. Ethel was gracious enough to call me. For God's sake, she could've called the police. And to be perfectly honest, I'm a little afraid of Brendan myself. We don't know him very well. We don't know what he's capable of—well, actually, we do now—we don't know what else he's capable of." Brian took a deep breath.

"Man, if I miss much more work on family matters, this place will be going down the tubes. All right, Keogh, I'll be home by about six thirty. I'll call Hal and ask him to cover for me. Try to make sure the tough guy doesn't wander off."

After briefing Hal on the status of available units and reviewing a short 'to do' list with the part-timer, Brian left the office and made his way across the yard toward the pickup.

"I suppose this means our lunch is off for tomorrow," called out a voice from the door to the laundry room. It was Mary Porterfield.

"Not on your life. The people at Billy's already know to keep that intimate table for two overlooking the bridge for me and my rookie employee of the year," said Brian. "I'll get things squared away and be back tomorrow—and that's a promise, princess." He tossed the woman an affectionate wave and jumped into the cabin of the Ford. Within seconds he was motoring south on Route 1 toward the New Hampshire border.

Margaret was standing inside the front door when Brian entered the house. Delayed by unusually congested traffic, his mood was uncharacteristically edgy. He gave his wife a peck on the cheek and awaited an update.

"Brendan doesn't know we've spoken or even that we know about the whole Randy Jeffords matter," she said.

"Where is he?"

"He's up in his room."

Without hesitation, he climbed the stairs and made his way directly to the back of the house and Brendan's bedroom. Reaching the closed door, he decided to forego the formality of a polite knock and pushed it in.

"Excuse me," called out the young man from the desk at the far end of the room. "Did you ever hear about knocking?"

"Why don't we go for a little walk," suggested Brian.

"I'll pass," responded his son.

"That wasn't an open request. I insist." The eighteen year old rolled his eyes but did rise to his feet. His father escorted the teenager downstairs and out the front door, not stopping to announce their departure to the rest of the house. "I thought we'd walk down the road a piece and maybe clear the air." There was no response from Brendan. "Margaret and I have been informed that you worked over Randy Jeffords at the mall yesterday."

"I don't know what you're talking about—and I don't even know anybody named Randy Jeffries."

"It's Jeffords—and don't be a smart ass. Anyway, I've had to drive all the way back here from Wells to inform you that you'll be calling him tonight—apologizing, and letting him know nothing like that will ever be happening again," he explained in a tone void of compromise.

"In your dreams," mumbled the teenager before turning away.

"What did you say?" Brian asked, placing his hand on the young man's shoulder and turning him back to re-establish eye contact.

"Man, spare me your concerned-father bullshit."

"Brendan, the Jeffords could have called the cops on this. That kid is no where near your size—and now he's afraid—or maybe even humiliated—about going back to school." The eighteen year old looked at his father and only half suppressed a chuckle. "Oh, you think you're quite the tough guy, don't you? What a brave man he is—belting around a kid half his size and too afraid to fight back. Was it to impress the girls he was with? Well, if it was—and they were impressed—they're not worth too much themselves."

"Man, get lost," snarled Brendan before turning and walking back in the direction of the house.

"Where do you think you're going?" his father called out, running up behind the teenager. An instant later he spun the eighteen year old around. "I want to see this tough guy everyone saw at the mall yesterday. Show me how tough you are. I'm not half your size. In fact, I'm a little bigger than you. Now you can really show me something." Brian planted himself directly in his son's path. "Show me something," he ordered.

"Screw you," shot back the boy before turning to walk away. His father's response was to cuff him on the side of his face, his hand making a loud, smacking sound. The action caused the boy to freeze in his tracks, anger quickly building in his eyes.

"Go ahead, Brendan, hit me back—because I'm not feeling very tough picking on someone smaller than me." The young man stood still, merely glaring back at his tormentor. A second passed and Brian struck again, slapping the boy on the other cheek with a lightning quick strike. Brendan lashed out instantly but his blow was blocked by his father. Off balance, the eighteen year old was easily wrestled to the ground, rendering him vulnerable. Kneeling over his son, his arm preventing a counterattack from below, Brian attempted to further reason with the young man.

"Any coward can do what I just did here—or what you did yesterday. Now, I'm asking you to do something that takes some guts—call that kid and apologize. Let him know you won't be pulling any of that shit again. You're not doing it just for him—you're doing it for yourself. My wife—she doesn't invite just anybody into our house. She sees something in you Brendan. And in case you haven't noticed, this is a pretty nice place to be living. Bedford is a hell of a nice town and that's a hell of a nice house back there. You've got a baby sister who, by all reports, is nuts about you. Count your blessings and don't fuck this up." He relaxed his grip on the boy and gradually helped him to his feet. Brendan remained silent while his father brushed the last, few blades of grass from his arm. That left the two men facing each other, eye to eye. Brian broke the awkward pause, wrapping his arms around the teenager. "I love you, Brendan." His son did not return the embrace or the sentiment. Brian turned the two and started them back toward the house.

A car sped up Joppa Hill Road and passed by them. Brian, his arm hung over his son's shoulder, spoke following an extended silence.

"Now, I want you to know that you can go back to the house with your head held high. What just happened here goes to the grave with us. There isn't even any redness on your face so no one has to know what went on. Get it? Just so you realize that that's a luxury Randy Jeffords didn't have. You come out of this with your pride intact. Understand?"

"I understand."

"And you'll call the Jeffords boy—tonight?"

"Yeah, I'll call—but mostly cause I like it here."

"That's all I ask, Brendan. You don't have to like me—just mind me when you're under the Kelly's roof."

Arriving back at the house, Brendan went in search of Margaret. Together, Brian would learn in a pillow conversation with his wife that the two called the Jeffords' household and mended fences with Brendan apologizing and personally promising Randy Jeffords that there would be no repeat of his terrible behavior.

XIV

Brian checked his watch while speeding through the intersection of Route 1 and Mile Road. It was nearly twelve thirty. A hundred yards further up the road he directed the pickup between the expanse of stockade fences and into the complex. Forced to spend additional time at home ironing out the detail of his son's stay, he was running late for a luncheon appointment. The Ford's suspension groaned as he took the cement speed bump too quickly, then rolled the vehicle into a parking space by the motel. Vaulting from the cabin of the pickup, he sprinted to the main building and into the office.

"You two haven't started lunch yet, have you?" Brian called out to an empty lobby.

"Well, look who finally decided to make an appearance," shouted Millie, her voice echoing down from the top of the stairs. "It was nice of you to call in and let us know what your plans were. That poor girl's been on pins and needles all morning. I told her you were probably detained over in New Hampshire—and that you'd make lunch up another time."

"She didn't eat, did she?"

"No, probably cause she's sick from disappointment."

"Where is she now?"

"Down below—somewhere in the new section."

"Hey, Mill, you aren't up there goofing off are you? Maybe propped up in an easy chair filing your nails?"

"Of course I am. You know me. Oh, and don't lock the door on the way out—my pedicurist arrives at one," she hollered back. He shook his head in amusement and headed in the direction of the newer cottages at the eastern end of the compound. Descending the gentle, grassy slope, his eyes picked up on Mary's favorite, red vacuum cleaner parked out on the deck of the second to last cottage.

Making his way to the lowest point on the nearly five acre complex, he slipped up onto the stained, gray deck and peeked inside the building. The young woman was not in view but, following a moment's hesitation, he picked up on the rustling of linen from an interior bedroom. Quietly, he stepped inside and toward the sound. Reaching an open doorway, he snuck his head around the corner and eyed Mary, kneeling at the foot of the bed, painstakingly folding a top sheet.

"Am I being stood up for lunch?" he asked, startling the girl. Her head turned, a strand of blond hair cascading down over one eye.

"You did make it back," she called out, bouncing to her feet in a single motion.

"The princess doubted me?"

"After you got that call yesterday and had to rush home, I told myself not to get my hopes up," she confessed, her face beaming up into his. "It's the story of my life. I've stopped looking forward to things because something always happens to ruin it."

"Well, not this time sister. It's off to Billy's where you'll be inundated with one boring story after another from me. Be careful what you wish for young lady—you might just get it." Mary broke out in a giddy laugh before stopping abruptly.

"No, no, no—you're all dressed up in a shirt and tie—and look at me. I didn't even bring a nice thing to slip into because I knew it would only jinx me and you wouldn't come back. I'm going to look stupid next to you, Brian—like a poor, little chambermaid—which I am."

"My wife dressed me today. Come on now, Mary, there's no way you could look bad—even in rags." She stared up at him, an expression of apprehension blanketing her face. She followed this by closing her eyes, almost appearing to be holding back tears.

"Okay, would you feel better if I dressed like a bum? What about if I looked like some indigent who doesn't know where his next meal is coming from?"

"What do you mean?"

"You know that pair of pants and shirt I wear when I'm painting—the ones with the ten shades of paint all over them? The ones Millie likes to make fun of when I put them on."

"Yeah."

"I keep them in the utility shed. I'll go up and put them on—and then we'll go to Billy's. In your tee shirt and jeans you'll look like someone who just bought me at a flea market." The young mother burst out in laughter, her face lighting up behind a row of white teeth.

"You'd do that for me?"

"Absolutely," he answered definitively.

"You wouldn't mind?"

"I've worn worse."

The drive to Billy's Chowder House took less than a couple of minutes. Brian, decked out in his paint-splattered shirt and jeans, escorted his young employee into the restaurant with a flourish of old world manners.

"See us to your best table, my good woman—and don't let my shabby appearance deceive you. I've been hard at work painting masterpieces—and when my next canvasses are completed, Jackson Pollock will be reduced to a mere footnote in art history," bragged Brian. The woman extended a courteous nod.

"This way, Mr. Kelly," directed an attractive woman in her thirties. The two were led to the exact table where Brian, Bobby and Perez had been seated a week before.

"As you can see, I have my own table here, Mary," he announced.

"It would seem so," added the hostess, apparently remembering his visit from the previous week.

"I don't want you worrying about what you can or cannot order. If it costs too much, I'll just take it out of your profit sharing check in the fall." The diminutive young woman laughed but Brian was not sure she understood the meaning behind his humor.

"You know Mr. Kelly—you're a very smart man."

"And why do you say that?"

"Oh, I don't know—it's just the way you say things—like when you came in and you made the crack about painting artistic stuff. I know it had some real smart idea behind it, but I didn't have the slightest idea what you meant."

"It wasn't a big deal, kid. I just tossed out a name of a painter I'd heard of."

"No, you're smart—smart as a whip, as my mom would say." They were interrupted when the waitress approached the table. It was Betsy.

"Wow, it gets even better. Mary, I have my own table and, see here, I have Betsy, my own waitress."

"It's turning into a habit, isn't it?" she answered.

"We'll start with two glasses of white wine. Pick out something for us—a little bit on the sweet side," he suggested.

"I'll need to see some identification from you, miss," stated Betsy routinely. The request sent Mary scurrying inside her purse.

"And, of course Betsy, you'll be needing to take a long, hard look at my license and picture I.D."

"No, Brian—not unless you're looking to buy a handgun too." Mary passed the woman her license. They both looked on as the attractive waitress's eyes poured over the relevant information.

"You're a young looking twenty-three," she blurted out before returning the card.

"Oh, my God—it's like being back at Lowell High and dating one of the cheerleaders!" Brian announced with the exaggerated giddiness of a teenager. "I feel all the years washing away and here I am sitting with the prettiest girl in the freshman class," he teased.

"You better stop making fun of me here or—I swear—you'll have a food fight on your hands," she warned, dipping a spoon into her glass of water.

The conversation grew more meaningful over the course of the meal. Brian learned much more about the life of Mary Porterfield. A native of Beals Island off the coast of northern Maine, she became pregnant in her mid teens. Her baby's father was old enough to enlist in the Navy, and did, leaving her and her family to provide for, and bring up, her son. In 1993 she pulled up stakes and moved south with her son to York County on the word that jobs were more plentiful. Shortly after arriving, she became involved with a local cook by the name of Duane Cross. Cross had had the good fortune to inherit his father's house a few years earlier. In making the acquaintance of Mr. Cross, a man nearly ten years her senior, Mary had stumbled upon the remedy for her greatest problem, affordable housing. So, as she saw it, a pact was made with the devil.

"When someone ain't well educated—and I ain't—the combination of rent and child care is just too much. I won't stay home and sit around like some fat welfare mom but there ain't enough hours in the day to work to pay for both. That's where Duane came in—free rent and all I had to do is put up with his drinking and his temper tantrums," she lamented, pausing between spoonfuls of chowder.

"He doesn't hit you, I hope," asked Brian.

"No, it's mostly all screaming. He'll raise his hand once in a while but he's never hit me or Roddy. It can be scary, though, when he blows up." Brian extended Mary a concerned, sideways glance and continued with his meal. A few moments passed before he noticed the young woman was consuming her lunch at a quicker pace than him.

"Why are you in such a hurry to finish your meal? Is my company that painful?"

"Am I rushing down my food? People tell me I do that. I think it comes from growing up poor up on the island and thinking the food'll be all gone before I get mine," she explained.

"Princess, you don't even know the meaning of being poor," he suggested, pretending to be angry.

"I do so. I could tell you stories about not having enough to eat and some nights spreading ketchup on bread for sandwiches."

"Well, let me tell you—you rich little Washington County debutante. I can remember the time I had to nail my shoes together to go to school—cause the top part's stitching had totally unraveled from the sole—so when I walked it looked like my foot was opening it's mouth and yawning."

"How could you nail shoes together?"

"Very simple—my ma pounded the nail up through the sole and into the top part, you know, to keep the shoe mouth from opening. And when the nail stuck out through the top she told me not to, under any conditions, kick anyone in the bum, cause the nail would go right up their bum." The blonde exploded in laughter. "And as far as them sandwiches, my ma had us praying to the Blessed Mother at night for Her to grant a miracle and send us the money for ketchup and bread so we could have those wonderful ketchup sandwiches—and to be like the rich Porterfields up on Beals Island." Mary continued to laugh, extending her hand and placing it warmly on Brian's forearm.

Lunch was drawing to a close. Brian thought he noticed his employee growing increasingly relaxed as the meal progressed. For him, this lunch, something he looked forward to throughout the week, proved to be even more enjoyable than anticipated. After paying the tab and tossing out good-byes to a few of the staff, particularly Betsy, he escorted Mary to the pickup, stepping ahead to open the door for her when they reached the vehicle. His actions brought an expression to her face, a look of appreciation and something more.

"It's been a while," she said forlornly. He knew enough not to respond to her heartbreaking statement. Millie's caution from the previous day came to mind.

XV

The summer of 1995 was underway. It was late June and Brian had cause for optimism with projected revenue and earnings up as the country showed a complete recovery from the recession earlier in the decade. However, in spite of all the good news on the economic front, he faced a brewing crisis. A few weeks earlier, he was contacted by his two partners and informed they were interested in selling the business. With the stock market heating up and their equity in the corporation substantial, it was their intention to dump their interest in the small business and reinvest the proceeds in equities. They had presented Brian with a proposition, offering him first refusal on buying their two thirds interest in real estate and operations. In recognition for his years of service as operating manager, the property was offered to him at one and a half million dollars, a discount of two hundred thousand dollars from the asking price on the open market.

Millie looked up from the front desk as Brian cleared the door and walked toward the kitchen. His body language spoke volumes. She heard him grab something from the fridge and fall onto a chair. She walked across the room and stuck her head through the doorway.

"No luck?" she asked.

"That's the third bank I've sat down with and still nothing. Too risky with just you applying for the mortgage, that's all they've come back with." The woman let out a sigh of frustration. From behind, Mary entered the kitchen from the back door and walked up to the man. Without hesitation, she brought her hands down on his shoulders and gently massaged his back.

"As much as I've tried to avoid it, I'm going to have to ask Maggie to sign off on this thing. The banks have been totally straight with me in saying that this thing will literally fly through with her signature on the note. I'm going to have to bite the bullet and ask her to come in with me. Millie, as much as you may hate this, she's going to have to be brought in as an equal owner. I can't even imagine her just signing off on this without something in return—but, who knows, maybe she'll surprise us."

"You know, the thing about this that makes it stink to high heaven is that I know you'd sign off for her in a moment if it was her in this position—and never ask for a nickel in return."

"Yeah, you're probably right."

"Not probably—you would, Brian."

"Mill, this doesn't mean you'll be giving your notice I hope?" Mary asked.

"Well, it doesn't suit me at all, if that's what you mean. And I know I've said

I'd pack up and quit if that woman ever had anything to do with this place—but as long as she's back in New Hampshire where she belongs—and not in our hair—I'm sure I can live with it."

"Mary, as much as I could sit here all afternoon with your fingers kneading into my shoulders, I'm afraid I have to get on the horn and call Maggie May. I'll see if she will see me this afternoon and begin running this by her."

"Please tell me you're not going to call and ask for an appointment," barked Millie.

"No, I'm just calling to make sure she has some free time. I'd rather do this in the privacy of her office than at home where the kids might overhear something, you know, like if I have to sweet talk my way through this."

"More like if she decides she wants to see her husband do a little groveling, isn't it, Brian?"

"It won't come to that, Mill, I know it won't."

"God, I dislike that woman," cried out Millie as she turned in the direction of the front desk.

"We're not all going to lose our jobs?" asked Mary, her voice sounding childlike in its uncertainty.

"Don't worry kid, nothing like that's going to happen," he reassured, his hand reaching back and clasping hers.

Brian caught a break when he came upon an open parking space on Stark Street, arriving in downtown Manchester just before four o'clock. His good fortune seemed to be holding up when he saw there was over an hour of time left on the meter. Crossing the street, he strode into the brick building housing his wife's accounting firm and approached Gretchen at the front desk. The attractive, middle-aged blonde flashed him a warm smile and instructed him to proceed straight to Margaret's office on the second floor. Entering the room, he approached his wife, planted a platonic kiss on her cheek, and took a chair.

"I have to admit, Kelly, I'm intrigued. My husband visiting me at the office in the middle of the week—and carrying a satchel full of documents—what could this mean?" Brian sensed she was treating his visit as a joke but withheld a reaction.

"First, can I close the door—for the sake of a little privacy?"

"If you mean *may* you close the door—well, the answer is yes." He bit his tongue and closed the door. He hated it when she corrected his grammar but stopped short of a comment at this time.

"There's been a lot going on in Maine over the past few weeks that I've sheltered you from—for obvious reasons. My two partners have given me first refusal on buying them out. They want out of the business sometime in the foreseeable future with the hope of reinvesting somewhere else. I've been visiting banks over in Maine and, so far, I haven't been able to get financing completely on my own."

"Were you surprised by that, Brian?"

"No, I know it's a common practice to have both spouses sign off on debt instruments of this nature."

"Debt instruments—aren't we polished," she said sarcastically.

"Maggie, cutting to the chase here, the banks have been quite frank in telling me that my purchase of the business will fly through with your signature. I've brought along—"

"And why do you think they've said that?"

"No doubt because of how much you earn."

"Thank you, Brian."

"As I was saying, I've brought along a recent appraisal they had on the business and some year-to-date numbers. The taxes you do here—so you know we make money. I also have the terms and rates the banks have offered for the refinancing. As you can see, my partners have discounted the purchase price by a couple of hundred thousand in the event I can buy them out."

"Now let me get this straight—you don't expect me to just sign the dotted line on this note or notes, do you?"

"No. The way I see it, we'd become equal partners, sharing the outstanding stock fifty–fifty."

"Fifty percent share to me—fifty percent, even though they won't even finance you so much as a toilet bowl seat without me."

"Jesus, Keogh—will you stop busting my balls here and act a little more like my wife! This is a good deal. I don't deserve having you work me over here like some poor bastard off the street! This whole thing will not take a dime out of your pocket but will increase your net equity by a hundred grand, given you share in the two hundred thousand dollar allowance they're giving me on the purchase price. My equity in the current business satisfies the bank insofar as a down payment. I just need your signature."

"No, Brian, you just need my signature—and for me to share in the risk with you."

"I've run the numbers. The risk is not that great!"

"The banks don't seem to agree."

"Keogh, this is my livelihood," acknowledged Brian, his voice showing the first sign of duress. "The numbers work, Maggie May."

"I'll be the judge of that. Is there anything else?"

"No, that's it."

"And I won't keep you hanging. I'll put everything else aside and review your numbers. I'll give you an answer tonight when I get home."

"This means a lot to me, baby girl."

"It's business, Brian. I'll run the numbers and give you my answer tonight." She rose from her chair and escorted him to the door, signifying their meeting was over.

Brian was running a repetition of curls with fifteen pound weights when he heard the sound of Margaret's BMW from out front of the house. Out back, Jenny, Brendan, Colleen and Moira were still poolside where they had shared dinner an hour earlier. It was nearly seven o'clock. It took only seconds for Margaret to clear the front door, kick off her shoes and slip into the living room. Brian sauntered down the hall and joined his wife on the couch where she already had her feet propped up on the coffee table.

"Where's everybody?" she asked.

"They're all out at the pool. They've already eaten. I waited for you." He noticed at once she was holding his papers.

"Brian, let me get right to the point here—and before we have an audience. I have no interest in owning, running, or otherwise having any attachment to your motel."

"We're more than a motel, Keogh."

"Having said that, and knowing that this thing has been part of your life for over twenty years, I will co-sign with you—"

"Maggie May, you won't be sorry—"

"I will co-sign with you on the mortgage—in exchange for fifty one percent of the voting stock." His mouth dropped open. He followed this by shaking his head in disbelief.

"No, Keogh, fifty percent."

"Fifty one percent, take it or leave it," she reaffirmed, staring into his eyes behind an emotionless expression.

"Fifty percent—even partners."

She handed him his papers. "Those are my terms. Take them or leave them."

"Stick it up your ass!" he lashed out.

"Fine. I'm going for a swim," she announced, hopping to her feet and making her way toward the hall.

"God, you can be a miserable witch! What's wrong with you? We're married. We have a daughter outside. We've made vows to each other—in front of God. This mortgage is just fucking business, Keogh. This is shit compared to everything else we have together." She stopped in the doorway and turned back toward her husband.

"Fifty-five percent. And the more sentimental horseshit I hear—the higher it goes."

Husband and wife joined the family in the backyard a few minutes later. Brian, unnerved by the exchange in the living room, was quiet, content to bounce his daughter on his knee and make small talk with her. Margaret, on the other hand, joked openly with most everyone, her spouse being the lone exception. Later, they shared a bed but nothing more.

There was a noticeable chill in the air at breakfast the next morning. Jenny provided practically all of the limited banter with Brendan tossing in a comment or two, mostly of the needling variety and exclusively aimed at Jenny. Rising from the kitchen table, Brian made haste to visit Colleen in front of the television where he showered her with a barrage of kisses. Returning to the kitchen, he found only his wife still sitting at the table. She made no attempt to acknowledge his return. He leaned down and placed an innocent peck on her cheek.

"See you Sunday night. Love you," he said softly.

"Drive carefully. Love you, too," she answered, in a tone more empty than cold.

By late morning, Brian had fielded questions from both Millie and Mary on the success of his visit to Manchester the previous day. He had deflected them as best he could in an attempt not to lie to either woman. However, his general mood gave away the relative failure from the day before. Finally, Millie approached him during the first lull of the morning.

"I'm guessing it didn't go well yesterday," she said, trying to pry some information from him. He looked up at her and shook his head. "Mary was practically in tears this morning after speaking to you. She knew things hadn't gone well, even if you didn't say so."

"Have you ever had to do something, knowing you were going to hate yourself after?"

"I'm sure I have."

"Well, that's what I'm about to do. I'm going to run down to Deptula and make a call. I don't want anyone walking in on me while I'm doing this. That should give you an idea about how much I hate what I'm about to do." Millie closed her eyes, shaking her head knowingly.

Brian wasted no time. Following a three minute drive, door to door, he sat in front of the phone and summoned his strength to make the call. Finally, he told himself the sooner he called, the sooner it would be behind him. He punched away at the keypad and waited for the ring.

"Margaret Kelly and Associates, LLC," answered the friendly voice.

"Gretchen, would you ring me up to my wife?" he asked.

"Right away, Mr. Kelly."

"Margaret Kelly," answered the no-nonsense voice.

"Hey, Maggie, just me—just checking in to tell you that—you can go ahead with that thing we discussed yesterday—on the stock distribution and all." She did not respond immediately. "Keogh, are you still there?"

"Oh, I'm still here Brian. I'm just trying to remember what percentage we wound up settling on. Do you remember?"

"Good old Maggie May. She doesn't believe in *hitting* a man when he's down—she *kicks* him." She reacted with one of her assortment of feminine giggles. Most times he found this habit endearing, but not on this occasion. "You put down whatever percentage you want. I'll sign it."

"You can be a total juvenile about this whole matter, Kelly, or you can look at it in a positive light. In the end, it all stays in the family."

"That's right, Maggie May, now all I have to do is outlive you." His statement brought more laughter from her end.

"I'll fax you over a draft of the shareholder agreement. I took the liberty of sending Bill Eggleston's office some of the information. This is real cookbook stuff and he's already had one of his flunkies shoot me off a copy."

"You were that sure of yourself?" he asked.

"That sure," she answered emphatically.

"One small favor, though—if you don't mind. I'm calling from the cottage. Could you wait fifteen or twenty minutes before you fax the agreement? I'd prefer it if Millie doesn't see the specifics of the draft. I'm sure you can understand my reasoning."

"Ah yes, the fragile, male ego."

"So you'll wait?"

"Maybe."

"Come on, Keogh, you won. Anything else is just kicking the corpse."

"I'll walk very—very—slowly—to—the—fax—machine."

"Keogh!" There was silence from the Manchester office, followed by a dial tone.

Brian took a deep breath, relieved the call was over. Then, after dousing his face with cold water, he quickly returned to the pickup and raced back toward Route 1. Rolling the Ford to a stop directly in front of the office, he jumped from the vehicle and rushed through the door.

"I'll be taking all faxes for the next couple of hours—some highly confidential material is due in," he called out.

"That woman has to be the boldest, brassiest thing on God's green earth," exclaimed Millie from the TV room. Brian's heart sank. Taking a few steps further into the building, he spotted her seated by the far window.

"I was hoping to get back here before that came." He watched as the woman's eyes scanned the page, then flipped to the next one. He walked over to his assistant manager and collapsed in the chair beside her. "Millie, I was out of options. It was cave in or let the place go. I took the lesser of two evils. I love it here—and I love the people around me—and trust me, I've been dragged over the coals—"

"She has the unmitigated nerve to put her name before yours—you, who's been here for over twenty years—"

"Millie—Millie, that's the least of what she's done to me! Who cares whose name is first?"

"But, Brian, there's a principle here."

"That's not important. It's the number of shares that's important." She looked up at him with a baffled expression before returning her eyes to the page. "Well, you didn't actually expect her to be gracious about this whole thing, did you?" He shook his head in disgust.

"I've seen a side of my wife in the last twenty-four hours that has made me sick inside. I really thought I knew her better." The woman laid the pages on his knee and rose to her feet.

"Equal partner indeed—she'll get a piece of my mind if she tries throwing her weight around here while I'm in the building."

"Millie, she's more than an equal partner—she's controlling partner."

"Fifty shares her, fifty shares you—that's equal in my book." Confused, Brian squinted his eyes, then flipped through the pages resting on his lap. On the first page it read: Margaret Kelly...50 shares, Brian C. Kelly...50 shares.

"Am I missing something here?" Millie asked before answering an incoming call.

It was just shy of eleven o'clock and Brian was preparing to turn off the office lights. The NO VACANCY sign by the road had been lit for over four hours and his duties had been limited to refilling the ice machine and answering renter's questions at the front desk. Taking a chance on someone being up, he punched out the digits to his home phone.

"Hello," answered the female voice.

"First ring, Maggie May, you must have still been up."

"I was reading in bed—if you must know."

"I'm calling to say thanks."

"It took a while. What, twelve hours?"

"I must say—I have never—ever been worked over like that before." She laughed. "But you really carried that whole thing a little far."

"Sometimes I get the impression you don't really know who I am and what I do. I tell you stories from the office and from my other business dealings but I'm never sure I'm connecting with you."

"You weren't too nice."

"Brian, I haven't accumulated everything I have—I'm sorry, we have, just by running numbers and preparing tax returns. I'm a savvy businesswoman and I enjoy what I do. I like to take toys from the other guy's pile and put them in my pile. That's what I do. I look for opportunities and I exploit them."

"But, Maggie May, you were screwing around with my livelihood."

"I was proving a point. I take from the other guy's pile—like I did with you, and put the nice toys in my pile. The difference here was—I gave you back your toys. I did it for the pure joy of watching you break—and teaching you a little something about whom I am and what I'm capable of doing. However, and thankfully for you, I'm in love with you and so your toys came back."

"I did crack, didn't I?"

"Like an egg."

"Is everybody okay at home?"

"They couldn't be better."

"How's Brendan doing with the pool?"

"Good—keeping it clean and the water clear."

"Do you miss me?"

"I miss you terribly."

"How does it feel knowing you're going into business with me?"

"Wow—half owner of a no tell, motel. Be still my heart."

"Good night, Maggie May."

"Oh, Kelly."

"Yes."

"This morning when you kissed me on the cheek in the kitchen, in spite of the fact I was jerking you here, there and everywhere—"

"Yeah."

"It reminded me why I love you so damn much."

"Good night, Maggie May, until Sunday."

"Good night, partner."

XVI

The peak season for beach communities in Maine had arrived. It was mid July and that meant heat, humidity, long lines and extended waits at restaurants and traffic lights. For Brian and the Atlantic Coast Lodge, this was when a season's success or failure was decided. The formula was simple: top, in-season rates along with zero vacancies equaled maximum profits. This was the time of positive cash flow, when dollars could be stashed away for the extended winter. A bad May or October was regrettable but a bad July was disastrous. In the heart of the summer it was not unusual for Brian to go three or four weeks in a row without setting foot in Bedford, prompting Margaret to pack up Colleen and spend weekends at the cottage, just for the opportunity to catch a fleeting glimpse or break bread with her husband. However, on a late Monday morning in mid July, Brian scheduled himself out of the daily operations in order to accompany his two closest friends to Manchester, New Hampshire where they would sit with his wife and begin the process of formalizing their partnership.

The three men were crammed into the front seat of his pickup when they turned onto Elm Street and made their way north in the general direction of the offices of Margaret Kelly and Associates, LLC. The decision to merge these two, free-spirited individuals had not come easily or quickly. The proposed two week trial period for the potential partnership had ballooned to two months with Perez showing reluctance to commit until just a few days before. With Bobby functioning as forward observer from his position between his friends, they were able to grab a two hour parking space about three blocks from the accounting office.

"We're early," announced Brian while parallel parking.

"Maybe we have time to grab a bite. I'm starved," said Bobby, already pushing on Perez to vacate the vehicle.

"Jerkoff, I told you Maggie May's buying us lunch after the meeting," stated Brian.

"Then maybe a cold soda or something?" whined Bobby.

"One of you guys feed the meter, seeing that it's my gas that brought us down."

"Nothing," offered Bobby, pulling his pockets inside out as evidence.

"Useless fuck, what else is new," added Perez as he fished change from his back pocket.

With the meter fed, the trio made their way from the side street to Elm where traffic sped by them in both directions and a brisk, humid wind blew into their faces from the south. Following Brian's lead, they walked toward Stark Street and their noontime meeting.

"We've got a half hour to kill, unless you'd rather go to the princess's office and have her glare at us—cause we're early," said Brian.

"I'll pass on the extra time with the accountants," Bobby answered.

"Same here," chimed in Perez. When they reached a corner where the traffic caused them to pause, Brian solicited some feedback from the two men.

"So, what's your first impression of the city?"

"Doing nothing for me so far," remarked Bobby.

"It doesn't have the kind of character Lowell has," added Perez.

"Well, Lowell has more going for it—like the national park—and the history and all the canals," explained Brian.

"What do they have here?"

"They've got a shitload of lawyers—and panhandlers coming out their collective asses," joked Brian.

"No canals?" Perez asked.

"They filled them all in—a long time ago."

"So they *had* a place to *drown* their lawyers—and they screwed up," piped in Bobby to the other's amusement. "No fucking shortage of garbage either," Bobby added in response to the litter at the edge of the sidewalk.

"Maggie told me once that Elm Street acts like a giant wind tunnel and sometimes the garbage will blow down from the north or up from the south—and it's like you're caught in the hose of a gigantic vacuum cleaner."

"And no one here in town has jumped on this potential tourist attraction?" Bobby asked whimsically.

"Man, people'd pay good money to see shit like that," added Perez, deciding he wanted in on the wisecracking. The trio caught a break in the flow of cars and jogged across the intersection. Reaching the far sidewalk, they were confronted by a man in baggy clothing leaning against a building.

"Got any money?" sang out a voice best described as listless.

"Sorry, all my money's in real estate," wisecracked Bobby while his cohorts merely shook their heads no. The three continued to walk into the gusting wind while Brian guided them closer to Margaret's office.

"Man, as I said before, I'd like to duck in somewhere and grab a Coke or something," repeated Bobby. The friends paused and scanned the storefronts for a variety store or diner. It was then that a young man with yellow, bleached hair approached. Bobby's attention was captured when he noted the individual had a large boa constrictor draped around his neck. Immediately forgetting his thirst, he approached the pasty, white male.

"Is that damn thing alive?"

"Yeah, sure it is, but it's sluggish right now cause it ate not that long ago," he responded. Immersed in their own conversation, a few seconds passed before Brian and Perez noticed their friend and the young man with the snake.

"Bobby, what are you doing bothering this gentleman? Can't you see the young man is busy—conferring with his attorney?" said Brian. His friend, busy rubbing his hand along the reptile's scaly surface, let out a hoot and returned to his buddies.

"Man, this damn wind is wicked," exclaimed Perez, placing his hand up to shield his eyes. The men reached another intersection and paused.

"Maggie's office is just a little way down that street over there," directed Brian, pointing west to Stark Street. It was at that moment when the three visitors spotted an oversized pizza box bouncing along the sidewalk in their direction, propelled by what had to be a twenty-five mile an hour wind. They all stood transfixed as the cardboard container rolled, flipped and careened toward them. Frozen in their tracks, as if hypnotized by the approaching litter, all three watched as the object flipped along on all four corners. Then, drawing near, it opened and attached itself to Bobby's pant leg like an eighteen inch folded, cardboard set of teeth.

"What the fuck?" Bobby cried out, causing his friends to explode into laughter. The pizza box stayed wedged against his leg by the wind until he reached down and pulled it away. In an instant, he noticed that the box had left its mark on his leg, a six inch, red line on his light brown slacks, no doubt the remnants of tomato sauce.

"Are you kidding me?" Bobby howled. This brought even more laughter from the others. "I gotta get some water to wash this out before it sets in."

"There's a place up the street there," said Brian, pointing up a side street to a sandwich shop called Albee's. "Go up there and get some water—and wash that red shit out before it dries."

"You're turning into a god damn embarrassment," called out Perez while his friend walked toward the shop.

The old friends decided to wait on the street corner until Bobby returned. Brian grew quiet as he looked up and down the busy street, his eyes darting from building to building.

"You know, Buddy, I can remember the first time I walked down this street—back when I was in high school. There were a lot of cool stores and stuff then—nothing like the shit today. Man, I remember even getting the living crap beaten out of me not that far from here. Oh, and remember that Christmas I came back to Lowell and you finally came over and visited and had Christmas dinner with us?"

"Yeah, and I got to actually meet your mom—and Jimmy and your aunt."

"I swear that was my best Christmas ever. It was the last one I had with my mom. Plus, I was back in Lowell and saw you and the guys from the neighborhood. You took me down to the Cathay Garden and I told you about this girl in school up in Manchester who treated me like a piece of garbage. Yeah, a girl named Maggie May. There were real stores all along this street then, and I bought almost everyone presents here—even Maggie May. Now look at this crap—empty stores and pizza joints coming out the ass. It's like the land where dreams go to die."

"Nothin stays the same, Bri—nothin," lamented Perez, his voice dropping off in such a way that Brian knew his words were taking in more than the immediate surroundings.

"Hey, McQuade's is still here," called out Brian, pointing up the street a short way. "It's nice to know that something's survived."

"I got a cup of water and some paper towels," announced Bobby as he approached them from the side street. "The people in that place were real nice but it was jammed and there was no way I was going to try to get cleaned up with an audience." Reaching his friends at the corner, he slumped down to the ground and began dabbing his stained pants with a moistened towel. This went on for the next thirty seconds.

"It looks like the shit is just spreading. It's gettin worse instead of better," observed Perez.

"It's like this tomato shit has already penetrated the fabric. Man, it is getting worse!" At this point the man was frantically rubbing the spot and using up the better part of his water supply. "Man, this sucks to high heaven," he finally exclaimed, the futility of his undertaking now evident.

"Got any money?" asked a familiar voice. Bobby glanced up into the face of the homeless man who had tried to pan handle change only minutes before.

"Are you kidding me? You're back? Don't I look the slightest bit familiar to you, you freaking moron! You asked me for money less than ten minutes ago," exploded Bobby.

"Yeah, Pal—all of his money's in real estate—remember?" heckled Brian.

"It's the change in wardrobe, Bobby. He doesn't recognize you. The pants make you a new man. You're a changed man," needled Perez.

"I look like a freaking idiot. I went out of my way to dress up for this—for your wife and all—and I'm going to look like a freaking idiot. Do you think she'll notice?"

"We'll make a game of it. Let's see if we can keep her distracted and not notice—because if she notices, she will, sure as shit, bust your balls," predicted Brian. The two friends agreed to come to Bobby's aid and try to mask the problem.

The three men arrived at Margaret's building early and were immediately directed upstairs to her office. Proceeding upstairs and led by Brian, they walked single file into her office and made themselves comfortable in three leather chairs spread out in front of her desk. Brian, after claiming the chair closest to the door, leaned over and gave his wife a peck on the cheek. Once all three gentlemen were settled in their chairs, Margaret rose and closed the door to her office. Walking back to behind her desk and without so much as a sideways glance toward Bobby, she spoke.

"Cut yourself shaving, Bobby?"

"I'm sorry. What did you say?"

"The blood stain on your pants—I was wondering if you cut yourself shaving. I know I have a terrible time some mornings—particularly on the calves."

"It's tomato sauce, thank you. I'd tell you how it got there but you wouldn't believe it anyway."

"Now you live in Ogunquit, don't you?"

"Yeah—with my wife and four kids. Get her off me, Brian." His call for help brought laughter from the other men as well as Margaret herself.

The conversation turned exclusively to business for the next hour as Margaret tossed questions at Perez and Bobby. On occasion, Brian provided additional information for his wife, knowing his friends did not understand a question or lacked the knowledge to answer it properly. The minute hand on the clock was straight up on one o'clock when the CPA flipped her legal size note pad closed and made an announcement.

"Gentlemen, it's time for lunch—and lunch is on me. Do you have any suggestions or requests?"

"Nothing too fancy if you don't mind—not with these pants," asked Bobby. Margaret considered the request and made her own suggestion.

"Classical Food and Grog—it's down in the mill yard. It's not upscale but I'm not going to be embarrassed showing my face there," she added.

"It's your town baby girl. We'll go on your cue. I take it the grog means the boys can have their beer," asked her husband.

"It was my first consideration," she answered, giving her husband a discreet pinch on the rear end as they filed from the office.

The party of four traveled the short distance in two vehicles with Margaret inviting Perez to share the front seat of her BMW. The restaurant and pub was located at the far end of a mill building and in the shadow of the Granite Street Bridge. A few yards away, the Merrimack River flowed leisurely by. A patio off the red brick building was open with about half of the dozen tables there occupied. The strong winds from just an hour before had diminished, prompting Margaret to request seating out of doors. Escorted to a table on the river side of the patio, Bobby took an opportune moment to whisper into his new partner's ear.

"Looks like a fucking yuppie hangout if you ask me."

"Elbows off the table and no swear words—you'll be fine," counseled Perez.

The four were seated, ordered beverages, and were reviewing their menus when Bobby spoke up.

"Now, Margaret, nothing's going to come crawling up from the river and take a bite out of one of us, right?" The woman looked up from her menu and calmly responded.

"And Bobby—you would find that *pleasing* or *displeasing?*"

"Displeasing me—pleasing anyone else." Brian glanced across the table at Perez and faintly shook his head. Margaret's attention was drawn away from her companions a moment later when a group of individuals were seated at an adjacent table.

"Don't look now, but we're being graced by one of the city's beautiful people." Close by, six young professional types sat down with a measure of self-generated fanfare. "That's Angela Masterson, our local news anchor, and her entourage."

"Which one is Angela?" whispered Brian into his wife's ear.

"She's the one with the auburn hair and the smirk permanently etched on her face." With all eyes shifted in the direction of the adjoining table, the drinks arrived and the waitress took orders for lunch.

"Someone's apparently trying to save money on glassware," observed Brian, holding up his wife's plastic wine glass.

"It's their policy out here on the patio—with the brick floor and all. They don't want any glasses falling and shattering all over the place," she explained.

The following few minutes had Margaret pepper Perez with questions about Brian in his youth. Perez obliged, providing the table with two or three stories of the young man's tribulations back in his Lowell neighborhood. Their meals had just arrived when a minor skirmish erupted at the next table.

"Take the wine back and bring me a fresh glass in just that—a glass. I'm paying too much for this chardonnay to be drinking it out of some plastic piece of junk," exploded Miss Masterson to a flustered waitress.

"I'm sorry miss but it's the restaurant's policy—"

"I don't care whose policy it is! No, never mind—just bring me the manager." The waitress retreated on the spot as other members of the television personality's party voiced encouragement. "Do you believe this shit? Welcome to Mayberry." The young woman's words brought a quiet roar from her table while others seated nearby looked on in silence.

"Does the floor show come free with the meal?" asked Bobby in a low voice. Seconds later a visibly unnerved, middle aged man, presumably the manager, approached Miss Masterson's table. She was on the offensive before he could utter the first word of an explanation.

"I want this plastic junk replaced with proper glassware—for everyone at the table. Perhaps I should remind you how much business the station brings down here every week—our people and many of the guests we have in. I'm sure there are a dozen other pubs that would be more than willing to take on our business—and who would have no problem serving us properly." Her voice, laced with authority, carried across the patio, designed as it was for public consumption. The manager's reply to her demands was made in a tone barely above a whisper. However, his body language spoke volumes. He turned to the distressed waitress and issued an order. It was clear to all looking on that an exception to the establishment's policy on glassware on the patio was about to be made. Margaret looked on as a variety of cheeky smiles broke out on the faces at the next table.

"Yes, Mr. Perez, as I was saying to you earlier, we here in Mayberry are quite blessed to have an influx of outsiders who are, by their own admission, so, so much better than we natives," said Margaret, projecting her voice above the murmur from the other tables. "Now they may not be very well educated, and God knows they lack all the social graces—and, you know, if the rumor mill is accurate, they're not terribly well paid at that toilet of a TV station, either—but they are our self-appointed beautiful people here in Mayberry. Rules just don't apply to them." Margaret shifted her eyes from Perez to the Masterson table. There, as expected, every set of eyes was riveted on her.

"Bitch," spat out Angela. The one word insult only fanned the flames of the woman's antagonism.

"What happens is our illustrious television station here in town goes out and recruits flunkies from liberal arts colleges in the northeast. Starry-eyed losers are brought in to hone their nonexistent skills with the idea of moving on to bigger and better things. The station makes out by never having anyone on board for more than a couple of years and, therefore, salaries stay continually at entry level."

"It's amazing how bitter the middle aged can become—no doubt stuck in some dead end job with no chance for advancement—the glass ceiling and right there on the ground floor," answered Ms. Masterson, spoken to her cohorts but in a voice purposely projected over the patio. Her caustic comeback elicited a faint smile from Margaret.

"You know, I've always understood that the camera adds ten pounds. But, seeing this inarticulate heifer at the next table in the flesh, it appears bright sun and fresh air must add thirty," sniped Margaret, upping the level of attack.

"Okay, Keogh, cool down," prompted Brian. The anchorwoman rose from the table and stormed off in the direction of the restaurant entrance.

"Nothing like a nice, quiet lunch after your business meeting," quipped Bobby, picking at his fries and basking in a few moments of peace.

"I'm sorry, gentlemen, but I have a low tolerance for people like Ms. Masterson. This is where I choose to work and live and I won't have an arrogant New Yorker—or whatever the hell she is—come in here and mouth off," she added. Brian reached over and squeezed her hand.

"Right now you actually have that look you have just before we have biting sex," he whispered to her.

"Hey, no secrets at the table," called out Bobby. Finally, a smile returned to the CPA's face. She followed this with a flaring of her nostrils, another gesture she usually reserved for times of intimate foreplay. It appeared a cooler head had prevailed. The four had just begun to partake of their lunches when Angela Masterson reappeared in the company of the manager. They proceeded onto the patio and over to the Kelly table.

"I wonder if I could impose on you to move to a table inside the restaurant?" asked the manager. The question was directed toward Brian.

"You will impose nothing of the sort," came back Margaret, not allowing her husband to respond. "Number one, we were seated before the idiots at the next table. And number two—and more importantly—don't think we don't know what this is all about. We are quite conscious that we have a Hispanic gentleman in our party and this does not sit well with these people—and perhaps your restaurant."

"See here," responded an already flustered manager. Brian jumped to his feet.

"All right, let's stop right here," he stated emphatically, stepping into the fray. "Why don't we just do this: I will see to it that no further comments are made from our table—directly or indirectly—and I ask that this young lady see that the same is done at her table. Agreed?" The manager looked to Miss Masterson and received a weak acceptance. The woman shot Margaret a venomous glance and reclaimed her chair. Brian extended his hand to the manager, reassuring him the confrontation was over. Returning to his chair, he leaned down to within earshot of his wife.

"Keep a lid on it, Keogh—and I mean it," he whispered, then pecked her amorously on the cheek. "Buddy—I apologize for the Hispanic crack from the beautiful Mrs. Kelly. She only knows one way to attack—to the throat." Perez raised his glass to his friend's wife.

"My kind of woman," he said, a glint of admiration sparkling in his eye.

Brian's role as peacekeeper proved a successful one. The meal ended and the parties separated with nothing more than icy glances exchanged by the female combatants. Margaret drove the gentleman back to the pickup, wished her two new clients a safe trip back to Maine, then extended her husband an arms length handshake. His response was to pull her against himself and kiss her intensely on the lips. She did not resist, going so far as to laugh softly and whisper into his ear.

"The baby and I will be up for the weekend."

With the pressure of their meeting with the certified public accountant behind them, Perez and Bobby's mood lightened. Brian aimed the pickup toward the turnpike and sped toward Lowell. En route they relived the stressful lunch. They joked about the catfight that nearly took place with Perez stating emphatically that he would have offered three to one odds on the Kelly woman. At the end of a thirty minute ride the Ford proceeded up Lakeview Avenue toward Perez's rented room.

"I'm telling you guys, this is not going to take more than a half hour, honest to God," he attested of his soon to be vacated living quarters.

"A celebratory pop is in order and it's on me. Let's have a beer at the tavern to salute the new partnership, then empty out the apartment and bring everything back to Maine," suggested Brian.

"Wouldn't it make more sense to empty out the room first—then go for a beer?" Bobby reasoned.

"Let me get this straight partner—you want me to leave all my worldly possessions in the back of a pickup truck unguarded while we're inside having a beer?"

"Yeah, we'll only be inside for a half hour or so," contended Bobby. Brian and Perez scoffed in unison. Reaching his arm around his old friend, Brian yanked him close to himself.

"Oh, he's so young and so, so innocent," he exclaimed, giving his voice a mocking, childlike quality.

"I don't care if half of it is pure shit—it'd be gone so fast your head would spin," declared Perez. "Jesus, Bri, what the fuck have I saddled myself to here?"

"You heard what Keogh told you—partnerships in business are like marriages, minus the foreplay and sex," stated Brian.

Arriving at the end of Lakeview Avenue, the men poured out of the Ford and into the Tavern at the Bridge. Inside they grabbed the nearest three stools and ordered a round of beer. The suds went down quickly, prompting Brian to offer covering the cost of a second. Waiting on the next round, he glanced over at the corner table where he had spotted his lifelong friend two months before. He considered how the course of Perez's life had changed just on the almost chance meeting that day and his own stubborn desire to bring this man back into his life. He sat quietly while Bobby and Perez jabbered a few feet away, privately considering how the very outcomes of human existence can teeter on the timing of an arrival or departure, of a smile or gesture not reciprocated, of a slight or injustice not overlooked. The net outcomes of human lives are the product of what appears, on the surface, to be an insignificant decision. The next round of lager arrived and was dispatched of with little delay. Passing on Bobby's suggestion for a game of pool, the three men headed out and onto the task at hand, moving Perez permanently to York County in Maine. Crossing the parking lot and reaching the pickup, Perez stopped and looked back wistfully at the red brick building paneled in green.

"We'll be back, my friend—to celebrate our future victories. We're not saying goodbye to Centerville," stated Brian, picking up on his friend's nostalgic mood.

"There's a lot of fucking memories here, Bri."

With the pickup parked in an alleyway off the rear entrance to Perez's apartment building, the room was emptied of the man's furnishings and possessions in well under an hour. The three men had piled back into the vehicle and were about to pull out onto the street when two teenagers appeared from nowhere and stopped at the entrance of the alley. The teenagers, appearing roughly fourteen or fifteen, seemed to intentionally loiter in front of the Ford, paying no mind to the trio inside the cabin of the truck.

"Hey guys, we're in a bit of a hurry," called out Brian through the side window. One youth, a red headed kid with a smirk etched across his face, flashed him his middle finger.

"Move your asses you little cock suckers!" screamed Bobby through the windshield. The second teen, Hispanic looking and slightly smaller than the other, stared boldly at Bobby before making an invitational gesture toward the crotch of his pants. Instantly, the passenger door flew open and Perez exploded from the truck. The youths turned and bolted across the street in the direction of an adjacent alley. Perez remained in pursuit. The two punks quickly disappeared from sight along with their pursuer.

"Holy shit, what do you think he'll do?" Bobby asked.

"Probably chase them until he runs out of breath."

"He wouldn't kick the shit out of them—would he?"

"He's old world. You never know." The men did not have long to ponder the end result of the chase. Perez trotted back across the road and jumped back into the truck no more than a minute later.

"Let's ride," he called out, slamming the passenger door shut and banging twice on the side of the truck. Brian wasted no time, moments later speeding the Ford up Lakeview Avenue toward the boulevard.

"Did you catch the little bastards?" asked Brian.

"The little red headed fucker went right over a fence—no chance to grab him. But the other little prick wasn't so lucky."

"What the hell did you do?" Bobby asked.

"I kicked him up the ass so hard he'll have Shinola on his breath for a week." Perez's words caused Brian to chuckle.

"I hope neither of them got the license plate number," said Bobby, sounding uneasy from the incident.

"I doubt it. That would have taken an ounce of brains," Brian reasoned. The Ford hit consecutive green lights by the bridge and was soon roaring beside the Merrimack River toward Methuen. The front seat had grown quiet, each man considering the events of the last five minutes. It was Perez who shattered the silence.

"You know, growing up as a kid back home, you would never see children or even teenagers talking or acting that way around an adult. Young people showed a measure of respect for their elders. When did common courtesy and respect get replaced with this shit?"

"All this permissive, Doctor Spock bullshit has to have something to do with it—and, of course, the garbage on TV," theorized Brian, his words causing the cabin of the truck to grow quiet.

When Bobby leaned forward and turned on the radio he drew a moan from the other two.

"I've got to be in the mood for country and western—and I'm not right now," chirped Brian.

"So when do you start looking for your own permanent place?" asked Bobby of Perez.

"Tomorrow morning, first thing," he answered.

"Right now there's nothing east of Route 1—not until the fall," said Bobby. "Man, I think back to my days as a bachelor and some of the shit houses I lived in. Brian, remember that mobile home I rented out on 9 B?"

"That wasn't that bad. It was okay when you kept the place clean."

"I was thinking more of the neighbors and the barking dogs and shit."

"Oh yeah, the neighbors. Who were those real cockroaches who moved in across the way after Linda Birch and her family moved out?"

"You must mean the Swinconecks."

"How could I forget?" Man, those animals would've needed a year of etiquette classes just to raise themselves to white trash status. God, they were brutal."

"What was so bad about them?" asked Perez, not privy to any of his friend's common experience. The question brought an amused expression to Brian's face.

"Bobby, tell him about their houseguest." He shook his head and laughed.

"Man, I've tried to forget this chapter in my life. Okay, for my partner I'll relive it one more time. Back in the mid-seventies I was living in a mobile home out on Route 9 B. There was another mobile home just like it about forty feet away sharing the same driveway. Anyway, after one family moved out, another moved in, the Swinconecks. They'd been living there less than a month—along with their fucking dogs that barked eighteen hours a day and shit on anything that didn't move—and a few things that did. Anyway, one morning I'd gotten up and made my coffee—all the while listening to three dogs barking at every passing car and chirping bird—and I look out my window and across at their house and I see something not human with its head sticking out of their window. I did a double take, then probably a triple take, because I quickly realized there was a fucking horse sticking its head out the window. My neighbors had a fucking horse living in the house with them!" The proclamation brought a roar from the three men.

"Oh, Man, can you imagine the fucking stench in that place?" exclaimed Perez.

"Oh, well—I'm sure the horse eventually got used to it," added Brian to another chorus of laughs. He reached around Bobby and took hold of Perez's arm. "You know buddy—Bobby and I could make a couple of calls—you know, in case the mobile home is vacant—to put in a good word for you."

$\mathcal{XVII}$

$\mathcal{B}$rian sat in his undersized office in the corner of the main house while the air conditioner whirred in the window a few feet away. It was the second half of July and it was hot. He reached out and grabbed an orange from the edge of the desk. It had been left there by Mary Porterfield, part of a daily ritual. For a fortnight now she had routinely left him a single piece of fruit every day. Over the summer, a true friendship had developed between the young, single mom and her employer. She continued to join Millie and Brian at noontime for lunch, a courtesy not extended to the other employees. On some occasions, largely on Millie's days off, they would share stories of their personal lives, going so far as to seek advice from the other on matters involving the opposite sex. The summer season was proceeding well with gross revenue up over nine percent to date. This was particularly important this year with his wife now insisting on operating numbers on a weekly basis. Following a glance up at a photograph of Margaret and Colleen, he grabbed the phone and called her at the office.

"Margaret Kelly," announced an icy voice.

"It's me, Keogh. I just had to hear your voice."

"I can't believe I'm saying this but I'm actually glad you called."

"Wow, there's something I don't hear everyday."

"Come on, Kelly, I'm not all that bad."

"Hey, it's you—and I've come to accept it. I know you have to keep it hidden that you love me beyond belief—that you couldn't imagine living without me—and that you literally worship the ground I walk on."

"Oh, God, he's started taking drugs and now he's hallucinating. Brian, be strong, just say no."

"So—you were saying—you're glad I called?"

"Yes. Is there any chance you could come home, even for one night?"

"How soon?"

"How about tonight?"

"Is it my body you need?"

"Oh, God—I can't believe I'm about to say this—no, it's not your body, it's your mind."

"My mind?"

"I've gone into a funk—you know—one of those depressions I go into every once in a while. But, this time it's worse. If anyone can bring me out, it's you."

"I'm in your blood, Maggie May."

"Worse yet, you may be in my head."

"How about this—you give *me* a long massage while I talk you out of your funk?"

118

"No, that won't work. I'd just get more depressed because I don't give massages as well as you. What would work is that you give me a massage while we
work this out. Brian, you give wonderful massages. It's one of the few things,
maybe the only thing, you're better at than me."

"When, if ever, will I get a massage?"

"Your fortieth birthday—and I promise! So, will you come home? Jelly Bean
would love it."

"Oh, so now it's Jelly Bean. When she wants something it's Jelly Bean. All
right, I'll come—only one night though. How's Brendan coming along?"

"Good, a little better every day. Did I tell you, I've got him into Southside for
September? He'll get his diploma here. And—he's landed a part-time job at the
movie theatre at the Bedford Mall. He and Jenny snipe at each other all the time
but it's a good natured feud—no hostility."

"Like us in high school?"

"No, I remember that as more of a worshiper and worshipee relationship."

"Keogh, I will get over you one of these days, you know."

"Don't count on it. What time shall I expect you?"

"Seven."

"Thank you, Brian."

The front door to the Kelly household swung open at a few minutes before
seven o'clock and Brian did not hold back on his entrance, calling out to the
upstairs rooms.

"Where is my Jelly Bean?" From upstairs came the sound of a young child's
wild activity, followed by the scampering of feet.

"Daddy," called out the toddler. Seconds passed before Colleen appeared at
the top of the stairs, her nanny in tow. With assistance from Moira, she maneuvered down the flight of stairs and sprinted toward her daddy, falling onto the
plush rug once in the process. Reaching her father, she was rewarded by being
lifted high over his head, finally brought to rest on his shoulder.

"I have missed my little darling so much," cooed Brian, his arm enveloping
her tiny body and securing it to him.

"Everyone is out at the pool," said Moira. "We've all eaten." He extended the
teenager an abbreviated hug, making his way toward the back yard.

"Moira, if you'd like a little time in the pool before it gets dark, then feel free
to join us. I'll put Jelly Bean to bed tonight. It's almost that time anyway." The
Irish teenager turned and briskly ascended the stairs, taking him up on his offer.
Clearing the back door and out into the yard, Brian spotted Brendan skimming
thistles from the surface of the swimming pool while Jenny poked at a laptop
computer balanced on her lap. Lastly, his eyes picked up on Margaret as she cut
through the water, apparently doing laps. Brendan was first to spot him on his
approach, extending his father a courteous, if not warm, welcome. The crack of
the latch on the pool gate brought Jenny's eyes up from her computer.

"She's been asking about you all week Brian," she commented behind a sweet
smile. "Sorry, Brian, but we've eaten," she added.

"Yes, I've been told." Approaching Jenny, the toddler perched on his shoulder, he stopped directly behind his step-daughter and reviewed the material on the monitor.

"A travel piece on Nova Scotia," she explained, looking back over her shoulder. He tried to read on but was interrupted by the sound of falling water as his wife made her exit from the pool. She ascended the cement stairs like a pagan goddess emerging from a mystical, clear water spring, the curves of her body silhouetted against the blue sky on the horizon. Reaching the lip of the pool, she stepped from the water, met by Brendan who offered her a dry towel. Margaret glanced in the direction of her husband and daughters, her head tilted sideways as she dried her hair.

"How long have you been standing there?"

"I just got here."

"We've all eaten," she stated emphatically.

"Damn it, do I look that stinking hungry? How many people are going to tell me that? It's okay—I'll make myself a sandwich. Or maybe I'll just take a bite out of someone's soft, little leg." He turned his head and playfully bit tenderly on his daughter's calf. Colleen burst out laughing. "Oh, Moira's on her way down to the pool."

"Who told her she could?" Margaret asked accusingly.

"I did. It's hot. I'll put Jelly Bean to bed tonight." His wife lifted her eyes to the sky in a gesture of disapproval.

"She's help, Brian, not a member of the family."

"Lighten up, Maggie May. The baby loves her and that's good enough for me." She breezed by her husband, continuing to dry her hair, and made her way toward the house. Brian followed close behind, continuing to transport his daughter atop his shoulder. Inside, the woman made her way to the kitchen where she prepared her husband a sandwich.

"I'll put the baby down for the night," he announced while making his way to the stairs. He passed Moira on the way up, wishing the redhead a good swim.

"I'll bring you up a tuna salad sandwich and some potato salad," his wife called out.

Brian found his wife spread out on the bed, lying naked on the bed sheets, when he opened their bedroom door. Twenty minutes had passed since escorting his daughter upstairs and eventually to bed.

"Has Colleen been keeping up with her evening prayers?" he asked.

"Oh, I'm sure our little, Irish saint has been seeing to that in your absence."

"Good—it's important."

"You know, in retrospect, I made way too many concessions to you on this whole Catholic thing before we got married." He laughed.

"Blinded she was by his magnificent body and all the pleasure she knew she would derive from it," he clowned in his best Irish brogue. Crossing the bedroom, Brian sat down at the writing table where his meal awaited him. Margaret propped herself up against the headboard while her husband took the first few bites of his sandwich.

"Don't you have even the slightest bit of modesty when you lie there naked?"

"You're my husband for God's sake!"

"I know, I know, but you don't show even the slightest bit of modesty—none! I just find it curious." She rolled her eyes impatiently. "So what is it you wanted me home for, Keogh?" Her head fell back against the headboard, producing a low thud.

"Do you ever get the feeling your life is passing by too fast and that you're getting old?"

"Yeah, I know that feeling."

"Well, I've been getting that feeling a lot lately—like I'm losing it—or have even lost it. I'm feeling old all of a sudden. Three years ago when I turned thirty-five, I thought I could hear middle age scratching at the door. Now, it's like it's hitting the door with a fucking battering ram! Do you hear what I'm saying, Brian? I'm accustomed to men falling all over themselves around me. There was a time, not so long ago, when I could intimidate a man just by staring at him. I think that day is long passed."

"That's horseshit, Maggie May. You haven't lost a step."

"Brian, I can remember a time when I could literally make a man prostrate himself in front of me. And that's no bullshit!"

"Please tell me you never carried through with this power of yours."

"I would, but I'd be lying if I did."

"When was this?"

"It was back in college."

"What did you do—make some poor idiot beg for sex?"

"No, it was even worse than that. I set up this poor guy at the sorority house—and put him through the wringer while my sorority sisters looked on."

"Keogh, please spare me the details," he asked while shaking his head in disbelief.

"I've always had this thing in me that rears its ugly head every once in a while. It's a desire to really hurt people—to be really mean and walk all over them. I know I'll hate myself afterwards but I fucking do it anyway. It's almost like a sickness."

"Yeah, I've seen you when you get like that. I know it's not you and you'll come out of it soon enough—but it's no picnic being around you at those times."

"My mother saw it in me even when I was a girl. She kidded around and said I was her bad seed. She probably thought I'd grow out of it."

"I love you anyway, Maggie May. Besides, we all have that battle going on inside us."

"I just needed a little time with you tonight to help me get through this funk I'm going through—because I'm getting old and everything," she admitted.

"You're not getting old! Look at women like Raquel Welch and Lauren Hutton. They're a lot older than you and they're still as sexy as hell. My God, Lena Horne is ancient and she's still a very attractive woman. Why—if you ran into that poor bastard from the sorority house today, something tells me you could still have him at your feet begging for whatever you had him begging for before."

"Don't bullshit me, Brian."

"I'm not! Are you kidding me? Where is this shit coming from?"

"I think I was already feeling it coming on—and then we had that argument last week with those assholes from the television station."

"Why is that bothering you?"

"You heard what that bitch said to me—about being bitter and middle aged."

"She was just trying to get your goat. My God, you had just called her every name in the book, ignorant, uneducated, an overweight cow."

"I believe the word was *heifer,*" stated Margaret proudly.

"Yeah—heifer. And was it thirty or forty pounds overweight? I can't remember. Now she could afford to lose five or ten pounds, maybe—but thirty or forty?" The woman snickered, showing a slight sign of accepting her spouse's explanation. "She had nowhere else to go. She probably thought you were in your late twenties and decided to make you think you looked older. Keogh, you're the youngest looking thirty-eight I've ever seen. I sometimes worry that soon people will start thinking you're my daughter—and Colleen's my granddaughter."

"Really?"

"If you could have heard how the guys were talking about you last week—and how lucky I was to have you—your ego would have been up in the clouds." She reached out her arms for him and he reacted by joining her on the bed.

"I have this meeting with a potential new client tomorrow. He's blown me off twice in the last month. No one blew me off in the old days. I really want this client. He's been with Rose Dalton for the past few years but her people screwed up royally last tax season. Last year Rose was blowing her horn at a chamber meeting about how she landed one of my former clients. It was a piss ant client—less than a couple of grand a year. This client tomorrow, if he doesn't cancel on me again, is up around fifteen or twenty grand—and I do want to stick it up Rose's ass."

"Wear the red dress, Keogh. You're death in that red dress."

"I thought of that, but I'm almost afraid to. I've never failed in that dress and I'm not sure my ego could survive failure at this point."

"Wear the red dress. You'll wrap him around your finger." She slid her body down from a sitting position, bringing her torso along side her husband. He responded by laying his hands down on her perfectly flat stomach. "Your body's still cold from the pool," he observed.

"Massage my muscles—and make me laugh," she commanded in her best Shirley Temple impersonation. He laughed before bringing his hands up her torso, stopping at the base of her breasts.

"We need lotion for this to work," he stated, hopping from the bed and retrieving a bottle from his bureau. Returning to the bed, he took a position on the bottom half of the king sized mattress. "Over on your stomach. I'll start with these major league calves." He began the process of kneading the woman's highly muscled limb. She responded with a sigh, resting the side of her face on the pillow.

"Amuse me, Kelly. Get me out of this damn depression." He took a moment, his hands alternating between calves with an occasional pass over the arches of her feet.

"Okay, here goes—and what's more, it's about two of your favorite clients."

"A story about Perez and Bobby?"

"Exactly. First, I'll give you a little background. Bobby's been renting the same office and storage space for over three years now. He's rented from old man Hilliard up in Kennebunk and he's grown to like the old guy. Anyway, last winter this scumbag who moved into York County just a couple of years ago, decides he wants old man Hilliard's building. Hilliard's got the thing mortgaged to the hilt but is managing to keep up his payments with the building almost completely rented out. Well, when this New York outsider asks the old guy to sell him the building, he's told no. So what the prick does is float a story to the paper about negotiations and the paper prints it without checking with old man Hilliard—which is what the New York prick wants."

"Do you know this guy?"

"I met him once—a pompous asshole. Anyway, when the tenants in the building hear about this negotiation garbage, some of them get spooked and start looking. A lot are tenants at will, meaning there's no lease."

"I know what that means. I'm not an imbecile."

"Just making sure you're paying attention, Maggie May. Well, by the end of March the building is half empty and the old guy can't convince new people to come in. His cash flow is down the toilet and he has to crawl back to this bastard who chisels another twenty-five grand more off the price. Hilliard sold the building near the end of May."

"The guy's a sharp businessman, Brian, admit it."

"Anyway, after he's bought the building, the scumbag finds out that not all the tenants have no lease. It turns out that our own Bobby Copeland has a lease with over two years left on it—and the lease, which the genius from New York has to honor, has utilities included—electricity anyway. The new owner goes to Bobby and Perez and nicely asks them to consider vacating. They say no. He asks again and Bobby tells him to go fuck himself—they're staying."

"Did this clown actually think they were going to walk away from an attractive lease?" Margaret asked.

"Maybe he thought he was dealing with dumb Mainers. However, this New York genius's problems were only beginning. What happens next is that it's getting hot going into the Memorial Day weekend, so Bobby starts up the air conditioner, puts it on high, and decides to leave it on all weekend— twenty four hours a day. The boys have a few beers over the holiday and laugh it up over what's happening with the electricity back at the office. That Monday, Perez shows up with another air conditioner, which he puts in the next window to Bobby's, and away they go—twenty four hours a day—day in and day out. It becomes a competition. A week later, Perez gets the idea that these air conditioners are too new—too energy efficient. So he goes to Biddeford and picks up some second-hand, piece a shit air conditioner at

Goodwill or someplace and replaces the other one. Not to be outdone, Bobby finds some old piece of junk in Sanford and replaces his good one. So picture this, Keogh, they're running these two energy sucking units twenty-four hours a day, knowing they don't have to pay the bill!" Margaret began to laugh, a steady, unforced laugh.

"They're insane," she called out.

"They weren't done. Bobby comes in one morning in June with a space heater under his arm—and he sets it up facing right into one of the air conditioners and turns it on. So when they leave for their customer's places that day, a space heater is shooting hot air into an air conditioner. By the end of June there's an air conditioner in every window—four of them—cranking out the electricity twenty–four hours a day with a heater shooting hot air into every one of them. It's insane! That's about the time the scumbag landlord gets his first electric bill— and he can't stinking believe it! He must have thought he was lighting all of Maine! Perez actually told me that one morning he got to the office—opened the door to the two rooms full of pure, unadulterated energy, and couldn't believe his eyes. He said, *Bri, I opened the fucking door and, I swear to God, there was half an inch of snow on the floor and on top of the desks.* Maggie, they were creating mini weather systems inside their office!" The habitually stern woman laughed uncontrollably for a few seconds before catching her breath.

"What's going to happen with all this?"

"I think they plan on sticking it to this guy for as long as they can. Bobby said they might strike a deal with the landlord if he'll forgive some debt he holds on old man Hilliard. The poor, old guy had to sell for less than what he owed on the building and the New Yorker actually paid the extra debt for him and took paper back."

"Imagine if any of the tree huggers up there ever got wind of what your friends are doing. Think of what these maniacs are doing to the ozone layer."

"I really don't think they give a shit, do you?"

"No, they probably don't. Thank you for that bedtime story from Maine. It's nice to hear the bad guys take one up the ass once in a while." Brian smiled up at his wife and placed his open mouth down on her nearest calf.

"I do love the taste of chlorine on the skin. Not all skin—but certainly your skin."

"That's good, because I have chlorine *all* over me," she added.

"On the back of your knees?" he asked, running his tongue over her moist skin.

"All over," she said encouragingly.

"Up here on your inner thigh?" He pushed himself higher on the bed, biting softly on her tender flesh.

"Everywhere Brian, the chlorine is everywhere," she suggested coyly, closing her eyes and preparing herself for the thrilling pleasure his tongue was about to bestow on her.

XVIII

On a hazy, hot and humid Saturday in late July, Margaret, Jenny and Brendan were attempting to beat the heat by taking advantage of the family's pool. The three had vacated the house shortly after ten o'clock, setting themselves up with reading material and other amusements a few feet from the inviting water. Early on, the younger two had been psychologically bullied into games of chess by Margaret and suffered the same fate. Jenny, to her credit, had extended her mother for the better part of an hour. Brendan, on the other hand, lost his queen very early in his match and was forced to concede to Margaret shortly thereafter.

On this day, set aside as it was for relaxation and the recharging of her batteries, Margaret took particular note of the peculiar rapport developing between her daughter and their male houseguest. The two young people, thrown together under odd circumstances only weeks earlier, had spawned a relationship not unlike that of brother and sister. The two attractive young people were constantly the object of the other's sarcasm and quick wit, much the same as siblings vying for the approval of a parent. Following a five minute dip that had her swimming the length of the pool a dozen times, Margaret went in search of a towel and checked her watch.

"Hey kids, it's nearly twelve-thirty and the lady of the house is getting hungry. Who's going to volunteer to make lunch?"

"I think Brenda should. He doesn't do a thing around here as it is," explained Jenny, feminizing the young man's name in hope of getting under his skin.

"Anyway—I think I should be beyond consideration—given my performance in the chess games," reasoned the woman.

"I have an idea. What if Jenny and I race for it? How about six lengths of the pool, the loser brings the winner and the beautiful Mrs. Kelly, lunch at poolside?"

"Make it eight lengths of the pool and you're on Brenda," called out Jenny.

The challenge was accepted, as amended. Less than two minutes later, Jenny and Brendan were poised side by side at one end of the pool and awaiting the starting whistle from the lady of the house. At the sound of the whistle, the two hit the water in unison and propelled themselves forward. Margaret watched in amazement as Brendan, a marginal swimmer less than four weeks earlier, pulled out to a full body lead. He maintained this edge for the first six laps of the race, in spite of losing ground at each turn, and headed into the final leg with a comfortable lead. It was in these last, two laps that Jenny finally began to close the gap. In the final lap, an exhausted Brendan was barely able to hold off the oncoming Jenny, slapping the edge of the pool just before the young woman's hand made contact.

"Brendan's the winner—in a photo finish," called out Margaret, standing directly above the two swimmers.

"Another lap and I would have won—another two laps and Brenda would've drowned," called out Jenny before sending a spray of water into the winner's face. Brendan, out of breath and gasping for air, hung to the side of the pool and did not respond.

The two competitors climbed from the water, making their way back to their respective loungers and a towel. Following less than a minute devoted to drying herself off, Jenny slipped her feet into a pair of sandals and made her way back toward the house.

"There's a small part of me that feels sorry for Jenny, having to slave in the kitchen for us while we sit our here by the pool," admitted Brendan.

"Brendan, you're too soft. The truth is we're providing the girl with a life experience, and not all life experiences are pleasant," answered Margaret behind a pair of oversized sunglasses, her face directed up toward the afternoon sun.

"Maybe I should go help her."

"She'll respect you more if you don't—trust me on this."

The teenager's soul searching came to an end twenty minutes later with the sound of the screen door slamming at the back of the house and the sight of Jenny carrying a tray of food and beverages toward the pool area. Neither moved a muscle when the young woman reached the gate and struggled with the latch, the tray balanced precariously in one hand.

"We were becoming concerned," said her mother at the sound of her daughter's approach.

"If my sandwiches are on white and not wheat you can take them back right now," clowned Brendan with a hint of forced pretension in his voice.

"No, Brenda, I know you're watching your girlish figure and went with the wheat," answered Jenny, the needling apparently piercing her normally good-natured personality. After placing her mother's lunch on the table beside her chaise lounge, she walked behind Brendan who was still lying on his back, his face angled to one side as he worked on his tan. His eyes remained closed as she pulled up beside his stretched out body, clothed only in swimming trunks. He did not see her remove a large glass of ice water from the tray and extend it over his chest. She deliberated for less than a second, then tilted the glass, letting the frigid, ice water stream down on his chest, stomach and lastly into his crotch.

"Ahhh!" he cried out, bolting up from the chaise lounge and scattering ice cubes in all directions.

"I'm so sorry, Brenda—accident prone, that's me," admitted Jenny.

"Like hell—and stop calling me Brenda."

"Now children—play nice," counseled Margaret, sipping on her third martini.

"The truth is, you're a bad sport. I beat you at swimming and you can't take a little ribbing."

"Oh, please."

"But I'm going to give you a chance to redeem yourself. You're so proud of your diving and you know I can't dive for squat. Give me two weeks, and with your mother as the judge, I'll take you on at diving. Right here—five dives—and we'll each come up with a prize for the winner—from the loser."

"You're on, Brenda Starr" came back Jenny, extending her hand to make it official.

"Keep it up with that Brenda crap. It only makes me more determined to beat you."

"It'll take more than determination, Brenda Lee. It'll take talent—leaving you out. Mother, you'll have to help me out. What does junior here really dislike doing?"

"Give me a couple of days to mull it over, daughter. I'll see what I can come up with." With the wager set in place, a general peace settled in at poolside while all three had lunch.

By mid afternoon Colleen and Moira had joined the family around the pool. Margaret was now nestled under an umbrella, reading and keeping an eye on her toddler. Over the preceding two weeks, Brendan was providing Moira with swimming lessons. In that time, he had the Irish teenager master the breast stroke, an accomplishment she proudly reported to her family back in Doolin in their most recent phone conversation. Now she was back in the pool working on the mechanics of the back stroke under the watchful eye of her male mentor. It was at this time that the poolside phone rang, causing Colleen to call out in surprise. Margaret leaned back and removed it from its cradle. The hint of a frown came over her face as she listened intently. Brendan and Moira called a temporary halt to the swimming lesson and gazed up at the woman while the twenty month old slowly brought her crying under control.

"Jenny, it's for you. It's Roger," Margaret stated with bloodless frigidity. Jenny's head rose up from the lounger. Appearing startled, she walked to her mother, her beautifully tanned legs set off against her white bathing suit.

"Hello," she said timidly, taking the phone. Margaret peered up at her, searching for a clue to her reaction. Jenny, conscious she was the center of the family's attention, turned and walked toward the far end of the pool with the portable phone. At first content to speak in a whisper beyond anyone's earshot, she eventually retreated to beyond the fence, disappearing into the front yard.

"Who's Roger?" asked Brendan.

"Her old boyfriend—he walked out on her last Christmas," answered Margaret. The young man picked up on the negative overtone brought on by the call and wisely decided against asking the woman for any additional information. He returned to the swimming lesson. Twenty minutes passed without Jenny's return.

"Moira, make sure the baby stays out of the sun," ordered Margaret before picking up her articles and returning to the house.

Walking around to the front of the property where Jenny had vanished from sight some time before, Margaret entered the colonial in search of her daughter. She walked the length of the downstairs hallway, peeking inside each room as she advanced. In the kitchen, she noticed the telephone resting on the table. Convinced Jenny was nowhere on the first floor, she climbed the stairs. Seconds later she picked up on the sound of muffled sobbing from behind the young woman's bedroom door. She pushed open the door to find her first born stretched out on the bed, her face buried in a pillow.

"Anything you'd like to talk about?"

"He's engaged—he'll be getting married next spring," announced Jenny.

"He called to tell you that?"

"He called because he just realized he left a lot of personal items, like family pictures and video, behind in Newport. He was following up to see if I still had them."

"Do you?"

"I have most of it."

"If it were me I'd torch them."

"I didn't think I'd react this way. I was getting by fine without him."

"Honey, it's not your heart he's really hurt, it's your vanity," her mother reasoned, taking a seat on the edge of the bed and stroking her daughter's hair.

"In the back of my mind I thought he was coming back to me." The young woman pulled herself up from the mattress and rested her head on her mother's shoulder. "I loved him once—and maybe I still do."

"Brian has a theory about this sort of thing—that once you've loved someone—and then it ends—you're never quite whole again—that there's a piece of your heart you will never recover. Maybe he's right."

"I don't need to hear that right now," confessed the girl before letting out a long sigh. "I think what bothers me most is thinking how he always said he didn't believe in the institution of marriage—that it was archaic—something created by religious zealots to control the masses."

"Horseshit from Roger to cover up his own fear of commitment," theorized Margaret.

"Well he doesn't seem to have any god damn fear of commitment now! That's what really seems to be eating at me."

"Come back and join the family. It hurts the most when you sit by yourself and stew over it. No one else needs to know what's taken place."

"No—I don't think I've gotten all of the tears out of me yet. In fact, I know I haven't. Make up something to tell them—particularly Brendan. I'll rejoin everyone when I think I can be decent company again." Margaret cradled her daughter back onto the bed and rose to her feet.

"I know the kind of hurt you're going through. I only have to think back to the night Brad marched into my office and told me he was moving out. It isn't fun." On those words, the woman eased the door to the girl's bedroom closed, leaving her to grapple with the pain that only one who has loved in vain can understand.

Hours passed. It was nearly six o'clock when a series of gentle knocks on her door brought Jenny out of a light sleep.

"Who is it?"

"Brendan."

"Go away."

"Your mom wants to know if you'd like dinner."

"Go away. I'll come down and make myself something if I get hungry."

"Can I come in?"

"What is there about *go away* that you don't understand?"

"Are you mad at me or something?"

"This has nothing to do with you."

"I was hoping for a chance to run something by you."

"Do it from out there. Through some miracle of science, your voice carries right through the door."

"It's a little on the personal side, Jen." The young woman let out a restrained scream before rising from the bed and stomping to the door. Brendan took a step backwards as the door flew open and he was confronted by Jenny Keogh.

"Go ahead, I'm listening," she said in a tone laden with impatience.

"You're still in your bathing suit!" he exclaimed. "Have you been crying?"

"Brendan, it's been a lousy afternoon and you're getting the evening off to a bad start too. For God's sake, say what you have to say and leave me alone."

"I'll wait until you're in a better mood," he said before turning to leave.

"Oh, for God's sake!" she called out, grabbing the young man by the shirt and pulling him through the doorway.

"No, you're not just going to walk away—not after this whole production of yours. Speak!" The teenager walked to the far end of the room and fell back onto her reading chair.

"There is no way I can even begin to ask you what I wanted to ask you with you acting like this."

"Oh, God, please strike this idiot dead or something, but make this nightmare end," cried out Jenny, rushing across the room and grabbing the young man by the lapels of his shirt. With her body leaning forward awkwardly, the chair shifted to one side, sending both crashing onto the floor. The crash of their combined bodies was followed by a spurt of laughter from Brendan as he lay on his back under Jenny.

"What are you two fools doing up there?" shouted Margaret from a floor below. "All I needed to know was if Jenny wanted dinner."

"Now you've done it stupid, you've upset mother," warned Jenny, her words delivered in a horror movie dialect and tone. He responded with more laughter. Jenny thrust her hands around the teenager's neck and squeezed. "What—in the name of God—did you want to ask me? Tell me Brenda!"

"It's just that I know you weren't planning on seeing any of your friends this weekend—"

"Why can't he just come out and say it?" she roared, reapplying pressure on her would be victim's throat. His response was more laughter, genuine and prolonged.

"Your mother told me I could use the wreck this weekend—and I thought it might be fun if we jumped in the car and went to the Milford Drive-In. I've never been to a drive in—and it would look creepy going alone. I'll pay." Jenny, her hands continuing to encircle the teenager's throat, abruptly froze.

"Sweet Jesus, my life is even more pathetic than I could have imagined. Teenage boys are now asking me out."

Behind them came the sound of footsteps. Then, Margaret and Moira appeared in the doorway.

"What in the name of God is going on?" the mother asked of her daughter who, at the moment, sat atop Brendan.

"I think Brendan just asked me out on a date," answered Jenny. "A month from my twenty-second birthday and I'm being asked out by a teenage boy to go to the drive-in. You've come a long way, baby," she muttered.

"Well, as long as no one's being murdered up here," added Margaret. Following a moment's hesitation taking in the odd scene in front of her, she turned and guided the nanny downstairs.

"So, I guess that's a no on the drive-in idea."

"Brendan, it's really been a bad afternoon. Your timing isn't the best." The young man broke eye contact and began pulling himself out from beneath her. "I'm really kind of flattered—really, I am."

"No, it's okay," he answered, politely extricating himself from their tangled arms and legs.

"The girls around Bedford are going to flip over you once you start getting around," she comforted. "It's just that---right now I'd make terrible company for anyone. I got some pretty sucky news this afternoon and it's really got me down."

"Sometimes it's better not being alone when you feel like that. And as far as the Bedford girls are concerned—a few have gone out of their way at the mall to try to get my attention but I'm not interested."

"Why—do you think you're too good for the Bedford girls?"

"No, not at all."

"Then ask one out."

"I just did," he said, rising to his feet and making for the door.

"Do you really want to spend the night with someone who might break out in tears at the drop of a hat—and who could spend most of the evening running down men in general and one named Roger in particular?"

"Are all the jokes I hear about drive-in food true?" he asked, ignoring Jenny's question.

"Yes, they probably are."

"I'll put up with anything, your moaning and groaning, the food—"

"Don't forget the mosquitoes."

"The whining—the bugs."

"My mother will have a shit fit. Brian's son and her daughter out on something that could be loosely called a date."

"What's the big deal? I'll be nineteen in less than a week. You won't be twenty–two until next month."

"Oh my God, you've already done the math," she exclaimed.

"I'm not ugly!"

"You are anything but ugly."

"And you're about the most beautiful girl I have ever known—all kidding aside. I love it here—being able to see you every day." Stunned, she walked up to him, laying her hands on his shoulders.

"Okay, slow down now—slow and easy. Let me go change into sweats or something. I'll join you downstairs."

"Yeah, as much as the guys in Milford would love seeing you in that bathing suit, I'm not in the mood to be fighting them off all night."

"Don't worry—I'm easy to get over. Just ask Roger."

"He's an asshole, Jen—a total asshole."

At shortly after seven o'clock, Jenny, dressed in sweat pants and a halter top, appeared in the doorway to the living room. Margaret's eyes widened when Brendan hopped up from the couch and joined her daughter.

"Brendan thought it would be a good idea to get out of the house and not sulk all night. He's taking me to the drive-in."

"Margaret, you said I could use the wreck this weekend," he added.

"Yes, I suppose I did."

"And mother—just to let you know, I'm paying my own way. I don't want junior here getting any ideas."

"I'd say it's a little too late for that—the ideas, I mean. Drive carefully," she added, her mouth slightly open in disbelief. They turned and made for the front door. Margaret rose from the couch, making her way to a window where she watched this young man, a total stranger less than three months ago, open the car door for her daughter in true, gentlemanly fashion and climb behind the wheel.

XIX

*I*t was Thursday, August 10th, and Brian woke up in a positive frame of mind. Later that afternoon, he would be heading home to Bedford to see his family for the first time in nearly two weeks and the mere thought of this elevated his spirits. Margaret and the baby had stayed home the weekend before, choosing poolside in New Hampshire over the Maine coast, largely owing to the confined quarters of the couple's Wells Beach cottage. Two days before, in reaction to the summer's very positive operating figures, he had overloaded his staffing of chambermaids, scheduling all six women to report at nine o'clock. In addition, all were asked to work through lunch, causing more than an isolated sigh from one or two of the girls. On or about one-thirty, the six women congregated behind the main house. The day's work had been completed in record time, leaving them to question whether they were expected to punch out early or break for a long, overdue lunch. At long last, Brian stepped out from the office and onto the porch.

"Ladies, if I may have your attention for a few moments, I have some announcements." The women approached the deck with Mary Porterfield front and center. "As you all know, my charming, socialite wife is now a fifty percent owner of the corporation for which we all work, and she has instituted a set of new rules that I will now announce and explain—after which I will take questions from you. I take it you have all punched out?"

"We weren't told we were supposed to," called out Sally Hanrahan, a heavy set, middle aged woman.

"No mind, I will simply adjust your times by hand on your dismissal in a few minutes. Anyway, on to the matter at hand, Margaret, my wife, has instituted a few, new, corporate rules which will go into effect tomorrow morning. I'll read them off, one at a time, and take questions and comments at the conclusion." The half dozen women standing before him exchanged curious glances before focusing back on Brian. Directive one, effective August 11, 1995, individuals acting in the capacity of chambermaids shall not wear any of the following during working hours; shorts, culottes, skirts, casual dresses, sneakers, sandals, boots, hip boots, waders, socks, knee socks, galoshes, blouses, coats, overcoats, raincoats, tee shirts, g strings, gloves, hats, caps and bathing suits." Brian tilted his eyes up into a small sea of open mouths.

"What in the name of Jesus H. Christ does that leave—panties and a bra?" roared the Hanrahan woman to a chorus of laughs.

"Come on, Sally, I'm expecting everyone to get on board and take this seriously," admonished Brian, a serious expression creasing his face.

"I am serious," she answered, a more sober tone carried in her voice.

"Directive two, effective August 11, 1995, individuals acting in the capacity of chambermaids will collect all tips and gratuities in a central location daily, whereupon seventy-five percent will be reserved for charitable purposes. The remaining twenty-five percent will be distributed equally among the active employees that day after taxes are withheld for both federal and state purposes. A charitable cause for purposes of this undertaking is defined as the Bedford Republican Women's Guild, the monies to be applied to help defray the cost of instruction for classical dance and equestrian pursuits, all recipients the sons and daughters, grandsons and granddaughters, of the citizens of Bedford, New Hampshire." He raised his eyes from the paper and into the half dozen, muted faces, mouths reopened in astonishment.

"Brian, you've got to stand up for us here. We can't go along with something like this," called out Mary. He froze before shaking his head in disbelief.

"I can't go through with this. It's just too cruel," he confessed. "Ladies, I'm sorry, there is no new set of rules or proclamations from my wife. I was just pulling your collective chains. However, what we are about to all take part in is the first annual Atlantic Coast Lodge Chambermaid Appreciation Day. Right now down at the pool we have our own Hal Newdecker, part-time assistant to the assistant manager—we give out titles like banks—preparing steaks for you. Now Hal may be something less than an award winning motel manager, but he is an accomplished caterer in his other life. Now if you will just begin the walk with me down to poolside, I will fill you in on what you can expect. From now until five o'clock you will be wined and dined—totally on the clock—no one has to punch out until then. There's an assortment of bathing suits left behind by our gracious guests in cabin fourteen that you may try on and use—all sizes and shapes. And yes, they've been thoroughly washed! Now besides steak, Hal's told me he brought some lobsters, corn on the cob, steamers, beer and tonic. Tonic is what I called soda growing up in Lowell. Old habits die hard. It's Millie's, Hal's and my way of saying thanks for a job well done. Oh—and a warning—some of the bathing suits we're providing are pretty funky, but after a couple of beers will anyone really care?"

His announcement sent a jolt of energy through the group of women who began the short walk down to the pool. Peeling off from the others, Mary made her way to Brian's side, extending her arm around his waist and accompanying him in step down the grassy hill. Nearly a foot shorter than her boss, she tucked her head under his arm and playfully bumped his thigh with her hip on every step.

"You have to be the best darn boss in the whole, freaking world," she muttered.

The group was about twenty feet from the pool area when the aroma from the grill reached them, bringing on a chorus of ahhhs.

"We'll eat first—then get the bathing suits. While Hal's taking your orders, I'll find a way to get some music out here. This is your day ladies—well, at least, half day. You can celebrate having no dress code and not having to hand over three-quarters of your tips to my wife."

The customarily reserved Hal proved to be a gregarious co-host and qualified chef. The women rapidly got caught up in the surprise social gathering, arranging pool furniture in a half circle and celebrating as a group. Steak and lobster proved to be the main course of choice while beer was consumed by a ratio of six to one over soda. Brian assisted Hal, functioning as a waiter, insisting that none of his employees should have to lift a finger. Following on a lead from Mary, all of the women giddily kissed Brian on the cheek as he served each individually. A majority of the guests were a mile away at the ocean, leaving the poolside open for the chambermaids but on one or two occasions when a paying guest made their way inside the fence, they were offered food and drink and encouraged to join in the festivities.

It was almost three o'clock when Mary and Sally meandered up the hill to the cabin and took advantage of the inventory of abandoned bathing suits stored there. It was not long before the others in the party of six followed suit. Brian was occupied helping Hal put away some perishables when his attention was captured by an outburst of laughter from atop the hill. He turned to see Mary parading around on the lawn in an undersized, two piece bathing suit. Making her way down the incline in his direction, the petite, young woman called out to her boss, drawing attention to the print on her bikini, a blend of seahorses and smiling whales.

"I actually remember the eleven year old girl that left that suit here," clowned Brian in a loud voice. "It had to take more than two beers to give you the courage to put that on, Mary." The girl gave off a giggle and raced toward him.

"Come on now—there are a few pairs of men's trunks up there. You can't just let us be the ones parading around in bathing suits," she argued, taking hold of his arm and tugging him away from the fence.

"Hold on here. I've seen the sort of renter who leaves behind his trunks. I'll join you gals in a few minutes—but it'll be in my own trunks. I have a pair up in the office. Just give me a couple more minutes helping Hal." Mary accepted his proposition with a leery stare before pointing a finger in his face.

"I'll be watching," she promised before walking to the cooler for another beer.

It was not long before the half dozen women were enjoying themselves in and around the pool. Brian took notice while performing busboy duties and clearing the furniture of all evidence of the recent meal. At some point, he paused behind the barbeque grill and observed the women, most middle aged, while they temporarily blotted out the burden of their daily rituals and acted in the manner they must have as teenagers twenty-five or so years ago. Their families did not expect them or anything from them until after five o'clock. Their lone responsibility until that time was to take advantage of the circumstances at hand. Mary, being the youngest, was providing the spark for the festivities as she organized a cannonball competition. As each woman took her place at the edge of the water, the others taunted her good-naturedly, their catcalls fueled by the consumption of beer.

The pool activities soon took on a life of its own, allowing Brian to slip away from the good natured craziness undetected. Returning to the office, he thanked Hal for his efforts and took a breather with Millie.

"So would you rate this little experiment in employee relations a success?" she asked.

"Beyond my wildest dreams—the girls seem to be having a ball down there. The food and drink cost maybe two hundred bucks. On top of that we're paying about twenty extra hours in wages. Big deal! Can you hear them down there? They sound like boy crazy teenagers the way they're hooting and hollering."

"There aren't too many bosses in these parts that'd even think of doing something like this. I hope these girls know what they have here."

"Hey, Mill, don't make it more than it really is. It's a few steaks and some fun at the pool. It's not like donating someone a kidney."

"It's good—and it's decent—and it's Christian. It has nothing to do with money."

"I can see it now—in a hundred years they'll be canonizing me in Rome, Saint Brian, the patron saint of chambermaids."

"There you go again—poking fun when I'm being serious. Brian Kelly—you're a good, decent man and a fine Christian. It's unfortunate that you're not totally enlightened and a Congregationalist, but I suspect I'll be seeing you in heaven someday nonetheless."

"Whoa, it's after four-thirty. I promised the girls I'd change into a bathing suit and join them. Plus, I'll have to bring the curtain down on this in about half an hour." Jumping to his feet, he made tracks to the closet in his office.

A roar went up from the women at poolside at the sight of their boss walking in their direction dressed in only swimming trunks, a towel draped over his shoulder. His entrance through the noisy gate heralded the end of the cannonball phase of their celebration and the beginning of the Brian Kelly segment. After a few exaggerated stretching movements, he spoke to the women.

"You know, girls—on second thought—I'm not much in the mood to go in the water. In fact, I think it's fair to say that nothing—and I mean nothing—or no one could *make* me go in the water." The challenge voiced, he knew full well what his statement would touch off.

"Okay, everyone, you heard him. We've been challenged," called out Mary, walking to her bottle of beer and chugging down the remaining contents. Seconds later, she charged a determined Brian, his hand gripping one of the wooden posts anchoring the fence. She reached him first, bear hugging him around the waist. The others followed close behind, grabbing his arms and legs and pulling at him.

"Someone tear his hand from the post," Mary ordered, clearly taking charge of the mission.

"This is too easy," he taunted. "It's like having a half dozen feeble, old men try to take down Hercules—it's laughable." The joking on Brian's part caused the burly Sally Hanrihan to take an even more active role in dislodging him. His grasp finally broken, the women were able to slowly move him toward the water.

"I'll have my wife fire you—all of you—if even a drop of water touches my person," he yelped.

"We've got him, girls—keep pulling," urged Mary.

"Millie, call the police!" he hollered, approaching the edge of the pool. Over the next few seconds, the hopelessly outnumbered man staged his last stand, teetering on the rim of the pool for a moment until he felt his feet literally lifted from the cement. His initial sensation was that of hitting the cool water and descending a full body length below the surface. His second sensation was of the warm body riding him downward. Mary Porterfield, her arms reaching around his neck and legs tightly ankle-locked about his waist, was in tow. Reaching the floor of the kidney shaped pool, he looked through the water into her beautiful, youthful face, only enhanced by the curious circumstances. They remained fully submerged for a moment, totally apart from the din only a few feet away and above the surface of the water. Brian became aware of Mary's pelvic bone pressuring against his body and providing a trace of warmth. His mind reeled from her closeness, this grown woman so much an impressionable girl. Still grasping his neck, she drew her face closer and pressed her lips to his. He returned her affection, for the moment under the influence of her delicate, female form and the spontaneous arousal it was igniting in him. It was a moment of absolute bliss, helpless surrender, pleasure bordering on ecstasy. Their entwined bodies began the slow ascent, reaching the surface of the water to a chorus of hoots and catcalls. Her face was against his, prompting her to press her lips to his a second time. He puckered his lips, communicating to her that the interlude could not continue.

"Hey, you two, get a room," came a voice from the onlookers. He answered with a sheepish grin, kissing Mary on the cheek and tactfully pushing her away. Her response came through a wounded expression, her eyes reflecting hurt.

"Hey, what time do you folks have?" he asked.

"Ten minutes to five," answered Sally.

"Okay, just time for my harem to change out of their bathing suits and punch out for the day," he announced, happy for the opportunity to disperse the crowd of witnesses. Taking hold of Mary's hand at the wrist, he guided her through the water to the ladder. He watched as her petite body emerged from the pool, a shower of droplets from her one hundred pound frame cascading down on him and the surrounding water.

"Are you coming?" she asked, her tone unable to mask a degree of frustration.

"In a couple of minutes, baby girl. I don't get a chance to take a dip too often. It feels good." He wondered if she accepted his explanation or saw through it. In truth, he was aroused and his body attested to it. He required a brief interlude for it to return to normal size.

Brian's eyes remained on Mary while she stepped away from poolside and walked toward a lounger where her towel laid strewn across the back rest. A few steps into the short walk she staggered to one side, catching herself by grabbing hold of the fence.

"Hey, kid, are you okay?" he asked.

"Yeah, I think so," she replied behind a hollow stare. Disregarding the state of his body, he bounded from the water and rushed to her side.

"Let's take it slow and easy back to the office. How many beers did you put down this afternoon?"

"I lost track—one more than Sally."

Following a minute of rest and breathing exercises, Brian guided his employee up the hill, past the other women now emerging from the cabin and makeshift dressing room, and toward the office. Millie was at the front desk attending to the needs of two families of guests when Brian and Mary came through the door. He ushered the young mother into the kitchen and away from the visitors. When a hastily brewed cup of coffee had no effect on the chambermaid's lack of lucidness, he decided she should be escorted back home to Sanford.

"My son's at daycare today. We'll have to go there first," she directed. It was just after five-thirty when the office was finally emptied of paying guests. Brian enlisted Millie to drive the young woman and her vehicle back to Sanford, pick up her son, and deliver both home. Following close behind the two women, he had ample time to replay the events of the afternoon in his head. He was not surprised that a young, impressionable woman under the influence of one too many bottles of beer would become forward with him. After all, a comfort level between them had grown into a warm friendship. It was understandable that, in the heat of the moment and given the warmth each had for the other, a spark of passion could and did flash between them. What caused him to pause and reflect was his reaction to the exchange. Up until the incident at the pool, he had steadfastly believed that his love for his beautiful and successful wife was so powerful as to leave him immune to any and all temptation. However, on this afternoon and in the company of a handful of employees, he had watched that belief crumble like a house of cards, shattered at the hands of a struggling, uneducated, single mom.

Brian followed in close formation to Mary's ten year old vehicle, following the car first to daycare, then to a small, poorly maintained single family house in Sanford. Emerging from the vehicle with the boy, she was greeted from the front porch by an unshaved, unkempt male. The greeting was neither warm nor prolonged, the man disappearing into the house after taking an extended swig from a can of beer. Following an embrace of the young mother, Millie walked back to the pickup and joined Brian for the ten mile drive back to Wells.

"I would feel a whole lot better if those two were coming home with me instead of staying here," commented Millie while Brian turned the Ford around and started the trip home. "Did you see the likes of him standing on the porch?"

"Yes, I saw him."

"I've told her she could come stay with us in York. The poor thing started to shake as we approached the house. And what's this stuff she started talking about, you being mad at her about something at the pool?"

"Did she say that?"

"Yes, like she didn't already have enough to be worrying herself about."

"God, how could she think that? I'll sit her down first thing tomorrow and put her mind at ease."

The phone was ringing as Brian and Millie arrived back at the office. She raced to the front desk while he struggled to disengage the key from the door. With the key finally removed, he looked up to see his assistant manager beckoning him to the phone.

"It's Linda Turcotte—and she sounds upset," she whispered, her hand muffling the mouth piece.

"Linda—is everything okay?" inquired Brian.

"I hate to always be calling you when something's wrong or I need help."

"Don't be silly. What's going on?" Brian winced as he heard the woman struggle to hold back tears.

"I tried reaching Brendan at the house but your wife said he was at work. I didn't say anything to her because I feel I've already heaped enough on her shoulders. She's a good woman, Brian."

"Linda, what's wrong?"

"It's time for Brendan to come home and say good-bye to his step-father."

"Oh Linda, I'm so sorry," he consoled, his words prompting a short period of weeping at the other end of the line.

"If you can see to it that Brendan gets back to Albany quickly, I'll reimburse you for the cost—but he must know that he has to come quickly. Jack is very ill. The other kids are on their way."

"He'll leave tonight—I'll see to it."

"You've done a wonderful job with him. I can't get over it. He's sounding like the old Brendan when we talk these days. How did you get him to go back to high school?"

"That's all Maggie May's doing."

"I owe that woman for all her kindness."

"Wow—I don't hear that said too often—not about my Maggie May. It's hard to explain but she's just taken a liking to the kid. She's much closer to him than I am. It's bizarre."

"You're being much too hard on her, Brian. So I can depend on you to get him back as quickly as possible?"

"Linda, don't worry, I'm on it. Would it help if I came over?"

"No, I know how busy you are this time of the year. Thank you anyway. Just get our son home to me—that'll be enough."

The conversation over with the mother of his only son, Brian dropped down on the office couch and let out a sigh.

"Is it me or has this been a wicked year for family problems?" he asked, glancing up at Millie. "Remember things back in the late eighties when I'd go for walks along the beach at night—and meditate?"

"Wasn't that about the time you latched on to that spoiled, little lunatic from Kennebunkport who'd come over here whenever she felt the urge?"

"You must mean Molly?"

"Oh, she was quite the piece of work! You've got a family now. That's the way it should be. But a family means responsibilities. You count your blessings, mister, that's what I say."

"I haven't thought of Molly in ages. Come on now Millie, she wasn't a lunatic—just a little eccentric."

"And don't I remember a certain someone complaining about scratch marks all up and down his neck. No sir, a godless lunatic—and that's all I'll say on that subject."

He dialed the house in Bedford a few minutes later, only to get the answering machine. When a second call got the same result, he made his way to the pickup and set out for home. It was seven o'clock. The ninety minute trip gave him ample time to consider the circumstances. He said a prayer for Linda, asking God to help her through this ordeal. When the thought of attending to Maggie May under similar circumstances came to mind, he had to push it from his head, so painful was the thought. Linda's crisis harkened him back to the day he received word of Angelique's accident and the rush to Quebec City. He had been too late for even a hurried good-bye. For him, the loss had come quickly. Only the recovery was prolonged. At eight twenty-five the pickup turned onto Joppa Hill Road and he followed the rows of stone walls to the house. The windows were ablaze in artificial light when he reached the driveway leading to the huge, white colonial.

The Ford rolled to a stop directly in front of the granite steps. Jumping to the ground, he made haste to the front door. From inside, noise from the television echoed through the house. Cartoons, he thought, the baby is still up. Stepping inside, he called out.

"Brendan." His voice was loud enough to reach the far end of the second floor.

"He's still at work," called out Jenny from somewhere downstairs.

"Where's your mother?"

"Mom's over visiting grandmother," replied the young woman, sticking her head out from the kitchen.

"When's Brendan due home?"

"I'm supposed to pick him up in about a half an hour. The junk's in the garage."

"I'll pick him up. His mom called. He's got to get home. His stepfather is near death." His words robbed Jenny of her smile as she stood hand-drying a glass.

"Why are there cartoons on in the living room and no one watching?"

"The baby was watching them before they left. Mom just forgot to turn them off." He joined Jenny in the kitchen, nervously examining the contents of the refrigerator.

"Everything okay here at home?"

"I suppose."

"How's everything in the slam bam world of freelance journalism?"

"I had one hit last week—made a whopping two hundred and fifty dollars," she reported.

"Well, Kid, that'll keep you in bubble gum the rest of the month," he joked, feebly keeping the conversation going with his stepdaughter. "By the way, I take it Brendan's still working at the movie theater in the Bedford Mall." She nodded yes.

"Are you mad at me or something? You're awfully quiet."

"Does this mean he'll be moving back home?"

"No, but he has to go home to be with his family—particularly his mom—and to say good-bye to his stepfather." Brian detected a note of relief on the girl's face at the clarification of his son's status.

It was still a few minutes before nine o'clock when Brian pulled off Route 3 and into the parking lot of the Bedford Mall. The marquee sign by the roadside announced *Batman Forever* and *Clueless* as two of the features playing. His son was expecting Jenny to chauffer him back to the house, assuring Brian he would not disappear with some third party at the end of his shift. With a few minutes to spare, he wandered around a bookstore across the hall from the cinema. It was an independent store called Booksmith. He had recently read an article about the plight of small bookstores and chains. Many had been forced to close their doors in the last ten years, according to the piece, forced out of business by two or three major chains. He distinctly remembered the essence of the article: that professional service and knowledgeable salespeople were no match for superior capitalization. While roaming the aisles, he wondered how long the attentive, middle aged woman at the cash register would have her job. Exiting the store, he glanced down at the bargain table and spotted a discounted, coffee table book dedicated to the beautiful, Maine coast. He picked it up and flipped through the pages. Near the back of the hardcover was a full page, color photo of Beals Island from the air. Brian tucked it under his arm and walked to the checkout. It would be a gift to Mary, proving beyond a reasonable doubt there were no bad feelings on his part from the episode at the pool.

Brian's eyes lifted from the book of photography at the approach of two males from inside the movie theatre. They walked side by side toward him along the cinema's widened corridor. Brendan, the taller of the two, peered out into the mall, his eyes likely scanning for Jenny. Stopping just short of the hallway, he bid his co-worker goodnight and rested against a railing ordinarily used to direct the flow of moviegoers. It was not until Brian rose to his feet that a visual connection was made between them.

"Where's Jenny?"

"She's at home. I had to bring you a little solemn news and the drive home seemed as good a time as any to do it," answered Brian, careful to keep his voice low. His son's eyes grew wide with anticipation. "Your mother called me this afternoon. She's calling everyone in your family home to say good-bye to Jack. I'm afraid he's not going to make it, Brendan—and he doesn't have too much time left with us." He placed his arm on the teenager's shoulder, steering him out of the building and toward the pickup. He watched while his son's eyes grew moist. "To hear your mom talk, he's been doing some suffering over the past couple of weeks and this could be for the best."

"Is he awake—you know, alert?"

"He's under a lot of medication, but my understanding is he'll know you're there." Father and son reached the vehicle and Brian wasted no time getting them on the road. "It's not just important to go home and say good-bye to Jack—your mom needs all of you—and you in particular. You're her youngest and probably her favorite. You've got to be there for her, guy. She'll need someone to lean on to get her through the wake and funeral. None of that's a picnic. If you're strong, you'll make it a little easier for her. You follow me, right?" The young man nodded yes before turning away and staring out the passenger seat window.

"Does Jenny know?"

"Yeah—when I left to pick you up she was the only one home. Everyone else was over at the Keoghs." Conversation on the ride home was sparse, Brendan's mind, by all appearances, someplace else, perhaps focused somewhere in the past and remembering time spent with the man who largely functioned as his father.

"Let me get the Ford out of sight before my wife rips my head off—again," joked Brian, albeit restrained. They were home. Brendan hopped from the vehicle and made his way into the house.

Conscious of the developing bond between his son and Jenny, Brian prolonged the time needed to satisfactorily shield his truck from the eyes of passing neighbors, allowing the two to communicate openly for at least the next few minutes. He entered the house to find the two sitting side by side in the living room, the fingers of her right hand interlaced with Brendan's.

"Run upstairs and grab a few things from your bureau. Do you have a dark suit?"

"I do back in Albany."

"Good, that's one less thing to worry about." The headlights from the BMW appeared through the window, announcing the return of mother, daughter and nanny from the Keoghs.

"I'll get packed," said Brendan, turning and making his way for the stairs.

The front door flew open with Colleen scrambling toward the living room, obviously having spotted her father through the front window.

"Daddy," she called out, her arms extended.

"Jelly Bean—my teenage queen," he answered in rhyme before lifting her high above his head.

"Kelly, if you're expecting dinner—forget it. The kitchen is closed," announced Margaret. "And what the hell are you even doing home?"

"Brendan is being called home. His stepfather is very ill and Linda's calling the family home to say good-bye." She dropped her eyes and walked toward the kitchen.

"Where's Moira?"

"She's staying with my folks. Tomorrow's her day off and mom and dad are going into Boston for the day. She'll be going in with them—to shop and stuff. Outside of flying into Logan, she's never seen the city. Besides, my folks love her."

"Your folks love her—I love her—Jelly Bean loves her—Jenny loves her—Brendan loves her—"

"Brendan tolerates her!"

"Brendan loves her. Everyone loves her except Maggie May Kelly, Bedford's yuppie from hell," he needled. She shot her husband one of her well practiced, squinted glares and retreated to the kitchen. Having won the brief skirmish with his wife, the proud father celebrated by bouncing his daughter between his knees.

Trot, trot to Boston
Trot, trot to Lynn
Look out little Jelly Bean
Cause you might fall in. He sang to Colleen, opening his knees before catching her on the last bar as she dropped toward the floor. The toddler burst out in uncontrollable laughter with each repetition. This went on until Margaret re-entered the room and took a position behind father and daughter.

"For the life of me I don't know why I'm walking around with a glass of wine in one hand and a glass of ice cubes in the other," she lamented.

"Perhaps the ravages of advancing years?" theorized Brian. The woman withheld comment, choosing to place the glass of wine down on the end table.

"Or perhaps just being married to a total asshole!" she cried out, pulling at his shirt collar and pushing the cubes of ice down against his warm, exposed flesh.

"Sweet Jesus," he called out as she rode his twisting body to the floor, careful to cradle his daughter from harm. "No mas, no mas," he cried as she continued to apply pressure on the ice against his skin.

"Ravages of advancing years—is that it, Kelly? Say you're sorry, you insensitive bastard!"

"Enough, Keogh—please."

"Say you're sorry."

"I'm sorry, beautiful lady."

"You mean beautiful, young lady, don't you?"

"Beautiful, young lady," he conceded. She dismounted him and reclaimed her wine glass.

"God, sometimes you two are worse than twelve year olds," observed Jenny.

The mood was broken by Brendan's footsteps descending the stairs. Margaret reached down and scooped up three or four ice cubes from the carpet which she brought to the kitchen sink for disposal. She returned to find the young man standing awkwardly next to Jenny.

"I need a ride to the bus station in Manchester. Jen said she'd give me one," he explained. Brian rose to his feet, fidgeting to remove something from his front pocket.

"Oh Man, don't go through all of that, Brendan." He pulled a single key from its chain and flipped it to his son. "Take the pickup. Bring it back when you've finished your business. Be good to your mother—and make your dad happy." The teenager froze in his tracks, noticeably astonished by the man's generous offer. "Do you have enough money?"

"I've got a couple of hundred bucks."

"I'm sure that'll get you to Albany. Drive carefully. Try to be home for the start of school." It was Jenny who walked him to the door and ultimately all the way to the garage.

With the baby sound asleep and Jenny caught up in a classic movie down-stairs, Brian and Margaret prepared to retire for the night. He sat propped up in bed, observing his wife's grooming habits as she applied moisturizer to her skin while seated in front of a half length mirror.

"You never told me how that combination presentation and lunch went—the one you were so nervous about. I remember I told you to wear that ruby red dress of yours. What happened with that?"

"Piece of cake," she announced. "And that was a damn good client."

"How well did it go—and did you wear the red dress?"

"If I had brought along a hula hoop he would've been jumping through it for me—that's how well it went."

"So you were all worried for nothing?"

"Are you interested in hearing what else I did?"

"I'm interested in everything about you, Keogh. What else did you do?"

"You know that little bitch who broadcasted to the whole city about how she stole this little, piss ant client of mine a few months back?"

"Yeah, I seem to remember you mentioning that."

"Well, once I had a signed engagement letter in my hand, I sent the bitch a god damned sympathy card—like for someone who's just lost a relative. The difference being that that's how she'll find out I just took a fifteen thousand dollar a year client from her." Her story prompted him to break into song.

You don't tug on Superman's cape
You don't spit into the wind
You don't pull the mask off that old Lone Ranger

"And you don't fuck around with Maggie May Keogh," interrupted Margaret.

"It's Kelly, Keogh—Maggie May Kelly."

"You had to remind me."

"Maggie, you still haven't answered my question. Did you wear the red dress the day you walked all over the new client?"

"Yes, Brian, if you must know—yes."

"You're death in that dress. And speaking for the rest of us mortals—we salute you."

Brian abruptly rolled himself out of bed and approached his wife. Turning her moisturized face, he placed his mouth on hers, his tongue purposefully swirling around her own as if exploring its surface for the first time. He pulled back for a moment before running his tongue along the surface of her lips. She did not respond.

"I was thinking about Linda driving back from Wells—and how it must feel to watch someone you love slip away from you. Maggie May—promise me you won't die first."

"I promise to do everything in my power to outlive you, Kelly."

"Thank you."

"If you like, I'll even go so far as to take dance lessons on your grave," she added.

"Keogh, I was being serious."

"No, you were being overly dramatic."

"God, you can be so cold sometimes."

"And you can be so fucking dramatic."

"Are you telling me you can't feel for someone suffering through what that woman is right now?"

"Shit happens. We come into this world alone and we leave it alone," she remarked in a voice void of feeling, as if reciting her maxim for the hundredth time. He leaned over and kissed her bare shoulder.

"Can I do anything to relieve tension and take you out of this mood?"

"Yes, you can. How about sleeping downstairs on the couch tonight?" He pulled back from her and returned to bed.

"I really hate it when you get in one of these moods. Where did this come from so suddenly?"

"Sometimes I can take your Mr. Wonderful disposition—and other times it makes me sick. Right now it's making me sick."

"Fine—have it your way. I'll be getting up early in the morning. I'll make myself coffee."

"Whatever," she answered before walking from the bedroom and slamming the door behind her.

Ten minutes after being abandoned by his wife, Brian descended the stairs and found Jenny and her mother sitting in front of the television, a bucket of popcorn propped up on the couch between them. He walked up behind them and bent down over Jenny.

"Any chance of you giving me a ride to a car rental place in the morning?" he asked.

"Sure, that won't be a problem. What time?"

"They probably don't open until seven-thirty anyway. Eight will be okay." Jenny gave a thumbs up, never removing her eyes from the television. "That looks like *All About Eve*—good movie. And to quote the great Bette Davis, *Fasten your seat belts, it's going to be a bumpy night*—and this has been one—stinking—bumpy—night."

"Brian, this movie is so great. I've never seen it before. Marilyn Monroe's in it too," exclaimed the girl.

"Bette's from Lowell, Jen. I'll bet you didn't know that."

"It's nice to know someone from that godforsaken place made something of themselves," sniped Margaret.

"Stick it, Keogh—stick it where the sun don't shine," he came back before turning and leaving the room.

Millie did a double take while glancing out the office window when Brian pulled up to the main building in a compact car. It was beyond mid morning and he was just returning from his unscheduled trip to Bedford.

"Trouble with the truck?" she asked as he came through the office door.

"I let Brendan borrow it. He's back in Albany by now."

"And how's Linda holding up?"

"She's a wreck—but I think having Brendan home for a while will help."

Brian breezed by his assistant manager and instinctively made his way through the kitchen to his office. There, as always, a piece of fruit, today a pear, sat on the corner of his desk. Millie appeared in the door behind him.

"That poor child came in this morning—head hung low and embarrassed. She thinks you might be mad at her for the episode yesterday." He shook his head in disbelief.

"Mill, will you hang around just long enough for me to go find her and tell her to stop being silly?" The woman gestured him to action and walked back to the front desk.

Making his way back to the car, he retrieved an oversized, plastic bag and began the search for Mary. Coincidentally, he located her in cottage sixteen, the unit he first laid eyes on her a few months before. Pushing in the door, his eyes met hers as she knelt in front of the vacuum cleaner, snapping on an accessory nozzle.

"What's this crap about you thinking I was mad at you for some reason?" She blushed, her eyes dropping to the floor.

"I made a fool of myself."

"No you didn't. If I had tossed you across the pool instead of melting on the spot, then you would've made a fool of yourself," he reasoned.

"You're married. I knew that. Brian, I'm sorry. And it was in front of all those people." He stepped over to her, applying an innocent hug that found the top of her head barely able to make contact with his chest. He held on for an extended moment before pushing her to arm's length. He handed her the bag.

"What?"

"Look inside," he instructed. She reached inside the plastic bag and pulled out the coffee table book.

"The Coast of Maine," she read off the cover.

"Flip to page forty-four." She flashed him one of her assortment of adorable grins and proceeded to turn the pages. He gazed down and watched the smile come to her face.

"Beals Island," she said wistfully.

"From the air—the birthplace of the sweetest girl in Maine.

"Can I keep the book long enough to make a photocopy of the picture? It'll be in black and white but that'll be okay."

"Baby girl—I bought it for you. Forget the photocopy." Brian took a step backwards, retreating slowly from the cottage. "Join me later at the main house for lunch. Is it a date?" Mary nodded yes.

Summer was on the wane in New Hampshire. It was early September and with it brought the end of vacation time for Margaret's employees. At present, her staff was toiling largely on write-up work and the annual audit engagements for the firm's non-profit organizations. The Labor Day weekend had just concluded. On this day, a sunny Tuesday, the most significant item on the business calendar was the arrival of two, new employees, Amanda Boisvert and Christopher Treadwell. Both young professionals had been recruited the prior winter from their respective colleges with Ms. Boisvert having completed a single semester internship with the firm. On this morning the pair of recruits would begin a week of orientation starting with an hour apiece behind closed doors with Mrs. Kelly.

Miss Boisvert was first to sit with Margaret. She came to the organization with an impressive 3.88 grade point average and a short stack of glowing staff evaluations from her few months in house as an intern. Amanda, somewhat over-weight and pale of complexion, arrived perfectly dressed on her first day of regular employment. Ms. Boisvert's hour with her new employer was uneventful. The cornerstone of discussion was Margaret's absolute authority on company policy and decision making.

Second to sit with her was Christopher Treadwell. The handsome, young man from Massachusetts was greeted with a warm smile from Mrs. Kelly as he entered the office and claimed an upholstered chair across the desk from her.

"So the day has finally arrived," she announced, tossing out an open ended statement and waiting on a response.

"Yes, it's here—and the jitters right along with it." Margaret stared coyly across the desk at him. Chris Treadwell was pleasing to the eye, from his perfectly styled, medium length hair to his flawless, tanned complexion. She had spotted him nine months earlier out of a multitude of interviewees at Bentley College. At that time she had overridden Vern Butler's negative appraisal and invited the young man up to Manchester for a second interview. So strong were her instincts for the young man's charisma that an exception was made to the firm's manda-tory 3.5 minimum grade point average, Margaret going on to explain to Vern that Christopher's intangibles outweighed any arbitrary minimum requirement.

For Margaret, the time spent in isolation with Chris sped by when compared to the same period played out with the studious Boisvert woman. When the all important subject of the CPA exam came up, she was quick to share an anecdote with her youthful, male employee.

"The year I passed all four parts of the exam, I went so far as to take advantage of anything and everything I could. You see, Chris, back then it wasn't just that you needed a seventy-five on all four parts of the exam, it was also important to do well in relation to the others taking the exam with you. So that May when I sat, it didn't matter whether the weather was warm or cool, I wore a pair of mint green, short shorts along with a pair of sexy sandals. When they opened the doors and let us into the examination hall, I grabbed a desk at the very front of the room. Now I may not be the prettiest girl in the world—"

"No, Mrs. Kelly, you're an extremely attractive woman," interrupted the young man.

"Thank you, Chris. As I was saying, if nothing else, I had a terrific pair of legs. So what I did for the two and a half days of the exam was to put them on display at the front of the room—knowing the seventy percent or so sitting with me were male and within eyeshot. As I saw it, they would be, at minimum, inconvenienced—if not downright distracted." Young Treadwell roared with laughter at the story, complimenting his new boss on her resourcefulness.

An hour after his arrival, Margaret stood up and reached across the desk, shaking Chris Treadwell's hand and officially welcoming him to the firm. He offered her a warm, borderline flirtatious smile in return and exited the office. She turned and walked across the room to a window, glancing out at the alleyway between Stark and Market Streets, and considered matters of both a business and personal nature. A floor below, a destitute, likely homeless female walked awkwardly by, careful not to put any appreciable weight on her right foot. Reaching a spot on the pavement affording an open view of the building, the shabbily dressed individual stopped abruptly and gazed up at the window. In a split second the two women found their eyes locked in what could be described as visual combat. Margaret stared downward, making no effort to hide her revulsion for the woman's condition. On closer scrutiny, she thought how this pathetic creature might not be too many years older than herself. The test of wills went on no more than ten seconds before the woman dropped her eyes to the ground and hobbled away, but not before breaking out in an almost hysterical laugh. Returning to her desk, Margaret glanced down on the comprehensive work schedule for the month of September. Of special interest to her was the week long preliminary audit work up north in Gorham, New Hampshire. The client, a large auto dealership, was one of the few in the office requiring overnight travel. Jim Doucette, Claire Gagnon's steady boyfriend, was listed as the in-charge on the engagement. Margaret thought back to a recent conversation with her friend. Claire had come across a credit card receipt for an engagement ring in Jim's apartment. She saw an opening, a legitimate excuse, to put a plan in motion. She buzzed Doucette in his office.

"Jim, would you have any problem with me pulling you off the audit up in Gorham and rescheduling you somewhere closer to home?"

"Is there a problem, Margaret?" he came back, a hint of anxiety in his voice.

"No, no, no—I'm just not sure my best friend in the whole, wide world could survive a week away from her honey, that's all."

"Actually, it would take a little pressure off of me if you did."

"It's done then. Drop the files in my office when you have a minute. I'll plug you into this little non-profit in Exeter in its place. Where do you generally stay when you're up there?"

"I stay at the Town and Country Motor Inn. It's a couple of miles down the road from the client."

"Nice?"

"Quite."

Amanda Boisvert and Christopher Treadwell were the guests of Margaret and Vern Butler for lunch on this day. Most of the conversation was provided by Margaret and Vern. The new employees were content to listen and learn and, most importantly, not shoot themselves in the foot through an inappropriate comment or opinion. Immediately upon returning from lunch, Margaret called down to the front desk.

"Gretchen, have you already booked Jim Doucette and his assistant up in Gorham for later this month?"

"I was planning on getting it done later in the week."

"Well then, don't bother with it. I'll take care of it myself. Please get me the phone number for the Town and Country Motor Inn, will you?"

Armed with all the information she needed, she closed the door to her office and punched out the number for the White Mountain inn. She made her booking instructions clear and precise.

"I want two of your best rooms—adjoining, they must be adjoining—and by that I mean an inside door connecting the two units. Can you accommodate me on this?" she asked.

"Yes, Mrs. Kelly This will not be a problem."

"I want four nights, September twenty-fifth through the twenty-eighth. You have the company credit card on file. I'm told we use the facility for all our work up there." In seconds the reservation was made and the details finalized. She put down the telephone, leaned back in her chair, and closed her eyes. A moment later she reached down and scratched in a change to the September schedule. It now read: Coos County Motors, Gorham, NH, M. Kelly & C. Treadwell.

XXI

By mid September, Bedford's Kelly household was functioning in as close to normal fashion as could be expected. Jenny was enrolled at nearby Saint Anselm's College, allowing her to live at home while working toward her bachelor's degree. Following the death of his stepfather, Brendan returned and began his senior year at Manchester's Southside High School. Days before, Margaret shocked the household by announcing she had signed a one year lease on an oceanfront home at Wells Beach. Commencing on October 1st, the family's second home was a two and a half story beach house on the ocean side of Atlantic Avenue. As she explained it, the owner's recently inherited a house at Boothbay Harbor twice the size of their Wells Beach residence. They planned to spend the next year living in Boothbay Harbor. If the new residence proved to be to their liking, Margaret would be given first refusal on the Atlantic Avenue property with the year's lease payments applied towards the sales price. Since Labor Day, Brian's visits home had become more numerous and for longer durations. However, during this period he had grown concerned over what he perceived to be a wall thrown up by his wife between them. For this reason, he was pleased when she unexpectedly turned to him one evening as they lie in bed and asked for his assistance.

"Kelly, if you wouldn't mind, I wonder if you could cover for me at home the week after next. I've got to be out of town—up near Berlin—and I'd like to know you were here holding things together," she said, rolling onto her side, her breath warming his neck.

"What are we talking about here, every night?"

"Could you manage that?"

"Yeah, I could, if it's only for a week. Is this a new client or something?"

"No, it's one of Jim Doucette's—but I told you he's popped the question to Claire, and I didn't have the heart to separate them so soon after." She augmented a soft, seductive quality in her voice with the movement of her fingertips down the middle of his chest and through his pubic region, her fingers coming to rest on his penis.

"Does this mean you're finally coming out of the funk you've been in lately?" he asked. Her response was non-verbal, gently biting his ear. She studied her husband, watching his breathing grow deeper by the second and feeling his arousal within her fingers. With each passing moment she sensed him grow weaker as the need for her touch intensified. She covered his mouth with her own and felt him reach full erection. Paralyzed by the arousal she brought to him, Brian remained still while she mounted her helpless partner, directing him deep inside her. Seeming to summon every ounce of remaining strength, he reached up and

149

pulled her mouth back to his own.

"I do love you, Maggie May. You are my everything."

"And I love you, Brian. I love you."

By the third week in September only two chambermaids remained on the payroll. The marketing efforts over the winter assured the Atlantic Coast Lodge more than its share of bus tour traffic, keeping the complex's vacancy rate under thirty-five percent between Labor and Columbus Days. The slower paced off-season also allowed the manager and his assistant to take entire blocks of days off at a time. On the Friday preceding his wife's weeklong business trip, Brian sat at his computer, inputting financial data and generating payroll. It was what he considered the first real autumn day of the year, the temperature not expected to exceed sixty degrees. On this day, Mary had broken her long string of leaving him a piece of fruit. In point of fact, he had not set eyes on his young friend all morning.

The thirty-two members of a bus tour had just departed when he decided to pay a surprise visit to his favorite chambermaid. Tearing her payroll check from a series of disbursements, he set off down the hill to the lower cottages. In time, he found her inside a cottage near the extreme northeast edge of the property.

"Where's my dream girl?" he called out as he entered the two bedroom unit.

"Hard at work in the bathroom," she answered.

"Well, I've brought you down your paycheck and I'm bored as hell up in the office. I could use someone to talk to for a few minutes."

"You can leave it on the kitchen table. I really wish I could take the time to gab, but I can't." Brian reflected on Mary's words and grew suspicious. Crossing the living room, he planted himself in the doorway to the bathroom.

"You don't even have two minutes for your old swimming partner?" he inquired, staring down at the back of her head.

"Sorry," came her reply. He crouched down beside her. Placing his hand on her cheek, he turned her face toward him. His eyes widened at the sight of swelling around her left eye and an upper lip split and caked with dried blood.

"It was an accident, Brian. There's no need to get upset."

"It was that prick you live with, right?" he roared.

"Stay out of it. Duane said he was sorry." He jumped to his feet and stormed from the cottage. "Stay out of it. I need that house for me and Roddy," she called out to him as he raced up the hill. He met Millie at the door to the office.

"I don't look too desperate, do I? Is the ink dry on my check yet?" she joked.

"Millie, I need you to cover for forty-five minutes. I know it's your day off. Just this once for me," he urged excitedly.

"Go ahead—go ahead."

Brian hustled to the Ford and sped off in the direction of Sanford. Fifteen minutes passed before he turned the pickup off Route 109 and up a short series of side streets. Exiting the truck at full speed, his spirits soared at the sight of Duane Cross tinkering with a car engine in the yard beside the house. Brian sailed over the property's dilapidated, picket fence and was on the man in seconds, striking him on the temple with a fist and causing him to drop the wrench held in his right hand. He reeled backwards, falling against the side of the vehicle. Dragging the man by a straggle of hair, he pulled him twenty feet behind the house and away from the eyes of any passing motorists or pedestrians. Convinced they were adequately hidden from sight, Brian drove the side of the man's face into the ground.

"If you ever—ever lay a hand on that girl again, it'll be the last thing you ever do. Do you fucking understand me?" When there was no response, he drove his knee to the side of his victim's face. "Do you fucking understand?" This time the man responded, albeit weekly.

"I understand," muttered Cross, spitting soil from his mouth in the process. Still not through, Brian dragged the side of the man's face along the gravelly soil another two or three feet, finally bringing the full weight of his knee down on his victim's jawbone.

"If you so much as touch that girl—or if our little discussion here is reported to anyone—the authorities—anyone, you won't hear from me, you'll hear from a couple of pricks who will make you wish you were never fucking born! This is fucking child's play here. If anyone so much as asks me about our discussion, I will see to it that you get to meet these two pricks. Now tell me what's going to happen," ordered Brian.

"Nothing, please, I've had enough," he mumbled, his spirit evidently broken. Brian rose to his feet, relieving the pressure being brought to bear on his victim.

"Remember everything I've said here. Oh, and stay down where you are until you hear my truck drive away. If I see you pop up even a second early, I'll come back and repeat this whole fucking exercise." Returning directly to his vehicle, he wasted no time loitering on the scene, knowing Cross could have a firearm somewhere on the premises.

Using the drive back from Sanford to regain his composure, he entered the office while Millie was in the process of registering an elderly couple. Brian shot his friend an approving smile and proceeded to the kitchen. He barely had time to pour himself a cup of coffee when his assistant manager stuck her head through the doorway.

"Is everything okay?" He lifted his eyes from the rim of the mug and nodded. "Mission accomplished—I think."

"And what mission was that?"

"I paid Mary's roommate a visit."

"Why?"

"Mill, she came in to work all busted up. He must have belted her around last night. She stayed away from the office this morning. I happened to go down to the cottages to visit her and give her her check. That's when I saw what she looked like. So I went over and paid the cowardly bastard a visit."

"You didn't hit him, I hope."

"Oh, I hit him all right. I also dragged him around the yard and told him what would happen if he raised a finger to her again."

"Brian, you can't be doing things like that. He can have you arrested for something like that."

"My hunch is he won't be doing that anytime soon." The woman moved from the doorway, pulling a chair up next to her friend of fifteen years. She looked squarely into his eyes, alerting him she was planning to do more than make small talk.

"We've known each other a long, long time now—and I think we can both level with each other. Am I right?" He nodded yes. "All I'm telling you here is you've got to be a little more responsible on matters like this, particularly matters involving pretty, young women like Mary Porterfield. Now heaven knows I'm not saying a bad word about that little girl. She is one of the sweetest, little things I've ever met. What I'm saying is that a female like her can turn your head and have you doing things you wouldn't normally do."

"There's nothing like that happening—"

"I didn't say it was. But word got back to me about you two the day of the chambermaid party—in the pool, I mean. That little girl is quite fond of you, fond enough to act up with people looking on and all. She sees in you all the things lacking in *all* the men she's known in her life—and in the back of her mind she knows she has the power to turn a man's head."

"Millie, you have to know how incredibly much I'm in love with Maggie. You, more than anyone, know how much crap I have to put up with because of her. And I put up with it because I love her so very much. I wouldn't risk what I have for anything."

"I'm glad to hear that," she said.

"Is Maggie perfect? No, she's far from it. There are a thousand things I'd like to change about her. I don't like being married to an agnostic. I don't like her caustic mouth. I could go on and on."

"I can only imagine what she has to say about me."

"Don't think you're alone. It's my entire circle of friends. She's a snob! But that's *who* she is and *how* she is. We're married—married in the house of God, and I love her so much it hurts."

"I'm sure all that is true. I'm just saying I've seen you act differently around our Mary—different than around anyone except Angelique—and your wife of course." The conversation paused with Brian appearing to regroup his thoughts.

"Okay, I'll be totally honest. If this were five years ago and Maggie wasn't in my life—yeah, I suppose Mary is someone I could have embraced. I'd be a liar if I said anything different. But it's not."

"I'm not going to belabor this. That little girl has charms. Think of what just happened in the last hour—and how you reacted when you saw her harmed. Be very careful."

XXII

Brian arrived back in Bedford late on Sunday afternoon, fulfilling his promise to his wife. For the next week he would function in her place as the authority figure at the house. His arrival found everyone at home. Quietly, he tiptoed upstairs to the second floor. Down the hall, he stopped in front of Colleen's bedroom. He picked up on her voice from behind the door, intermittently mouthing words and singing a tune. He pushed on the door, slowly swinging it inward. The sound of the movement was picked up by the toddler, prompting her to stop singing and glance in his direction. Her mouth dropped open from curiosity. The proud father burst into the room.

"It's Jelly Bean and she's saying terrible things about her daddy!" he called out in a frenzied voice, grabbing her from atop the bed and swinging her around the room at arm's length. The child cried out in surprise, one long scream followed by a steam of laughter.

"Colleen, your daddy's home for a whole week. It'll be just you and me. Does that sound good to you?" The toddler excitedly attempted to form the words and voice her pleasure.

"Daddy—you'll push me in the wagon outside and down the street?"

"Absolutely—and maybe we can chase Moira around the house until she falls down."

"Moira fall down in the grass," added the twenty-one month old.

"And we can make Brendan sleep out in the pool shed on the Astroturf—and make Jenny wash the dishes all day and vacuum all night."

"Jenny will vacuum the floor for us," repeated the girl to Brian's delight.

"When mommy's gone tomorrow this becomes daddy and Jelly Bean's house, right?" he asked, drawing his daughter to him.

"It really sounds like this house will be in the hands of a real adult," sounded a voice from the hall. Margaret had heard her husband from the bedroom and decided to investigate.

"Keogh, by the time you get back on Friday you won't recognize the place. This house's in desperate need of a man's touch—and with my cultured, gentrified upbringing in Lowell, there's no telling what I can have this place looking like. The ordinary is about to become the extraordinary."

"Kelly, if I so much as find a throw pillow out of place you'll pay in blood," threatened his wife.

"Did you hear that Colleen, mommy is trying to get tough with me. She's already forgotten the countless beatings she's taken over the past three years."

"You heard me—no funny stuff. And I'm dead serious," warned the woman before returning to the master bedroom.

A few minutes had passed before Brian meandered up the hall and joined his wife in their bedroom. He found her busy packing. She did not acknowledge his appearance in the doorway.

"You know you'll be sorely missed this week, don't you?"

"Well, I certainly hope so."

"It's going to be great spending all this time with Jelly Bean and the gang, but I'm going to miss having you around. It's amazing how our lives seem to be out of sync so many times of the year."

"Brian, I do appreciate you coming to my rescue here on short notice."

"That's what love will do for you—sacrifice, sacrifice, sacrifice," he responded, sending a stabbing knot of guilt through her stomach.

"On Friday, I took a few minutes to make you a 'to do' list. It's taped to one of the kitchen cabinets."

"You laid out a work schedule for me? Are you kidding me?"

"Well, it's too late to use the pool! Don't bitch, I've allotted twenty minutes a day for time with Colleen," she teased, tossing him a sideways glance. He crossed the bedroom, wrapped his arms around her, and peppered the side of her face with kisses. In the process, his eyes dropped to the articles being assembled for the trip.

"You're bringing your racket?"

"I should have some time for relaxing—although probably not a whole lot." He released his wife, falling backwards onto the bed.

"Now are you going up there by yourself or will someone be with you?"

"I'll be dragging along a grunt—one of the new kids we brought in a few weeks ago," she replied, providing the information in a matter-of-fact manner.

"Male or female?"

"Male. Why, are you jealous?"

"Damn right I am! What does this guy look like? This guy has to have the cushiest assignment on the face of the earth." Brian rolled from atop the mattress and maneuvered himself directly behind his wife. Placing his hands on her hips, he drew himself up to her backside and kissed it repeatedly through her jeans. "Yes, Mrs. Kelly. I'll do whatever you say, Mrs. Kelly. Did you say *jump*, Mrs. Kelly? How high, Mrs. Kelly?"

"Let me get this straight, Brian—are you impersonating my assistant or just being yourself?" He paused for a moment before placing a final kiss on her buttocks.

"It's a little of both, unfortunately—a little of both. So Maggie May, you didn't answer my question, what does this guy look like?"

"He looks like every other male accountant on the face of the earth. What do you think he looks like?"

"Claire's engaged to Jimmy Doucette—and he's one of your accountants," countered Brian.

"Jim's an exception. You know—someone's beginning to sound very insecure here," she suggested, turning from her packing and staring her husband square in the eye.

"It would seem so. Oh well, given our advancing years, who in their right mind would give either of us a second look?"

"Do I hear a challenge here?" she shot back. "And on the subject of advancing years, speak for yourself and not for me."

"Come on, Keogh, you know damn well you're still death on wheels—looks wise. Lighten up." Brian, still kneeling on the floor beneath his wife, snaked his way around her body, applying a final peck to her inner thigh. She resumed packing without acknowledging the affection.

Unexpectedly, Brendan materialized in the doorway. He appeared not to have witnessed the exchange of words seconds before.

"Brian, if you have a few minutes to speak with me this evening I'd appreciate it," he requested. The man rose to his feet, leaving his wife with an affectionate squeeze on the shoulder.

"This would be as good a time as any," he said, joining his son in the hallway.

"How about if we go for a walk outside and get some fresh air?"

"A walk outside, huh. Not if it means another go around down the street, kid. I'm not anywhere near the fighting machine I was a couple of months ago," he kidded. "I'm two months older—two months slower—two months softer." His son laughed while they descended the stairs, making their way out the front door and down the driveway.

"It's just that I haven't had much time here at the house with you since school started and with my job. I'm not sure I even had a chance to thank you properly for letting me use the truck to go home. I want you to know how much I really appreciated that. Man, when I told mom about it, she couldn't believe it. She really respects you. I guess she always has but couldn't talk about it considering the way things were."

"Maggie told me that you were really glad you went home to see Jack and be with your mother."

"Yeah, he was my dad for most of the time I was growing up—until he got sick a couple of years ago. It wound up being a good thing I left when I did. He didn't hang on very long after I got back. Anyway, after the funeral and after my sister and brothers had left, I had some time to spend with mom—just talking and, you know, keeping her company. One thing I really found interesting was her telling me the story about how you brought her to the dentist when she had a bad toothache—when Bubba was away fishing or something—and paid for the dentist out of your own pocket. What was really cool was the way she talked to me like I was an adult, telling me how you brought her home and put her to bed after she passed out from exhaustion—and never touched her even though you sort of had a crush on her at the time. She told me how she came to you the next night to thank you—and how you guys made love that night—which led to me. She explained to me things like they were—like I was a close friend and not just her youngest."

"Your mother was a beautiful lady—and she still is, I'm sure. We were both lonely at the time and just needed somebody. Our personal situation was hopeless but only she was smart and mature enough to end things. Brendan, I can still remember how much it hurt when she moved away. It would have hurt even more if I'd known about you. By the time our paths crossed again, she had met Jack and was in love with him. I was still alone. Do you remember coming to my place in Wells and using the pool? That was the day I found out you were my son." Walking abreast, the two men proceeded down the country road and away from the house.

"I've been way too hard on you, Brian. That time at home with mom got my head clear. I'm just taking this time to say I'm sorry for all the shit I gave you."

"Apology accepted—and the matter forgotten," he declared, reaching around the teenager and pulling the young man against himself. "Can we turn around now before we reach 101 and have to call the house for a ride back?"

The walk back up Joppa Hill Road was passed in casual conversation. For the first time, Brian shared with his son some of their common, family history. This included a description and account of his paternal grandmother, Elizabeth. At Brendan's urging, he also recounted events from the summer of 1991. That was the summer Jenny spent working for Brian at the complex.

Margaret kept a low profile on this Sunday evening in September. Content to sip quietly on a glass of wine in the corner while the rest of the room buzzed with activity from other family members, she mentally visited the circumstances about to unfold in the White Mountains over the next few days. The thought of her time away with her young employee excited her. She drew solace from the fact that the family, particularly Brian, would never have any knowledge of the well orchestrated events about to play out in the shadow of Mount Washington. It would be fun, she thought, a challenge for her womanly wiles and a possible step into the heretofore unexplored province of infidelity.

When Margaret excused herself from the room the group was in the final stages of a hotly contested game of *Trivial Pursuit*. Brian assured his wife he would join her upstairs shortly, but first needed to help teammates Moira and Colleen dispatch of Jenny and Brendan. She was already under the covers and feigning loss of consciousness when her husband discreetly entered the bedroom and leaned over her.

"It's amazing how brilliant I look when your enlarged brain is on the sidelines," he whispered under the covers.

"Happy to be of service," she answered through a faint yawn.

"Keogh, I've decided to make you an offer you can't refuse. In recognition of your tremendous sacrifice on behalf of the family—venturing up into the wilds of the mountains—facing incredible hardships—"

"Kelly, I'm staying at a luxury resort for God's sake—a little less drama if you will."

"In recognition of your sacrifice, I am submitting myself to you on this night—submitting myself for your pleasure. I will not refuse you any pleasure, even it will debase or dehumanize me. Anything, even if I won't be able to look myself in the mirror for a month. You ask for it, and I'll perform it. Nothing is beyond your request."

"God damn it! I've got my alarm set for five-fifteen. Give me a fucking break here. I just want to go to sleep," she spat out. He hoisted himself from the bed and walked to the door. She heard his hand grip the doorknob. An extended pause followed. She knew an apology of some kind was fitting under the circumstances but withheld one. The door opened and closed in the next instant and the time for action had passed.

XXIII

*T*he sporadic, pulsating sound of the alarm clock split the air in the darkened bedroom. Reaching to the night table, she made contact with the OFF button on her first attempt. Margaret raised herself to the sitting position and extended her arms. The room was absolutely silent. She reached down to the mattress, expecting to pick up on Brian's body beneath the covers. Instantly, she realized she was alone in bed. After allowing her head to fall back onto the pillow, she rolled herself sideways, her bare feet making contact with the carpeted floor. Through half opened eyes, she stumbled toward the master bathroom.

The grandfather clock in the downstairs hallway was striking six while Margaret hauled her luggage downstairs, staging it by the front entrance. Chris was expecting her in the parking lot of his condo at seven. The drive to Manchester would take no more than twenty minutes. On a hunch, she walked down the hall and stuck her head through the living room doorway. She expected to find Brian sprawled out on the couch or propped up in the recliner, no doubt having fallen asleep in front of the television. The empty living room caught her by surprise. Thinking back on what transpired in their bedroom a few hours earlier and pushing thoughts of her husband to the back of her mind, she stepped across the hall and into the kitchen. There, she assembled everything she needed to prepare a pot of coffee. With the brewing light of the coffee maker on, she fell back into a chair and allowed her mind to play with events about to take place. Her stomach was literally fluttering with anticipation of the trip north to Gorham and her time with young Chris Treadwell. Closing her eyes to the sound of brewing coffee, she savored the feeling of anticipation, excitement, adventure, and even a degree of nervousness. This was uncharted territory for her. Her pleasant daydream was interrupted by the sound of footsteps moving down the hallway from above. Convinced it was her husband, she planted herself squarely at the table, the picture of poise and resolve. Her eyes widened in surprise at the sight of Moira stepping into the room.

"And sure I thought I heard someone moving about," said the nanny, decked out in flannel pajamas.

"Early departure for the White Mountains—I want to be up there and on the job no later than nine-thirty," explained Margaret.

"I noticed the guest room door was closed, Mrs. Kelly. Did someone come in after I retired last night?" The teenager's question answered the question of Brian's whereabouts.

"Mr. Kelly wanted a full night's sleep and decided to isolate himself from my racket in the morning," she answered, pleased with the credibility of her lie. "Any last minute questions before I go?" The Irish girl shook her head.

"He's going to let me prepare a few dishes from home. I'll be interested to see if the rest of the family enjoys them."

"Don't tell me—let me guess—lots of lamb and even more potatoes," she cracked, shooting the young woman a combination smirk and grin. Her employee of eighteen months granted her a half-hearted smile and moved toward the door.

"I'll be seeing if I can get a wee bit more sleep before the angel begins to stir," she said.

"It was a joke, Moira. Don't go getting all teary eyed over it. It was a joke." The teenager turned back to the lady of the house.

"Sometime the hurt's in the tone and not the words, Mrs. Kelly." Margaret looked up at the teenager and narrowed her eyes.

"Don't you go and get huffy with me, missy. You do and I'll have you out on your ass so fast your head will spin. And while I'm at it, here's a reminder: you're here because of Mr. Kelly—and not me. It was his idea to bring some little harp over here, not mine. So you're walking on thin ice when you pull this victim shit with me. Am I making myself clear?" Avoiding eye contact, Moira nodded yes and retreated for the hall. "Oh, and while I have your attention—drop that whole family thing when you talk about the household. We hired you—we didn't adopt you. You are not—nor will you ever be—part of the family." Her words still echoing through the room, Margaret picked up on the sound of the girl's steps as she raced back to the second floor. She already realized she had been hard on the young woman. This was indisputable. A part of her was sorry for the attack but there was something in her, a dark force that caused her to lash out at others. She had a compulsive need to break down other individuals. It did not bring her pleasure but more a state of contentedness. As she saw it, it was evidence of her person, position and power. On this occasion, her lashing out was probably attributable to Brian's decision to sleep in the spare room and away from their bed. A night spent on the living room couch could be rationalized away as accidental. A night in the spare room could not be.

After pulling the BMW out of the garage and in front of the house, she loaded the vehicle with her luggage. She followed this with a final pass through the house. She had now been up nearly an hour and a half without a sign of any family members. She was angry at Brian. She fought off an impulse to return upstairs and confront him but settled on a different strategy. When he finally awoke, he would find her gone, no good-byes and no words of apology. Gulping down the remaining coffee from her cup, Margaret walked to the front door. From upstairs came the sound of Colleen's voice from behind her bedroom door. She ascended the stairs, ducking into the baby's room with her arms extended.

"Mommy," cried out the child. The woman raised her finger to her lips. She gave the toddler a kiss and backed away.

"I'll be back in a few days sweetheart," she whispered before disappearing from the room.

Margaret steered the vehicle out of the driveway and down Joppa Hill Road, her adventure rolling into motion. The morning was cool and clear, the precise weather that made autumn her favorite season. Sunlight was catching the top of the trees as she drove the two plus miles to Route 101. Reaching the state road, she was forced to wait on a stream of cars traveling eastward. She took this opportunity to check her makeup in the mirror. She was pleased with what she saw. Not even a hint of tiredness under the eyes, she thought to herself.

Her male assistant was standing by the front door of his condominium when the BMW turned into the driveway. His apartment was in the north end of the city, the section considered most desirable by a majority of Manchester's residents. The young man was impeccably dressed in a tailored suit, charcoal in color, white shirt and tie. His appearance cried out conservative which pleased her immensely. Chris was tall, approximately six feet, with sandy colored hair.

"I've left enough room in the back of the car for your suitcase," she called out to him. Following a brief struggle angling his luggage into place, the trunk was closed and the handsome twenty-two year old joined his boss in the front seat.

She found the first twenty minutes or so of the trip awkward, each uncertain of the other's personality. It was Chris who tore the conversation away from the mundane and predictable and initiated some meaningful dialogue.

"Can I share something with you from way back last year when I was interviewing with the firm?" he asked, his tone relaxed.

"I think you mean *may* I share something with me, don't you?"

"I'm sorry, may I?"

"Why not—it's a long drive to Gorham."

"Back when I was interviewing with the firm—and sitting across the table from you, I remember thinking to myself if I'd ever be working one on one with you and what it'd be like." She tossed him a sideways glance, a faint smile on her face.

"And you didn't have the same thoughts in the course of your other interviews?"

"God, no! Most of the others I sat with were old, gray haired partners who seemed as uninterested in me as I was in them. Man, you were different. I probably shouldn't tell you this but a lot of the guys, the accounting majors I mean, were talking about you for the next couple of days."

"What do you mean—talking about me?"

"You know—about you being so attractive and everything—and how it would be working for you everyday."

"Well, it's nice to know my presence on campus was taken so seriously."

"But, Mrs. Kelly, it was. More than one of my profs talked about you and how sharp you were—that working under you at your firm would be a great learning experience. Not all the professors are real high on working for the large firms."

"That's nice to hear," injected Margaret as the car made its way through the capital city of Concord.

The sound of classical music reverberated through the automobile for the next few minutes with nary a word spoken. Chris seemed only half interested in a magazine he balanced on his lap.

"I thought I'd stay on 93 right on through Franconia Notch—then go up through Twin Mountain and hook up with Route 2 in Jefferson. Do you have any other suggestions?"

"Whatever you say, Mrs. Kelly. I don't think I've ever been above the notch—at least not as an adult. I'm more of a beach bum than a climber. Just give me a warm beach and lots of sun and I'm happy."

"Well then, this will interest you. I've just leased a house at Wells Beach over in Maine. It's for one year with an option to buy at the end of twelve months," she boasted, omitting the approval of the owner as a prerequisite.

"That sounds pretty exciting. Is it oceanfront?"

"Yes, we're talking the ocean side of Atlantic Avenue," she added proudly.

Following an hour of non-stimulating, highway driving, the car began the slow ascent into Franconia Notch. Chris became particularly attentive, peering out the windows at the walls of the adjacent mountain slopes and craning his neck to snatch a glimpse of the Old Man of the Mountain rock formation. Exiting the notch, the automobile sped northward through tree lined roads until it reached Twin Mountain. Margaret stopped and consulted a map, needing to find her way to Route 175 and ultimately Route 2. The auto traveled the remainder of the trip to Gorham in the shadows of Mounts Adams and Madison which towered above them from off the right side of the road. This leg of the trip had driver and passenger peering out at the colorful foliage surrounding them. Finally, they cruised down a two mile stretch of road leading to their destination, Gorham, New Hampshire.

"The Town and Country Motor Inn is about a mile in the other direction," she said while turning left onto Route 16 and heading due north toward the client's dealership. "We'll put in about six hours on site and excuse ourselves to check in at the inn. You are still up for some tennis, I hope? I noticed you packed a racket."

"Absolutely—and I've been warned about you, Mrs. Kelly—your tennis game, that is."

"Oh, please, I'm an aging ham and egger up against a college stud."

"I don't thing *aging* is a word that fits you. In fact, when someone told me you had a daughter in college I nearly flipped."

"I do my best—to fight off Father Time, that is," she answered behind a modest smile.

Day one of the audit work at Coos County Motors went smoothly. After being escorted to the conference room which would serve as their working area over the course of the audit, Margaret assigned her associate responsibility for updating and reviewing the client's internal control system. She spent the majority of the first day of field work reviewing the prior year's work papers and arranging meetings with key personnel over the course of the week. The two auditors did not break for lunch, limiting their intake of food and drink to a series of cups of coffee and a fruit cup. It was two-thirty when Margaret gave the order to begin packing up. The order given, she made her way to the levorotary, leaving Chris to put away the permanent and working files, straighten up the room, and await further instructions from his employer. Returning to the conference room, she found her assistant standing at attention next to the leather briefcases that held the audit work.

"You don't have them in the car yet?" she asked, gesturing to the satchels and the set of keys she left on the table.

"No, I guess I thought—"he muttered, seeming flustered by the critical tone in her voice. He made a clumsy pass at picking up both briefcases, dropping one on its side in the process. She took note, anxious to observe his outward reaction to her first show of absolute authority. They walked from the building side by side, the young associate laboring under the weight of two satchels and his own briefcase while Margaret strolled alongside encumbered by nothing but her designer handbag.

The plan for the remainder of the day was simple but structured. Thirty minutes after checking into their individual rooms they were to meet in the hall dressed for tennis. They would proceed to the public courts near the center of town and play best two out of three sets. It was autumn in the heart of the White Mountains and they expected the temperature to fall as the sun dropped toward the western horizon.

Chris was standing in the hallway when Margaret emerged from her room. Instinctively, his eyes were drawn downward to her long, sculptured legs on display beneath her tennis whites. She, too, sized up her male associate. He did not possess the classical, male body of her husband, broad shoulders tapering down to narrow hips and waist. Chris was built more bull like, very broad shoulders with muscular arms and a thick torso. He was probably destined to fill in during middle age and develop a rounded stomach and oversized backside. But for now, in the prime of his life, he was quite appealing.

"The time for talking has passed. Bragging rights are on the line, my young friend, and may the better man—or should I say person—win," she proclaimed with lighthearted bravado.

"Those of us who are about to die salute you," chimed in Chris, mimicking the words spoken in so many gladiator movies. The response brought a chuckle from his boss who wrapped an arm around his broad shoulders and guided him down the hallway and out to the parking lot. It was only a momentary drive down the road to the town center. As expected, they found Gorham's public courts empty. Wasting no time, Margaret opened a can of new tennis balls and motioned Chris to the far end of the court. For the next five minutes they volleyed, neither putting appreciable pace on their shots. Following a particularly long rally, she walked back to the service line and practiced her serve, concentrating more on putting the ball in play than delivering with any velocity. Chris, on the other hand, delivered his practice serves at maximum speed. By the close of the ten minute warm-up, Margaret had sized up her opponent. Chris had played the game before, that was evident. He brought a strong serve and a reasonably good forehand to the competition, she thought. She would have to analyze the remainder of his game under playing conditions.

Margaret offered Chris his choice of serving or receiving first. He chose to begin the first set at the service line. His decision proved a wise one. She was only able to win a single point in the first game. Her twenty-two year old adversary won the first game by virtue of an ace ripped along the center line so hard she was barely able to flick at it. At the sound of the ball hitting the chain link fence behind her, he pumped his arm in triumph. She, too, was able to hold serve on her first attempt, although it did require more effort. Already analyzing his game, she deduced Chris had played a fair amount of doubles just from his propensity to work the ball at sharp angles during rallies. With the score knotted at one and Chris on his way to winning another easy game on serve, Margaret's probing ground strokes seemed to expose a chink in the young man's game. After purposely avoiding the corners of the court, negating his talent for playing sharp, difficult angles, she began driving the ball continually to his backhand. His response was merely to block the shots and send the ball back weakly. After losing two consecutive points to his employer, he did manage to salvage the game with a powerful ace driven wide to Margaret's backhand. However, in her mind, the genie was out of the bottle. She tested her theory during the next game, sending ground stroke after ground stroke to his backhand. She breezed through the game, not allowing him to take a point. Seeing his female opponent's strategy take hold of the tempo and course of the match, Chris tried making adjustments but with no positive results. His attempts at revamping his backhand proved erratic, his shots carrying long, time and time again. Meanwhile, Margaret beat up on his game with workmanlike precision, successfully driving the ball over and over to his left side. She completely dominated the last four games of the set and took it six games to two.

The second set picked up where the first ended. Margaret thought she detected telltale signs that the air was coming out of her Generation X employee. To make matters worse for the young male, a mixed group of teenagers had gathered nearby, seating themselves on a picnic table. The girls in the group began letting out roars of approval on those occasions when Margaret won a contested point. For her part, she played to the crowd, intentionally allowing rallies to drag on by removing pace from the ball and requiring Chris to run back and forth behind the end line. For forty-five minutes she toyed with her overmatched challenger, like a cat playing with its captured prey. She ended the second set and the match with an ace, her first of the afternoon. Chris almost appeared relieved as he walked to the net to congratulate his boss. The gesture prompted a cheer from the teenagers seated nearby.

"That was an ugly, ugly beating, Mrs. Kelly," he conceded good-naturedly.

"I had to keep the heat on Chris—you're a good player."

"I just didn't have an answer for what you were doing."

"Tennis is a physical game of chess—which is why I love it so." She reached over the net and applied a hug. His body was moist with perspiration. "What if we catch something quick and light for dinner—maybe have a pop in the lounge back at the inn, and then I'll let you do a little studying back in your room." He agreed and the pair found a restaurant nearby on the main street.

Over the course of the meal, Margaret began to question whether she had the resolve to follow through with her fantasy and mount an assault on the young man's virtue. She was tested when thoughts of Brian and Colleen drifted into her consciousness. Following brief periods of doubt, she dismissed these second thoughts. As she saw it, her game plan was airtight: an indiscretion far from the eyes of family and friends, no one to be hurt, no harm done. She saw this undertaking as just another challenge, a much needed boost for her slumping self image and ego. Her ability to seduce a young man barely older than Jenny would go a long way toward extinguishing the bonfire of self doubt created by the onslaught of middle age. She had already reasoned away any guilt from this small indiscretion. It meant nothing beyond the thrill of a seduction and a night, or two or three, of sexual pleasure.

"Do you want to hear something pretty funny?" Chris asked as they walked across the parking lot after dinner.

"Sure, go ahead."

"For the last few days I've been struggling with whether to go all out and win the tennis match up here or let you win—because you're my boss and all and not to upset you." She hooked her arm around him and tugged him against her.

"Think of all the stress you put yourself through for nothing," she said behind a flirtatious glance. It was only a short drive back to the inn, no more than a mile. When Chris grew quiet she subtly employed her peripheral vision and thought she caught him admiring her legs as she maneuvered the car pedals below. They were almost back to the facility. Looking out the side window, Margaret caught sight of a pair of golfers attempting to squeeze in the final, precious minutes of dusk on the nearby course.

"I've already instructed my husband to retire me to the dog track if he ever catches me with a golf club in my hand. That would be a sure sign I was over the hill." The words barely out of her mouth, she regretted them. What was she doing talking about her husband under these circumstances? She glanced across the front seat. Chris showed no reaction to her statement beyond a polite smile. With the sign for the Town and Country Motor Inn just ahead, she steered the BMW up the driveway and into the general parking area.

"Chris, I hope I can depend on you to join me for at least one drink in the lounge. Keep in mind, it's on the company."

"Yes, of course," he replied, but with little enthusiasm. They stepped out into the brisk, autumn air, still dressed in their tennis attire. The path to the inn's lounge led them through the main lobby. A middle aged woman behind the front desk looked up from her paperwork and flashed a smile. Beneath their feet, the plush, green carpet felt good after the pounding from the tennis court. Reaching the door to the lounge they paused, surveying the large, open room. To their immediate right was the bar, the stools less than half occupied. Margaret's eyes scanned the room, eventually locking in on a vacant table about midway along the far wall. She beckoned to Chris and strode across the floor, mindful that a majority of the men in attendance were following her progress. Wearing tennis whites and her legs still taut from two sets on the court, her presence literally commanded their attention. She led her assistant to a three foot square table surrounded on three sides by chairs but offering a small, cushioned couch angled against the wall. Reaching the far side of the spacious lounge, Margaret claimed the couch and motioned Chris to the chair facing her, his back to the room. It was only seconds before a waiter approached them. Introducing himself as Jeff, the well-groomed man in his mid to late twenties took their beverage order, his eyes never leaving Margaret the entire time.

"I'm afraid I don't have a good track record drinking Singapores. I'll have to watch myself," she confessed. Her assistant groped for a clever response but came up empty.

"I stuck with light beer—considering my study time later on." Following a day spent in relative ease, she thought he might be tightening up.

The table fell quiet for what was no more than thirty seconds but long enough to spread a veil of awkwardness over the proceedings.

"Chris, I know you've only been with the firm less than a month but maybe long enough to provide me with some feedback. What do my employees think of me? What do they say about me when they gather together and I'm not around?"

"They respect you a lot as far as I can tell," he answered diplomatically.

"By *respect* do you mean *fear?*"

"I'm not sure fear is the right word. Early on you hear about who's really sharp and all—and everyone agrees you're the sharpest person in the office—hands down." Pleased with his response, she smiled at the young man, her blue eyes riveted on his. At that moment the waiter arrived back at the table with the beverages.

"Will there be anything else?" he inquired, flashing Margaret a broad grin and the hint of a mischievous wink. She responded with an expressionless stare, her eyes frozen with condescension. It was a glance honed to perfection over the years fending off unwanted attention from the opposite sex. Following a moment of uneasiness, the waiter paved the way for his retreat.

"I'll check back with you folks every so often to make sure everything's okay." Outwardly flustered, he turned and made his way toward another table.

After spending a few moments fiddling with the fruit slices balanced atop her Singapore sling, she sampled her drink. She responded with a facial acknowledgement that it met with her satisfaction, then lifted both legs up onto the sofa and fell back against the rear cushion. From the far end of the room there arose an audible reaction from a table of men. Involuntarily, Chris's eyes shifted from Margaret's to her long, tanned legs, now extended across the length of the furniture.

"I have a confession to make. Last night while I was packing, my husband was running a few questions by me. When he asked me about the associate who was accompanying me up here I implied you were just another typical, male accountant. Anyway, in all fairness to you—that is not true. That was just one of the many factors that went into my decision to make you an offer last winter."

"I'll be honest—I went into that interview seeing myself as a long shot."

"I learned the hard way some years back that just because someone has a 4.0 grade point average doesn't mean they'll be successful in public accounting. You have to have some amount of people skills, too." Abruptly, Margaret realized she was letting the conversation drift away from personal matters. "Pardon me if I'm getting too personal here, but I haven't heard you make mention of your life away from the office. I'm assuming a good looking kid like you has a girlfriend— or three."

"Not even one—not even close. I dated the same girl in college for the better part of three years—and that fell apart the summer between my junior and senior years. I spent my senior year mostly going to frat parties—which led to a few one night stands. But that's it."

"What a waste," she responded, hoping to send the right signal and perhaps pique his interest. On those occasions when she let her eyes shift over to the table of businessmen in the far corner of the room, the group of men she had caused to outwardly stir with the raising of her legs from the floor, she caught no less than half of them leering in her direction. She took a sip from her glass and beckoned to the waiter she had emotionally neutered ten minutes before.

"Another Singapore—and don't have the bartender change a thing, it was perfect. Chris, I hope you won't let me down and you'll have another beer?" He nodded an unenthusiastic yes.

"I have to allow myself some studying time," he confessed before excusing himself and leaving for the men's room. Her associate had scarcely cleared the door when one of the gentlemen from the far table rose to his feet and walked in Margaret's direction. She locked eyes with him as he casually made his way toward her. Dressed in a well-tailored suit, he exuded confidence. The man, appearing to be in his fifties, had a tanned, handsome face and thick, silver hair. She thought he resembled one of those middle aged models commonly seen in clothing catalogs, awkwardly posed in sportswear and holding a dumbbell or golf club.

"Someone's been playing tennis," he quipped while flashing a wide smile and gesturing toward her outfit and outstretched legs.

"Oh, don't tell me, you're a private detective—such powers of observation." There was no playfulness in her reply. He smiled down at her, a hint of apprehension already cropping up on his face.

"My name is Jim Urquhart and I'm extending you an invitation—"

"Please, stop right there with your invitation. I have absolutely no interest in your invitation and, to be honest, I'm a little insulted by it."

"The invitation goes for your son, too. There's no cause to be insulted." His words drove a spike of rage through her abdomen.

"A stranger old enough to be my father approaches me the moment my escort leaves the room—and I'm not supposed to be offended?"

"I'm prematurely gray," he said defensively.

"And prematurely wrinkled?" The man took a step backward from the confrontation just as the waiter arrived with the next round of drinks. "Thank you waiter—and while you're here I want to offer to buy Jim here his next round—not the whole table over there—just Jim. Oh, and I'll also cover the cost of a Geritol chaser." The waiter shook his head, glanced over at the man, and stepped off to an adjacent table.

"You are one, rude bitch," he declared in a hushed voice.

"And you are dismissed—Jim," she answered, dropping her eyes to the Singapore on the table in front of her.

Margaret played idly with her drink awaiting Chris's return. From across the room she picked up on grumbling, no doubt stemming from Jim's account of the verbal exchange only seconds before. Thankfully, Chris appeared in the doorway and made his way back to the table. Following his progress, she became conscious of his relative inexperience in social settings and youth in general. He reclaimed his chair and immediately found Margaret's legs propped up on him, her tennis sneakers coming to rest in his lap.

"I'm afraid my legs, bony and shapeless as they are, are getting a little too much attention from across the room," she contended, her attempt at humility coming off as insincere.

"Shapeless, huh?" he responded without further commentary. Margaret became aware that the young man was now avoiding direct eye contact with her. She was becoming discouraged. A voice from the back of her mind hinted to her that at age thirty-eight, and in a public setting, she was making a spectacle of herself. She was Margaret Kelly, mother of two, and not Margaret Keogh, who sixteen years ago walked off a college campus and into a major, Boston accounting firm, impressing and making use of male partners from day one of her employment. That young woman could break a train of thought with a simple, suggestive smile or stop a sentence at its midway point with a casual crossing of her legs. Now she was being forced to bear witness to her own clumsy attempt at a seduction. This train of thought caused her to consider what Jim from across the room was feeling at the moment. Did he feel anything akin to the mild depression settling over her? She glanced across the table at Chris. He responded with a peculiar smile. He appeared uncomfortable, if not on edge. She thought back to the hours of planning and scheming to pull this week off—and felt foolish.

It was shortly after eight-thirty when Margaret and Chris stumbled along the slightly arching hallway together, both feeling the effect of the two sets of tennis earlier. Reaching the adjacent doorways to Rooms 136 and 137, they let out a simultaneous sigh of relief and embraced.

"It's time to hit the books. Remember, if you need help with anything, don't be afraid to ask." She planted an innocent kiss on his cheek and entered her room. Her unit was spacious, large enough to easily accommodate the queen sized bed and two large bureaus. Behind the adjoining door, she made out the sound of Chris opening and closing the closet. Resisting the television set, she fumbled inside her briefcase and put her hands on some light reading material. *This is what people past their prime do—they read,* she thought. The events of the past two hours had dispirited her. Suddenly, unquestionably, she felt old. Alone in the quiet room, she remembered back to her time in high school, in the ancient 1970's. She thought back to times in her junior and senior years when she practiced yoga. She had brought a leotard with her on the trip, for no particular reason. She located it in seconds at the bottom of her underwear drawer. It was as if a voice from inside was directing her. It only took seconds before she had removed her tennis outfit and footwear and was clothed only in the purple leotard. She instructed herself to search out inner peace and escape the shroud of gloom this evening had brought upon her. Taking a seat on the floor, she assumed the full lotus position and concentrated on projecting her mind to a peaceful place, a place where women approaching their fortieth birthday did not foolishly delude themselves into thinking they were the same femme fatale they were twenty years ago. She sat, still, relaxed, palms up, blocking out everything around her. That was until a knock on the adjoining door from Chris's room brought her out of the trance.

"Margaret, is there any chance of getting a little help on something that's just not sinking in? I'm working on consolidations and I've always been weak in that area." He inched the door open but did not stick his head in, respecting her privacy.

"Yes, Chris, give me a second," she answered, managing to bring herself back to the mundane here and now.

After scrambling to her feet, she made her way into Chris's room, finding him seated at a small desk over an open study guide. Joining him, she remained standing, peering down at the material. Margaret trained her eyes on a sample test problem, reading the text completely before attempting to help her assistant. Focused on the material, she did not pick up on the relative position of their bodies. Seated low on a folding, metal chair, the young man was at eye level with her athletically sculptured thighs, exquisitely highlighted by the cut of the leotard over her pelvis. She was not aware of anything out of the ordinary until her concentration was interrupted by the crash of the metal chair hitting the floor. It was at that moment that she felt Chris Treadwell's hands clutching her while he sank in slow motion to his knees. His collapse was analogous to the plight of a prize fighter who, after absorbing a beating round after round with no outward damage, collapses unexpectedly in a later round from the cumulative effect of his opponent's onslaught. So it seemed to be for the young Chris, the mere proximity of Margaret's female form being the straw to break the camel's back.

"I don't care if it costs me my job—or a beating from your husband, I just need to tell you how incredibly beautiful you are—and that I will do anything you ask of me," he confessed through exaggerated breathing. She did not speak, limiting her response to nothing more than passing her fingers caressingly through his hair. He remained kneeling before her, now passionately tasting the skin just below the cut of her leotard. His message was unmistakable: his desire to perform oral sex on her.

"Please," he whispered.

"Are you sure? I haven't showered from the tennis. Are you sure, Chris?" There was almost a measure of cruelty buried within her question, knowing full well he had lost control of his actions but requiring him to make his admission a second time.

"Yes, Margaret—oh yes. Please, I need to taste you and make love to you or I'll explode." She methodically guided him back toward the bed where she seated herself. He followed, never regaining his feet.

"Take your clothes off, Chris. I want you undressed before me," she insisted, her voice insinuating it was a condition of acceptance. The young man rose to his feet and tore the clothing from his body, his eagerness again reminding her of his relative youth. Seconds later, he was standing before her in the nude, waiting on her instructions. Margaret sat thoughtfully and surveyed the twenty-two year old. He impressed her. She thought he might be better endowed than Brian. After reaching up and pulling the leotard down over her shoulders, she eased herself backwards onto the bed. Her wishes could not have been more apparent: remove the garment and stimulate her. Following her cue, Chris dropped back to his knees and pulled the leotard from her body. Within moments his warm, moist tongue was exploring her vagina. Margaret instinctively reacted to the current of pleasure passing through her body, calling out the young man's name. Within seconds she had raised her legs and rested them on his back, enveloping his head with her thighs. He countered by intensifying his probing within her. She moaned in reaction to the pleasure, her erotic journey underway. The depression from her apparent failure earlier in the evening was lifting, replaced with a superb invigoration, her ego restored. The ripples of pleasure passing through her body caused her mind to soar. The pleasure, the intoxicating pleasure, spirited her back to people and places from her past. This was a common experience with her. She was in an erotic freefall. Unexplainably, an afternoon from her early years of high school came to mind. Visiting her friend Cindy's house, the two teenagers had come upon issues of Playboy pigeonholed in her brother's room. Free to peruse at their leisure, the teens had read aloud parts of the magazine they found particularly sordid. She remembered the experience as an enjoyable one, with one exception. The young Maggie May took offense at cartoons depicting women kneeling before men at their desks, in bedrooms, wherever. Hard pressed to find men depicted in a reciprocal position, and the girls had tried to on this day, she formed resentment toward the prevailing norms and mores of society, at least in matters involving sex and the genders. When Chris's tongue touched upon an exceptionally divine nerve ending deep within her, she tightened her thigh muscles around his neck, sending a message to linger in that spot. That reflexive act brought Chris back to the woman's consciousness. Her thought process flying free of her body, Margaret flashed back to the young man's interviews the prior winter and the seedling of an idea created at that time, a fantasy molded into a plan and carried to a successful conclusion. The image of a pair of proud parents seated in the audience at graduation ceremonies only four months before came to mind, replacing the interviewing process. His parent's sacrifice must have seemed immaterial to them on that proud day in the face of his achievement. How could they have even imagined the greater good to come from their unselfish efforts? For Christopher Treadwell's educational accomplishment over the prior four years was only part of the final product: he was also being nurtured for services of a more personal nature, services to be rendered for the sole benefit of one Margaret Kelly, prey in the guise of a recruit. In spite of herself, she laughed aloud, causing the young man to pause.

"Is everything okay?" he asked, confused by her outburst.

"Never been better, Chris—please continue," she insisted. He resumed, and she returned to her state of near ecstasy, for her state of mind went far beyond the magnificent pleasure emanating from her womb. It was also the realization of power over another human being. This specific act, perhaps more than any other sexual act, established a pecking order, a dominant individual. All self doubt about her status as a sexual creature in the face of the passing years was being put to rest. Her absolute power over this human being and the circumstances surrounding them reassured her. For Margaret, it was far more important than the sex. For at this moment and owing to their relative positions, she had imposed her will on him.

A cool wind swirled around their legs as Margaret and Chris made their way across the client's parking lot to her car. It was Friday afternoon and the week of interim work was behind them. The air was crystal clear and the colorful foliage glowed from the sunlight. In the back of Margaret's mind was the immediate need to have an earnest talk with her assistant. The last four nights had seen her share her bed with a human being she barely knew less than a week before. Gorham, the White Mountains, the Town and Country Motor Inn, this had been her playground over the past week, far away from the prying eyes and wagging tongues of Bedford and Manchester. However, it was time to return to the real world, her family and her husband. In the last ninety-six hours, she had managed to put to rest her insecurities stemming from the advance toward her fortieth birthday. For this, she owed Chris Treadwell a great deal. The preceding night, Margaret thought she detected a heightening of affections on his part. She hoped she was wrong.

Margaret had the BMW cruising along a remote stretch of road in Jefferson beneath Cherry Mountain when she guided the conversation to the matter in need of addressing.

"Chris, just in case I haven't told you, this was a wonderful week up here with you, for obvious reasons."

"For both of us," he replied.

"And now we're faced with returning to the real world." He stared over at her and nodded. "I'm faced with going back to my family and acting like nothing has happened. It's what I'll do—what I have to do. What I'm saying is that our experience up here together must remain our wonderful secret. Everything, particularly our lovemaking, must remain between you and me—and no one else."

"You're talking like we'll never be together again—ever."

"There's a strong likelihood that that will be the case."

"What about when we come back for the final work?"

"There's a good chance I'll put Jim back on the engagement for that." She reached over, taking hold of his hand. "Please tell me you're going to be all right with this." The young man closed his eyes as the pain caused by her words took hold of him. She brought her hand up and played with a strand of his hair, much as she had prior to their lovemaking.

"Margaret—I'm totally and hopelessly in love with you. I'm sorry, but it's true."

"Oh, Chris, we both know you can't let yourself feel that way," she reasoned, feeling sincere empathy for him.

The car fell silent as Margaret motored southward toward Franconia Notch. From Twin Mountain they were able to glance back at the already snow capped summit of Mount Washington, each knowing this chapter of their lives was drawing to a close. Chris brooded for much of the two hour journey home. Conscious of his delicate mental condition, she exited Route 93 in Concord, opting for the less traveled Route 3A for the last leg of the trip. She took this opportunity to pull the automobile to the side of the road beneath a crop of white birches.

"A final kiss from an incredible lover?" she asked, leaning her body toward him. He responded with a prolonged, passionate kiss, his eyes filled with tears he would hold back until hours later in his deafeningly quiet apartment. "And a promise to keep this wonderful week our secret—for as long as we both shall live?" Her words caused him to chuckle through the heartbreak.

"I do—promise, that is."

XXIV

The sun was just disappearing behind the trees at the back of their property when Margaret arrived home on Friday evening. Twenty minutes before, goodbyes in front of Chris's condominium building had been unpleasant with Margaret forced to reiterate the finality of their relationship. Perhaps for spite, Brian had left his pickup in the driveway directly in front of the door. In front of his Ford was the family junk, almost exclusively Brendan's mode of transportation. Following a deep breath and a check of herself in the mirror, she pulled her luggage from the car and hauled it up to and through the front door.

"I'm home—not that anyone should care," she called out, dropping her luggage the moment she entered the house. From up the hall came the sound of voices. Seconds later Brian appeared followed by his daughter.

"Our driveway looks like an outtake from the *Beverly Hillbillies*," she exclaimed, but not with the usual venom.

"It was my way of saying thanks for not getting a single call from my better half all week," he answered.

"Sorry about that—out straight." He walked up to his wife and embraced her. She returned the hug and beckoned to her daughter. Colleen was standing a short distance away, almost appearing afraid to approach.

"Darling, come here," beckoned the mother, extending her arms. The toddler responded, albeit hesitantly.

"I'm in the final stages of making my exquisite Irish fish chowder—from my mother's recipe—care to join us, Mrs. Kelly?"

"Oh, my God, this isn't the recipe where she left the haddock, and any other fish—out of the chowder, is it?"

"Partly—there is a real shortage in the chowder of anything that ever lived in a body of water—but I've compensated by putting magnifying glasses at every setting—so you can appreciate the fish on those rare occasions you do find it on your spoon." Brian looped his arm around his wife's shoulder, pulling her toward the kitchen.

"Did you miss me, Kelly?"

"I'll say I did. All those other women I brought in every night—none of them could hold a candle to you." His words caused a stabbing in her stomach. She smiled through it.

"I hope you at least changed the sheets."

"Of course—I had to hide the evidence."

Margaret entered the kitchen to a full house. Moira did not bother to raise her eyes from the table. Jenny and Brendan, both leaning side-by-side against the sink, greeted her with a hug as she made her way around the room. Brian gave his wife a squeeze on the arm as he broke away, returning to the stove. His daughter followed, all the while clutching his leg.

"It may look like I've been doing the lion's share of the cooking this week but Jenny and I have pretty much taken it easy. Brendan, as we know, is totally useless in the kitchen and so, it goes without saying, has provided nothing." In acknowledgement, the teenager rose to his feet and whimsically called off any applause. "It was our little Rose of Tralee who stepped up to the plate and knocked the ball out of the park. Maggie May, this little girl can cook." She extended the nanny a cursory nod and changed the subject.

"Did I get any mail?"

"There's a stack of it on your desk upstairs," answered Brian while adding haddock to the pot.

"Did anything at all exciting happen in my absence?"

"Brendan's getting calls at the house from girls—and from the sound of them—real barracudas," chirped Jenny.

"Ah, yes—the girls of Southside—the shy, little girls of Southside."

"It's not just school—but from work, too. Teenyboppers, girls in their twenties, they're all interested in our little Brendan," added Jenny, clearly out to get a rise out of him.

"It comes with the territory—me being in the motion picture business and all," he joked.

"Well, I can honestly say I never had that problem back in high school," said Brian while attending to the chowder.

"Hey, Kelly, let's revisit those days at Southside—crappy clothes, no car, borderline personal hygiene, lame, geeky friends. Jesus, you brought so much to the table. It's amazing with all that going for you—you weren't able to attract a single girl," ribbed Margaret.

"Actually, there was one little gal—a pathetic little thing I took pity on. Coincidentally, she lived in Bedford—on Ministerial Road. She was the brainy type—always getting straight A's—but God, what a little loser!"

"Is that the little loser you used to travel out to Bedford to see on weekends, on foot, in the freezing cold of the winter—like a lovesick puppy dog?"

"I'm not sure. It was a long time ago."

"Was that the little loser who dumped you in the fall—not for another guy—just because she was so freaking bored with you?"

"You know, I think it was. Boy, I was pretty hard up in those days. The important thing is—eventually—she crawled back to me," he answered, peeking over his shoulder at his wife.

"That's funny—I seem to remember a certain loser proposing—borderline begging me to marry him. Tell me Brian, am I getting one loser mixed up with another?"

"No, any guy begging the former Maggie May Keogh to marry him—that is a bona fide, first class, unqualified loser," he confessed to a chorus of howls from those in the room.

"I love it when you two go at each other," confessed Brendan. "You two are so perfect for each other."

Husband and wife retreated upstairs for the evening after the eleven o'clock news. An hour earlier, she had hinted that she needed to talk something over with him. He hoped this meant addressing their recent communication problems, something he saw as a possible cause for her moodiness in the last few weeks. In addition, he needed to speak with her regarding Moira. During the week, the nanny had confided in him on the matter of her employment. Emerging from the master bath after brushing his teeth, he found his wife camped in front of her bureau mirror applying moisturizer.

"God, it's going to be nice having you beside me in bed tonight," he confessed.

"Yes, it will be nice. Having said that—I want to remind you that we take possession of the house on Atlantic Avenue next week. I'm going up Monday to get the keys and be shown where everything is. You do know you'll have complete access to the house, don't you?"

"I sort of assumed that—seeing that we're married!" he called out, a little put out with her declaration.

"Well, that being the case—I don't think it would be such a bad idea if you thought seriously about putting the shit box on the market. The building may not be worth much but the land is probably worth a fortune."

"Sorry, Keogh, that's not going to happen. I love that place."

"We don't need it anymore. We don't need *two* places at Wells Beach. It's excess baggage. We have a bigger and better place."

"First of all, you have a one year lease—it's not yours. When the year is up you may be out on your ear."

"I've seen pictures of their place in Boothbay—they'll be offering me the house in a year if not sooner."

"Next topic—because this topic is closed for discussion," he declared.

"Don't you talk to me like that in my house. I'll tell you when the subject is closed for discussion. We don't owe squat on the shit box and will probably walk away with two hundred grand after taxes. That's money we can roll into the new house."

"Did I stutter when I said no to this whole idea. No is no! I'll consider renting the little house if we wind up buying the big one. Until then, everything stays the way it is. Now—can we please stop arguing and make peace?" There was no answer from her side of the room.

Crossing the bedroom, he sidled up to her, placing his hands on her shoulders. She remained perfectly still.

"The other thing I needed to speak to you about was Moira. She confided in me that she doesn't feel wanted in the house—by you. She feels like you're always upset with her."

"Oh, for Christ's sake—she's hired help! What does she want me to do—sing her to sleep every night?"

"Keogh—relax. Lighten up. She just needs to feel like she's wanted. We want her here. The baby loves her. Do it for Colleen."

"God, you are such a doormat, Brian," she said, her blue eyes flashing disapproval.

"Being civil to people is hardly being a doormat."

"Civil to everybody but me," she countered.

"There's no point arguing with you when you're in one of these moods. Let's just both keep our mouths shut before this escalates anymore. Just a warning though, I'm not sleeping in the guest room tonight. If you want to be alone— you sleep there." Margaret screwed the cap back on the moisturizer and made her way to the bed. Before clicking off the light, he leaned over and kissed his wife's cheek. She did not respond.

XXV

*I*n early October the foliage bordering the wildlife sanctuary in Wells usually begins its annual slow explosion to color, and 1995 proved no exception. The southern coastline of York County is the last place in Maine to reflect the change of seasons. This Monday morning carried a frosty snap in the air with the television weatherman predicting the temperature would not reach sixty. Brian's mood was upbeat, having returned early this morning to learn the complex had maintained an eighty percent occupancy rate over the weekend, unheard of this late in the season. It was a few minutes after noon. He was picking at his lunch at the front desk while Mary Porterfield lay sprawled out on the couch on the other side of the room. She was in the midst of a full day of work, the only chambermaid on duty. Her soup and sandwich already consumed, she was spending the remaining quarter hour of her lunch break chatting with her boss. From the walkway behind the building came the sound of leather to pavement. Brian looked up from his tray as the office door swung open. Simultaneously, Mary bolted to an upright position at the intrusion. It was Maggie May.

"No need to jump, Mary—it's family," reassured Brian.

"I thought you might want these," called out his wife from the door. An instant later, a set of house keys flew across the room at him. He snatched them out of the air.

"Wow—Brian Kelly, oceanfront property owner—or lessee," he exclaimed. His wife did not seem to hear, her attention already occupied by the petite blonde seated on the couch.

"Mary, this is my wife, Maggie—love of my life and mother of my little Jelly Bean. Maggie, this is Mary Porterfield, one of our newest but already one of our most valued employees."

Margaret stepped toward the girl, prompting Mary to spring to her feet. Standing a half foot taller and impeccably dressed in a perfectly tailored business suit, the professional woman's persona should have intimidated this young girl from northern Maine. However, on the surface it did not. After brushing it along her jeans to remove any remnants of lunch, she extended her hand to Margaret. They shook hands, the girl staring intently into the woman's eyes the entire time.

"Yes, Mary, this is the lady that owns the other half of all the stock in the company. So be very nice to her." She flashed Mary the dimmest of smiles and turned back to her husband.

"And you'll be home when?"

"Wednesday and Thursday nights, then the gang will join me up here at the new house, right?"

"Yes, I'm anxious for you to spend a little time there with me," she replied while moving behind the front desk toward him. "Until Wednesday," she said before leaving him with a meaningful kiss on the lips. "Mustn't dawdle, work at the office," she exclaimed as she turned from her husband. "And nice to meet you," she called out to Mary before exiting the building.

The phone rang while the two stared across at each other. From outside came the sound of leather heels on pavement before the slam of a car door. For the next five minutes Brian reviewed rates and details with the caller, inserting his personal charm in the process. The discussion over, he hung up the phone and turned to his friend.

"Harriet Karpinski—and her sisters—three nights over the Columbus Day weekend—four cottages in total. Thank you Baby Jesus," he cried out while extending a hand skyward.

"She is a very beautiful woman," announced Mary from the couch, her first words since Margaret's departure.

"Who is? Mrs. Karpinski? How would you know that?" he asked with a straight face.

"Your wife is stupid. She's really beautiful, Brian."

"That she is—that she is. But truth is—I think you made her a little insecure. Listen Mary Porterfield of Beals Island—you're a little heartbreaker yourself. Don't let anyone tell you you're not."

"She actually scares me. She's really—oh, what's the word?"

"Overdressed?"

"No, what is it?"

"Overbearing?"

"No. Intense! That's the word—intense. Your wife is intense."

"Yeah, she's intense all right."

"She has this power to just look at you and make you feel like you're dirt."

"That's funny—because I didn't get that feeling from you at all. You handled Maggie May just fine, my little Mary." The young woman flashed her boss an appreciative smile. By now she had returned to lying on her back.

"This couch is so very comfortable. It's better than the one we have at home. When the time comes to replace it, let me know—because I'll buy it from you and put it in my house."

"Oh, we're never going to replace that couch. Someday it'll be a tourist attraction. I'll be able to tell our guests that the famous movie actress, Mary Porterfield, used to lay on it all the time. Of course, that'll be a couple of years from now after your movie career takes off." Her response was a sweet, childlike laugh.

"Movie star, huh."

"Uh-huh—you're a cross between Meg Ryan and Marilyn Monroe." Mary had closed her eyes, taking full advantage of her last few minutes of lunch break.

"My mother called me last night. It was nice hearing her voice cause—it's been a while."

"Is everybody okay at home? Is everybody in good health?"

"Yeah, sounds like they are."

"Because, without your health everything else is just so much dog shit." She opened her eyes for a second to flash him a knowing smile.

"Rod's been discharged from the navy. He's back in Jonesport."

"That's Roddy's dad, I take it."

"That's him. Eight years away—you'd think the idiot would have stayed the full twenty for the pension."

"Maybe he just got sick of it. People do."

"He's called the house more than once—even dropped by to say hello to my parents."

"And I'm sure he's asked about you and Roddy."

"Of course. He wants to know where we're living. They wouldn't tell him."

"What was he like? You must have felt something for him once, right? He wasn't abusive I hope?"

"No—not abusive. He's a decent guy—quiet and decent. Of course, he wasn't decent enough to stick around when I got pregnant." Brian observed a certain sadness overtaking his friend as the subject of her teenage years was introduced, prompting him to move the conversation elsewhere.

"Oh, before I forget, you know that your hours will have to be dramatically reduced after Columbus Day—right? Anyway, I've used what little influence I have down at Billy's Chowder House to get you twenty to twenty-five hours a week over the winter—to help get you by. I'll be able to give you eight to ten hours here when we close everything except the main house. And—you know you can always come to me for help if you get in a bind. You do know that, right?"

"I was beginning to worry about the winter. I was putting it out of my mind and praying for help. It's hard looking for work when I'm still working here."

"And there's always unemployment compensation. In my youth I was an expert at collecting that. I think they dedicated an entire wing of the Unemployment Office in Sanford to me—I was that good at collecting," he boasted.

Mary rose from the couch and strolled across the room, stopping directly in front of her employer and friend. Without hesitation, she wrapped her arms around him, resting the side of her face on his chest.

"You are, without a doubt, the most wonderful, generous, good-hearted man I have ever known—and I thank God every day that I know you," she whispered.

"You're my precious angel," he whispered back, accentuating his words with a kiss on the top of her head. Reluctantly, she pulled herself back and made her way across the room. Reaching the door, her hand already on the knob, she stopped and took a deep breath. Brian's eyes had not left her.

"I love you, Brian Kelly. There, I said it—it's out." Her back was still turned to him.

"And I love you, too, Mary Porterfield." Brian looked on as her head dipped slightly, signaling to him that she was in tears. Her back remaining turned, she forced herself to speak.

"Duane is talking about buying a pit bull. I think it's because of you," she said, introducing a strange change in subjects.

"Tell him if he harms a hair on your head—I'll drive to Sanford, shoot the dog, and beat the crap out of him again." She raised a single finger in the air, indicating she understood the message.

"I'll let him know." With that, she left the building, never bothering to glance back at him.

XXVI

*O*n a Thursday morning in late October while the ocean water retreated through Wells Harbor and back to its home in the cold, blue Atlantic, Brian took a call at the front desk that would alter his life. It was the off season, a time when the summer voices had long since echoed away and the beautiful strand of land clinging to Maine's southern coastline returned as the exclusive province of local residents. It was the magnificent quiet descending on the landscape at this time that caused the words from the telephone to hang in the air around him. On the clock, the phone call ran no more than three minutes. At its conclusion, a shaken, heartsick Brian Kelly wandered from the main house and down the slope to the swimming pool where he propped his back against the wooden, security fence and gazed out at the harbor and distant ocean. He remained seated there until three that afternoon, processing the painful message from an anonymous caller.

At five o'clock Brian joined Perez and Bobby in Kennebunkport at Alisson's Restaurant. They sat together at the bar. He did not confide in them the details of the earlier conversation. He just needed to see them, to know he still had them, friends for life. Both men picked up on the strain present in their friend but respected his decision not to confide in them the cause of it. They reminisced on times gone by, on Brian's childhood in Lowell and on his young adulthood in Wells. There was laughter and some soul searching. At six o'clock, and at his insistence, he paid the bar tab and left for Bedford.

Arriving at the house shortly before eight o'clock, Brian placed a phone call to his in-laws, asking them if they minded an unscheduled visit from their granddaughter. He was happy when their response was an enthusiastic no. From downstairs in the basement came the sporadic sound of weights hitting the floor and the thud of impact on the heavy bag. Margaret was home and working out. He climbed the stairs and made his way down the hall to Moira's room. Following two gentle taps it swung open.

"Mr. Kelly, what are you doing home?" she asked, a paperback held in one hand.

"It's an unscheduled visit. Moira, I'm afraid I need a big, big favor from you."

"I'll try. Is everything all right?"

"No—and that's all I can say right now. What I'm hoping you will do is take the baby over to her grandparent's house for a visit. They're over on Ministerial Road. You've been there before, right?"

"Yes—sure it's been a while, but I think I can find it."

"I need you and the baby out of the house for an hour or so. I think there's going to be a real explosion here in a few minutes. I'd like to have a little privacy in the next hour—in case it gets really nasty."

"Mr. Kelly, you're scaring me."

"Nothing physical, but I'm sure it'll get very loud. By the way, where are Jenny and Brendan?"

"They're at a lecture at St. A's. Do you believe it? She's got him attending a lecture on nineteenth century authors or some such thing. Do you believe it?" The revelation actually forced a laugh from him. "I'll get the baby all bundled up and we'll be on our way in no time."

"I saw the junk parked out next to the garage. You'll be okay driving that, right?" The young woman laughed.

"If you saw what I was driving around County Clare just before I came to the states, you wouldn't ask that question."

"One more thing, Moira—if in the next few days you find me temporarily out of the house—please, please make the best of things around here. I know I'll be back—one way or the other. Colleen loves you—and I know I'll feel much better knowing you're here for her."

"Of course, Mr. Kelly."

After assisting the young woman with the baby and sending them off to the relative quiet of the Keogh household, Brian collapsed into a chair in the corner of the master bedroom and waited for his wife. She would head upstairs for a shower after her workout. That was her routine. Waiting on Margaret gave him time to organize his thoughts. His stomach was in a knot, a product of rage, anguish and disappointment. Fifteen minutes into the vigil, she appeared in the doorway, her body defined like a comic book superhero and glistening with perspiration.

"What the hell are you doing here?" she called out in astonishment, stopping dead in her tracks.

"I needed to talk and it couldn't wait."

"That's why we have telephones," she answered, resuming her walk toward the bathroom.

"This should be done in person—face to face."

"Well, it'll have to wait until I've had my shower," she insisted.

"Right now—not later. I have a simple question—requiring a simple answer." He watched as a look of concern came over his wife's face. It only took seconds before concern was replaced with defiance.

"Go ahead," she replied, crossing her arms and staring squarely at him.

"Were you unfaithful to me last month on that trip up in the mountains?"

"How dare you ask me a question like that?"

"Just tell me no, Maggie May—and that'll be the end of it."

"Where did you get an idea like that?"

"Just look me in the eyes and tell me you weren't unfaithful—and that'll be the end of it," he stated, still remaining calm. Her eyes broke from his and moved to the windows lining the far wall of the room. She took in a series of labored breaths but made no reply. "Oh fuck—it's true," he said, a pained realization present in his tone. She turned abruptly and strode out into the hall. "Get back in here or I'll drag you back in here," he ordered. She reappeared in the doorway seconds later, her eyes squinted with anger.

"I want to know who the fuck you've been talking to," she said.

"It was a female. I didn't recognize the voice. She sounded fairly young. Now, let's get back to the matter at hand. Keogh, my first impulse is to go to your office tomorrow—and confront this prick."

"Brian, he's not a prick—and there's no way I'm having you come to the office and lay this on me. Jesus Christ—be reasonable."

"Oh, so you're even standing up for the little bastard now. I didn't say I was going to beat the crap out of him. I just want to talk to him—man to man."

"No, Brian—absolutely not."

"Well, then that leads us to alternative number two: I want this prick off your payroll, out in the street and out of your life—immediately."

"It was a one time thing. It's over."

"Maggie May—he has to go," he said, still calm.

"I'm sorry, that's non-negotiable."

"Non-negotiable! Non-negotiable! We're not working out a fucking lease here, Keogh. This is our marriage."

"I told you—it's over, Brian. It was a one time thing."

He turned from his wife and crossed the room. Pulling a suitcase from the closet, he threw it down in front of his bureau and began emptying the contents of the upper drawers into it.

"If this is intended to scare me—then think twice." Ignoring her words, he hastily rammed as many articles of clothing possible into the one piece of luggage, then slammed it shut.

"Call me when you get serious about putting our marriage back together again," he said hastily on the way to the door. She moved forward, blocking his path.

"You may leave *my* house when I'm done talking to you—and say you may leave *my* house," she stated defiantly.

"Are you saying you're getting rid of him?"

"Brian, for the last time—that's not on the table."

"Okay, step aside, Keogh. No more of your horseshit." When he tried stepping around her, she blocked his path, going so far as to grab his arm, her nails penetrating his skin. In response, he took hold of her by the waist and lifted her up from the floor. Her legs dangling freely beneath her, Margaret struck her husband on the side of the face in retaliation for the indignity. Shaking his head in disgust, he brought the skirmish to a close by tossing the woman onto the center of the bed. The angle of the fall combined with the spring of the mattress caused what could be best described as a trampoline effect, sending her hurtling sideways toward the edge of the bed. The second, unintended landing came on the very edge of the king sized mattress and saw her tumble awkwardly to the floor. He stood frozen momentarily, surprised by the actions played out before him. Seconds later, Margaret rose to her feet, appearing more surprised than injured.

"Are you okay, Keogh?" he asked, relieved to see her standing upright so quickly. Her expression turned from surprise to hostility.

"You abusive prick—get out of my house," she said, spitting out the words. "I don't want you anywhere near me or my daughter." Hurdling over the bed and past her husband, she ran to Colleen's room and pushed open the door. "What the hell have you done with my daughter?" she cried out.

"Relax—she's over with your parents. Moira will have her home in an hour. I didn't want her around for this."

"Go—get out of my house. Go to your teenage trollop over in Maine. Run to your jailbait. I suppose you expect me to believe that nothing's going on there. Bullshit!"

"Sorry to disappoint you, Keogh—but nothing has."

"You are so full of shit, Kelly. Oh, and while we're on the subject of Colleen, when I'm through with you, you'll be lucky to see her fifteen minutes a year—and don't think I can't. It's what I do best, remember? You see your Honor, my husband has, of late, become violent. He literally threw me across the room, your Honor. I'm afraid for me *and* the baby."

"I'm warning you—no one keeps me from my daughter—no one."

"Don't threaten me, you bastard. Oh, that's right—you're a real life bastard. Sorry for striking so close to home." He turned from her and started down the stairs. Reaching the first floor, he spun around. Margaret was glaring down on him from the top step.

"You know what's amazing? You did and said everything under the sun—but you never even once bothered to say you were sorry," he stated wistfully. For once, she had no reply. He shrugged, turned, and walked from the house.

XXVII

*M*argaret spent the remainder of Thursday evening analyzing the confrontation with her husband. Of particular interest to her were the circumstances by which he had learned of her infidelity. Putting her analytical mind to work, she reviewed the fact pattern known to her, thinking through every bit of information and considering who had possible access to it, and when. Shortly after arriving at the office, she put a call through to Chris Treadwell. This week he was working out of town in Portsmouth. During the twenty minute conversation, he denied telling anyone of the short lived affair. It was only in the final five minutes of quasi interrogation that he admitted to one exception, leaking word of the tryst to his brother. He qualified this by informing her that David, his brother, worked and lived in Burlington, Vermont, far from Manchester and even further still from Wells, Maine.

At four o'clock on this Friday afternoon Margaret buzzed Debbie Dunfey, a staff bookkeeper, and asked her to report to her office at five. Debbie, an overweight woman of approximately thirty years of age, shared office space with Chris Treadwell, their work stations separated only by a partition. Glancing away from her computer monitor, Margaret spotted Debbie standing in the shadow of her office door. The time on her computer screen read 4:57 PM.

"Come in, Debbie—and close the door," she ordered. The woman complied, and sat herself in the nearest chair. Margaret paused and took stock of her employee, instantly noting that the woman's hands were trembling. "As you probably realize, it is never a good sign being called to a supervisor's office late in the afternoon on a Friday—and this occasion is no exception. I'll preface my remarks by saying that your complete honesty will go a long way toward retaining your position here. I take it you value your position here."

"Yes, Mrs. Kelly, I really do."

"Then it will behoove you to provide me with the absolute truth when I ask you a question. Do you understand me?" The woman gestured in the affirmative, appearing almost unable to speak.

"I have reason to believe that a nasty rumor is circulating around the office, a rumor concerning Chris Treadwell. Do you have knowledge of the rumor I'm referring to?" The Dunfey woman froze, transparent in her desire to answer the question in an acceptable manner.

"I think I do."

"And that rumor would be what?"

"That would be that—that he may not have conducted himself properly during his audit work up in Gorham."

"During his time up in Gorham with me—isn't that what you mean to say?" The woman dropped her eyes to the floor before answering the question.

"Yes ma'am."

"What's more, I have good reason to believe that this rumor grew legs in your office—from your side of the partition."

"Oh no, ma'am. Really, it's nothing like that. Chris and I are barely on speaking terms. He wouldn't confide anything like that in me."

"Then where did you get wind of this ugly lie?"

"I can't be absolutely sure, but I think I might have overheard it in the staff room," confessed the woman.

"The staff room! Are you saying this thing is circulating as common knowledge?"

"I'm afraid it is, ma'am," answered the woman before sneaking a glance at her watch.

"You look at that watch one more time while I'm discussing something with you and you'll be out on your ass so fast your head will spin," roared Margaret. The tirade caused the woman to burst into tears.

"I've done nothing wrong, Mrs. Kelly, you must believe me. I only checked my watch on account of my son in daycare—and the people there wanting him picked up no later than five-thirty," explained the woman as she fumbled for a handkerchief.

"You do know you make about five thousand dollars more here, given your experience and skills, than you could most anywhere else locally? You do know that, right?"

"Yes ma'am."

"I have a way of checking your story. That'll come on Monday. If what you say does not check out Monday morning—I'll be standing over you at your desk as you empty it out and you'll be unemployed by noontime. Do you understand me?" Debbie closed her eyes and nodded yes. "You may leave now," added Margaret, signaling the woman to vacate her office.

Brian locked the door to the main house and made his way across the yard to his pickup, parked in its customary spot by the storage shed. The complex was empty of guests, the last having checked out two days earlier. It was Friday afternoon, less than twenty-four hours since he packed a suitcase and moved out of the Bedford house. On a whim, he pulled the Ford off Mile Road on the trip home and into the parking lot of Billy's Chowder House. He was hoping Mary Porterfield had caught a Friday shift. Learning she had not, he made quick work of his beer and continued home.

Pushing open the front door of the cottage, his eyes were quick to pick up on the single, flashing light from his answering machine. One flash, one message, he thought to himself. He hit the rewind button and waited for the playback. *Hello Brian, it's Margaret. I had no desire to speak to you today so I went this route. On the matter of keeping you away from Colleen, consider that retracted. I was way out of line. You're a good father. I think we both know that. Also, all that about being an abusive husband, again, way out of line on my part—consider it forgotten, at least at my end. When you're ready to apologize for your behavior at the house, then maybe we can begin putting things back together. Until that time I prefer no communication. One lone exception, call me, preferably at the office, to arrange to see and have the baby. That's all from this end.*

Margaret charged into the office on Monday morning, thirty minutes behind schedule and outwardly irritable. She stopped at the front desk, waiting for Gretchen to wrap up a call. The conversation, possibly personal, was brought to a rapid conclusion.

"Gretchen, if you would, find someone to man the desk for the next half hour, pour us both some coffee, and join me in my office," she barked. Margaret was already climbing the stairs before the attractive, middle aged woman could respond. Reaching the second floor, she picked up on Chris's voice from down the hall. Back from his assignment in Portsmouth, he was scheduled to work in the office on this day.

It was ten minutes before Gretchen Karrer, an employee of the firm for a half dozen years, made her way into the office balancing a pair of coffee mugs on a notepad.

"You won't need the pad," announced Margaret, gesturing to the woman to close the office door behind her.

"Gretchen, I've called you in here behind closed doors because I know you and I trust you. Right now I need feedback that I can rely on—and I'm hoping you can provide that feedback."

"I'll do my best, Mrs. Kelly—but wouldn't you be better off asking one of the guys?"

"This has nothing to do with finances or number crunching. Besides, I don't trust any of the men in this place as far as I can throw them—and that includes Vern." The receptionist took a sip from her cup, clearly more at ease around Margaret than most of the other employees.

"I want feedback on the scuttlebutt around the office about Chris and me. How widespread is it?"

"Quite widespread—in fact, I'd be surprised if there was someone working here that hadn't heard the rumor." Margaret took a deep breath while her body tightened with rage.

"And do you believe it?"

"No," replied the woman.

"Gretchen, answer me this, how do you think this whole, ugly thing got started?"

"Chris."

"You're sure?"

"I'm quite sure."

"And why is that?"

"I saw it—and I heard it with my own ears."

"Would I be out of line to ask you for details?"

"No, Mrs. Kelly, you wouldn't. A couple of Fridays ago a lot of the gang from the office went out for drinks after work. It was a good time. We did a lot of drinking, particularly the younger people. We hooked up with some people from another firm, the one Rose Dalton is partner in. She was right at the table with us for the second half of the night. Chris was talking about hooking up with you up in the mountains. Rose seemed to get a real hoot out of that. I know she doesn't like you very much. So you see, I saw him talking about it, myself. That's why I say I'm quite sure he's the one who's spreading the story." Gretchen paused, took a deep breath, and drew in another sip of coffee. Across the desk from her, Margaret sat practically motionless, deep in thought. It would be nearly a full minute before she rose from her chair and approached her employee.

"Thank you for your honesty—and your insight," she said before awkwardly wrapping her arms around the woman. "You're very valuable to me. I appreciate everything you do here," she confessed, unaccustomed to expressions of this nature. Gretchen thanked her for the compliment before retreating back to her desk.

Margaret intentionally avoided any contact with Chris throughout the morning, leaving her office door three quarters shut at most times. It was nearly noontime when the voices, Chris's among them, of two or three of her male employees passed the door, presumably heading out for lunch. Taking advantage of the opportunity at hand, she walked down the hall and into the office Chris shared with Debbie Dunfey. She found the woman hard at work entering data into her computer. Standing directly behind the woman, she spoke to her in a tone more civil than a few days before.

"Debbie, I think I owe you an apology for last week. I'm sorry about the whole scene in my office on Friday. Please accept my apology." Her employer standing behind her, out of view, the woman nodded her head twice in acknowledgement and continued working. Margaret followed her words with an affectionate squeeze to the woman's shoulders. It was a gesture that did not come natural to her. She had an aversion to coming in contact with people who were overweight. However, she knew she had humiliated this single mother the preceding Friday and groped for a way to exorcise her guilt.

"You're doing a fine job," she finally whispered before tapping her warmly on the back and walking from the room.

There was a note taped on Chris Treadwell's computer when he returned from lunch this day, asking him to report to Margaret's office on or around five o'clock. It is safe to assume that the possibility of an amorous reconciliation with his attractive employer must have passed through his mind. In fact, this thought and the reliving of his time spent with Mrs. Kelly in the picturesque setting of Gorham, New Hampshire, probably danced through his head throughout the afternoon. These optimistic dreams would not prove to be anything near the agonizing reality he was about to face.

Following a quick series of taps, her door swung open and Chris Treadwell presented himself. He was smiling, the identical smile that had caught Margaret's attention nearly a year before. She rose from her desk and casually made her way to the door, pulling it shut and, to some extent, isolating them from the outside world. Walking back behind her desk, she could feel his stare attach itself to her body.

"I will try to make this as quick and painless as possible," she stated, her words erasing his boyish smile and replacing it with a look of concern. She reached inside her desk and pulled out a single sheet of paper. "I'm asking you to resign, effective today." She slid the sheet of paper across the desk to within arm's length of him.

"I am offering you a month's severance pay. In addition, I've spent a good part of the afternoon lining you up job interviews. Your reference from me will be solid. Chris, I'm sorry it came to this but you've given me no other option." The young man fumbled in his chair, his mouth hanging open from shock.

"Margaret, I don't get it—"

"You didn't keep up your end of the bargain. You broke your word. I've got a husband who walked out on me. I'm looking like a perfect fool."

"I didn't talk to anyone about this—except my brother," he exclaimed.

"And, on top of everything else, you're a liar!" The twenty-two year old leaned forward in his chair, burying his face in his hands. She looked on in silence while her lover from only a month before foraged for a tactic, an angle, anything to extricate himself from the circumstances at hand.

"I love working here," he mumbled, his voice taking on a pitiful quality.

"You should have thought of that before you started running your mouth off." She pulled a pen from her desk and placed it down on the letter of resignation. "Sign it, Chris," she demanded. The room grew deafeningly quiet. "Sign it, Chris," she repeated, her voice absent any hint of compromise. Slowly, his head rose until his eyes met hers.

"Sexual harassment—what you did to me is a form of sexual harassment," he said.

"Don't go there, Chris. I'm warning you—don't go there," she warned, her tone carrying a cold determination.

"I'll charge you with sexual harassment. The last thing you need is to have our dirty little affair played out in a court of law," he stated boldly. She had anticipated a possible tactic along these lines and already prepared a counter attack.

"Okay, seeing that it was you who brought it up—we will go there. Let me set the stage. We have a courtroom full of people—and your mother and father seated in the front row. Your Honor, it happened like this: I was minding my own business in my hotel room when there was a knock. It was the plaintiff, asking me if I'd help him with his studying. Your Honor, as God is my witness, I was standing by his desk reviewing a problem from his book when he, he being Mr. Treadwell, dropped to his knees and professed his love, or was it adoration? Your Honor, it was pathetic. I must admit I felt pity for him, kneeling as he was. Your Honor, I must plead guilty to selfishness—the way I let the plaintiff grovel—and ultimately used him. I'm guilty of selfishness—but not of sexual harassment."

"It was you who seduced me," he murmured.

"Seduced, maybe—but not harassed!"

"A jury would see right through this," he argued, albeit weakly.

"Christ! He still hasn't heard enough," she called out, now standing directly in front of him. "Shall we revisit the whole episode involving your fondness—no, your devotion, to my buttocks, Chris? Shall we, Chris? How do you think your parents, a jury, and a courtroom would react to that, Chris? My husband's walked out on me, Chris. I don't give a shit what comes down in court, Chris. This harassment shit is just that—a crock of shit, Chris." She stepped back from the young man, his expression reduced to a blank stare. Her verbal assault had seemingly drained his spirit. Margaret felt something akin to heartache for him and softened her voice.

"Please Chris, sign the paper," she asked. It was the voice he would always remember from his time spent in Mount Washington Valley, in the lounge of the Town and Country Motor Inn, from the captivating woman who spent five days and four incredible nights with him. The young man leaned forward over the desk and scratched out his name and date on the form, not even pausing to read the specifics.

XXVIII

November roared into York County off the gray Atlantic Ocean like an express train, bringing with it sub freezing temperatures overnight and the disappearance of all but a few of the out-of-state vehicles from the roadways. On the first Friday of the month, it was Brendan who delivered his father a much appreciated gift, Colleen for the weekend. With her half-brother towing an oversized, plastic, play vehicle behind her, the nearly two year old made her grand entrance into the main office of the Atlantic Coast Lodge, only to find no one in sight and the building deathly quiet.

"Brian—anyone home?" called out Brendan while the two slowly approached the front desk. It was when the toddler walked within a few feet of the registration stand that her father sprang out from behind the desk, crawling on all fours and hollering a blue streak.

"Ahhhh," cried out the little girl as the man grabbed hold of her ankle and squeezed.

"Jelly Bean for supper—yum, yum," he snarled. The toddler reacted with hysterical laughter.

"Daddy—I'm not for supper, now stop that," she insisted, a smile covering her face.

"Okay, okay—but give me a big hug," he replied, extending his arms from a kneeling position.

The two men unloaded Colleen's articles from the BMW while the little girl familiarized herself with the first floor at the inn. It would become her racing track for the next two days. Father and son eventually collapsed onto the sofa and watched as the energy-charged little girl pedaled her vehicle through the series of rooms completing a full circle every forty-five seconds or so.

"So, when the hell are you coming home?" asked Brendan, not one to beat around the bush.

"That's completely up to my wife. She knows why I left and what I expect of her to return."

"No one in the house even knows what all this shit is about? Can you share that with me anyway? Jenny keeps asking her mother, with no success—and I'm sure she'll be asking me when I get home. What do I tell her?"

"I know this makes me sound like a perfect asshole but it's just—I can't. It's up to Maggie to bring everything out in the open—not that I'm looking forward to that."

"Daddy—watch me," called out Colleen as the three-wheeled cycle rolled by.

"I see you, Jelly Bean, Daddy sees you," he answered.

"Dad, are you seeing another woman?" inquired the teenager. The bluntness of the question was lost on his father. Instead, he felt moisture seeping into his eyes, never having been addressed by his son in this way. He saw it as an acceptance of his parenthood beyond that of purely biological.

"I take it by that you mean—have I had sex with another woman? And the answer to that question is no." Brian watched as his son scanned the room with his eyes, appearing more like a nervous habit than a review of the furnishings. He studied the young man's face. He was taken with Brendan's resemblance to himself, hair and eyes. His smile, though, was Linda's.

"Margaret's a stubborn woman—a very, stubborn woman. She doesn't give an inch. Couldn't you make the first move? No one at the house would think any less of you. We know what she's like," he reasoned.

"Son, I can't. You don't have all the facts—if you did, you'd see where I'm coming from."

"I mean, the holidays are around the corner and we have this shit hanging over our heads. Dad, I miss you. We all miss you. Give in—for us." Brian shook his head and rose to his feet. When Brendan followed suit, he was greeted with an enthusiastic bear hug from his father.

"Next time you talk to your mom, tell her I was asking for her."

"She has the house on the market back home. She says she's probably moving back to Maine, at least for the time being."

"That's good. These days I can use all the friends I can get," laughed Brian.

XXIX

*T*he Portland weathermen had gotten it right. Brian sat propped up on his couch while the cottage was buffeted with gusts of wind approaching forty miles an hour and rain coming down in horizontal sheets. Outside his windows, the estuary was filling up with water, the high tide due in another ninety minutes. It was a good night to be hunkered down and out of the elements. He tried to remember the television schedule for Wednesday nights, and whether any programs were of interest to him. It was just a few minutes before ten o'clock. From behind the cottage came the sound of metal scraping along a second surface, telling him his garbage cans were being tossed by the wind. It wasn't the first time, he thought. He could rescue them in the morning. He found himself wondering if the weather was this chaotic back in Bedford. A swirl of wind rattled the back windows and he was reminded of an old Gordon Lightfoot song, *The Wreck of the Edmund Fitzgerald.* The words were not coming to him, just one bar; *when the winds of November come early.* Presently, a few feet away and outside his windows, they were not early at all, but right on time.

Of late, evenings such as this, the ones spent alone, were particularly difficult. Three weeks had passed since he walked out of the house. This passage of time away from his family came unexpected. Now, each day, he waited on word from Bedford, word from his wife, in the form of an apology, to return home. But each day passed without so much as a call or recorded message. Recently, a new possibility had arisen, the possibility of a letter from an attorney's office. In his mind, his Roman Catholic beliefs caused him to place far more significance on the couple's wedding vows than her. As he saw it, her bloodless, sectarian perspective on life, marriage, and ultimately divorce, translated to nothing beyond concerns over legal fees and the division of assets. In the game of life, his Christian faith, the belief system that formed the pillar of his everyday existence, was a handicap, at least in the arena of life pitted against the likes of Maggie May. That was how Brian saw it.

He was on the verge of dozing off when a commotion erupted at the front of the house. Jumping up from the couch, he unlocked the front door and stepped out onto the porch. There, two figures were visible to him on the deck. The larger figure, barely more than an outline on this contemptible night, was banging frantically on the door. He reached behind him and flicked the light switch, illuminating the front of the building. A girl and a small boy stood out in a torrent of driving rain at the door to his porch. He threw open the hook lock and pushed out the door. The two individuals rushed in passed him and out of the elements.

"Oh, God, Brian, I'm so glad you're home. I'm not sure what I'd done if you weren't here," exclaimed a young woman though gasps of breath. It was Mary Porterfield.

"Where did you guys come from?" he asked as rainwater cascaded from his visitors onto the porch floor.

"The car—Duane's car is stalled in the middle of the road on Webhannet. It won't start—I can't get it to start," exclaimed Mary, out of breath and fighting back tears.

"Relax—get your breath—we'll go get the car."

"I took it without his permission—and now it's dead in the middle of the road. I'm screwed, Brian—I stole the car," she blurted out.

"Don't worry, Baby Girl, it'll be all right. We'll go get the car and get it back here," he assured her. "Let me get my rain slicker and you can bring me back to it. We'll leave Roddy here where's it's dry."

"No, I don't want to be alone," the seven year old cried out, clutching his mother.

"All right, all right, Roddy, we'll put you in the truck with your mom and me and take you with us." Brian bounded into the cottage and emerged a few seconds later wearing rain gear and holding a poncho.

"Mary, put this on and let's go get the car," he instructed, ushering mother and child out into the driving rain.

Brian backed the Ford onto Deptula Lane and proceeded up the road. By now, the torrential downpour had carved deep pockets of rainwater into the gravel surface of the tiny, private road. Following her directions, he turned the vehicle right onto Webhannet Drive and drove south for approximately a quarter mile, spotting the woman's Toyota, its emergency lights flashing, mired in a low spot on the road. The rain, pummeling the pickup in a nonstop deluge, was dropping more water on the windshield than the wipers could manage to disperse. He pulled the truck off the pavement at the edge of an immense accumulation of puddle water and stopped. Twenty yards beyond the disabled vehicle, the wind-driven ocean struck at the granite retaining barrier and sent a wall of seawater spouting twenty feet in the air.

"Maybe later we can go for a walk," called out Brian, his body halfway out of the truck's cabin. His attempt at humor was lost on the nearly hysterical woman. "Where are the keys?" he hollered, prompting her to rifle through her rain-soaked jeans and come up with them. "Stay here," he instructed forcefully.

Following five minutes of futility trying to turn the engine over, he sloshed his way back to the pickup.

"Not even close," he reported to Mary and the boy. "That means we go with plan B. Mary, you're going to have to get out and help me. The car's in neutral. You get behind the wheel and steer. I'll push from behind. Once we get the car out of the puddle, you run back and get Roddy. I'll keep it rolling. We'll push it home. Once Roddy's in the car, you resume steering—except this time from the side of the car, helping to push. Got it?"

"Got it," she responded. Already the water had completely penetrated Brian's leather boots. His feet were painfully cold and wet.

Brian took a deep breath and gripped the rear bumper of the vehicle. The car and he were standing in nearly a foot of water. From behind, gale forced winds pushed at his back. He had to get the car rolling, he thought, there was no plan C.

"Ready?" he called out. Mary yelled back. Her response was unintelligible. He assumed it was 'yes' and prepared to push. A moment before attempting his fete of strength, he was reminded of something—Saint Christopher, the patron saint of travelers and a favorite of his mother. Vatican II had ruled this saint a figment of everyone's imagination and busted him. He remembered his mom hearing this and dismissing it, saying the good men had been tired from all their holy work and made an honest mistake. So there was the difference of opinion, the pious, all knowing theologians of Vatican II versus Elizabeth Kelly, his sainted mother. No contest, he thought to himself.

"Saint Christopher—I need you here," he called out before exerting his entire upper body strength into the car. He thought he felt movement, slight, but movement. Digging his feet into the pavement, he found a pothole and pushed off from it. The Toyota bucked and then began to move. He plowed forward through the water, the vehicle rolling noticeably faster with each step. Seconds passed and they had cleared the puddle.

"Get Roddy," he called out to the boy's mother, now putting the power of his legs as well as one shoulder into the undertaking. They were on level ground and, gratefully, had the wind at their backs. Continuing to push, he finally caught sight of Mary rushing by him with her son.

"Jump in the back seat," she hollered, her words barely audible over the howling wind.

"We've got to get this thing rolling as fast as possible—on account of the rise in the road up ahead. It's not much of a rise but we better get over it on our first try. Understand?" he shouted out. He was applying laws learned in physics class from years before—inertia: the tendency of a body in motion to remain in motion.

"Yes," she answered, conserving words and energy. Brian pushed off with his legs in an all out effort to increase speed. Forty yards in front of them a vehicle, the first they had encountered, turned the bend in the road and rolled toward them.

"Don't let up, Mary—keep pushing," he called out. The car, its headlights temporarily blinding them, approached and passed with no hint of deceleration. "We're almost to the rise—don't let up," he cautioned. The rise in Webhannet Road came just before the right-of-way down to Crescent Beach. A few feet later Brian felt the resistance on the vehicle from the upward slope. He let out a roar and pushed his shoulder into the car. It was at the exact moment when all momentum seemed to be lost that the two felt the crest of the small hill and the vehicle slowly began to regain some speed.

"It's done—we're over the hump," proclaimed an exuberant Brian as the Toyota slowly rolled alongside the one hundred foot break in oceanfront homes. Here, the action of the waves sent water up over the seawall and onto them. The salt water splashing down onto the car elicited screams of terror from the little boy.

"It's okay, Baby—it's okay," reassured Mary. Twenty seconds passed and the Toyota was coasting down the moderate slope in the direction of Brian's cottage. The remaining two hundred yards to the end of Deptula Lane took another ten minutes with the final, agonizing fifty feet made over the potholed, gravel road.

"Leave the car in the road Mary. It's okay. I own this end of the street—and—well, I'm drained. You guys go in the house. I'll go back for my truck." The woman pulled her young son from the back seat and hustled him inside while Brian trudged back the quarter mile to the site of the breakdown.

Fifteen minutes later, Brian burst out of the darkness and rain and onto the porch, his body soaked to the skin. When he turned the doorknob and pushed open the living room door, he found the boy huddled in a dry blanket, his rain drenched clothes tossed in pile in the corner of the room.

"Not a bad idea," he commented, closing the door behind him. His raincoat already off and on the floor of the porch, he walked past mother and son, through the kitchen and into the bedroom. He returned with two garments in hand. The first was a pair of oversized, flannel pajama tops which he flipped onto Roddy's head. The second was an extra large tee shirt with the inscription *I'm with stupid* on the front along with a horizontal arrow pointing out the direction in which the imbecile could be located. "This was the rage one year up at Old Orchard Beach. The French Canadians couldn't get enough of them. Now why don't you guys use the bedroom to change into these and I'll crank up the heat." Her shirt caused Mary to laugh out loud, albeit through chattering teeth. "I'll also put on hot water for tea. It's all I have in the house right now."

Mother and son disappeared behind the knotty pine door of the bedroom while their host, his clothing completely soaked, puttered in the kitchen. "Mary, check out the bottom drawer of the bureau. I may have something else you can slip on under the 'stupid' shirt in there," he suggested.

"It's okay—the 'stupid' shirt will be fine," she called out. "I just feel terrible leaving all these wet clothes on your floor."

"If you feel that bad then you could always run out to the back yard and hang them on the clothes line—you know, to let them dry overnight," he wisecracked.

"Now why didn't I think of that?" she came back.

His guests emerged from the bedroom seconds later and made their way though the small kitchen and back into the combination living room and dining room.

"Oh, Butler, master Roddy and I will be having our tea in the dining room tonight," Mary instructed, injecting snootiness in her voice.

"Forgive my boldness, Ma'am, but is there any reason why you won't be having your tea in the library tonight?" asked Brian, deciding to play along with the joke.

"I cannot tolerate boldness in servants! You will be replaced in the morning, do you hear? And if you must know—the library is currently under four feet of water. That is why we are having our tea out here—my soon-to-be-fired butler."

"Well, now I can see how things will be when you buy me out at the lodge and I become fulltime groundskeeper—hell on earth."

It was only a few minutes later when Brian carried a tray of hot beverages into the room, placing it down on the table. After preparing each cup of tea to specifications, he excused himself, slipped into the bedroom, and returned in five minutes dressed in flannel long johns. "No snickering from the peanut gallery—they're dry. That's all that matters right now." He fell back on the couch beside Mary and began sipping on his tea. It took only a moment for him to realize that the woman's mood had turned serious.

"Are you okay?" he asked.

"With all the excitement I'd forgotten how much trouble I was in."

"What do you mean?"

"I told you. I took the car without permission. Duane was drinking and starting to act up. I was afraid for Roddy because he seemed to be mad at him for something. I panicked and stole the car."

"It'll be okay. We'll get the car started in the morning and bring it back to him. It'll be okay."

"It's his car, Brian. I took *his* car without his permission. Isn't that grand theft-auto?"

"Oh, please, you live with the guy. We'll get it running in the morning and bring it back."

"God, he's going to be pissed at me."

"I promise—it'll be okay, so stop worrying." Her son had already finished his tea and was now embracing his mother. Mary, balancing her cup on one knee, had slumped sideways with her head resting on Brian's shoulder. The room grew quiet except for the roar of the wind from outside and the sound of rain pelting on the windows. Brian sipped intermittently on his beverage while his guests seemed to fall in and out of a light sleep. Leaning against him, Mary's body gave off a shiver every thirty seconds or so, as if attempting to shed the effect of the time spent out in the cold rain.

"You know kid, I think it'd be a good idea to get the little guy in bed and under the warm covers," he suggested.

"We can stay the night?"

"Yes, of course. Is that okay with you, Roddy?" The little boy nodded yes behind sleepy eyes.

"Now, Roddy, you'll be sleeping in the small bed next to the window. That's the bed my little daughter, she's not even two, sleeps in. The only bad thing about that is she's just a little girl—and sometimes she has an accident—an accident that doesn't dry all the time."

"She spills stuff?" he asked. His question brought laughter from the adults.

"I was only kidding with you. The bed will be nice and dry," confessed Brian.

"Oh, God, feel my feet," exclaimed Mary. He reached down and clutched her right foot.

"Cold feet, warm heart, that's what they say," he commented. "We'll work on that next—but first things first, put the big guy to bed." After directing her son to thank their host for the use of the cottage, she escorted the boy into the bed-

room. She spent the next ten minutes tucking him in and reassuring him everything would work out fine.

Returning to the living room, she found the television on but with the vol-
ume set on low. From the kitchen Brian instructed her to get comfortable on the
couch and wait for him. Seconds later, he stepped back into the room carrying
an oversized towel in his hands.

"Turn sideways, feet up," he ordered, gesturing to her to lift her feet. Turning
herself to one side, she lifted them as instructed. He joined her on the couch,
propping her feet up on his lap and wrapping them in a heated towel, no doubt
just removed from the oven door.

"Oh, oh, thank you, Brian—that feels so, so good," she whispered. She closed
her eyes and allowed her head to roll back. "I could really get used to treatment
like this." No words were exchanged by the two friends for the next few minutes
while he pressured the heat from the towel against her skin. "You know, you've
gotten the coldness out of my feet but I'm still half frozen everywhere else," she
commented, following her declaration with an exaggerated shiver. He responded
with a devilish, sideways glance followed by an almost undetectable shake of the
head. "What I need here is a few minutes of body heat," she declared, pulling her
feet away and scrambling across the couch. Within seconds she was seated in his
lap, her left arm resting on his shoulder.

"Mary, wait now, we've got to be careful here, I'm—" She stopped him in mid
sentence, bringing her mouth to his. He returned the kiss, his body already experiencing the same pleasurable arousal it had the past summer during their
embrace in the pool. Incredibly, he realized, he was already fully erect as the
weight of her diminutive body, a body clothed only in a light tee shirt, pressed
down on him. He tried to speak at the end of an extended half minute kiss, only
to have her reengage their lips and reassume full control of the goings on. When
the young woman sensed he was beyond the point of mounting any further
resistance, she pulled her lips away.

"Besides being the sweetest man I have ever met in my life, you have a fan-
tastic body," she whispered, pushing her hand beyond the waistband of his long
johns and examining his erect penis. She dallied there, watching her manipula-
tion register on his face. "Besides the obvious," she stated, clutching tightly to his
erection, "you have practically no fat around your waist or anyplace else—and
you're so tall." She brought her eyes back to his and searched for evidence of any
resistance. She saw none. "I want you to make love to me," she said.

"Are you sure you know what you're doing?"

"What do you mean by that?"

"I mean—I'm married."

"You're separated."

"Millie warned me that I was getting too close to you."

"So why didn't you listen to her warnings?" He shrugged. She pressed her lips
to Brian's, reminding him of how he arrived in his present circumstances.

"I'll make love to you—but just so I know it's absolutely what you want—
and that I'm married—lie down in the bedroom for fifteen minutes and think it

over. Come back for me then and it'll be done—because at this point there's nothing or no one I want more than you." She looked deeply into his hazel eyes and knew he was sincere. She left him with a final, passionate kiss and disappeared into the bedroom. He walked into the kitchen and checked the clock. It was exactly eleven-thirty.

Brian opened his eyes to the sound of the television droning softly behind him. He had nodded off. Jumping to his feet, he stepped into the kitchen and checked the time. The clock read twelve-fifteen. He stood for a moment, questioning his inability to remain awake. Clearly the lateness of the hour and the exertion from the rescue of the car had contributed much to his loss of consciousness. Quietly making his way to the bedroom door, he threw the latch and swung it open. The room was dark, illuminated only by a night light he had resurrected from the bureau for Roddy's benefit. In front of him, Mary lay sprawled out on the full-sized bed, her body half exposed as the bed covers laid threaded between her legs. The lines of her petite body and the exposure of her perfect skin immediately re-ignited his passion.

"Mary, have you changed your mind?" he whispered in her ear as he knelt beside the bed. She did not stir. "Mary, have you changed your mind?" His words brought a fluttering from beneath her eyelids.

"Brian, I'm sorry—I'm just so tired. I'm sorry, I can't stay awake. But you can have me if you want. You know it's all right," she murmured back. He leaned forward and kissed her on the mouth. She responded weakly. Her face looked beautiful as she drifted into unconsciousness. The fire from within him only increased. He moved down her body, taking her exposed nipple into his mouth and caressing it with his tongue. Her breasts were small, as he knew they would be, and exceptionally soft to the touch. He saw no possibility of reversing himself. He felt his stimulation increase while he ran his tongue along the white skin of her stomach, stopping and delicately kissing her navel. His heart pounded with excitement, knowing in moments he would lie with her, embrace her, feel the warmth of her body, and join it with his own. His eyes widened. He reached down and ran the tips of his fingers over her moist, flaxen pubic hair. His body shook with anticipation. From across the room, a sound caught his attention, causing him to glance up from Mary's body. There, he caught sight of Roddy. The seven year old appeared frightened, his eyes frozen wide open.

"Is my mommy dead?" he asked pathetically, the nightlong trauma to him seeming to culminate in this last, unimaginable nightmare. Brian raised his head from the woman's body.

"No, Roddy—of course not. She's just very tired from pushing the car and all." The boy seemed unconvinced as tears appeared in his eyes. "No, it's all right," reassured Brian, pulling himself to his feet and pulling the covers over the young mother's nude body. When the child began to weep, he circled the bed and went to his side. "What's this crying stuff? If I can prove to you that your mom's okay, will you stop crying?" The boy indicated yes. The child was then brought over to the edge of his mother's bed and encouraged to feel the beating of her heart. "If she was dead you wouldn't be feeling that," stated Brian. "Would you feel better sleeping right next to mommy?" Again, the boy did not speak but indicated yes. He slipped the seven year old into bed beside his mother, giving each a kiss on the top of the head. "Now if you start getting any crazy thoughts about her being dead again, just reach over and feel her heart beating," he counseled before leaving the room and settling in on the couch for the remainder of the night.

Brian awoke Thursday morning to the sight of Mary Porterfield standing over the couch, a cup of fresh brewed tea in her hand. The storm had passed, now well beyond the Gulf of Maine and pounding Nova Scotia. Following a few minutes of meaningless chit chat, the two friends talked in earnest. Not wanting the woman to place herself back in harms way, he suggested she and Roddy move into the cottage, at least for the time being. He would move up to the main house at the complex. Mary would only be expected to pay him whatever rent she could afford. For transportation, they would share access to the Ford, the only time he would need sole control of the pickup being when he had Colleen visiting.

The Porterfields took possession of the cottage on Sunday, November 12th. On the day before, Mary was escorted to Sanford by Bobby and Perez where the pickup was loaded with all their worldly possessions and moved to Wells Beach. The entire experience passed without incident.

XXX

When Thanksgiving Day approached and no invitation was forthcoming from his wife in Bedford, Brian made the best of his circumstances and enlisted Mary to put together a holiday celebration at the cottage. Hosts and guests only numbered four, Mary and Roddy, Brian and Perez. Perez became available when his steady girlfriend decided to accept an invitation from her eldest daughter and traveled to Connecticut for the day. The festivities at the tiny cottage on Deptula Lane went well. Brian thought he detected a trace of detachment in Mary's demeanor, particularly near the end of the day, but did not question her on it.

When the phone rang Friday morning, the day after Thanksgiving, and Mary unexpectedly invited Brian down to the cottage for a talk, he suspected something of importance was on the horizon. Southern Maine was riding out the final few weeks of autumn. The air was cold and the first traces of ice were beginning to show up in the harbor and estuary.

The pretty blonde had a half pot of coffee already prepared when Brian came through the door and claimed a chair at the dining room table.
"You look sad, Kid," he commented. She dropped her eyes.
"I am."
"And you need to share this with me, right?" She nodded yes and walked to the kitchen, returning with a tray and two cups of decaffeinated. She sat down beside him, placing her hand on his.
"I'm afraid I've been running up a wicked phone bill over the past week. I've been on the phone with Beals Island—my mom and dad—and Rod. They've been encouraging me to come home—to start again—to give Rod a second chance."
"And you've told them you would?"
"Yes, just before Thanksgiving. I didn't say anything then, cause—I didn't want the holiday spoiled for you," she explained.
"I'm going to miss you more than you'll know," he confessed, his eyes moistening.
"You know how I feel about you, Brian—and I know how you feel about your wife, your daughter, and your marriage."
"It isn't just that—there's also a few years separating us."
"That never bothered me—so it shouldn't have bothered you," she insisted. She drew in a sip of coffee and continued. "You have done more for me than anyone, except for maybe my parents—but I'm going to ask you for one more favor."

"Consider it done."

"Take us home—take me home in the pickup. Be there with me when I go home."

"Come on, Mary—anything but that."

"It means everything to me, Brian."

"To go up there and hand you over to another guy—and then drive home alone. Oh, Jesus, don't ask that of me."

"I don't want to make the trip up there without you. Say you'll do it for me." She sprang to her feet and embraced him. "Please, I'll make sure he's nowhere to be seen until you're gone."

"When?"

"Sunday."

"Well, this isn't my weekend to get the baby, so that's not a problem."

"It means a lot to me," she added while holding the embrace.

"We'll leave early in the morning and make a day of it," he said, unable to deny her this final request.

At seven-thirty on the morning of November 26th, the pickup pulled out from Deptula Lane and began the long drive up the Maine coast to Beals Island in Washington County. Most everything had been packed the night before and protected with a blue tarp spread across the back of the truck. The plan called for them to stay with the highway from Wells until Brunswick and then rejoin Route 1 for the better part of the trip. Early on, Mary surrendered her window seat to her son. She was happy to sit beside Brian for the remainder of the journey.

The trio's first stop did not come until Thomaston where they found a cozy café in which to grab a late breakfast. Entering the town, Brian pointed out the state prison to Roddy and made a bold prediction.

"Look, Roddy, in two or three years that's where Duane will live." His humor was lost on the seven year old but not on Mary who gave him a playful elbow to the ribs. It was not long after their breakfast stop that they pulled off the road again. They were in Rockland. The sidewalks were mostly deserted, a far cry from the spring and summer when tourists stream through the town, exposing themselves to the art of the Wyeth family. Window shopping was the order of the day on this Sunday as the three patrolled the main and side streets, searching out samples of the great, and not so great, painters and sculptors of the region. Brian, a lifelong critic of abstract art, delighted in minimizing most all this 'work' exhibited in the windows of small galleries. When Mary grew cold they retreated back to the pickup and continued northward.

Their next stop in an itinerary of random stops was Camden. Not so much a working town as Rockland, there was a sad tranquility to this harbor village in the off season, its sidewalks accustomed to the constant foot traffic of gentrified tourists, but now quiet.

"As your tour guide for today it is my duty to point out to you that quality motion pictures like *Peyton Place* and *The Man Without a Face* were shot on location here in Camden," announced Brian, pretending to speak through a megaphone. Having no problem finding a place to pull over, they strolled through a public park. Carved out from a densely commercial neighborhood, it rested on the side of a hill, affording visitors a splendid view of the harbor and adjacent waterfall. Brian glanced down at his watch while mother and son walked ahead for a better viewing of the cascading water.

"One-thirty guys, we've got to get back on the road." Remaining in town only long enough to purchase three cups of hot chocolate, they rejoined Route 1 and continued toward Washington County. "I can't help but liken our movement north on this road to the falling of sand through an hour glass. When we get to the end, it's good-bye," declared Brian, prompting no response from Mary but causing her to rest her head on his shoulder. There was no lighthearted banter for the remainder of the journey. Banter was replaced by human touch, some-times subtle, but in all instances meaningful.

"Turn here, Brian, right onto Route 187," called out the woman. Following her direction, he turned the Ford off Route 1 and pointed it due east to Jonesport. "It's been two years since you saw grandpa and grandma, are you excited?" Mary asked.

"I don't remember what they look like," the boy answered.

"I've shown you pictures. Don't you go and get all shy with them now," she warned. "And don't you get all shy with them either," she counseled Brian, inject-ing a trace of humor to the conversation. As they drove this last leg of the trip home, Brian made note of his surroundings. The sides of the road were largely lined with trees, the occasional single family or mobile home only popping out from the tree line every half mile or so. Washington County was far more rural than York County, he thought.

Ten minutes passed and he lifted his foot from the accelerator. They were approaching Jonesport. Following a complete stop, he turned left and slowly drove in the direction Mary indicated. Catching his first glimpse of real water less than fifty feet away on the right, he looked beyond to an arching bridge.

"That's the bridge out to Beals—we'll be taking it," she announced, simulta-neously tightening her grip on his arm. Seconds later, the Ford reached an inter-section. At the corner, a residential home displayed a set of ceramic toilet bowls in the front yard. He gestured toward them. "They were there when I left two years ago. There are a lot of free spirits in Jonesport and Beals," she added laugh-ingly. The pickup headed up and onto the bridge. "Over there on the right, facing that small island—that's Barney's Cove—where I grew up," she stated proudly.

"It looks beautiful from here," he commented.

The summit at the arch of the bridge afforded a panoramic seascape on both sides of the vehicle. The pickup crept along as Brian took in these new sights, all the while envisioning Mary growing up in these surroundings.

"I can actually picture the teenage Mary Porterfield walking over this bridge and searching out the boys in Jonesport," he said, sharing his thoughts with her.

"And you'd be picturing right," she added. The Ford rolled onto Beal's Island less than a minute after leaving the mainland. She directed her friend to turn right and drive straight up and over a hill. A few hundred yards up the road, they broke the crest of the hill and were staring out through the windshield at the hamlet of Barney's Cove. The late afternoon sun glistened over the blue water visible between and over the houses built along the waterline a short distance in front of them.

"My house is the cedar shingled one down to our right." Following directions, he steered the truck onto a paved driveway and behind a newer pickup. "That's my daddy's new truck. At least we know their home." Mary and Roddy piled out of the Ford just as the side door to the house swung in and a woman appeared on the small porch. Mary ushered her son toward his grandmother who had already descended the three steps from the porch. Brian watched as the three exchanged hugs. Shortly after, they were joined by a large man with snow white hair. Following a brief hesitation, father and daughter embraced. Moments later, and after her parents gestured her toward the house, she led the family members in Brian's direction. Still seated behind the wheel, he quickly pushed open the door and jumped down to the pavement.

"Mommy, Daddy, this is Brian Kelly, the man I told you about who I worked for and helped me so much," she said proudly. The man and woman stepped forward and shook his hand, thanking him for his efforts on behalf of their daughter. Brian appeared embarrassed by their gratitude and praise. Aside from the couple's down to earth attitude, he was struck by their ages. They did not appear too many years older than him. When the Porterfields invited him inside they were waived off by Mary who explained that she and Brian needed to go for a short walk and that he needed to leave for Wells soon after. When Roddy showed resistance to being separated from his mother, he was informed that no less than three toys were on the table in the house awaiting his attention. Assured his mother would rejoin him in a few minutes, he bolted from the family and made for the house.

Following another series of brief expressions of thanks, Mary took Brian's hand and led him out of the yard and onto the road.

"We'll walk the circle up by the cemetery and then I'll let you head home," she explained. He had grown quiet. The moment he dreaded had arrived. For the first few minutes she was content to point out properties and landmarks, the most notable being a rusting, long abandoned gas pump standing by the edge of the road.

"When I was carrying Roddy there were times I felt like that gas pump—alone, abandoned, useless, worthless. I'm over that now," she announced. Two cars drove past the couple in the course of the stroll and both acknowledged Mary's return home with a short greeting. It was dusk when she pulled him over to the edge of a small cemetery.

"That's the grave of Barney Beal. He was a great man and I'm descended from him—somewhat. My mom's a Beal."

"Well, I knew there was something that made you special," he replied. Mary drew herself next to him.

"Now you—hear what I have to say. I didn't ask you to drive me up here just because I'm nearly broke and wanted to save on bus fare. Well, maybe partly, but that was a small part," she confessed, laughing and beginning to cry simultaneously. "You're here, Brian Kelly, because I wanted you to know exactly where I am and where I live. I wanted you to know that you can call me anytime—for any reason. Now, in your mind, I won't be in some strange place you can't even picture in your head. You know I love you and I know—in your own sweet, sweet way, you love me. I understand everything more than you think—me, this little hick from Washington County. I know you love your wife—and that she is really, really beautiful. I know how important your marriage is to you because of your daughter—and your religion, Millie explained to me about your religion. I admire that, I really do. It's rare—and it's special. But life is crazy. So I want you to know I'm here—just in case life doesn't work out the way you planned. Have I made a big enough fool of myself yet, Mr. Brian Kelly?" she asked, her head tilted downward staring at the ground. He reached down and lifted her chin.

"Nothing Mary Porterfield says to me could ever be foolish. You own too much of me."

"I won't be kissing you good-bye in front of the house—with my parents and the neighbors looking on—not a real kiss. But we can do that here," she declared. He bent down and they kissed, neither knowing if it would be their last.

"Can we make a promise to each other?" Brian asked amidst a last embrace. "Like what?"

"Six months from today—that would be May 26th, we contact each other, and find out how the other is doing. Seriously, we make a commitment to reach the other, no matter what."

"I promise," she said, placing a final kiss on the side of his face.

Mary turned from the vehicle and walked toward the house as Brian turned the ignition key. She did not turn back to him. The beams from his headlights allowed him to make out her final gesture, a poignant wave delivered over her shoulder.

XXXI

Margaret swung open the front door to the house and called out to anyone within shouting distance.

"I want everyone packed and ready to leave in thirty minutes," she ordered. From upstairs came the sound of scrambling feet.

"Mrs. Kelly, did you say something about leaving early?" called down Moira.

"Yes, I've had a very bad day and the sooner I can get to the coast to unwind, the better."

"It shouldn't be a problem, Mrs. Kelly. I already have Colleen and I packed and it's just a matter of getting us cleaned up a wee bit for the trip." Having abandoned the office five hours early, her and everyone else's schedule was turned upside down. She stormed upstairs and into the bedroom. Seconds later her suitcase was on the bed and she was cramming in clothes for a two and a half day weekend. Her heart was pounding frantically inside her chest. At the moment, she needed the peace and isolation only her oceanfront retreat could provide. She paused for a second and considered whether to ask Brian to take Colleen for a second, consecutive weekend. Would he mind? Her husband had become a mystery to her. Astonished by his stubbornness and resilience, she never imagined he could or would drag the separation out to what was now nearly two months. She missed him, terribly. Margaret crossed the room and stood in front of his bureau. He had not returned to the house since October. It was now December 8th. Somehow, he had survived the separation through Thanksgiving, but Christmas would be different, she thought. Pulling out the top drawer, she fumbled through small, incidentals of his life; an expired license, his passport, a few family pictures. Her eye picked up on a vaguely familiar envelope leaning against the back panel. She pulled it out and removed the card tucked inside. She remembered it. She remembered it well. It was the congratulations card she had given him back at Southside High when he had made the honor roll. Brian had held on to it for twenty-two years. *Take away your great intellect, tremendous good looks, family fortune, creative genius and charismatic personality—and you're a nobody like the rest of us! Congratulations Brian…Maggie May.* She shook her head in disbelief as droplets formed in the corner of her eyes.

"Oh, Christ," she whispered just above her breath before slipping the card back into the drawer.

Maine was blessed with unseasonably warm temperatures on this weekend and the shoreline at Wells Beach was no exception. However, with the warm flow of air came thick fog along the coast, a bi-product of the warm air and cold ocean water. This was not lost on Margaret as she pulled the BMW up to the garage door at Wells Beach. Instructing Moira to unload the car, she took Colleen in tow and climbed the steps leading onto the two-sided porch. The air hung stagnant around them, the temperature fluttering around sixty degrees. Pushing in the kitchen door, she threw her keys on the table and made her way to the living room. There, ordinarily, the picture window would have afforded her a full, one hundred and eighty degree view of the Atlantic. However, at the moment, she could barely make out the wooden steps leading onto the sand just twenty feet from the house. She let out a frustrated sigh, undoubtedly willing to sacrifice the warm temperatures for a mile of visibility.

Margaret was perched comfortably in a living room chair when the phone rang from out in the kitchen. Raising her eyes from her book, she was curious to learn who was trying to reach her. She had purposely restricted the number of people privy to this line. Unaccountably, her mind hastened back to the office and the events that day. Her stomach knotted from just the thought of those earlier events, she pushed them from her mind.

"Mrs. Kelly, it's Millie Pierce wanting to speak to you," cried out Moira.

"Tell her I'm sorry but I really can't come to the phone." She threw her head back and waited for the sound of the phone deposited on its cradle. It did not come.

"She says this call cannot wait," announced the nanny nervously.

"Oh, God, make it stop," she muttered under her breath, pulling herself out of the chair and walking to the phone.

"Yes, Millie," she said in a foul tone, making no attempt to mask her irritation.

"I'm about to do you a favor so I'd appreciate none of this sassiness," replied the woman.

"It's been a very trying day, Millie—and I'm quite on edge at the moment."

"I've called to give you a warning about something—and a suggestion." Margaret let out an exaggerated sigh.

"Yes."

"There's been some trouble in your marriage of late, trouble Brian has kept to himself. There's also the matter of a young girl who has taken quite a shine to your husband. Now you may think you're God's gift to the male gender but I'm calling to tell you that you've got competition for that man and you're only a baby's breath away from losing him."

"Please, Millie, I do appreciate—"

"Listen to me now! It's clear to me you don't know how close you are to losing your husband. You know, you may think you're a beautiful woman but you've got more competition than you ever dreamed of—and I think you know who I'm talking about. As I see it, it's this simple: you act now, tonight, or waive good-bye to a man who's probably too good for you in the first place. And let me be honest—and I think you know that's something I believe in—being open and honest. It's your marriage that I want to see stay intact—for Brian's sake—because I think it means a damn more to him than to you. I don't know what caused this whole parting of the ways—nor do I care to know. I'm simply saying for his sake, for your daughter's sake—and yes, even for your sake, do something! He left the lodge a couple of minutes ago and if I know him, and I think I do, he'll be starting on his walk up the beach to the jetty as soon as he gets back to the cottage. That means he'll be passing right by your house there on the ocean in a short while."

"Thank you, Millie. You've certainly given me something to consider," answered Margaret thoughtfully.

"Don't just sit there on your can thinking about it—do something!"

"Is there anything else?"

"No, I've spoken my peace. I'd say the rest is up to you."

"Well, thank you for your candor and frankness."

"Oh, please, stop it with the college words. Just wake up missy, or you'll lose something you'll regret for the rest of your life. And with that said I'm out of advice and patience."

"Good night, Millie," she said, hanging up the phone and screening out any last response from the woman.

Margaret walked through the living room and out onto the porch. The fog showed no sign of lifting, hanging over the sand and distant crashing waves like an eerie shroud. The air temperature was cooling but still was likely on the plus side of fifty degrees. She ducked inside and grabbed a light jacket.

"Moira, I'm going for a short walk along the beach. Answer the phone if it rings."

"Yes, Ma'am, I won't even lift a finger for dinner till you get back."

Margaret descended the porch steps and a shorter set of stairs down to the beach. Hidden by the fog, waves crashed an indeterminate distance in front of her. On this evening the lights from neighboring Kennebunkport, the harbor jetty, even the bank of lights at Wells Beach's main parking area, were hidden by the fog bank that hugged the shoreline. She walked toward the crashing surf, only able to make out depressions or swirls in the sand twenty feet out in front of her. Margaret paused and reflected for a moment, her surroundings empty of anything resembling a reference point. The packed sand beneath her feet was not in complete darkness. The previous night saw a full moon and a small amount of lunar rays were managing to penetrate the thick fog. She turned to retrace her steps back to the house but could not pick up on any light, artificial or otherwise, from behind. She moved ahead, her eyes becoming adjusted to the muted light. She was picking up on the subtle movement of fog banks, something that lent itself to thoughts of sinister deeds and people.

"Brian," she called out meekly. She listened for a response over the sound of the waves crashing nearby. There was none. She followed her instincts, hoping to move away from the surf and toward the ocean front homes. A few seconds passed and she realized she was sloshing through a stagnant pool of ocean water, no doubt left behind by the last high tide. Moments later, the cold from the water penetrated her flat heeled shoes.

"Brian! Brian, are you there?" she bellowed, the sound of distress making its way into her voice. Again, there was no reply. "Brian, can you hear me!" she hollered at the top of her lungs.

"Hello," echoed a response from a considerable distance.

"Brian, is that you?" she answered, straining her voice.

"My name's Brian," answered a familiar voice.

"It's Maggie. You are Brian Kelly, right?"

"How many stinking Brians do you figure are out on the beach here tonight?" he came back, sounding measurably closer.

"Brian, stop clowning and find me over here."

"Keep hollering and I'll hone in on your voice."

"I'm standing out in the middle of the thickest fog I've ever seen—trying to find my husband because he walks out in this shit I'm told—and I haven't got the first idea of where the fuck I am—only that my feet are soaked and I've probably ruined my shoes thanks to the salt water all—"

"I'm right behind you, Keogh." She spun around to see her husband standing ten feet away, partially hidden behind a slowly drifting wave of fog. She ran to him, placing her head on his chest and wrapping her arms around his shoulders. Her embrace was not returned.

"I had it on good authority that I might connect with you out here," she said.

"Yeah, I'm out here quite a bit these days—just like in the old days."

"It's been almost two months since we had any kind of a talk. I could use an ear about now," she confessed.

"Why not," he answered with an uncharacteristic lack of enthusiasm. She tucked her arm under his and set off walking.

"Wrong way, Keogh," he interrupted, turning her around. "Why don't we walk toward the jetty." She extended an understanding nod and switched directions.

"Brian, I'm coming off one of the worst days of my life. Things are getting out of control at home and—today in the office—that was the crowning jewel of this whole month."

"It sounds like my whole fall."

"We're not just talking bad here—we're talking in the toilet. My life's in the fucking toilet right now—big time."

"Well, if nothing else, you've raised my curiosity on this thing at the office," he admitted.

"I'll need a little time to build up my courage to the point where I can even talk about that shit in the office today. Brian, it was fucking awful." She tightened her hold on his arm, dropping her head onto his shoulder. "Let's start with something smaller and work up to that. First of all, Moira's given me her notice. She's given me a month. I offered her more money, less hours—it didn't make a difference."

"Has she found something else?"

"No, I asked. She just wants out of the house. It has something to do with me, no doubt. Colleen's going to be devastated."

"When did this happen?"

"About a week ago." He shook his head and continued walking, his wife continuing to lean against him.

"Jenny and I have been at each other's throats of late. Cross words here and there led to a handful of shouting matches. She's sided with you, and that's without knowing anything about why we separated. Brendan's tried to smooth things over but with only limited success. I've been stressed without you—and it's shown. Jenny's gone so far as to threaten to move out. She's grown into quite the independent little thing."

"You've got to guard against things like this. It threatens the family—and the family is everything. I know—I've learned the hard way. The family is everything, Keogh," he counseled. His wife nodded her head and let out an exaggerated shiver.

"I do believe the temperature is dropping," she observed, yanking him closer to her. Brian stopped long enough to peel off his overcoat, draping it over her shoulders. "Are you sure?" she asked, pulling the garment around her.

"Maggie May, is there anything else?"

"He's gone you know."

"I know."

"Where are we?" she questioned, the fog continuing to keep most everything around them shrouded in gray.

"The jetty should be no more than twenty yards in front of us," he predicted. She grew more sober.

"Brian, I want you back."

"Is this an invitation to supper?"

"Kelly, I want you all the way back in my life—all the way." He glanced down at her, then out into the shapeless, gray mass in front of them.

"Are you sorry? Would you ever pull anything like this on me again?" She burst into tears.

"Never."

"It wasn't just me, Keogh—you did this to the whole family."

"I know that," she admitted, sounding genuinely contrite.

"If I decided to take you back, I'd insist that you make a concession to me, something that you'd feel a sting from."

"Like a whipping?" Her question caused him to chuckle.

"No, I'm actually afraid you might enjoy that too much." It was her turn to laugh.

"How much of a sting are we talking about here?"

"This is more in your area of expertise, but I'd estimate eight or ten grand."

"You want me to write you a check or buy you something?"

"No, there's no cash involved." She stared up at him curiously.

"Something worth ten grand and it won't cost me anything in cash," she repeated.

"Exactly."

"I give you this and we put this whole mess behind us?"

"That's the deal." She looked up at him. Her blue eyes searched his face for sincerity and, upon finding it, prompted her to action.

"Done." He leaned down and kissed his wife for the first time in over two months. "Now what have I just bargained away?" Margaret asked.

"Is it really important? Isn't the important thing that we've ended this insane time apart?"

"What have I bargained away, Kelly?" He looked down and smiled.

"One share of stock in the corporation, that's all." She looked into his eyes, surprised by her husband's demand. They had reached the jetty. "Okay, let's turn and head south."

"I can live with the stock thing. It's really only a formality. You're the one there most of the time and running it." He reached around his wife and pulled her closer.

"Have we reached the part in the program where you tell me about what happened in the office today that has you so shook up?" She closed her eyes and let out a prolonged moan.

"It is so horrible that just the thought of talking about it puts a knot in my stomach."

"It'll probably be therapeutic getting it out in the open—and sharing it with your lifetime mate." She glanced up, rolling her eyes.

"I was sitting at my desk this morning working on the notes for a financial statement, when I was suddenly interrupted. Chris Treadwell's mother, believe it or not, had made her way into the building—got by Gretchen downstairs—and was standing across the desk from me. And Brian, this bitch was breathing fire. Oh, God, was she upset." Margaret kept her head down while relating the story, not raising her eyes for so much as an instant. "She slammed the door to my office shut behind her, leaving us quite isolated. She began screaming at me about the mental condition of her son and how I was responsible for pushing him to the brink of a nervous breakdown."

"Ouch," he exclaimed. "Could the whole office hear her?"

"The entirety of Stark Street could hear her. Anyway, following a full two minute tirade, I tried to calm her with words of consolation."

"Oh, I'm sure that's exactly what she wanted at that point."

"My words were scarcely out of my mouth when this deranged woman lunged at me across the desk, actually grabbing hold of my collar."

"What did you do?"

"I grabbed for her hair—wrapping my fingers through her frizzy black hair with its visible gray roots—and pulled."

"You pulled her hair out?" asked Brian.

"No, I pulled her over the surface of my desk and onto the floor beneath me. She hit the floor with a hell of a thud, I'll tell you. At this point, she let out a shriek, from pain, from surprise, I'm not sure. I just knew she wasn't done struggling and so I set out to restrain her. I brought my knees down on her chest—and then I lost it—pounding the back of her head against the floor over and over until Vern and James rushed into the room and pulled me off of her. By this time, she was hysterical, in tears—wailing."

"Is she all right?"

"Vern called me on my cell phone from the hospital at about three. The tests had come back negative—no concussion—and Mrs. Treadwell had been sent home."

"Holy shit," murmured a dumbfounded Brian.

"I'd already put a call through to my personal attorney, Bill Eggleston. He advised me not to worry. She was the aggressor—she had come to my office after me. She lunged at me. I merely protected myself."

"She's okay, right?"

"Oh thanks, Brian—thanks for all the concern about me. I'm only your wife. She's fine, Brian—please, no more worrying about the unfortunate Mrs. Treadwell." He felt his wife's body shake with anxiety after recounting the incident back in Manchester. "So, how does it feel coming out on the winning side of one of our confrontations?"

"There were no winners here, Maggie May. We all had to give blood at the office. It sounds like the little boy toy didn't come out of this too good either."

"I feel really bad for Chris—maybe more for him than anyone. By the way, do you know exactly where we are and where we're going?"

"Absolutely, Keogh—absolutely." They continued to walk. He thought to himself how wonderful it was to have her back by his side. "You know, I've been thinking over your account of what went on in the office today. I don't know if you realize it, but there's an incredible coincidence buried in the details of your story."

"I know I'm going to regret asking, but, what coincidence is that?"

"Think about it, Maggie May: you pile drive this poor creature to the floor, kneel on her chest, take a firm grip of her by the hair and pound her head on the floorboards."

"Go on," she insisted, bracing herself for his observation.

"The kneeling on the chest—the tearing at the hair—the pounding of the head against a hard object—it's amazingly similar to the early stages of *biting* sex," he said. She broke out into a fit of laughter, causing him to follow suit.

"If I don't laugh—and that's my first real laugh of the day—then I'll cry." She stopped, turned, and buried her face in her husband's chest.

"Now will you be obliged to report this little incident to the board of accountancy up in Concord? I mean, what do you say? I'd like a determination on whether I've violated the code of conduct. Is it a violation to hammer the head of the mother of a former employee into the floor boards of my office? Somehow, I don't believe your actions are specifically covered under the rules of conduct," he teased. The woman shook her head but remained silent for the moment, allowing her husband to work his sarcasm on her. Eventually, her dim smile grew serious.

"You know, there does remain one more painful issue to address."

"And that would be?"

"That Mary girl—the chambermaid. My sources, limited as they are, tell me that you two did some bonding over the past two months."

"I grew very fond of her."

"I'll bet. Anyway, I'm going to have to ask you to curtail—no eliminate—all contact with her. I won't be able to function knowing you're around her."

"That won't be hard—she's living at the other end of the state."

"She's what?"

"She moved back home to Beals just after Thanksgiving."

"You're sure of that?"

"I should be. I'm the one who drove her there."

"Does Millie know?"

"Of course she does." Margaret closed her eyes and shook her head in disbelief.

"The nightmare continues. I've been outfoxed by the holy roller."

"What are you talking about?"

"Millie called me just before I came out here. She warned me I was about to lose you. It's what got me off my ass and out on the beach on this miserable night. I panicked."

"She probably sensed I was weakening—that I missed you guys so much and that I might do something I'd regret. With Mary gone home, I had nobody. Thankfully Millie stepped in and it's Maggie May groveling here instead of me," reasoned Brian aloud, taunting his wife with the exaggeration.

"Are you having fun, Kelly?"

"No, Keogh—fun will come later." She reacted with a playful bite to his shoulder.

"Hey, look, we're home," he announced, gesturing toward a house visible through the heavy fog.

"Wait until they see who I'm bringing home—particularly Jelly Bean," she said.

"And Keogh, give me ten minutes with Moira. She'll stay after I sweet talk her for a while and let her know my wife will be subjected to disciplinary action if she gives her any more crap." He stopped and turned straight on to his wife. "Do you have any idea how much I've missed you?"

"So the day's not going to turn out so bad after all," proclaimed Margaret, leaning forward and pressing her lips to his. They drew from the other's mouth, only pulling back after Brian let out a shudder from the cold air around them. They turned and took their final few steps to the porch.

"You know, Maggie May, I must admit you are taking the matter of that share of stock really well. I fully expected you to go through the roof on that. I'm proud of you kid—for showing maturity."

"Don't get too lavish with your praise, Kelly. I don't expect you to have that share of stock too long."

"Forget it, Keogh, you're not getting it back."

"Oh, really?"

"Yes, really." She shifted her blue eyes up at him as a devilish grin broke over her face.

"Let me set the stage for you: A certain stunning thirty-eight year old slips into an exquisitely formfitting, *red* dress—wearing no underwear. This woman, let's call her Maggie May for the sake of argument, positions herself in the lap of some helpless sap and commences to whisper baby talk in his ear, her voice taking on a Shirley Temple quality. This pathetic male, let's give him a name and call him Brian, squirms helplessly in his chair, knowing this woman will take his share of stock—and anything else she damn pleases—before she is done."

"Keogh, I happen to know that techniques like this are in direct violation of the Geneva Convention."

"Like I give a shit! Take me to the World Court. I'll wear that red dress and when I'm done with them their gavel will be sitting in my trophy case and the bailiff will be washing the BMW out in the parking lot."

"How long will you let me keep the share of stock?"

"You'll have it for Christmas—and I'll take it back on New Year's Day."

"So you'll wear the red dress on New Year's Day?"

"Yes, I'll sit in your lap during the Rose Bowl Parade and take back my share of stock. That'll start 1996 off on the right foot." They had reached the stairs leading up onto the porch.

"Are you sure you want me back?" he asked.

"Kelly, you're the only man who's any competition for me. You're a challenge."

"If you want, Monday morning we go to your office together, Maggie May—and show everyone the Kelly's are back—and the carnival is over."

"You'd do that for me, really?" He kissed her on the bridge of the nose. Brian smiled and looked up toward the living room picture window.

"It's going to be crowded," he said.

"Not really."

"Where are you putting Jenny and Brendan?"

"Nowhere, they're home."

"You left those two at home in Bedford—alone?"

"Yes, so what?"

"Knowing how they feel about each other?"

"What are you talking about?" He reached down, applying a head lock on his wife.

"Hello, McFly, is there anybody home in there? Hello," he called out, tapping the side of her head with his knuckles. "Earth to McFly, those two kids are falling deeper in love every day. I can't believe you haven't noticed it."

"You're crazy, Kelly!"

"Wake up, McFly, your daughter—my son—it was inevitable," he declared.

"Nooooooooo!"

If you enjoyed reading

Obscene Bliss

by

Thomas E. Coughlin

Look for his other works of fiction

Maggie May's Diary

Brian Kelly: Route 1

The Odyssey of Sheba Smith

The Messenger

A Short Story By

Thomas E. Coughlin

*I*t was just after one o'clock on a seasonably warm Saturday afternoon when a lurch from the brakes of the bus brought me out of a semiconscious state. I opened my eyes to behold my first view of the city where I would spend the next five hours and twenty minutes of my life. I had been slipping in and out of a daytime nap for the past three hours, ever since our bus crossed the state line from New York into Massachusetts. I was in the middle of a painfully long journey from Albany, New York to Camden, Maine, and now faced an extended layover in Lowell, Massachusetts. This inconvenience was the price I was paying for not hitching a ride with my roommate after college finals two weeks earlier.

After climbing down from the bus and claiming my luggage, a duffel bag and small, laundry satchel, I tried to locate a comfortable spot in the terminal to wait out the afternoon. It was early June and the waiting area within the terminal felt the effects of the sun's rays pouring through the nearby wall of windows. The air in the building was stagnant, borderline oppressive. It only took a few minutes of loitering on the wooden benches to convince me to find another way to occupy myself for the next five plus hours. So, after procuring the use of a locker for my belongings, I set out to explore the city of Lowell. I was advised by the attendant behind the main desk that the downtown area was a ten to fifteen minute walk away. This did nothing to dissuade me, not with five hours at my disposal.

Emerging from the terminal and into the front, loading area, I was immediately taken with a weather-beaten building standing not more than a hundred yards from me. The sun bleached, brick structure was likely a relic from the nineteenth century. What made it particularly interesting was the faded lettering still visible on its side. *Hood's Tooth Powder, Hood's Olive Ointment,* proclaimed the dated advertising, the advertisement far outliving the products themselves. For some unexplainable reason, the information contained in the lettering stayed with me over the course of the fifteen minute walk downtown.

Guided by directions from an attendant in the terminal, I was able to find my way to the heart of the city. It proved to be a pleasant experience, walking over cobblestone streets in the shadows of wonderfully preserved, nineteenth century buildings. From observation, I learned that Lowell was home to a national park, a park dedicated to this country's industrial revolution. Although tempted to take in some of the history surrounding me, I was limited by funds. Instead, I decided to browse some of the shops in the area.

After poking my head into a handful of retail establishments, I settled upon an antique shop. The aisles were cluttered with an assortment of hodgepodge, some of it interesting. I settled upon a display of postcards. In doing this, I was able to isolate an assorted group of cards from New Hampshire. From childhood vacations with my family, my interest and curiosity in New Hampshire's White Mountains caused me to search out items from that region. I removed postcards from behind index cards marked Lincoln, Woodstock, Conway, Twin Mountain and Mount Washington, always watching for locations that looked at least vaguely familiar. Careful to keep each group separated from the next, I methodically reviewed one after another, eventually setting aside a small quantity that interested me. The cards were individually priced. I culled out one or two higher priced ones, then counted up the total cost of the remaining five. The cards were dated, some appearing hand painted. All were priced at fifty cents. Finally, after picking myself up from the dusty floor and paying the proprietor, I exited the store and set off for a cool place to sit down and examine my purchase more closely.

Retreating down another in a series of cobblestone streets, I wandered onto Market Street and into a large, brick building identified as the Visitor Center for the Lowell National Historical Park. Lacking the funds for anything else, I made a cursory review of the lobby before fulfilling the primary purpose of my visit; the purchase of a soft drink from the cafeteria. I strolled back onto the sidewalk and down the street to a small park on the suggestion of a staff member. There, I settled in on a patch of grass behind an iron fence while traffic roared by me only a few feet away. It only took seconds before my attention was captured by an impressive statue depicting a group of female, mill workers. The steel figures were spread out in a mystical formation, seemingly in flight. No doubt, the monument was in tribute to the many girls and women, tragic and ill-fated, who passed through this city during the industrial revolution. Eventually, the piercing sound of a car horn from the street behind me jolted my attention back to my purchase from the antique store.

The June sun radiated warmth as I stretched out on the grass and removed the postcards from my pocket. With the city of Lowell bustling behind me, I glanced down at each of the cards in turn, closely examining the picture on each. Of the lot, the most intriguing was the one titled 'Agassiz Basin, North Woodstock, White Mts., NH.' I recognized the location to be 'The Basin' in Franconia Notch. Following a drawn out period of close scrutiny, I turned the card over and noticed, for the first time, it contained a hand written message and cancelled stamp. The cancellation date was August 3, 1928 and was processed in Berlin, New Hampshire. The card was addressed to Miss Ida Burke, 78 Second Street, Lowell, Massachusetts. My eyes strained to make out the words scratched in longhand. They were written in a cramped style to allow the message to fit in its entirety.

Ida,

It was just today I learned of your engagement to Sam Dillard. I am beside myself. I will return immediately if there is anything I can say or do to change your mind. Please write. Mail is brought to us every third day. Sorry for the card and not a letter. I could only scratch up a one cent stamp and I was without an envelope. I can still be reached at the Berlin address. Please know I still love you.

James

I read and reread the message, trying to arrange the circumstances of this relationship from long ago in my mind. I glanced back at the date stamped on the card, August 3, 1928. Nearly seventy-three years had passed since the emotional crisis spelled out before me had taken place. I ran the date through my own historical references. At the time James had sent off his plea to Ida, Calvin Coolidge occupied the White House, Babe Ruth was in his prime, and talking pictures were just bursting onto the scene. Inexplicably, I felt a certain attachment building in me for these two individuals from the distant past. But, why wouldn't I? Here I was, in their city, reading this heartfelt message, a message clearly of tremendous emotional importance to James. Ironically, it was a heartfelt message just purchased by a college student passing through their city for the grand sum of fifty cents!

I peered down at my watch. It was nearly two-thirty. My bus to Maine would not leave for another four hours. Leaning back against the park fence, I tried to imagine the images of Ida and James. James was difficult, but I saw Ida as a pretty, dark-haired girl with large eyes and a perfect, milky complexion. Next, I tried to picture the house at 78 Second Street. It surely had flowers in the yard, I thought, and perhaps a wooden swing mounted on its large, front porch. It was at this moment that an urge swept over me. It was an impulse, in the form of an urge, an insane, crazy urge, to locate the house addressed on the postcard. Was this possible? The desire to locate and set eyes on the house that Ida Burke called home consumed me. Collecting my belongings, I jumped to my feet and made my way out of the park. A short distance down the street, a meter maid stood beside a vehicle and punched information into a hand held device. I approached her as she tore a slip of paper from the small machine and slipped it under the vehicle's windshield wiper.

"Ma'am, I wonder if you could help me with some directions?" I asked. The woman lifted her head and gestured to me.

"I'm not from around here and I was wondering if you know where Second Street is?" She pointed down the street, instructing me to take an oblique left at the traffic light and head straight until I crossed a bridge over the river. That would take me to Centerville and Second Street was just past the Dunkin Donuts shop.

I could not believe my good fortune. Was it possible the house was still standing? So it was, prompted by the availability of time and, no doubt, genuine curiosity, I stepped off in the direction of Second Street. The walk took me through the heart of downtown Lowell, and ultimately over an impressive, steel bridge. Reaching the far side of the Merrimack River, I looked back at a lengthy expanse of mills crouched beside the quick flowing water. The buildings, clearly long abandoned, had a foreboding quality to them, quietly resting there at the total mercy of the elements.

After making my way across a busy intersection, I was rewarded. There, before me, was a weathered street sign declaring SECOND STREET. I turned onto the sidewalk and proceeded onward. It was not a long street, appearing to end two or three hundred yards in the distance. The left side was lined with multi-family houses, as I could see it, while the right was made up largely of empty lots. I continued to move in the direction of the ascending street numbers until the tenement houses ended, replaced halfway up the street by single family homes. It was when I reached an upward slope in the road that a particular house stood apart from the others. Well maintained and elevated above the roadway, it stood out from the rest of the neighborhood. Walking up to the base of a series of granite steps, I strained my eyes to make out the digits attached to its wooden door. Not surprisingly, it was 78 Second Street. I crossed the road and took in the former home of Ida Burke from a wider angle. I gazed hypnotically up at it. A screen door at the front of the house prominently displayed the letter 'M' to the outside world. The house was larger than I had envisioned it. Glancing up at the second floor, I tried to imagine Ida sitting in the window, reading and rereading her card from James in August of 1928. Around me, the neighborhood was surprisingly quiet.

I had been standing frozen in place for nearly five minutes when the screen door to 78 Second Street swung open and a husky man stepped out onto the landing. He was tall with black, curly hair. He appeared to be about thirty years of age. Standing firmly on the landing, he made a point to lock eyes with me.

"Can I help you with anything?" he called out, sounding more challenging than helpful. I froze at the sound of his voice before managing to force out a response.

"No, it's nothing." I was a stranger in his neighborhood and he clearly saw me as up to no good. Teetering on the brink of turning and walking away, I instead gathered the courage to press on and possibly gain a shred of additional information about Ida and James. Unaccountably, in my mind, I had forged a bond with these two individuals from the distant past. I stepped down from the sidewalk and strode across the street in the direction of the house. "This is going to sound a little crazy but I actually came up this way to see your house," I confessed. The husky man descended the stairs, his curiosity apparently aroused. "You see, I bought this old postcard earlier today here in Lowell, and it raised my curiosity. This postcard is made out to your address and it really got my imagination going about the lady who used to live here. You see, the card has this real deep message on it, and I started wondering about the people. It's from a real, long time ago and I began wondering if there was any way someone in the neighborhood might know something about this lady."

"What's her name?' asked the man.

"Ida Burke, but she lived here way back in the nineteen twenties." The man stared down on me, then toward my hand and the postcards.

"Would you mind if I took a look at it?" His voice showed the first sign of civility.

"No, go ahead," I answered, lifting the cards up. I peeled Ida and James's card from the top of the stack and handed it to him.

"Jack Mason," he said, introducing himself as he took the card.

"Jimmy Ouellette," I answered, returning his terse introduction. These courtesies were followed by a ritualistic handshake. Mr. Mason's eyes dropped down to the postcard. Turning it over, he read the message scratched out on the back, straining his eyes to decipher the cramped lettering. "As you can see, the card was mailed to someone living in this house at this address." He lifted his eyes but did not respond. "I knew it'd be a long shot but I took a chance coming here in case there was maybe some way of finding out something about Ida Burke and James.

"And where did you get this card?"

"At an antique shop downtown." Mason allowed himself to lean back against the granite wall. For the next few seconds he looked off into the distance, as if mulling something over in his head or trying to recall a fact buried far back in his memory.

"Now I know you're probably way too young to remember these people, but have you ever heard anything about the families who used to live here, particularly Ida Burke or some fellow named James who knew her? Read the words on the card. You can see why I'm curious about what might have happened to them."

"Would you like to meet my grandmother?" Mason asked.

"Do you think she might have known either of these people?"

"Nana's maiden name was Burke, Ida Burke," he acknowledged. A surge of nervous energy shot through my body while the man led me up the stairs and into the house.

"Are you saying—?" I asked, my voice breaking off in mid sentence.

"She's in poor health, you see, bedridden for a couple of years now."

"Ida's here?"

"If you're really interested then I could let you speak to her."

"Yeah, if you think she wouldn't mind," I answered. He motioned me to a flight of stairs and we climbed to the second floor. My mind was racing like a teenage boy on his first date as I was escorted down the hall to a bedroom at the back of the house. Following the man into the room, my eyes were drawn to a woman lying in bed in the room's far corner. A dated table lamp provided the bedroom's only light, the shades completely drawn.

"Nana, I have a man here that has something that was mailed to you a long time ago. Do you feel up for some company?"

"Something sent to me?" she responded, her voice sounding simultaneously strained and curious. We approached the bed, providing me with my first clear look at Ida. Her face appeared more tired than old. Her skin was wrinkled but not deeply grooved. Ida had the appearance of a woman who must have been attractive in her younger years, perhaps even through middle age. After setting aside a photograph album, she lifted her eyes up to her grandson and me.

"This young fellow here brought over an old postcard he got downtown. It was mailed to you from a man named James." The old woman stared blankly into my eyes, not responding at once. "Here, I'll pull him up something to sit on and maybe he'll let you take a look at it." Mason walked across the room, picked up a well worn vinyl covered chair, and placed it by the bed. He then excused himself and made his way downstairs. It was at that moment that it occurred to me: I was sitting alone with Ida Burke, James's precious Ida.

"Ida, I know it probably sounds totally insane but when I read this card from James to you, it raised my curiosity." She did not speak. Instead, she reached for the postcard. I handed it to her. She fumbled her hand atop the night stand by her bed, eventually coming up with a magnifying glass. I studied her face while she manipulated the card under the magnifier and began reading the message. I watched as her eyes opened widely and, remained rounded, as she read the message on the back of the card over and over. "I know it's probably none of my business, but when I read James's words I got caught up in your relationship. Ida, what happened between you and James? The woman took another brief glance at the card, then pulled it up to her chest. Following an extended pause during which she might have mulled over whether to share this information with me, she proceeded.

"James and I fell in love the very day his family moved onto Second Street in 1924. I was only fourteen, James sixteen. His schooling was all done when he got here from Maine, so he went to work in the mill right away—and started courtin' me. I wasn't marryin' age, not yet, but we started plannin' a life together. He was still obliged to give his family some of his wages cause they were poor—even poorer than most—and they needed it. But James hated his work in the mill—hated the people and hated the dye and textiles. When he heard about a chance to work in the outdoors, up in the mountains of New Hampshire, he jumped at it. First I asked him not to go. Then I asked him to marry me and take me with him. That was 1927 and I was seventeen. He'd have none of it—said he'd need to give his family money for another year—then we'd get married. That'd give me time to finish high school. I was young and the time seemed to drag by, but I waited. He came home for Christmas that year, and stayed on till January. When he left, he sort of left our marryin' plans up in the air. We fought about that. He was never a good writer but after that it got worse. I kept writin' and beggin' him to bring me up to him. My sisters, particularly Jane, told me I was crazy but James was my first love—and I believed in him. Then again too, everyone knew Jane had taken a shinin' to him." Ida's words broke off abruptly, as if she needed a moment to recover her breath. She took this time to lift the postcard back to within sight and reread the message. I remained silent.

"In the spring, that'd be the spring of 1928, I began to receive attention from Sam Dillard. Sam had a good job in the mill and, unlike James, was quite happy there. There was some pressure at the house by now to pick up stakes. I was the oldest and the house was crowded. I was out of school and working at the 5 & 10. I was ashamed to write to James by now—ashamed cause I was seein' Sam and ashamed cause I'd already begged James to have me and bring me up north with him. But I asked my mother to send off a letter and tell James of Sam's marriage proposal. I still loved him and I hoped he still loved me—and I couldn't believe he'd leave me to another man. That letter went off in July and I never heard from James again. I married Sam the following spring. I lost Sam to tuberculosis in 1932, makin' me a widow at the ripe old age of twenty-two. I was still wearin' black when word came that James had been crushed to death in a lumberin' accident in the town of Milan. I still remember where it was he died. He was buried in a family plot here in Lowell and I attended the funeral— dressed in black for the man I loved who couldn't seem to return that love."

"But he did love you, Ida. It says so on the card," I interrupted. "Didn't you ask him to come back?"

My question caused the old woman's expression to change. She shifted her head towards me while she appeared to run the events from long ago over in her head.

"Young man, I've never set eyes on this card from James before."

"You mean you never got this! How could that be?"

"That's what keeps runnin' through my head. Where did Jackie say you found this postcard?"

"I'm not sure he did. But, I picked it up in an antique shop downtown. It was just there in a pile with a thousand other postcards."

Ida broke eye contact with me and rested her head back on the pillow. It was evident she was running something through her mind as she lay before me, her eyes now closed. Following a half minute of silence, she turned back to me.

"I lost my sister, Jane, last year. I remember, a short time after she died my niece let a man from the antique store come by the house and pick over anything he wanted before the house went up for sale. I know a lot of things made their way into his antique shop. Doris didn't have a whole lot of sentimental attachment to her mother's things, even family things going back to her parents and grandparents. Jane was a real pack rat most of her life. She never threw much of anything away. The more I think about it, the more I start to think that the card may have come from Jane's things." The elderly woman stopped for a moment as the trace of a tear showed in the corner of her eye. "My sister had a shinin' for James back then. Jane was a year and a half younger than me but he never took her interest seriously. My folks went so far as to tease her sometimes when the subject of James came up in our company." Ida's voice tailed off as her recollections came to an abrupt end. She raised the card in front of her face once again. Lifting the magnifying glass from the surface of the bed, she reread the postcard. I rose to my feet. "Young man, if you would be agreeable, I'd like to buy this card from you."

"No, that won't be necessary. Please keep it, Ida," I replied. I did not have to offer the gift a second time. By now, I had lost all eye contact with the woman. Her attention was riveted on the dated postcard of Agassiz Basin.

"On his last visit home, James took me to the Strand Theater. We sat in the balcony even though we really didn't have to. He told me that he loved me halfway through the picture. When the picture was done, we walked home the long way, even though it was cold, just so our time together would last longer. James insisted that we sit in the balcony, even though they had the velvet cord hangin' across the entrance. That night he told me that he loved me and that he would forever," added Ida as her mind began to lose its direction and fluency. I reached down and squeezed the woman's hand.

"I've got to be running along now, Ida. It was really nice meeting you. Thank you for sharing your stories with me," I added, inching my way toward the door. She did not answer. "I'll be seeing you, Ida. Take care of yourself, okay?"

"Thank you, James. Thank you for this. And yes, I will be seein' you soon, James," she replied before turning her head away.

I descended the stairs with Ida's words clinging to me. Meeting Jack Mason by the front door, I extended him a fleeting good-bye and began the walk back toward the bus terminal. It seemed fitting that my route would take me back along the cobblestone streets of Lowell. Walking in the shadows of the nineteenth century buildings, I thought only of Ida Burke. She and James had been young and in love so very long ago, a time when F. Scott and Zelda Fitzgerald presided over the Jazz Age. And, in this setting, a city whose buildings and roadways resonate with echoes of the past, I had journeyed across town and, incredibly, made contact with one of an era's last, glowing embers, an experience which left me both enriched and disconcerted. Forty minutes after leaving Ida Burke's side, I was back in the bus terminal.

A week after my long bus trip from Albany, and on an impulse, I went to the web site of the Lowell Sun and learned that Ida (Burke) Mason, 91, had died in her home at 78 Second Street. The notice was worded in predictable text. The paper reported that she was a graduate of Lowell High School, Class of 1927 and was survived by three children, seven grandchildren, and two great-grandchildren. The general public was also informed that Ida had distinguished herself during World War II through hundreds of hours of volunteer work. However, the true story of the life of Ida Burke went largely unreported. That story included one very special man, James. Unfortunately, Ida's obituary read as most all do: a compilation of accurate dates and vigilantly gathered names, but no more a reflection of her life than the letters chiseled on her cold tombstone.

I pushed my chair away from the computer while the events from a week earlier in Lowell, Massachusetts returned to me. Had I not delivered a message of profound importance to a woman, an absolute stranger to me, less than a week before her death? I sat back and wondered what role James played in my actions and the ultimate delivery of his profession of love to Ida. Could my actions have been guided by some force over and above my own curiosity? There was no way to know, but I put my mind to rest, trusting that James and Ida were finally together, assisted in some small way by this unlikely messenger.

Cover model, **Shelley Collins,** is a married mother of
three who resides in Manchester, New Hampshire.